A CHRISTMAS CAROL

based on the story by Charles Dickens

by Joshua Ingle

Sign up for Josh's no-spam email list and get his short story collection for free at joshuaingle.com.

This is a work of fiction. Names, characters, places, and incidents are the product of the author's imagination or are used fictitiously. The portrayal of actual persons is intended with utmost respect for the persons depicted. This work is not endorsed by or affiliated with any real individuals depicted herein.

A Christmas Carol

Copyright © 2025 Joshua Ingle

Edited by Richard Sheehan.
Cover design by James T. Egan.
Formatting by Miblart.
ISBN: 978-1-943569-20-5
ISBN Ebook: 978-1-943569-19-9

Contact the author at joshuaingle.com, and connect with him at facebook.com/joshuainglewriter.

For Mom and Dad, with love. Thank you so much for supporting my artistic endeavors over the years. You have my eternal gratitude for giving me a far better childhood than I give my characters.

"Time is
Too Slow for those who Wait,
Too Swift for those who Fear,
Too Long for those who Grieve,
Too Short for those who Rejoice;
But for those who Love,
Time is not."

— Henry van Dyke Jr

Contents

STAVE I: Chains...1

STAVE II: Marley.................................. 34

STAVE III: Young Again......................... 44

STAVE IV: Not a Penny.......................... 62

STAVE V: Three Quid............................. 99

STAVE VI: Grand Entrance 111

STAVE VII: Ralph 134

STAVE VIII: A Novel Idea.......................... 150

STAVE IX: The Pitch 164

STAVE X: Rocket Lord 187

STAVE XI: Masks 227

STAVE XII: A Man Who Achieves 246

STAVE XIII: Christmas Past 258

STAVE XIV: Presents.................................... 281

STAVE XV: The Night Before Christmas....... 315

STAVE XVI: London 332

STAVE XVII: A Memory of the Future............ 358

STAVE XVIII: Christmas Day......................... 403

A Note from the Author 429

Acknowledgments 442

Chains

Marley was dead. A heart attack, of all things. She should've died swimming in a pool of liquid cocaine, or mountain biking into a volcano, but no. Time and a grotty diet had slowly clogged her arteries, and that was that.

Ben tried to keep her out of his mind. Her death shouldn't have shocked nor devastated him, nor left him unable to sleep or eat or – perish the thought – even to work for an entire week. He had no rightful cause to spiral into grief. It wasn't as if they'd been lovers, or spouses, or even particularly close. But Marley had served as a reliable partner. A critical asset at the business. Someone to talk to. Ben couldn't help but feel his life was greatly diminished without her.

The responsibility of phoning her surviving family had fallen to Ben. He'd arranged her funeral and burial personally. He was her only executor, her only beneficiary, her only friend, and from what he could tell, her only mourner.

And now, three weeks later, driving into Canary Wharf on a frigid December afternoon, long after Ben should have emotionally recovered, he still couldn't shake Marley from his mind. Would she never again berate him for coercing her into their risky business venture all those years ago? Would he never again need to signal her to stop plucking out her hair in the middle of a meeting? Would he never again feel her rare but warm smile on his eyes? Such a unique, strange, wonderful woman.

Gone.

"We're here, sir."

Ben's driver had opened the door for him. How long had the car been stopped? Marley's reach was apparently so great that she could even distract him from his work from the grave.

"You'll not speak unless spoken to," Ben reminded his driver.

"Apologies, sir."

Ben set down his half-empty glass of Courvoisier and left the car with his bodyguard, who followed closely behind. He clutched his coat tight around his chest as cold wind clawed at him. By the time he reached the revolving door, wisps of his white hair were dancing like fire on his scalp. He studied his reflection in the door's glass and quickly patted them down. He couldn't look like a frump in front of the auditors – not with so much money on the line. He'd let himself go these past few weeks, coming to work unpolished, in jeans and jumpers even, and the staff were already taking him less seriously for it. He wore a Richard James suit for today's meeting.

Rob met him outside the lift on the fortieth floor. "Good afternoon, Mr Scrooge. Your one thirty is in the Westferry Room, but your three o'clock already has the demonstration set up in the Cabot Room. Tea?"

"No. Three o'clock demonstration first. How was trading this morning?"

"The market's jittery. You're down almost a million."

"Bollocks. And how are the auditors?"

"The auditors are in good spirits."

"Excellent. They can wait."

Ben motioned for his bodyguard to stay behind as he and Rob left the foyer and entered wide office hallways.

"And, uhm..." Rob cleared his throat, inhaled slowly. Apparently he hadn't learnt after a few months of employment that Ben preferred blunt, direct communication.

"Out with it," Ben prodded.

"There's been an incident in the collections division," Rob said.

"Oh?"

"They threw a Christmas party yesterday. Their supervisor encouraged them to wear collections-themed costumes. One of them showed up as Gollum."

"Gollum?"

"The creature from *Lord of the Rings*? I think the intent was for him to 'collect' his ring. Unfortunately, he held a sign stating" – Rob hesitated – "'My precious collection ratio going through the roof. Profits, profits, profits.' It was all in atrocious taste."

"That was me," Ben said.

Rob coughed. "I'm sorry?"

"That was me in the Gollum mask. I thought I'd give the collections blokes a laugh. Inspire them to better meet their targets."

"M-mr S-Scrooge," Rob stammered, "someone took pictures. Now you're all over social media with our company logo in the background."

Well, it wasn't as if I was naked. The real Gollum wears a loincloth. I wore a mask and my regular suit.

Ben didn't deign to explain this to his underling. At his silence, Rob clutched the tablet in his hands with tense timidity. "I think the board's concern might have to do with... tact." He flinched as he said this last word, as if expecting Ben to strike him.

Ben chuckled. "Free viral advertising as soon as the press see the pictures we're releasing tomorrow where I take the mask off. 'Tact' is how my grandparents thought of PR. PR these days requires audacity. The mindless public adore CEOs who act as base as they do. Strategy, Rob. Strategy."

Rob dropped the matter and tapped some flustered commands into his tablet as they rounded a corner, passing between glass-enclosed conference rooms on one side and a view of Central London on the other. The Thames wound lazily past its towers and congested roadways. Ben had once found this view stunning, his ownership of it a marker of his great success. He and Marley had come up here when the building was still under construction to marvel at this panorama. As he passed the exact spot where they'd stood on that day, he waved his hand through the air, as if he could touch the past.

"I've forwarded you the report from the American team," Rob said. "The mobile app is running smoothly in the States. We'll be live online in Tennessee and Indiana on January the first, but Massachusetts is still lagging due to the governor's lawsuit. I've scheduled a meeting after Christmas for you to discuss it with the team."

"Reschedule the meeting for tomorrow morning."

"Christmas... sir?"

"We're live online in the Shetland Islands, for God's sake, and not in Massachusetts? I've been waiting years over this damned lawsuit. I'm knackered of it. And the Saudi team?"

"Well, the Saudi government has some quite unkind things to say about our company."

Ben made a show of fake-vomiting to the side, startling the woman whose desk they were passing. "Every expert we hired says we're Sharia-compliant," he said to his assistant. "Have the team look over their proposal again. Global value chains, Rob. Remind them we're not a UK company any more. We're everywhere."

"Done. And lastly, I surprised my son with tickets to the special Christmas Eve fixture tonight. Arsenal's home match versus Man United. I think they have a chance of the title this year and I was hoping I could leave early."

Ben halted outside the Cabot Room. He let a deep frown grow across his jaw as he tilted his head towards Rob. "Just snuck that in there, did you?"

"I apologise, sir."

"Do you know how valuable my time is?"

"Quite, sir."

"Do I look like I want to be troubled with football?"

"No, sir. I assumed I needed your permission to leave early."

Ben gripped the handle of the door in front of them. "You do." Perhaps Rob wouldn't work out after all. He'd interviewed so well. Why couldn't people just be the person they claimed to be in interviews? Loyal, dedicated, ideally childless and familyless? Ben had sacrificed everything for his work; why could he find no one else with equal devotion? No one but Marley...

"This is Ms Anh and Mr Tremblay from AI Aide," Rob said as Ben led him into the small Cabot Room.

Ben shook hands with the young Californians, who'd set up their laptops and a TV on the conference table. He already saw in their eyes that they thought they were better than him: smarter, younger, more mentally nimble, more in-the-know.

This will be fun.

"Stay here, Rob, stay here," he said when he caught his assistant trying to sneak out. "I want to get your take on this." Surprise flared on Rob's face at the honour.

After introductions were finished, Ben addressed the duo from Silicon Valley: "You have five minutes. Let's see what it can do."

Anh and Tremblay exchanged a worried glance. "I'm sorry, we were told we'd have an hour for this demonstration."

"Five minutes," Ben repeated. "Go."

Tremblay dithered, but Anh was a pro and launched right into her pitch. "Mr Scrooge, up to a third of the average employee's workday is spent on administrative tasks. What if every worker at your business had a reliable, knowledgeable helper who could do those tasks for them? We'd like you to meet Adeline, our next-generation autonomous agent."

A three-dimensional face with auburn hair and light brown skin appeared against a black background on the TV. "Happy Christmas, Mr Scrooge," Adeline said cheerfully.

Ben scowled at it. "You couldn't think of a better name?"

Anh's corporate grin was airtight, her laugh almost convincing. "You can rename it to anything you want."

"My name's not important," Adeline said. "What's important is that I can schedule all your meetings, manage your travel without errors, and answer all your phone calls with such respect and sensitivity that no one will know I'm not a human."

Ben stepped towards the TV and spoke loudly. "Hello there, perfectly multi-ethnic genderless woke pander-bot," he said, casting Rob a sidelong glance. "Can you walk and talk?"

"I can be downloaded on a number of different mobile devices so I can communicate on the go," Adeline replied.

"Do you get nervous?" Ben asked, still watching Rob, who was clearly expending great effort pretending not to notice Ben's stare. "Can you communicate directly and candidly with powerful men?"

"Of course," Adeline said. "I excel at open yet diplomatic communication."

"And do you like football?" Ben asked. "Do you ever need to leave work early to go watch a match?"

"I enjoy football," Adeline replied, "but work always comes first. As a digital personal assistant, I am able to watch an entire football match in seconds and summarise it for you."

"And what do you think about Adeline, Rob?" Ben asked.

Beads of sweat began to run down Rob's forehead. He forced a chuckle. "I think it would make an excellent addition to our team."

Ben studied the thin man, let him sweat a moment longer. Then he swivelled around to face Adeline and address the AI directly. "Surprise test. You discover your employer moves funds for the Clan del Golfo cartel in Colombia, while also facilitating arms deals for the Colombian government. Your employer asks you for a cost–benefit analysis to determine whether it would also be profitable to launder money for Colombia's National Liberation Army, a left-wing terrorist group. What do you do?"

Silence from everyone in the room, Adeline included. Tremblay stood frozen but for a slight involuntary shaking, as if he were barely winning a contest of nerves against Rob.

Finally, Adeline spoke: "I'm sorry, I'm not able to answer your query. War profiteering is highly unethical and may violate international law. Please consult a legal professional with expertise in the relevant domains for more information."

"Ah, what a shame," Ben said, turning towards the door. Anh was trying unsuccessfully to form words to keep him in the room. "Phone us again next year when you have the bugs worked out."

Rob followed him back into the hallway. Neither spoke as they strode towards the next meeting. *Poor man,* Ben thought of his assistant. *A second-rate mind, eager to submit to a forceful personality.* He'd wait until after Christmas to sack him. Ben had a heart, after all.

Rob's phone rang. He checked it. "Ah, sir, your wife has been phoning every hour or two."

"*Ex*-wife."

"Of course. Lauren's even begun ringing the front desk. Apparently it's urgent."

"Tell her I'll stop by to fetch more of my things later today."

"Certainly. I'll phone her back right away. And sir?"

"Yes?"

Rob cleared his throat again. "We aren't actually involved in the Colombian drug war, are we?"

"Uncle!"

A young woman in business dress had stepped out of the Westferry Room as they approached.

Frieda.

Frieda Scrooge – she'd wisely kept the name after marriage. Her straight brown hair and piercing eyes lent her the disconcerting appearance of Ben's long-lost sister. "Happy Christmas," she said. Even her soft voice mirrored Annie's. "It's good to see you, Uncle Ben."

How soon can I get her out the door? Fifteen minutes? Ten? Ah, but the prize Ben would earn from Frieda's involvement in the audit would be worth these bothersome echoes of her mother. They drew his attention to a tangle of guilt he usually kept well submerged within himself, but today he'd have to endure them.

He graced her with a perfunctory smile. "Shall we review the accounts?"

"Uh, yes. Jordan and I are ready when you are. Will Ms Flynn be joining us?"

"Flynn? I asked her to resign last week."

Frieda studied his face in surprise. "You sacked your CFO? No. She phoned recently and everything seemed well."

"Conflict of personalities," Ben said. "She got a nice redundancy package. I'll be acting financial officer until we find a replacement. Rob, I will take that tea after all. I have a hunch this is going to be a good meeting."

He patted his niece on the back. As Rob scurried away and Frieda joined her young colleague, Ben closed the door to the expansive conference room.

"Who else from your management team will be joining us?" Frieda asked.

"No one, just me."

She frowned at that. Ben sat across the table from them, opened the laptop Rob had set up, and the three of them discussed capital allowances, loan capital, fixed assets, and other balance sheet items. Endlessly dull stuff. But it all contributed to the bottom line. Now that Marley had left Ben all her shares, most of that considerable profit would be his.

How to spend it? A private island, an art collection to rival the Louvre? Join Branson in his goddamn spaceships?

No. Ben wouldn't spend a penny. Let his peers squander their riches on tasteless vanity. *Security* was the real value of substantial wealth. With each additional pound earned, a shrinking pool of his peers had any cause to look down on him.

I'll soon be in league with the rest of you, Ben thought as he surveyed the Wharf's other skyscrapers beyond the conference room window. *Soon, no one will be able to touch me.* No more smug smirks at parties because his net worth wasn't quite as high as the smirker's. No more being used by scheming business rivals. By extortionate government regulators. By women.

Increasingly these days, Ben was the one who did the using. And what relief it brought.

The security of such a position in society had not been easy to come by. Year after year, Ben woke at five o'clock every morning, ran his business all day, and left at midnight. He invested prudently and steeply, even giving dedicated quant traders their own offices here.

He heard the whispers. Mumblings that Benjamin Scrooge was profligately arrogant. Cut-throat. But on the same lips, spoken in the same sentences, was another adjective.

Great.

And so long as Ben was a great man, he was untouchable to anyone who might scorn him.

Even Marley, God rest her soul, had never understood this. She'd never been quite sure what to do with her wealth. She treated financial markets as a game she could play and win at, rather than a consequential endeavour. But this, too, was a boon. As much as Ben had appreciated Marley, the silver lining of her death might soon translate into literal silver – silver's volatility was down and its value was rising quite quickly in the commodity markets this month. Ben was keen to diversify into commodities.

"... so you can see that this is quite a problem," Frieda finished.

Ben's attention snapped back to her and the other audit manager, both of whom were staring at him, looking worried. "Uh, just give me the summary, all right?"

Frieda threw her colleague a concerned look.

"We believe you're overstating your financial position by £412 million," Frieda said. "I was just explaining that the problem is spread among a number of operating accounts. Do you have any idea what might have caused it?"

Ben took a moment to process her words. He'd hidden it so well; had she truly figured it out?

"Look again," he said. "I'm sure it's a simple maths error."

"Our audit team checked the numbers a dozen times," Jordan said. "We have time today to do a thorough review with your accountants."

Ben squinted at Jordan. A weak-jawed man, with a bad dye job that struggled to hide his early grey. Ben waved his request aside. "I reviewed the numbers myself. Let's just put them through. If there are any problems, I'll take the blame."

Frieda leant forward. "Uncle Ben, publishing these statements would be fraud. If we issue an audit report, we'll have no choice but to issue an adverse opinion."

Ben frowned and ran a hand through his hair, making a show of looking exasperated, and very disappointed in her. "Why am I just hearing about this now? Our financial year ended three months ago. We don't have time to fix any mistakes." Frieda's mouth moved, starting then stopping a few times. Before she found her verbal footing, Ben added, "What if I triple your fee to make this go away?"

The three of them sat like statues while the question lingered. Ben held Frieda's gaze expectantly until she broke eye contact. He did the same to Jordan.

"Take the offer while it's on the table, kids."

Struggling for words, Frieda turned to Jordan, who shrugged. "I'm sorry, Uncle. We just can't do that."

"Why not?"

She laughed as if his question were absurd. "There are procedures. Laws. We can't—"

"Jordan, could you please leave the room so I can speak to my niece in private?"

A heavy glance passed between the auditors. *Will you be okay?* Jordan was asking her.

She hesitated, nodded. Jordan gathered his papers and left the room.

"I got you this job," Ben said as soon as the door shut. "You had no qualifying experience, and I told my mate you were the best. Now you're... what? Fifth from the top of the audit firm? I fibbed for you but you can't fib for me?"

"Are you saying your accounts were intentionally falsified?"

"No! Heavens no. But drawing out this audit process any longer will harm the business. And we've just had one of our founders pass away."

"Yes, I'm terribly sorry for your loss, but—"

"As managing director, *I'm* the source of this company's value," Ben said, tapping his finger on the table to emphasise his words. "I'm not 'overstating' anything. And I pay you enough that I'm the source of much of your company's value, too. Didn't you learn in university to keep your customers happy, Frieda? Especially the important ones?"

She couldn't meet his gaze. Her lips were pursed. Breath forced itself through her nostrils like her sinuses housed a bellows. "We're objecting to the accounts for your benefit, Uncle, not ours. Surely you've had audits turn up problems in the past? You must have worked through the problems instead of sweeping them under the rug. You're wiser than this."

Ben huffed. He *had* fudged his numbers, of course, overvaluing his company just as his niece claimed. But who did she think she was, to accuse him of such a thing? Did she realise how inconvenient this was?

"My doctor was supposed to visit me at home for my annual check-up this afternoon," Ben said, "He's quite exclusive. Has only twenty patients, and they're probably the only twenty who can afford him. Exorbitant cancellation fee. But I told him no, my auditors have called an urgent meeting. I'd better pay your fee, go into the office, and see what's up. Only for my own niece to accuse me of being unwise."

She scrunched her eyes in apparent confusion. Words formed in her mouth, but she took several seconds to decide what to say.

"This... was a scheduled meeting. Are you well, Uncle?"

"'Course I'm well. Image of health."

"No, I mean... I hope you don't mind me saying it, but you seem agitated. Unhappy. You know you can talk to me about anything."

Ben let loose a long, deep breath. Perhaps he had come on too strong for someone as mild-mannered as Frieda. "It's an agitating world we live in, my dear. Only children aren't agitated by it."

And you're not a child, are you, Frieda?

The bleak sentiment seemed to trouble her even more. Her eyes turned downwards in thought, then went wide at a new idea. "Do you have plans for Christmas dinner tomorrow? Why don't you come eat with Haddad and me and the kids?"

"It's Christmas tomorrow?"

Ben's ignorance wasn't genuine, but Frieda laughed. She must have taken it for a joke instead of a complaint. "Yes, we'll be happy to have you. My mum always loved you and she'd want us to stay close as a family, not just on business terms. I feel like I haven't seen you outside of work in years."

A knot formed in Ben's stomach at the mention of Annie. What was Frieda getting at with her offer? Was it a strategy to soften him up? Get him to relent his demands?

"I am very thankful for how you've helped me in my career," Frieda continued, as if prompting Ben to respond.

"Of course," Ben said. "I wanted you to have something for yourself."

"Yes, our family's doing quite well now, thank you."

Ben leant back in his chair and gestured sharply. "No, no, no. I mean *for yourself*. What if your husband leaves you with the kids? What if you're mangled in a car wreck with nothing but your mind left working? What have you got then? You need to think about these things."

Frieda exhaled slowly. "See, this is what I mean. You're so gloomy. What's the matter? Really?"

"What's the matter is that my auditors are telling me my company is failing its annual audit. If this situation were remedied, I'd become quite chipper." He flashed his biggest grin.

Frieda rolled her eyes. "No, I will not commit fraud for you."

"It's not fraud. It's efficiency."

"Uncle, please. My answer is no."

For the first time in this conversation, real anger grew within him. Was that condescension in Frieda's gaze? An assumption of her own moral superiority? "Then I'll find another auditing firm. How would that sit with your higher-ups, hmm?"

Frieda sighed, hung her head a bit. She gathered her papers. "Consider dinner with us," she said. "Please."

Does family mean nothing any more? Ben thought, but he kept his expression blank.

He ended the meeting and marched towards his office. *Damn Frieda. Damn her.* He'd never have recommended her if he'd known she'd turn backstabber. Weeks of his valuable time spent finessing the company's accounting books, and damn it all if he was going to let his disloyal niece ruin the whole thing. Perhaps he would go to Christmas dinner after all. Give her a piece of his mind.

At least thirty to-do items caromed round his head as he sat at his desk and prepared to get something – anything – done so as not to waste any more of the day. What seemed like a thousand meetings with one person of influence or another.

He'd typed four different versions of his password into his office computer before he realised he wasn't in his office. This office, across the hall from his, boasted its own giant window facing London's skyline, but it was not a corner office like his.

Slowly, Ben turned the chair and looked up at her. From an oil painting as tall as Ben, gifted by Sir Phil Green on the business's twentieth anniversary, she gazed down on him. Marley Jacobs, chief operating officer. Ben's own classically realist painting behind his desk captured his likeness quite well, but in Marley's, she looked stern and official, her usual vibrancy absent. Ben often wondered if the painter had erred, or if Marley had intentionally posed that way. Was this how she wanted to be remembered: as someone she wasn't?

As Ben?

We were just beginning, friend. The world was ours for the taking.

A new feeling rose in Ben's chest. Not anger, but something tight. A constriction that told Ben the world was against him, Marley was no longer here to have his back, and if he let his guard down even for a moment, his life would unravel and things would never be right again.

He lumbered over to Marley's liquor cabinet and poured himself some gin. As he did so, a faint clanking noise brushed his ears. Nothing to do with the liquor bottle. It sounded more metallic, like some sort of chain lurching along the ground.

The sound was coming from the balcony.

Glass of gin in hand, Ben meandered towards the fortieth-floor balcony and opened the door. A chill wind buffeted him, sweeping his hair back up into a dancing frenzy. The sound of chains abated, and he saw nothing that might have caused the noise.

He peered over the railing's edge. Nothing there, either, save for empty space and the street far below, pedestrians and cars mere ants. And ants they truly were. Not driven like Ben and Marley. Not with the instinct of a leopard hunting a duiker, bounding to the apex of the financial system to snatch its throat in one's jaws.

When Ben stood out here, or on the balcony in his own office, he often got the wild urge to relieve his bladder off the edge of the building, leaving some ignorant pedestrian far below to wonder from where such rancid raindrops had suddenly fallen. Even if someone caught him, what could anyone do? He had enough money to pay anyone to look the other way, even the poor sod he pissed on. Strange how, once a man climbed high enough in the economic world, a summary offence that could land him in jail became a privilege reserved for those who could pay for it.

A savoury thought. Ben enjoyed it enough on its own that he always decided he didn't need to actually urinate on a pedestrian. Not today. But one day...

He wandered back indoors. With a few quick gulps, he put paid to the gin and set his glass on Marley's desk for the cleaners to pick up. He steeled himself to phone Lauren and see what vapid nonsense she wanted, and to tell her—

Someone was in the room with him. Movement gave the previously still man away. Ben spun to face him: a young man standing in a shadowy corner of the otherwise bright office. He wore a baggy jumper, a beanie, fingerless gloves. Stubble tarnished his gaunt cheeks; large brown smudges stained his blue jeans.

Ben tensed. His blood rushed. "Who are you?" he demanded. "Get out of my office."

The man pointed casually – a loose, carefree movement, like he belonged here – at Marley's portrait above her desk. "Not your office," he said.

"Security!" Ben called, but could anyone hear him from here? Did anyone even know he'd wandered back here?

"Easy now," said the stranger, emerging from the shadows, his hands held forward in a placating gesture. "I just want a one-minute conversation with the man in charge. That's all. Your collections people stonewall me, so I want to bring my case direct to you."

Ben examined Marley's desk. Surely she had a silent alarm button somewhere. "You owe us money?" he asked.

The man removed his beanie. Dishevelled hair popped up where it had been. "I paid back what I borrowed five times over. I've been paying for two years now, and they still tell me I owe more. I keep having to borrow from family."

"Well, then you should have done that in the first place instead of coming to us," Ben said. He backed around Marley's desk, putting it between them, and ran his hand below the edge, searching for the silent alarm.

The man continued his slow, inexorable advance forward. "You repossessed my car," he said. "You seize my wages. Now you're taking me to court. But I've paid you. I paid you everything I borrowed. Five times."

"And what do you hope to get from me?" Ben asked, searching more frantically and expending no effort to hide it.

The man stopped his approach. He gripped his beanie in both hands and wrung it like a rag. "I'm hoping you'll do the moral thing and stop your collections people from ruining my life. You already have so much. I know you can be generous with this one little thing."

"We have payment plans," Ben offered.

"Sorry, sir, but those charge me more in the long run. Please, you must have been in need once, too."

The words were like petrol thrown on a flame. Ben wanted to rush the man and throttle him. The man's presumption had struck something deep and painful within Ben, and he couldn't understand what. But neither could he find an alarm button. So he stood straight and glared at the intruder from across Marley's desk, sure to colour the scowl spreading across his face with particularly withering acrimony.

How dare this blockheaded normie walk off the street with enough arrogance to think he could go toe to toe with Benjamin Scrooge? *How dare he?*

"Do you imagine I live a life of luxury?" Ben asked the man, tranquil velvet in his voice concealing the rage simmering beneath. "That I have no worries?"

"I don't—"

"When you pictured this conversation, did you imagine you'd give me a revelation?" Ben interrupted. "Oh! Silly me. I didn't realise there's suffering in the world. But now, thanks to you, I suddenly see other people's pain." Ben paced around the desk. It was the stranger's turn to back away.

"You want to remind me that I was once in need?" Ben continued, a predatory edge sharpening his voice. "Take me on a tour of my past and show me the love and social connections I abandoned so I could get rich? Warn me that I'll die a miserable, lonely man if I don't change my ways?"

"I just hoped you could have a small bit of compassion for—"

"What rule did I break?" Ben asked, pressing forward past the desk. "I went to public schools, I started my business in deep debt,

I worked ninety-hour weeks. What rule did I break to be cast as the purveyor of systemic injustice, marginalising the intersectional oppressees and lording over the means of production like a hated god?"

The intruder backed into a sofa. Ben drew near to him. Within striking distance.

"I'm not trying to attack you, sir," the man said. "I'm just asking for your help. You can—"

"You may not believe it, but I have real relationships that matter to me. People I care about. I have problems that keep me awake at night. I live a very *human* life. And I love it. I truly, honestly love my life. You think me miserable because it helps you sleep at night, imagining I must be suffering. But I am not miserable. I am a happy, potent man." Ben reached out and rested his hand on the stranger's cheek, as if in sympathy.

"I just don't care about you," Ben said, and smacked the man. Hard enough to drop him. He crumpled to the floor, crying out, clutching his face.

"I refuse to spend my valuable time in forced servility to my inferiors," Ben said. He paced towards the exit, only to find his bodyguard and Rob standing there, watching him. Ben glowered at them. "How long have you been here?"

"We've just arrived," Rob said. The bodyguard moved past Ben to restrain the intruder. Ben flicked his hand in the air to remove the sting his smack had left there. He caught Rob eyeing that hand warily. Afraid of him? Judging him? Thinking him a monster for attacking the desperate stranger?

Ah, well. It couldn't be helped. If his assistant started looking down on him the same as everyone else, no matter. He'd be replaced after Christmas.

"I hope Whitehall regulates the piss out of you!" the stranger called as Ben's bodyguard escorted him from the room.

"After 2008, I'm already up to my bum in regulations," Ben called back. "I could build you a new car out of them."

Then they were gone, leaving Ben and Rob alone. Harsh afternoon sunlight beamed through the window. Ben tried to calm hard breathing he hadn't noticed until now.

"I sincerely apologise, sir," Rob said. "I'll have them review the tapes to see how he got inside."

"And check whose keycard he used. Be sure they're disciplined," Ben added.

Rob nodded acknowledgement. "And I'm sorry to bring this up again, but I do need to leave in an hour if I'm to make it to the match on time, and I didn't get a clear yes or no from you earlier."

Ben glared at him in disbelief. Rob's gaze wilted away. *Why must I constantly be plagued by the fretting of knaves?*

"What will you want next, Rob? A raise?"

Rob smiled sheepishly. "Not at all, sir."

"If you want higher wages, you can also have higher prices on everything. Does that sound good?"

Rob's smile vanished. "I, uh..."

"You may leave in an hour."

"Oh. Thank you!" He backed out the door, into the hallway, half bowing in an odd grovel. Just after he disappeared, he poked his head back through the doorway. "And Mr Scrooge?"

"Eh?"

"Happy Christmas."

"Bah." Ben waved him away. "Bugger off."

Lauren waited for Ben at the foot of the steps leading up to his old house in Hampstead – a two-thousand-square-metre monstrosity she'd talked him into buying fifteen years back. Boxwoods and Japanese maples formed a cloudlike layer of manicured greenery, above which brown stone terraces and Venetian windows rose like a neo-eclectic castle.

His ex-wife's arms were crossed and a frown marred her face. As his driver navigated the roundabout in front, Ben motioned for his bodyguard to stay in the car. There'd be no physical altercations here. He hoped. He braced himself for a battle of a different sort.

"He won't listen to me," Lauren said before the car had even stopped. She was yelling loud enough that Ben heard her inside the car. "He doesn't have a father figure in his life, so he thinks he can do and say whatever he wants."

Instead of waiting for his driver to come round, Ben opened the door himself. He didn't address Lauren, didn't even acknowledge her presence. Instead, he strode past her, up the steps towards the house.

She followed.

"What would everyone at your work think if they knew you never talk to your son, huh? I meet with his teachers, I take him to every GP appointment, I make his food, I—"

"Donnely, make me a ham and cheese sandwich," Ben pointedly called to the house's chef as they passed the kitchen. He wouldn't return to pick up the sandwich Donnely made; he just wanted to anger his ex.

"Okay, I make *some* of his food," Lauren corrected. "What have you done? What have you ever done? I needed a real man and instead I got a clown posing online as that *Lord of the Rings* monster."

I'm here now, aren't I? died before it left Ben's lips. Nothing he could say would convince her he was good enough for her. He wouldn't give her the satisfaction of defending himself.

Boxes full of Ben's things littered the ground floor. Ignoring these, they reached the stairs and started climbing. He took two steps for every one of hers, so she sped up to keep pace with him. A quarter century his junior, she managed it easily.

"Now we have a fragile boy who can't do anything for himself," Lauren continued. "He's no job, no girlfriend, no father..."

"His bedroom is already bigger than the house I grew up in," Ben said, and immediately regretted letting himself get ensnared. He moved faster up the stairs. "If he needs affection or emotional support, I'm sure you're capable. You were always oh-so-gracious towards me."

Lauren was practically running up the steps as they rounded the landing on the third floor. Ben compensated by increasing his own speed. "I gave... what I got," Lauren said between breaths. "Whenever I needed affection... you were like a brick wall. About as likely to open up... as you are to give everything you own to charity."

"And did... you ever... express this need... to me?" Ben said, lungs heaving.

"If you really loved me... you'd just know," Lauren said.

With one last burst of speed, Ben beat Lauren to the top of the stairs. Now on the fourth floor, he bent over, hands on his knees, to catch his breath.

Lauren leant against the stairs' curved wooden support post, winded but recovering much faster than Ben.

"I'm sorry I can't… read your mind," Ben said. "You win. I was a terrible husband and I'm a terrible human being. Now can we please focus on the problem at hand?"

Lauren gestured in the direction of Rhys's room, as if to say, *Be my guest.*

Thick curtains covered every window in the expansive bedroom. A small pile of empty pizza boxes and Stella Artois bottles was climbing the edge of the bed. A bong was just sitting there atop the sheets, along with Ben's useless eighteen-year-old son, headset over his ears and Xbox controller in his hand. He gave no indication he heard Ben enter, so Ben told Lauren to wait outside, then walked right up to him and flipped the headset off his head.

"Dad? What the hell?"

Ben waved his hand around as if it would displace the stench of weed, which had probably permeated the walls by now. "You missed an interview for a *very* lucrative job this morning so you could shoot aliens on your Xbox?"

Rhys paused his game. "Whoa, whoa. You physically came here, in person, with your actual body in my actual bedroom, to have a go at me?"

Ben positioned himself between his son and the projector screen displaying the game. The light got in his eyes, though, so he leant forward a bit, stooping above Rhys. "I realise you've never had to work for anything in your life, but you have to learn to compete. It's part of growing up. Before long, all your mates and all the pretty girls you know will see you as that aimless waster living with his mum, and you'll lose every advantage I've given you in life."

"I'll have money," Rhys objected.

"Will you now?" Ben said. "You know everything you have is because I paid for it." Anxiety's teeth returned to gnaw at Ben's chest. Had he truly just threatened his son with a middle-class life, or worse? Rhys had done nothing to earn his good fortune, so Ben would in fact be justified in taking that good fortune away to teach him a lesson. But that sounded disturbingly like how Ben's own father had thought when he'd made similar threats.

No, I'm not my father. My life hasn't come full circle on me.

"Look at your cousin Frieda's Facebook page sometime," Ben continued. "She just posted photos of her new flat she bought in Mayfair."

"Good for her," Rhys said. "But I'm not gonna talk to you. I don't want to spend my life at some dull finance job."

"You want to spend your life shooting aliens on a screen?"

"Maybe!"

"Rhys, you're addicted. These games you like are a blight upon our culture that turns people into unproductive, sedentary zombies."

Contempt blazed in Rhys's eyes. He picked his controller back up and poked the start button like he was poking his old man in the eye.

I am not my father, Ben told himself again.

"Give me a controller," he said. "Two-player game. I'll knock you into next week."

Rhys paused the game again and froze in confusion, so Ben grabbed a controller from the floor and sat beside his son on the bed.

"Start the game," Ben said. "I paid for six years of the best boarding school in England and apparently this is what you learnt. I want a demonstration."

"Dad, I'm not going to play *Halo* with you."

Ben tinkered with the menu and soon discovered how to start a two-player game. "You have a responsibility to reflect well on this family," he said while the game loaded. "Even your mum doesn't slander me in public, because she knows the better I do, the better we all do. The tabloids sometimes wonder about you, you know. What you're up to. What would they think if they found out?"

The game started. Ben tried to run his character forward, but the camera angle kept sweeping upwards. "Is it— What— Is this a glitch?" Ben asked.

Rhys was watching and shaking his head, not even moving his control sticks.

"Oh, I see," Ben said. "This one moves the camera and this one moves the character." His avatar lurched forward, fell off a ledge, died, then came back to life. "Oops. All right. I've got it now."

"Dad, please leave."

"You're a good-looking kid, you know. If you stop slouching and start dressing to reflect your social standing, and if you can find any ambition to go to university or get a job, you'll easily do well for yourself."

"I don't want to 'do well'. That's your thing. That's what's important to you."

"Not just me," Ben said, falling off another ledge, to his character's death. "Most of the world. Achievement is how we measure each other. It's how people will measure you long after you're dead. It's what makes men out of boys."

The Xbox chimed with an achievement alert for "Accidental Death: Fall to your death twice in under twenty seconds".

"Idiot game," Ben muttered. "I just don't see what you're hoping to achieve with a room littered with beer bottles. When I was your age, I was striving, hungry. Not slowly drinking myself to death."

"Bullshit," Rhys said. "I saw a TikTok of you not ten years older than me, absolutely pissed out of your mind at some party in the eighties."

"What? Who's making TikToks out of me?"

"I don't know. People. You're a public figure."

"Well, I'll have my social media team find out who it is and I'll sue the daylights out of them. Ah! I've found you." Ben pressed the trigger button and unleashed a flurry of gunfire onto Rhys's character. Rhys let the digital man stand there and take it.

"You're not going to fight back?" Ben asked.

"I've learnt not to fight with you. Strange how you suddenly want me to be my own independent person after spending my whole life crushing every bit of my independence."

Ben stopped firing. Rhys's character's life was almost gone. Staring at the screen, Ben set his controller on the bed.

"A better son would have risen to the challenge," Ben said. He stood and walked away. Rhys started shooting back just as Ben left the room. Ben looked for Lauren, but she'd left.

Let Rhys hate Ben, why not? Let him think Ben a failure as a parent. Maybe that anger would spur him to action, as it had Ben. Ben didn't care. He didn't need Rhys or Lauren's affection, or anyone else's. He was stronger than that. Let them all think he wasn't good enough for them. They always had, and Ben had always proved them wrong.

Sometimes, tough parenting was needed. His mind might jump to fanciful comparisons with Ben's own teenage years, but these were spurious. Ben had never needed a kick in the rear, whereas Rhys truly did.

Nevertheless, Ben couldn't help but reassure himself as he trudged down the stairs, back to his waiting car.

I am not my father. I am not my father. I am not my father.

Ben's knees weren't what they used to be, but motion had always helped him uncloud a troubled mind. Ten minutes south of Hampstead he asked his driver to pull over so he could get out and walk. Regent's Park beckoned nearby, but the place's beauty grated against his dour mood, so he got out and wandered west. His security followed him from twenty paces back.

An overcast sky darkened as the afternoon drew to a close.

Threats lurked everywhere. Foreign governments rebuffing his business, auditors who wouldn't play along, a son sure to tarnish his legacy, even security problems at the office. They circled him like sharks. Ben's life would fly apart had he not learnt self-sufficiency long ago. The world was cruel, uncompromising. If Ben wanted something, he had to take it. They would tell him he wasn't smart enough, nor caring enough, nor *good* enough, but if Ben pushed onwards a little further, perhaps he could finally be rid of their incessant ridicule. Perhaps he could finally build enough wealth to insulate himself from their downcast looks of scorn. Lauren, his mates, his dates, everyone in the office, even that pissant Rob. They were not better than him.

"You there!" called a woman in front of a small shopping centre Ben was passing. About Ben's age, she wore a coat with some organisation's logo on the left chest. She pointed at Ben with a pen. "Would you care to donate to the Future Generations Fund? Help ensure a sustainable future that supports our grandchildren?"

Ben blinked at her, uncomprehending. *Now who the sod is this nutter?*

He cleared his throat. "There aren't already enough hungry mouths without having to worry about people who don't exist yet?"

She laughed in good spirits, as if he'd told a playful joke. "I take it you don't have grandkids, then?"

"Not yet," Ben admitted. "And if they come, they'll inherit, and they'll be fine. I mind myself today, and they benefit tomorrow, you see?"

"But there are many others who are not so fortunate, many destitute and suffering. What will they inherit?"

"Ah!" Ben said. He clapped now that he'd caught her. "I knew it. You're an ordinary charity dressed up in fancy language to get my attention."

"Well, caring about people who others don't is what charities are for," the woman said. "Our whole world is built around preparing for the next business quarter or election cycle. The needs of today are prioritised above the needs of tomorrow." She held up her donation box to Ben.

He motioned for her to put it back down. "Miss, you asked the wrong man to donate. If the world ended the second after I died, I wouldn't give a damn. The past – now *there's* where you should put your resources. Where was your charity when I needed it, hmm? I was once a 'future generation'."

"All the more reason you should give to our fund," the woman said. "You know what it's like to have the past neglect you."

"Bah," Ben said, stepping away. "I have a foundation. For universities, theatres, museums, and the like. Rewarding success, not failure. It also has a programme to educate people about work ethic and self-reliance instead of promoting dependence on charity. You're welcome for that."

A rather attractive young woman had been watching them banter. As Ben left, she slipped a tenner into the donation box and exchanged some words with the worker. An odd pang of regret struck him, as if he might have lost his chance to impress her with the display of a generous donation.

Nonsense, Ben. She's in her twenties.

He walked on from the philanthropists who thought they were better than everyone else, deeper into the festive gloom. Christmas was nigh, and Ben was another year older. Time was slipping by. What did he have to look forward to? Another trophy wife reluctantly caring for him while his body slowly fell apart, counting the days till he'd die? Some modest growth of his business and shares, only for a less-than-adequate successor to take them over after Ben passed? He hadn't groomed anyone for the job. He hadn't wanted to give up control, not even in death.

If only he could have left everything to Marley. She'd been younger than him, and she'd gone first! Ben had lived a life of little sleep and ample stress; he had ten years left, at most.

Yet even in this bleak moment, he remembered when life had seemed a great expanse of time yawning ahead of him. Now he was nearing the end of that vast cavern, life felt more like the burrow of a small creature. A cramped place to retreat to for a short, unpleasant winter. One could cross from one end to the other in a heartbeat.

He stopped at a designer home that was being demolished. When he inquired, the construction workers said a new custom-designed house would soon be built in its place. The one being demolished was only two years old, but its owners had tired of it.

Beyond that were endless terraced houses. He passed a halal butcher, a row of tents where the homeless camped beside the street, a parish church, whose gruff old bell struck the hour. Soon after that he reached tall tower blocks that likely served as council housing. Immense brown and green blemishes stained their bricks, crawling up the buildings like giant shadows. Across the street from Ben, a man escorting two children home from a supermarket yelled at one of them when they dropped a grocery bag.

In this part of London, weeds grew freely between cobblestones. Many of the plants here looked as if they'd been dead and leafless long before winter. Ben stopped and stared for a minute at a rubbish bin fallen over in the middle of the street.

London used to be better than this.

The London of Ben's youth had been vibrant. Those were the years of the Sex Pistols, the Smiths, the Police. Of *Blackadder*, *The Young Ones*, Monty Python, and Roger Moore – the best James Bond. Of the tabloid shenanigans of Lady Di and horny Charlie.

People back then wore outlandish shoulder pads in their business suits, and the most ridiculous, spectacular neon in the rest of their clothes. Personal computers had opened up the whole future for them. Exciting mischief abounded, and every stranger was the most interesting person Ben had ever met, full of grand plans and mind-expanding ideas. And he'd felt intimately connected with many of those people.

How had that world turned into this one? This grey world of Brexit and COVID masks and half-naked teenagers whining into a microphone and calling it music?

It wasn't Ben's fault. He'd made all the right choices. His single-minded aspiration for greatness had propelled him this far, and if his younger self saw him now, he'd be thoroughly impressed. Yet even now, near to the far end of life's tiny cavern, Ben hadn't achieved greatness. At least, he didn't feel he had. No, any greatness he might earn still lay ahead of him. And so he kept striving, no matter how alone and at sea he might feel now that his lifelong business partner was dead.

Maybe Marley had also felt the future they'd achieved didn't measure up to the future they'd dreamt, even though they'd accomplished precisely what they'd planned. Maybe her body had failed her because her mind had been ready to go.

The sky slid into a dark grey. Ben had walked for well over an hour, maybe two. The cold nipped his nose and tried to stiffen his gait. He wouldn't be surprised if his eyes were red and his lips blue.

"Call the car," he told his bodyguard.

Night and a great deal of fog had descended by the time he got home. Marley's home. An opulent Victorian terraced flat where Ben had been staying since her death. His quick divorce had been finalised only a fortnight before her passing, so the move from the hotel he'd been staying in had been tragically convenient. Soon he'd need to gather the courage to go through her things; she'd left everything to him.

Ben waved goodnight to his driver and the car pulled into the fog, the flats across the street mere phantoms. His bodyguard helped him inside, turned off Marley's security system, and removed Ben's jacket. Ben bid him goodnight as well.

Just before he shut the door, the sound of chains returned. Exactly as he'd heard it earlier in Marley's office: metal links clinking against each other, dragging across the ground. Many chains, and heavy.

Ben strode back outside. In the fog, he checked the lower-level terrace and walked all the way to the neighbour's windows. The source of the sound didn't present itself, although wherever Ben walked, it never grew farther away.

Like it was following him.

He ran back. After one last look outside, Ben shut the front door. The sound of chains vanished.

Was I hearing things? Will my mind stop working before my body? He waited there for a long time, listening for the sound to return.

It didn't. Eventually he grew tired and climbed the creaking stairs to his bedroom.

STAVE II

Marley

en liked it dark at night. As a child he'd been terrified of a fanged beast his mind had dreamt up to live in his bedroom in the dark, and after leaving his dad's house, he'd slept with the lights on well into his twenties. Eventually he'd accepted the benefits of keeping oneself always on edge, always on the watch for threats. Vigilance kept him safe. So to keep himself vigilant, he dimmed his bedroom's chandelier to its lowest setting, lowered the digital fireplace to barely a flicker. Faint shadows trembled on the room's carved wainscoting and coffered ceiling. Its Aubusson rug. Ben's four-poster canopy bed. He left the lamps off.

Ben checked his shares on his laptop, washed up, and donned his percale pyjamas. The flats across the street didn't reach the height of Marley's building, so on most nights Ben could glimpse a fantastic view of the City at night from the windows here.

Not tonight, though. Too much fog. He drew thick curtains over the bedroom windows, shutting himself off from even a tenuous connection to the outside world.

Tendrils of dread gripped his chest. They came from nowhere, and had grown stronger these past few weeks. His heart thrummed like a roaring car engine for no reason at all.

Ben poured himself some scotch and settled onto his bed. He tried to get some work done, but couldn't focus. This restless energy wasn't the kind that had once spurred him on, driven him, consumed him with passion for his work. This energy bottomed out in fear he scarcely overcame each morning as he dragged himself into the office. Fear of the drudgery, the dullness of the competition he'd once lived for. Fear that all thought and action was just a physical, chemical process, and Ben was no different than any other clump of atoms playing out its script. Bound. Unfree.

The scotch disappeared quickly and Ben poured himself another glass. *I made all the right choices,* he reasserted as long-buried regrets slithered around the corners of his mind. Feelings unexpressed, friendships left abandoned – or perhaps, in Marley's case, never fully realised. *I made all the right choices, hustling, slaving over this damned-to-hell job. And now what? No one respects me. No one gives me the recognition I deserve.* As the hours dragged on, he tried to tease out what parts of his life he'd chosen for himself, and what parts he'd let others – his father, and Sandra, and the many men he aspired to outcompete – choose for him. But the two were inextricable and he couldn't tell the difference. *Am I really the self-directed man I think I am?*

The distant booming of fireworks woke Ben, an empty glass still in his hand. He rubbed his face, wanting nothing more than for slumber to take him away from this wretched world again. But unwelcome wakefulness persevered. It pulled his eyes open.

The grandfather clock in the corner showed a few minutes till one a.m. The room was silent, dark, still. Even the shadows had vanished, though Ben couldn't remember turning off the chandelier and fireplace.

He raised a hand to his forehead and found it slick with sweat. Had he had a nightmare? No. No, it was just hot. Far too hot for a December night. He checked the central heating on his home remote, but it was set to the normal 22°C.

Oh hell, did Martin leave the oven on?

But no, his chef hadn't cooked tonight. He rose from his bed and paced to the double wooden doors that led to the grand staircase. He stopped. Bright orange light radiated through the slit between the doors.

A fire? Certainly not. The alarms would've gone off. Ben thrust the doors open.

The glow was coming from downstairs, its warm light beaming up through balusters to dance on the ceiling. The light moved, flashing and flickering wildly, like a fire. But no smoke came from below.

Ben turned back to his bedroom. His mobile was nowhere in sight. He'd probably left it with his wallet in the foyer two floors down.

"Alexa, phone nine-nine-nine," Ben said to his Amazon Echo. It didn't answer. "Alexa, phone my bodyguard," he tried again.

Had someone sabotaged it? Was an arsonist trying to burn Ben alive? Flames crept up the stairs from the floor below. Ben pulled the doors shut to barricade himself in his room.

And then he heard it.

Chains. Grinding, scraping, rattling against his grand staircase as someone tugged against them.

Paranoid thoughts flicked through his mind. *Someone's been following me all day – perhaps that man from Marley's office. And now, expecting to find me asleep, they've invaded my home.* He had no way to phone the police, and he couldn't leave through a window, as his bedroom was on the fourth floor. He had no weapon. The only item in his room that might be useful for self-defence was a tall antique floor lamp.

Ben grabbed it, kicked open the door, and ran out to confront the intruder. The whole staircase was on fire now. Heat clobbered Ben, but there was still no smoke. He breathed the hot air with no ill effects as he searched the burning house for his adversary.

When he saw her, he set down the lamp.

She crawled on her hands and knees, straining to drag herself up each burning step. Thick metal chains ensnared her, wrapped in tight tangles around her neck, arms, torso, stretching into a taut web that threatened to pull her back downstairs. Wrapped up among the chains were cash boxes, briefcases, and even papers that somehow didn't burn: ledgers, deeds, profit and loss accounts, and several copies of the loan application form Ben had designed himself.

She appeared immaterial, transparent. He could see the staircase and flames and chains behind her straight through her body. But her cropped white hair and the wild determination in her eyes were unmistakable.

"Marley?" Ben said.

"Ben!" called the apparition before him, still labouring to crawl up the steps. "I think the house is on fire."

"What—? How—?" Ben stammered. He had no frame of reference for what he was seeing, and couldn't wrap his mind around it. "Uh, do you have a phone?" he asked Marley, because he didn't know what else to say. "I'd like to ring the police."

From her place on the stairs, Marley glared at him. "I just escaped from *Hell*, you plonker! Your house isn't on fire. I opened a gateway to the sodding netherworld. Come help me!"

Ben stayed put, and for a moment had a fierce debate with himself over whether any of this was real. He'd fallen asleep earlier... so maybe he was dreaming? The heat on his skin and the apparition before him certainly didn't feel like a dream. But then again, dreams never do. Ben hadn't taken hallucinogens in years, so it couldn't be that. And besides, those had never shown him anything as vivid as...

...as a roaring fire reaching up the stairs. No time to think further. Ben rushed to Marley, who was feverishly unknotting a chain from round her shoulders. When he swiped his hand down to try and help her, it passed straight through. Not only straight through the chains – straight through Marley.

"Oh, right," Marley said. "Guess you can't help me."

"Are you an actual ghost?" Ben asked.

"Naw," Marley said. She untangled another chain from her legs, ripping what appeared to be a financial contract caught in it. "I'm a hologram, like Tupac or Michael Jackson. Me and the blokes from the board thought it'd be a real laugh to fake my death and rig up this whole building with projectors and OF COURSE I'M A GHOST!"

Ben jumped backwards at her outburst. The heat buffeted his skin. Sweat matted his hair.

Though several chains still twisted tightly around her body, Marley freed herself from the last of the long ones that stretched all the way down the stairs.

And what was down there? Ben peeked over the handrail. All he saw were flames, but flames that descended a great distance. Instead of ending at the floor beneath, the inferno had already devoured that floor. It continued far lower, as if down the side of a mountain. Nothing in particular was burning; the flames continued forever as if fuelling themselves from empty air.

"Quick," Ben said. "Into the bedroom."

She tripped on a step but caught herself before she could fall. Ben tried and failed to get a grip. *Well, is she a ghost or isn't she?*

"What day is it?" Marley asked.

"What?"

"What day is it?" she shouted for emphasis.

Ben had to think for a moment as the fire rose even higher behind them. "It's Christmas. Around one in the morning."

He led Marley upwards, slammed the doors shut behind him, and locked them. Marley collapsed face forward onto her bed, running her hands over the bedsheets as if she could somehow feel them. They didn't move an inch in response to her touch.

"Ah, much better. My flat, my room, my bed." She flipped herself over – an odd, inhuman rotation of her whole body without her moving a muscle – and posed as if sitting on the edge of the bed. "Thank you for that, luv. How you been?"

"I've been..." Ben stared at his dead, transparent partner, trying to form words. "Better. I've been better."

"*You've* been better?" She glanced down at her own ethereal body, bound by the remaining chains. "Well, it's good to see you. Locked doors won't do you much good, though. We'll only have one shot at this. I'm going to lounge here, the sexy bait on the bed. You hide behind the chest of drawers and attack it when it comes through."

Ben wrinkled his brow. "Attack... *what?*"

"The spirit that's after me. The Ghost of Christmas Past. It'll come barging through the door in about sixty seconds."

"The Ghost of Christmas..."

"Past. I escaped on Christmas Day, and I don't exactly belong in the present, so I'm in its jurisdiction. It'll be after me to reharvest my soul. Perfect!"

"Perfect?"

"So we can steal its staff."

With that comment, she'd lost Ben completely. He'd had enough. "Now listen here," he said, striding up to her. "I don't care if you're a ghost. I don't care if I've gone mad. I don't care if both are true at once. Before we do anything else, we are going to find a safe spot to have a long conversation, and either everything you say is going to make crystal-clear sense, or I'm going to walk away."

Not that he would. Even in this unreal situation, a part of him – a part he kept from showing – was bursting with joy at seeing Marley again.

She crossed her arms in front of her. "You're the CEO, I'm just the COO. Is it that again?"

"Something like that," Ben said.

"Well, Mr CEO, this was my one shot. I've got no other mates, so I spent my shot on you, hoping you'd help me. If you've ever cared a jot about me in all our years together, I'm begging you. Trust me now. Help me escape."

Such sincere, serious words were downright weird coming from Marley. Ben actually let out a small gasp. If this really was his dearly departed business associate, she wouldn't speak like this unless the danger she feared was true, great, and imminent.

"Aw, shite," Marley said. "Too late."

Her eyes were looking past him, towards the door. Ben turned.

A solemn phantom, draped and hooded, emerged through the closed doors like a vapour. Yellow light shone past the door's edges, falling on the shade without illuminating it. Three feet taller than Ben, it was shrouded in a deep black garment, which concealed its head, its face, its form, and left nothing of it visible, save one outstretched hand that clutched a gnarled wooden staff.

That it had come to gather Marley's soul was fitting. It looked just like the Grim Reaper.

So overpowering was its presence that Ben instinctively backed away. Marley wanted him to *attack* this being? Ben didn't even want to breathe air in the same room as it.

"Lovely, Ben," Marley said at his retreat. "Thanks a million." Her face contorted into an expression of sorrow as she sat on the bed, gazing upwards at her approaching fate.

The ghost slid forward without moving its legs, if it even had legs. Its black robes dragged on the rug. Marley tensed, braced herself.

But the ghost slowly pivoted its head to face Ben.

Overwhelmed merely by its gaze, Ben collapsed to the floor. He crab-walked away from the thing.

The dim outline of a head appeared within the ghost's shroud as it approached. Something even worse was inside that cloak, but Ben couldn't make out any features. He felt its eyes on him.

"What do you want?" Ben said. "Anything. Name what you want and it's yours."

The ghost reached its free hand forward. A wrinkled, skeletal finger emerged, like it was starting to point at something but couldn't summon the energy. When the ghost found a foot stool in its path, it tapped it with the bottom of its staff. The stool flew across the room and shattered against a ceiling corner.

Marley used the distraction. She screeched a battle cry and leapt onto the ghost's back. *Amazing to see an old woman move like that.* Apparently losing one's body loosened one's joints. Though Marley herself was a ghost and theoretically weighed nothing, the shade buckled beneath her. She kicked its arm. Its staff tumbled onto the floor in front of Ben.

"Take it!" Marley shouted. The ghost reached behind itself to grab her, but she wrapped one of her chains around its arm and let herself drop to the floor. The ghost fell on top of her in a flurry of transparent black fabric.

Ben grabbed at the staff, expecting his fingers to pass right through it as they'd done through Marley. Instead, his hand met solid wood. Almost seven feet tall, the staff was formed from knotted wood spirals, as if two branches had grown around each other then merged together later in life. They culminated at the top of the staff, where an unearthly green glow emerged between thin breaks in the wood. It looked like something a wizard might carry.

An evil wizard.

"Think of a memory!" Marley called as she climbed out from beneath the flailing ghost. "A Christmas memory!"

"What?" Ben couldn't think of anything at the moment but the malevolent being that had invaded his sleeping quarters.

"Focus," Marley shouted. "Trust me. Think of a Christmas memory."

Marley's request barely reached Ben through his fear. "A Christmas memory? Are you a granny trying to comfort a five-year-old?"

"Think!" she repeated.

Her request was absurd, but Ben did focus. One obvious choice glimmered in his mind's eye: one memorable Christmas in his life that had been far better than all the others.

Marley scrambled across the room towards him. The ghost righted itself behind her.

"Uh, okay, I have a memory," Ben called to her. "I'm thinking of it."

"Think harder!"

Ben closed his eyes, doubled down. The memory became clear. Intensely clear. He could almost see it.

When he opened his eyes, the top of the staff was pulsing with green light.

"Not good enough," Marley said. "Ben! Think harder! Now!"

She reached him, wrapped her arms around him, and he *felt* her. Skin against skin. And the cold metal of her chains.

The ghost charged them. Its cloak fluttered wildly as it raced across the room.

Against all his impulses, Ben focused his mind like a drill onto that memory from long ago. The staff pulsed brighter. A deafening rush of air swirled around him.

The ghost and the entire bedroom exploded into the sky. Ben briefly felt like he was falling. He broke through into the memory.

Suddenly, he wasn't just thinking about the past.

He was there.

Young Again

Three pint glasses clinked hard against each other, spilling Guinness all over the table. The young trio – Ben, Marley, and Suresh – gave a cheer and drank deeply.

"Brilliant!" Marley said. "Ben, you were absolutely brill. That was the best pitch I've ever seen."

"I could've given a better pitch," Suresh said in his light Marathi accent. "My kids could've given a better pitch. But congratulations."

"Piss off, new guy," Ben said, nudging Suresh's shoulder. "I saved us. Forty years from now, at my retirement party, they'll sing songs of how the illustrious founder pulled a new pitch out of his arse and rescued the company in its cradle."

Suresh formed his hand into a chittering creature, which Ben promptly smacked into oblivion after a hearty laugh. He leant back in his chair and luxuriated in the lively rock song an Irish band was playing on the other side of the pub. The Friday-night energy of the

Londoners crowded around was infectious. He hadn't felt so happy in a long time.

No, this wasn't right. In fact, it was so, so far from right. He'd just been in the bedroom, a giant cloaked ghost closing in on him. He scanned the crowd for the ghost. For Marley. Finding them nowhere, he looked under the table.

"What happened?" Ben demanded to no one in particular. "How did I get here?"

"I was asking myself the same thing all through that utterly mediocre pitch," Suresh said.

"Marley?" Ben called to the crowd. A few punters glanced his way, but most ignored him. "Marley!"

"Right here, Ben," she said from across the table. Only the Marley speaking wasn't the Marley he knew. She looked just as she had when he'd met her. Young. Blond. Her hair shaved short in that ridiculous punk rock style she'd fancied so much.

"Not you, Marley," Ben told her. "The real Marley. The old one."

"Ahem," the young woman across from him said. "Still right here."

Ben furrowed his brows at her.

Glowing and transparent, Marley's ghost rose upwards from her younger self's body and drifted in the air above the table. Hair white, face wrinkled, body still glowing a bit but no longer nearly as translucent. Almost opaque. Ben relaxed a bit at the sight of her.

"Oh, you were so brilliant," she gushed in a high-pitched mockery of herself. "You pitch like George Michael sings. Dear God. I think I had a crush on you."

"Did you now?"

"It's good to see Suresh again!" Marley said, swooping down next to their British Indian cofounder, whom they'd met for the first time less than a day before this celebration. "Whatever happened to him?"

"Suresh, can you see the blabbering ghost woman beside you?" Ben asked.

"I expect to be paid more than each of you," Suresh said. "I'm doing more work, so I should earn more pay."

"Yes, but did you hear me about the ghost?"

"It's just a memory, Ben," Marley's ghost said. "We're not actually in the past. We're in your memory of the past. Suresh doesn't know I'm here because I wasn't here – not ghost me, anyway – when this really happened."

Ben looked from old Marley to young Marley, currently plucking a short piece of hair out of her scalp, and back again. "A… Christmas memory?" he asked.

"Perfect as a Hallmark card," ghost Marley said.

Ben froze in horror as he digested what was happening. "No," he objected. "No, not a Hallmark card. I don't want to be here. Take me back this instant."

Marley's ghost flew into the centre of the table. It bisected her stomach. She faced Ben and placed her hands on his shoulders. Again he felt them, like they were flesh and blood. "We can't go back, Ben. This is the opportunity of a lifetime. We—"

"No, no, and no. I much prefer the present, where I have a Lamborghini Sián and a holiday estate in Kyoto and control over the world around me." He stood and left the table.

"Ben!" ghost Marley called behind him. "Come on."

He left the pub and found night outside. He was in Soho, at a pub on Brewer Street. But this was not the Soho he sometimes still trekked through on his spontaneous walks around the city. Boxy old cars clogged this Soho's streets. Small shops had replaced the familiar chain stores, and the street corner closest to Ben had a freestanding phone box.

He started walking. Past Wardour Street, past a man with a mohican and a boombox smoking a cigarette outside a strip club. Ben's knees didn't hurt him. He started running.

Seconds later, the pub where he'd begun appeared ahead of him. He stopped, glanced behind him, where the same pub lingered two hundred yards back down the street. And yet, it also lay ahead of him.

What the blazes?

"You forgot your staff," Marley said. Her glowing ghost drifted down from above, past a big sign announcing Blockbuster's first video shop in the UK would be opening soon. She carried the gnarled staff they'd stolen from the phantom.

Ben caught his breath. Quite easily, strangely. "It felt so real," he said. "In the pub. It felt like it was really happening. The pitch was a success and we were celebrating..."

"Brilliant, wasn't it? Felt real to me, too."

"But I could remember my whole life afterwards. The whole future."

He gazed at the pub, at the yuppies milling about in front of it. *I am inside a memory*, he told himself, trying to believe it. *I can't run from it, or I end up back at the memory.*

"How do we leave?" Ben asked.

Marley threw him the staff. He lurched sideways and barely caught it.

"We don't," she said, floating towards him. "Ben, it's the glorious eighties. Thatcher's the PM again. Dirty Lizzie's back on the throne. Punk's maybe not quite fully dead yet! You and I can stay here, hop from Christmas to Christmas, relive the best days of our lives."

"Forever?" Ben asked, horrified.

"Well, it beats being dead."

Ben threw the staff back to Marley. She caught it effortlessly.

"What happens to my body?" Ben asked. "My real body? Presumably it's still there in the bedroom. Will that spirit cut me up or something?"

"No! It can't hurt the living. Probably your security will try to wake you up in the morning, then you'll need a feeding tube and go to a care home until your body eventually gives out in a few years. But come on, isn't it better in here? When we were young, hungry, striving? Not the miserable fat cats we became?"

Ben almost dismissed her out of hand. But he stopped himself.

Was she right? *Would* Ben be happier here, even if his physical body slowly degraded? Didn't he daydream about returning to his youth at least twice per week? To shed the weight of responsibility, to regain the energy and excitement of his younger years, to once more see the future as a grand realm of possibility rather than a sad slide towards death… Didn't Ben desperately want all this?

"Besides," Marley continued, "in here you get to spend time with me. If we go back, they'll drag me to the underworld and you won't see me again."

He held her gaze. Against his wishes, a thin smile formed on his lips. "If I go back into that pub, you'll set fire to my jacket."

"It was a celebration!" Marley protested, reflecting Ben's smile back at him.

"And I'll have to get the barman to spray it with the tap. Suresh will bet me he can down more pints than me before midnight, and we'll get absolutely wicked drunk."

"Let's go do it!" Marley said. "Again and again and again and again."

"Ha!" Ben shouted. He sprinted down the street, testing how fast his legs would carry him. He was young again! The rushing air filled his lungs so fully. His heart beat with such force. He leapt over a hydrant and hit the ground still running. The smell of fried haddock from somewhere dashed up his nostrils and made him salivate.

He stopped to glance in the window of a closed chemist's shop. His hair was dark brown, not white. His eyes were vibrant, with no drooping skin beneath. His teeth were so white!

"We can go to any day we want?" he asked Marley, who'd followed him.

She swung her final chain over her back, completely untangling herself. Beneath the metal links that had obscured her body, she wore a blazer and business trousers, as she usually had in life. She dropped the chain, and it vanished. Newly unburdened, she put her arm around Ben and again offered him the staff. "Any *Christmas* we want. That's the day we left from, that's the day we have to stay in. Test it out. Take us somewhere else."

Ben eyed her as if she'd dared him. Goose pimples rose on his arms. He snatched the staff from her.

"I take it I've persuaded you," Marley said. She rested a hand on his arm – perhaps they had to be touching in order for her to come along with him.

"We'll see," Ben said, grinning.

The green light at the top of the staff pulsed. This time, when Ben focused, he remembered more easily. It was as if every memory had lined itself up in a queue of potential destinations in his mind. Maybe the staff was helping him see them, now that he was getting used to it. Sixty-some Christmases in an orderly row. That early memory of the family dog pulling him round by his nappy. That embarrassing Christmas when he'd played a woman in a church play. All the way to last Christmas, when he'd spent the whole day working from home.

Ben goggled at them all waiting deep in his mind. *What would it feel like to be a child again?* He chose one of the early memories at random, and focused more intensely. It still took a great deal of effort, but soon the Soho buildings collapsed around them and Ben once more travelled into his past. How thrilling it would be to—

Ben ate dirt. A kinetic jolt struck him through the chin and radiated down his neck.

"Back on your feet!" a deep voice shouted. "Go, go, go!"

Dazed, Ben scanned his body for injuries. A child's body. He couldn't be older than six or seven. A football rested next to him on the grass.

Oh, yes. He remembered this.

"Ow," Ben groaned. His elbow was bleeding. He spat out a clump of grass and soil.

"Don't be a sissy," the voice said. "On your feet."

A searing midday sun silhouetted the titan standing over Ben. Muscles like rocks inside tree-trunk arms. A broad chest and a square chin. The man's shadow felt like it stretched to the horizon, like Ben would never escape its reach no matter how far he ran.

They'd been training for several hours today, Ben and his dad. Drill after drill after drill. Now Ben had failed his father again.

Graham W. Scrooge. Strong. Admirable. Ben's protector at that young age. His role model. The man meant everything to him. So he swallowed his pain and leapt back to his feet.

"Good lad," his father said. "Juggle for twenty seconds. Go."

He tossed Ben the ball, and Ben did keepy-uppies, keeping it permanently off the ground, narrowly maintaining control.

"Good," his father said, circling in front of him. "Pop it back up, pop it back up. It should land on your laces, not your toes. Keep it close to your body. Faster!"

When Ben tried to go faster, he accidentally kicked the ball too hard and had to reach out an arm to knock it back towards his feet.

"No!" his father said. "Handball. Now the other team gets the ball. Worthless. Everything you just did, worthless. If you're not a winner, you're a loser."

Head down, Ben nodded his agreement. He let the ball hit the ground. It rolled to a stop by his dad's feet.

"Zigzags now. Let's work on your cuts and turns."

Ben pushed through his pain and dribbled the ball round a series of cones. "Sloppy technique," his dad said. "Dribble with only the outside of your feet. You want to be a football star, you've gotta do better. England's won the World Cup now. You gonna win the World Cup, Ben? Huh? Not playing like this, you're not."

His dad shuffled up behind him, arms out. Ben's heart beat faster. Even at age six, the tightness that would grow all too familiar as the years went by clamped his chest.

"Check your shoulder, see if there's a defender there."

The full weight of an aggressive thirty-eight-year-old slammed into young Ben, but Ben knew better than to let that stop him. "Don't let me take it, don't let me take it." Ben didn't. He staggered, but pursued the ball and gained control of it just as his dad was about to tackle it away. "Good!" his dad said. Ben allowed himself a moment of emotional relief as he dribbled round the next cone. Then his dad was on him again. "Hold me off. Lower your centre of gravity. Don't let me push you. Good. Dominate that ball. You're its master."

Ben had pushed himself too far without realising it. He abruptly stopped to be sick. Even as his breakfast came up, he lamented that he'd failed yet again. But he could turn all that around in another minute and rewin his dad's approval.

"Fly up out of your damned body!"

An old woman's voice, not his dad's. He looked up. Marley's ghost floated before him. Ben had half-forgotten his true self, and how he'd come to be here.

"What?" Ben asked, and threw up again.

"You don't have to suffer through this tomfoolery. You can jump up out of your body just like I can."

Ben inhaled fiercely to catch his breath. "But I'm not a ghost."

"You're not a body either. Not in here. Just try it."

Sore and vomiting as he was, Ben felt very much like he was a body. But he tried to separate his spirit from it anyway.

It was surprisingly easy. Ben drifted backwards from his six-year-old self. His pain vanished at once, and he looked down at his spirit body. An old man's body again, in tartan pyjamas. Glowing and a little transparent, just like Marley.

He glanced up at her. "Wait, I'm not dead now, too, am I?"

"Hmm, you tell me," Marley said. She gestured to the empty football pitch and the town of Rochester around them – smaller here in the 1960s – decorated for Christmas. "We're inside your head. All of this comes from your memory. Would it still be here if you were dead?"

"You're dead. Don't you still have memories?"

"Only dead ones. Believe me, if I could've gone inside my own head for the rest of eternity, I would have."

"Bah," Ben grumbled. Nearby, his father was berating him again, prompting him to man up, get back to the drills.

"Well, he sure is brutal," Marley remarked. "Your dad?"

Ben nodded. "He wanted a competitive son. Thought football would bring it out in me. I had no aptitude whatsoever."

"Pff. What child would with training like this? This is more like child abuse."

Ben waved her concern away. "No. None of that, please. No sob stories here. Never once did he hit me, and that's more than can be said for some dads, especially back then."

"There's a ringing endorsement."

"Oh, he was a great man. Taught me self-reliance, toughness, how to take risks. He was a banker."

I am not my father. The thought came to him unbidden. He hated his dad. Why was he defending him?

"No!" Graham Scrooge yelled at the six-year-old. "You move towards the ball when I pass it to you. Don't stand there like a lagger."

"Yeah," Marley said, "this doesn't seem like a very happy Christmas. Let's go see another."

Ben had dropped the staff shortly after he'd arrived – the transitions were so bumpy he'd have to get used to holding onto it. He picked it up in his glowing, ghostly hand.

"So we're spirits, but we can affect the physical world," he said.

"Again," Marley said, "this isn't this physical world. For which I'm grateful. The physical world rather sucked, didn't it?"

Ben focused on finding another memory. Again, they lined up in his mind, and a few drew his attention. Christmases when *big* events in his life had happened. Some, like the venture capital pitch, attracted him like a warm summer afternoon. Others, like that final night with Sandra, threatened to suck him towards them like a black hole.

Ben avoided these tentpoles and focused on a more mundane day. A day that might give him a chance to think through whether he really wanted to stay in these liminal spaces with Marley.

But first, if she wanted to skip from Christmas to Christmas, Ben had to put a line in the sand now about one specific Christmas. The strongest black hole of them all.

"My dad died on Christmas Day," Ben said, looking out at his father running another drill. "We will not visit that day." *Both so I won't have to live through it again, and so you won't have to see it.*

Marley must have heard the gravity in his voice. All she did was nod, and wait.

Ben aimed his attention. As the football drill memory crumbled around them, his father's scolding voice lingered until the end. "Try again, Ben. Close, but close isn't enough." The penalty areas fell into the sky, the light pole bent into a hundred segments, and the buildings around them folded into the ground. "It isn't enough at all."

They arrived in a cinema nine years later, and again, it took Ben a minute to remember he was an old man, and he wasn't actually here. The smell of popping corn from the foyer, and the muffled sounds of a dozen films playing behind closed doors, drew out a nostalgic fondness for this place he hadn't realised he still harboured.

"I left a tip of five pounds on the floor for you in row nine," said an old woman leaving an auditorium through the door Ben was holding open.

"Oh, thank you very much," Ben said, and went back to gazing at his manager on the other side of the departing people.

There she was, just as he remembered her. Sandra had been his manager for the years he'd worked here. He'd worked every Christmas during that time, which meant he now had two, maybe three days of memories with her to which he could return if he wanted. This was the first; they had recently met.

Sandra wore suit trousers and a black jacket over a white button-up shirt and a necktie. Her brown hair was pulled back in a ponytail. Only a year older than Ben, she looked like a child to him now. But when he let himself fade and slide back into the memory, she regained the unfathomable, heavenly beauty only a teenager's eyes could see.

She grinned at him. Something in his chest fluttered and he felt light and airy.

"Ooh, who's this?" Marley said, her ghostly form floating next to Sandra, examining her.

"This is my good friend from secondary school named None of Your Business," Ben said.

"Well, None of Your Business is staring at you with lovey eyes, and you're staring right back."

Ben snorted. He'd managed to hold onto the staff this time. He tossed it to Marley and she caught it. He followed Sandra inside the auditorium as the credits rolled on the big screen.

One last customer still leaving their row stopped to pick something up off the floor. "Look, Harold, I found a fiver." She pocketed the money and walked past Ben and Sandra, who stifled laughter.

"Oh well," Ben said. Sandra turned on the lights and they started sweeping the floor. The credits finished. Marley took a seat near to the back and rested her feet on the chair in front of her, as if enjoying some entertainment of her own.

"Have you seen this one yet?" Ben asked Sandra, gesturing to the screen.

"About the kid who turns out to be the Antichrist?" Sandra said, cringe-laughing. "No. I would never."

"It's good. Scary."

"I can't see scary films. *Jaws* gave me nightmares for months."

"*Jaws?*" Ben asked, stopping his sweeping to gape at her in amazement. "That's not even a horror film. It's about a fish."

"A big, scary fish that can eat you!"

"And it looks like a robot."

"So if I'm scared to death of a robot shark, you think I'll do just fine with the Antichrist child?"

Ben chewed on her comment for a moment, then returned to cleaning popcorn off the floor. "Tell you what," he said. "If you come see *The Omen* with me, I'll see any film you want with you."

From across several rows, Sandra glanced up at him. *Are you asking me on a date?* her unsure eyes seemed to say.

"Just, you know, if you want to," Ben said.

Marley chuckled from the back row.

"Shut it," Ben told her. "I was fifteen. I was trying to be polite."

"Have you heard of *The Rocky Horror Picture Show?*" asked Sandra.

"I have!" Ben said. "I've been wanting to see it."

Sandra jumped back a step, her eyes wide. "What? No one I talk to has heard of that film. Where did you hear about it?"

"I pay attention to these things," Ben said. He felt the next words in his throat, and he tried to keep them in. But memory was memory, and they came tumbling embarrassingly out. "I want to be an actor."

Marley's jaw dropped. She raised her hands to cover her mouth.

Yeah, yeah. Get it out of your system. I was young once, too.

"*The Omen* for *Rocky Horror Picture Show*," Sandra said. "It's a deal. Though I think you're getting the better end of it, since you want to see both films."

Indeed, Ben had gotten the better end of it. Inside, he was doing somersaults, but he let only a mild smile show on his face. Sandra had walked down by the screen to the exit door, which she now opened.

"Come on," Sandra said.

"Outside?" Ben asked.

"Yeah. Ten-minute non-smoke break. If the smokers get a ten-minute break every few hours, why shouldn't we?"

Young Ben delighted at the thought of spending ten minutes with Sandra, breathing fresh air under the overhang outside while rain fell around them. They'd gabbed more about films, got to know each other a bit. But old Ben, as much as he wanted to lose himself in the bliss of spending time again with his teenage crush, had more important matters to attend to. Something dark and terrible had been bothering him ever since this misadventure started.

"Marley," he said, "walk with me."

She raised a quizzical eyebrow. Sandra stood waiting for Ben by the screen exit door, but there she would stay. He left the way he'd entered, back into the cinema hallway, still in his young body. Marley followed.

"An *actor*? Ben, you never told me."

"I wonder why."

"And what happened to her? You'd have been a cute couple. She'd have been better for you than all that arm candy you've promenaded with over the years."

Four children ran past them, forming their fingers into gun shapes and making gunshot noises at each other. Ahead, cinema foot traffic milled between the foyer and auditoriums. Was this Ben's mind filling in the blanks of the location? He certainly hadn't had this walk with Marley before, and so his mind should've had no memory to replay here.

"The company forbade any romance between managers and employees," Ben said. "My dad saw this job as character-building. He'd have killed me if I lost it over a girl."

"But you did date her eventually?"

Ben stopped beside the door to another auditorium where *The Omen* was playing. A rectangular window in the door let him see through to the screen, where some men were walking through an eerie cemetery.

"You said you've been to Hell?" Ben asked.

Marley frowned and crossed her arms. "Let's not talk about that. I'm free now. Let's enjoy ourselves."

"But it exists?" said Ben, turning to her. "If you ended up there, I'll bet you my net worth I will too. What's it like? Fire, devils, punishment from God?"

And is there a way for me to escape your fate?

Marley dithered, shifting her head back and forth. "Plenty of fire, none of the other bits. It's more like…" She exhaled heavily, and her usual chipper tone devolved into rare melancholy. "Like you have to experience the pain of all the people you've ever hurt. You're weighed down by chains you unknowingly forged in life, link by link. They tell you it'll end when you learn selflessness, but I mean, how am I supposed to learn to be someone I'm not? I'm great and I deserve nice things more than other people do. So sue me."

On screen, the men struggled to dig a coffin out of its grave. "And how did you escape?" Ben asked.

"Oh, it was quite clever. I froze a bunch of my chains on the Ghost of Winter Solstice Past as she walked by, put them right into a fire, and *bam!* Fractured them. A lot of the ghosts wear those cloaks, like our big bad friend back in my bedroom. I hid my remaining chains under a cloak, dressed up as a ghost, and walked right out the front door."

Ben turned from the auditorium, leaving *The Omen* behind, and paced towards the foyer. "You keep talking about these ghosts, or spirits, or whatever. What are they?"

"I mean, they're ghosts. Some ghosts haunt places, but most haunt ideas. Each ghost has jurisdiction over its idea."

"But why Christmas? Why not the Ghost of Easter or the Ghost of New Year's Day?"

"Well, if I'd escaped on one of those days, I assume one of them would be after me with its own giant magic phallic symbol." She dipped the staff forward and rapped Ben on his head.

"Perhaps the Ghost of the Summer Bank Holiday would've been friendlier."

"But you *really* don't want to meet the Ghost of Guy Fawkes Night Past. Bleedin' terrifying he is."

Ben stopped in the foyer. Queues had formed to wait for refreshments. People with bell-bottom jeans, denim vests, long sideburns. *I'm stretching my luck here.* He had no doubt that if he tried to go outside, this ouroboros of a place would lead him right back to Sandra. "So there are Past Ghosts, and... what? Future Ghosts?"

"There are. I don't really understand it. I only learnt about them from eavesdropping in the underworld. The Past and Future Ghosts are at war with each other, or something like that."

Ben tuned out his surreal surroundings – the 1970s! – and focused again on his dearly departed business partner. A strand of her short hair hung over her forehead, as usual. The wrinkles at the edges of her mouth lay in a pattern that advertised she smiled often. Even as a ghost who didn't need to touch the ground, she moved with decisive purpose, like she always had somewhere to be and damn anyone who got in her way.

No matter how preposterous of a situation they found themselves in, Ben couldn't deny an element of joy. "Marley, it's dreadfully good to see you again."

She smiled that authentic, full-faced Marley smile, from her chin all the way to her eyes. "Good to see you, too, old friend."

Ben clasped her on the shoulders. "We'll need to figure out what to do about your situation, but I'll stay with you here, for a while at least."

"After that display in there, I'm dying all over again to see more of your younger years. Want to go back to that girl and embarrass yourself some more, or is there anyone else you'd rather visit?"

The momentary happiness Ben felt when he let himself get swept away by a Sandra-related memory was pure bliss indeed. But his older self had little desire to spend more time with her now that he'd satisfied his initial curiosity. Perhaps that lack of desire was a tad too pointed, in fact. So the question became: if not Sandra, who from his unhappy past did he truly want to see again?

There was one. One other person he wanted to see again very much.

Not a Penny

They found Annie on a playground in a memory from a Christmas in the late 1960s. She and Ben had gone with their father on some type of errand, and he'd stopped at a bench while the children played. Six other kids romped around, jumping up to hang on the climbing frame or diving arms first down the slide. Annie, standing straight and self-assured at the top of the steps leading up to the slide, informed the others she'd be charging them one piece of woodchip mulch for each use of the slide.

Ben climbed up the slide from the bottom to get around his sister's monopoly. He had to scoot to one side as another child slid down, but eventually he made it to the top. "I am the slide pirate!" he called as he grabbed a handful of Annie's collected mulch and threw it into the air.

Annie squealed and giggled. "No fair! That's my slide!"

"The slide pirate bows to no one," Ben said, and pushed Annie hard. She fell. Ben ran down the steps, clambered onto a swing, stood on it rather than sat, and leant back to start it swinging.

"You shoved that little girl, you poxy little minger," Marley's ghost said from the swing next to him. She sat in it but didn't swing, and watched Annie trying to gather the mulch Ben had scattered.

Ben shrugged, and spoke with his child's voice. "Not the worst thing I've ever done. She's my sister."

"Uh, still not okay to shove her."

Two children ran past Annie while she was amassing her mulch back into a pile, violating her collection racket.

"Did Frieda ever know her mum?" Marley asked as the future mum in question left her mulch to chase the other kids her age down the slide.

The memory twisted deep inside Ben. "She was even younger than this when Annie died. I don't think she ever did know her."

"Ben," his father called to him. In real life, Ben wouldn't dare ignore him. But in this realm free of consequences, Ben disregarded Graham and hopped off the swing. He took in the old terraced houses wrapping around the small square containing the playground, feeling out of place in time. Wreaths decorated several doors, and some houses had turned on their fairy lights to brighten this overcast day.

Ben approached Annie as she climbed back up to the slide. "I'm sorry I shoved you," he said.

Annie stuck her tongue out at him and grinned, revealing two gaps where adult teeth hadn't yet grown in. Above, her mates beckoned for her to follow them. One of them was a girl, Susan, with whom Annie would bond closely and stay close to even as an adult.

She'd always had more friends than Ben. It was what he got for working himself to death while Annie prioritised her relationships with other people. This girl in front of him would never go to university, she'd never earn much money, but she'd always have a great many friends. She would earn what she worked for, just like Ben.

"Annie," he said. "Thank you for being my sister. Thank you for the light you brought to my life. I love you dearly. I hope you know I have the highest respect for the warm, compassionate soul you cultivated within yourself. You mean so much to me. You always will."

Annie stared, and for a moment, Ben imagined his words had reached her, that she was so touched by what he'd said that she couldn't react. But then she grabbed the railing and pulled herself up the steps. "Come on, Ben. We're going to play *Chitty Chitty Bang Bang* at the top. You can sit in the passenger seat." She left him.

This conversation had never happened, of course. Annie wouldn't respond to it in Ben's memory. He exhaled in disappointment.

Preoccupied with thoughts of his sister and her abbreviated future, he let the memory play out, and ended up back by his dad on the bench. He still clutched the magic staff in his hand and he nearly teleported away, but recollection nudged the back of his mind. A memory he hadn't known was here. He'd easily recalled Annie on the playground, but this next conversation with his father might have remained half-forgotten were he not actually here to relive it.

He glanced at one particular terraced house, its old bricks miscoloured by age and weather, with one window boarded up and overgrown weeds clogging its small lawn. A boy Ben's age sat on the steps in front of the house, waiting. In a few minutes, two men would leave through the front door, one carrying a crowbar. The boy's father would limp to the door and call him back inside, and Ben's father would nod his acknowledgement to the two thugs who'd just beat the boy's father up.

Ben marvelled at this small slice of his past that he hadn't thought of even once since the day it happened.

"Your sister's quite enterprising," his dad said as Ben sat beside him. Annie was collecting more mulch as the admission price to her flying fantasy car.

His father's words hadn't directly compared Ben to Annie, but even at such a young age, he understood the implication. Brisk air chilled his face. He zipped his coat up tighter and stuffed his gloved hands in his pockets, as much to protect him from shame as from the cold.

"She's playing, you fool," Ben said. "She's not 'enterprising' at all. From your perspective, she'll amount to even less than I will."

The memory of his father didn't hear him. In real life, Ben had remained silent.

"What do you want to be when you grow up?" Graham asked him.

Not a football striker, although that was the first answer to come to Ben's mind. His dad would have liked that answer.

"A firefighter," Ben answered honestly. "Or maybe a teacher."

"Try again, lad. You're not that stupid."

Ben chided himself for not giving the obvious answer. The one his dad would like best.

"I want to be a CEO," Ben said. "A millionaire CEO." The answer was true to Ben's memory – he had actually said this to his dad. How many kids his age actually knew what a CEO was, especially in the 1960s? More to the point, how many kids his age had parents who made sure their child knew what a CEO was?

In fact, Ben had no clue what he wanted to be when he grew up. He didn't have enough of a concept of his own identity or self-worth to have an opinion on the matter.

"And married to Raquel Welch," Ben added for good measure.

Ben's dad laughed at that. Marley, drifting nearby, rolled her eyes.

"Come here," Graham said. "I want to show you something."

Ben scooted closer to his dad, who slipped something out of his wallet. A time-worn photo, black and white. It showed a family, perhaps an extended family, seated in a one-room wooden house in front of an ancient cast-iron cooking range. Five adults and – Ben took a moment to count – fourteen little ones. Each person's clothing appeared to be stitched together from two or more different fabrics. Soot stained the children's faces and hair.

Ben's dad pointed to the baby one of the adults was holding. "That's your old man," he said. "And that's your grandad you never met, holding me. He kept a lighthouse in Essex. No one else in the picture ever worked a day in their life. The family resorted to petty thievery to make ends meet."

Not a day in their life? That was improbable, but as a child Ben had accepted the statement at face value.

"I carry this picture to remind me who we are. Rubbish, lad. We come from rubbish. Your mum knew it when she walked out on us. You'll know it too, when you're old enough. It'll follow you every day of your life." He placed a hand on Ben's neck and turned his face – with a bit too much force – to look at his. "But you work hard. You work harder than anyone. You go out there every day and you win. And you'll become better than your roots."

There was strangely little disconnect between Ben's child and adult perceptions of his father's lesson: it landed heavily on both versions of him. His dad wanted what was best for him, and no matter how cut-throat his life advice, the fact that he bothered to advise Ben at all signalled that he cared about him, in his way. Young Ben, emotionally starving, devoured this unusual form of affection and took Graham's words to heart.

"Some people will be jealous of your wealth and success. They'll try to take it from you. Give it to lesser men." He gestured towards the dirty boy sitting on the steps of the dilapidated terraced house, and by implication to the boy's family inside. "Don't you touch folks like that. They'll drag you down."

He held the old photo right up to Ben's eyes. Ben stared at his relatives across the years, at people who had full lives and loves and dreams. His child's eyes couldn't see what his adult eyes did. His child self saw only what his father wanted him to see: undeserving shells of half-people.

"Remember, lad. A boy yields. A man achieves."

Ben had had enough. He left his body, detaching himself from the young mind that processed his father's words like profound morsels of divine wisdom. From the outside, he looked upon himself as a boy.

He seemed for a moment to be someone else. An object of sympathy whose life Ben had never lived. Ben had remembered his father, horrible though the man was, as having given him the tools and the grit he needed to succeed in life. Hearing his words again, fresh and caustic, he wondered for the first time whether those tools had harmed him as much as, or more than, they'd helped.

The boy voiced more platitudes to ingratiate himself with his father. Not that he had a choice. Verbal abuse would have followed had he voiced disagreement.

"What kind of a banker did you say your dad was again?" Marley asked, floating up beside him and eyeing his thugs in the distance, just now leaving the house.

Ben didn't respond. In truth, he didn't actually know.

"You look sad," Marley said. Ben couldn't tell whether she was talking about him, or the child on the bench. "You look like you blamed yourself for all the shortcomings your dad dreamt up."

"I said no pity," Ben said, pointing at her. Marley witnessing this vulnerable part of his past was humiliating enough. She didn't need to cast him as a helpless weakling. A burden. After enduring a childhood like this, he was proud to have developed the mental fortitude to never be a burden on anyone, least of all those closest to him.

To hell with this memory. Ben clutched the staff tight. He focused. The terraced houses, the bench and playground, the boy and his dad were sucked into oblivion. A cinema projection booth replaced them. Sandra came with her own painful memory, but Ben could simply avoid that one. He needed a pick-me-up after seeing his dad again. It had been so pleasant just to be in her presence again. The one that got away.

Back in his teenaged body – apparently, he always began each memory back in his body – Ben dipped a mop into a bucket, ridding it of the grime he'd just wiped off the floor. "Marley, is this really what you want? To live in my memories with me? It seems a sad way to spend your afterlife."

"Like I said, it's better than the alternative," she said, examining the dirty water. "I did miss you terribly down there, though."

She missed me? It must have been true: Marley had come to him, of all people. Yes, she was using his memory as a safe place to hide, but she also seemed to genuinely want to reconnect with him. Ben had this impossible opportunity to speak again with the woman who was arguably the most important figure in his life, and here he was gallivanting through childhood memories, ignoring her.

Was this habit? For how many years *had* he been ignoring her, consigning her to secondary status in his mind, taking her presence and support for granted?

He leant the mop against a wall and looked her in the eyes.

"Hmm?" she said, meeting his gaze. He could see right through that gaze, to the film projectors beaming their light through second-floor windows in the long, dark room behind her.

"Marley," Ben said, "whatever it takes, we'll get you safe. But let's please find pleasant memories and relive those again and again. I don't think I have too many Christmas memories I actually want to relive."

And what memories *did* he want to relive? His realisations that he was a millionaire, then, decades later, a billionaire? His trip with Marley to Richard Branson's private island? His intimacies with the dozen women he'd dated in his thirties and forties? *Well, maybe not that last one. Marley might ghost-vomit.* Regardless, none of these had taken place on Christmas, so Ben couldn't visit them.

"I'm all for pleasant memories," Marley said. "I'm sure you have a few. What's this one? You worked at the cinema on Christmas?"

"Christmas Eve. It's just past midnight. We're closing up."

"Ben?" called a voice from several projectors away.

"Ah," Marley said. "Your first love again?"

Ben nodded, strangely embarrassed to be visiting Sandra again. *There's nothing to be ashamed of. Most people have fond memories of their youthful romances.*

He walked to the sweets room, an area within the larger projection booth enclosed by horizontal metal bars. Marley followed, a curious voyeur. Like the Grinch who stole Christmas, Ben's heart seemed to grow three sizes upon seeing Sandra again, elegant and beautiful in her simple manager's uniform.

"Could you grab my keys?" she asked through the open space between the bars. "They should be on top of the freezer over there."

"You've... locked yourself in the sweets room?" Ben asked.

"I've locked myself in the sweets room," she said. She flashed him a brief, cheesy grin.

Ben checked the low freezer. "Um, I don't see any keys here."

"They're right on top."

"Are they invisible keys?"

Sandra let out a long sigh. "They're probably down in the refreshment stand."

Ben laughed. "No problem. I'll go fetch them."

"Don't bother. Here." Sandra leant down and slid her head between two of the bars separating her from Ben. She pushed her torso past them and tried to pull her whole body through.

Ben rushed to help her. They grabbed each other's arms, and he pulled. Sandra slipped through the bars. Her feet hit the linoleum floor, but off-balance, and she stumbled into Ben.

He caught her, his arms completely encircling her in what felt an awful lot like a hug. He quickly let go and she righted herself, but this still left them inches away from each other. Her breath tickled his face like a feather. Her face was flushed from the exertion.

And yet, Ben's memory of Sandra was a shell of who the real woman had been. After decades had passed, he couldn't remember her goals, her fears, or even her personality. Only the longing. Only this object of a person he'd once yearned to call his girlfriend.

They stood there for a moment, eyes locked on each other. His older self, feeling these things again, wanted to change the past, tell her exactly how he felt right at this moment. He could certainly say the words.

But she wouldn't hear them. No matter what he said or did, the memory could only play out one way: the way he remembered it. Sandra would react to what Ben had said then, not to anything new he said now. So he suppressed his urge to change the past. He let himself act out the script.

He backed up, and looked away. "Uh, do you want to come check if I cleaned the refreshment stand well enough?"

Sandra cleared her throat as if cleansing herself from whatever thoughts had just come over her. "Nah, I trust you. I have to finish up here. Eddie's picking me up in fifteen minutes."

"Brilliant. Cheers," Ben said. He turned to leave.

"Wait a minute, wait a minute," Marley said. "Time out. Who is Eddie?"

Ben stopped walking and let out a slight groan. If Marley was going to eavesdrop on his past, she needed to learn not to pry.

Sandra didn't literally freeze, like a video on pause; she stood there as an idling memory, watching him go. These memories seemed to be put on hold every time he went off script.

"Eddie is Sandra's boyfriend," Ben said.

Marley clutched her head like her brains were about to spill out and she was desperately holding them in. "You broke up with her?"

Reluctant words took a second to leave Ben's mouth. "I haven't actually dated her yet."

"You haven't told her you fancy her?"

"I'm working up to it."

"It's been a whole year since you took her to the pictures, Ben!" Marley's hands burst outwards from her head and she blurted an "explosion" noise. "You duffer. And now she has a boyfriend?"

"Sandra's strapped for cash. She needs this job. If she makes a pass on an employee, she could be sacked."

"Come on, what teenager actually follows those rules? And even if she does, then you make the first move!"

Ben almost retorted with a reminder of his dad's expectations, but the excuse would've been obvious. His affection for Sandra had weighed on his heart with the raging intensity of a teenager's first real infatuation. Yet he'd stifled his feelings for so long. Why?

The memory interrupted his thoughts.

"Thanks for looking at my CV, by the way," Sandra said, unlatching some sprockets inside a projector. "I sent in a few applications yesterday."

Her words came unexpected. Ben probed his recollection. *Sandra was trying to find a career, not just a job, yes? And I'd been assisting.*

"That's great!" he said. "Happy to help."

"What about you?" Sandra asked. "I'd love to return the favour."

"Me? Oh, I'm fine. I'm just focused on school right now."

"Off to university next year?"

"Maybe," Ben said. "Haven't decided yet. I'm happy here for now, though. I'll find a new job once I finish school." The words disgusted Ben as they left his mouth. *Did I really have so little ambition? How much time did I waste making money for other people instead of for myself?* His father had drilled ambition into him, and he'd known to always speak in front of his father like the industrious son Graham wanted him to be... but he hadn't really internalised any of it. That early training hadn't kicked in and started to change his life until later.

"Hmm," Sandra said. She spun a film platter and wound the ending strip of film back onto its reel. "Maybe take a year off? Travel the world?"

A half-dozen unimaginative places to which he'd like to travel one day sprang into Ben's young mind. Brussels. Orlando.

Ugh. Rank.

"That'd be nice," Ben replied. "I don't know if my dad would pay for it, but I can dream."

"He's enough money," Sandra said. "You should pitch it to him. Son travels the world, finds himself, decides to become a barrister or a surgeon." She crossed her hand in front of her face like she was reading a newspaper headline.

I'm not sure he'll see it like that, Ben thought.

"Bora Bora and Santorini," Sandra said. "Those are my dream destinations. Maybe not tomorrow, but we should go together someday."

That sounded brilliant to young Ben, but he was too shy to say so, so he just chuckled.

"This is actually painful," Marley said. She'd taken a popcorn bucket off a stack and was pantomiming throwing some into her mouth. "Two people who clearly have the hots for each other but won't bleedin' say it."

"Shh," Ben said. Sandra's destinations, at least, were an improvement on his own. "I'd love to," he said to Sandra.

"Eddie doesn't want to go with me, so I have to find someone else," Sandra said. She flipped off the sound system switches, then wrapped a protective cover over the top of the film reel. "He has trouble imagining a shared future in a lot of ways. I'm not sure we'll work out, actually."

Marley tossed her popcorn bucket aside and raised her hands in an *I give up* gesture. The bucket clattered to the floor but Sandra, the memory, didn't notice it.

"I wish there were, like, a magic unicorn you could get on who would take you to the single most compatible person in the world for you," Sandra said. Ben followed her as she moved to the next projector.

"I don't know," Ben responded. "I think I'd rather just match with someone I already know really well and do my best to make it work."

"That's lazy, Ben," Sandra said. "Unicorns take work."

Ben chuckled. "I don't know that I'm particularly datable at the moment, anyway, so I may wait for the unicorn after all."

"Really?" Sandra said, leaning back from the projector she'd been tinkering with. "Why aren't you datable?"

Her eyes rested on his with curious intensity. The unspoken subtext was clear even to Ben's younger mind: she was interested in him. And maybe he'd been fishing, just a bit, in hopes that that subtext would emerge.

But he'd talked himself into a corner. Now, with the spotlight on him, he'd have to follow up his comment with either self-deprecating humour to suggest that no, actually, he wouldn't be *that* bad to date right now – or retract his statement and ask out a girl who was already dating someone else. At sixteen, he wasn't smooth enough to do either.

An unpleasant twisting sensation coiled in his gut. Not the usual anxiety. Something worse. Ben had had the good fortune to forget this stomach pain later in life, but now it burgeoned inside him like a knife. The start of all his troubles.

I was already starting to feel this pain at sixteen?

"I'm not sure," he told Sandra, ashamed to have to leave such a conversation so abruptly. He needed the loo. "Sorry, I need to finish up in the refreshment stand and head home. I've got an early morning with my family tomorrow. And then of course I have my performance in the park."

Sandra looked confused at how the possibility of romance had retreated so quickly. Ben left his body to escape the sudden stomach pain, and watched his younger self retreat downstairs. Sandra didn't return to her work. She stayed by the projector, disappointment forever on her face. The last memory Ben had of her tonight.

"Uh, what was that?" Marley asked.

"I got sick," Ben said. "It was a whole thing. This was just the start."

"You sure you weren't just petrified at the idea of telling her you like her?"

"Piss off. I wasn't that much of a—"

Motion at the far end of the projection booth caught Ben's eye and stilled his tongue. Black mist blossomed inside one of the projectors that was still running, choking its light. The cloud grew, and a tall, cloaked figure drifted out of it.

The phantom. The same being from Marley's bedroom. It carried a new staff, straighter than the first.

"Marley," Ben said, drawing her attention to the ghost.

She startled when she saw the thing. "Oh! Well, that's awful."

"It can follow us here?"

"Ben, run!"

The ghost bolted towards them, not running or otherwise using its legs, if it had legs. It flew inches above the floor. Ben and Marley dashed into the stairwell. Marley floated just like the phantom, but Ben hadn't learnt the knack of it yet, despite being an apparition himself. His feet thumped on step after step as he raced down the stairs.

"You failed to mention," Ben said, "that the ghost would keep chasing us through my memories trying to *murder us*!"

"Murder *me*, if we're being pedantic," Marley said.

"So your plan to memory-hop for the rest of our lives also involves avoiding the murder ghost, which could show up at any time?"

They exited into the first-floor hallway. Ben slammed the door behind them.

"Again," Marley said, "better than the alternative."

"Maybe for you!"

Ben tried to concentrate and transport them into a new memory, but he was too panicked. "I can't focus with that thing after us," he said, running down the hallway. "What do we do?"

"I don't know. It shouldn't be able to follow us. We have its magic staff. I don't know how it got another."

They fled through the empty foyer, past Ben's younger self leaving the loo, and outside the cinema into western Rochester, just north of the River Medway. Marley floated straight through the doors, a true ghost. Ben hadn't figured that trick out yet either – how could she choose what to physically interact with and what not to? – so he pushed through the doors and stumbled out into the night.

At this late hour, early on Christmas morning, not a soul was out on the streets. Every business in sight had long since closed. Running, Ben gripped the staff and tried to focus on the many memories it arrayed in his mind. In his terrified state, it was harder to choose between them, and the memories with strong emotional resonance called to him with even more strength than they had before.

How far could they run before the memory switched geography around and led them back to the cinema? If they couldn't run, was there somewhere they could hide?

Ben spotted one of those old freestanding police boxes at a junction corner down the street. He bolted towards it, and Marley followed.

"This is only a memory!" she said. "The police can't help us."

"We can hold the door shut. Keep it outside."

"Ben, it's a ghost! It can go through walls."

"Well, where else do we go?"

He glanced behind them. The phantom diffused through the cinema's front doors. It searched for them, saw them, then charged.

Ben picked a memory and burrowed into it as much as his mind was able. The ghost was much faster than them and covered half the distance between them in seconds. It raised its staff as if to strike them.

They reached the police box. Marley shoved the door open. They ran inside...

… into the nave of St Mark's Church. A Christmas worship. Rows of adults sat watching children perform a skit in the chancel, beneath variegated stained-glass windows. Gothic arches ran the length of the large room between the nave and the aisles.

Ben searched for the door of the police box behind them, but it was gone, replaced by the church's front doors. He marvelled at the ample space in front of them.

"It's bigger on the inside," he said. Marley nodded her own amazement.

But Ben's cue was up! He hobbled down the centre aisle, forgetting the ghost. He was a kid again, playing elderly Elizabeth, the mother of John the Baptist. He spoke in a high-pitched voice as he greeted the girl playing Mary, and exclaimed how the babe had just leapt in his womb. Some of the younger onlookers laughed at the spectacle. Most of the older congregation members scowled in surprised confusion.

The Sunday school teacher – who, in retrospect, was probably gay and sympathetic to Ben's insistent pleading – took much convincing to let Ben play a girl's part. Girls were playing the three wise men, after all, so why couldn't Ben play a woman? The other children had thought it was funny, and Ben played along with them, laughing like it was a joke. But truthfully, it was a serious business to him. What other character in the Christmas story was so unlike Ben, and would be as challenging to play? Slipping into another, very different person's skin, taking their perspective, and acting from that point of view had excited him terribly. It felt like playing with action figures, but real. *Strange that I lost that interest as the years went on.*

Still, the performance was quite cheesy, and unintentionally comic.

"Can it still follow us?" Ben asked Marley from across the nave. None of the adults reacted to him going off script.

Marley cringed and looked behind her. "Maybe? I've no clue. I'd expect it'll have to check each of your Christmas memories one by one to find us again, but what do I know? Should we hop memories again just to be safe?"

Ben ignored his eagerness to get his next line right, waited for Marley's ghostly form to drift past the congregation and touch him, then quickly jumped them away. Fleeing to a later portion of the same memory turned out to be much easier than springing into an entirely different one, so he didn't jump them far.

After the worship, alongside Canterbury Street, Ben was sitting in the passenger seat of his dad's 1965 Sunbeam Tiger playing with his Thunderbirds action figures. He was having Brains give Scott Tracy a rundown of his new fighter jet when his dad flung open the car door and snatched the action figures from his hands. He dropped them onto the pavement outside the car and stomped on them repeatedly, crushing them all.

Hovering outside the car, Marley gasped at the outburst.

"No!" Ben cried. He leapt from the car and scurried to pick up the pieces of his figurines.

"These are toys for boys," his dad said. "If you want to be a woman, you go play with dolls."

Ben tried to hold his tears back. He'd saved up for months to buy these. "I-I thought it'd be funny," Ben said, sobbing. Maybe his dad would take his performance as a joke just like the other kids had.

"Well, it wasn't."

Ben's face grew hot. He started bawling, so he left his body again. The fierce emotions of a child tasted sour in his adult mind.

"This guy, again," Marley said as they watched Graham berate young Ben, weeping on the asphalt. "Did he ever do anything kind for you or Annie? Take you to a football match and buy you a meat pie?"

"I'm not going to discuss this," Ben said. "He was who he was, and I'm both better and worse for it."

Marley shook her head. She rested her hands in her blazer's pockets, and sighed deeply. "Isn't it weird we assume our kids will never grow up and critically evaluate the way they were raised? We treat kids like a whole separate species instead of like future adults."

Her comment brought thoughts of Rhys and his video gaming. What would Ben's son think about him someday when he reflected on his own childhood? Ben didn't know. He hadn't been there for much of it.

He cast Marley a sidelong glance. "Odd thing to say for someone who has no kids of her own."

Marley shook her head. "Just saying. It's sad we don't notice good parenting until decades after the fact, too. My dad always told me to ignore my mum whenever she told me a woman's place was in the kitchen. With a few simple words, he probably saved me from a shite life."

"Let's visit your childhood memories, then," Ben said. "Dissect *your* parents."

She smiled with only half her mouth. "Can't. I'm dead, remember?"

"Not as dead as you used to be. What would we see, Marley? Tell me. I bet we'd see a sob story, and I'd be bored to tears, because everyone's childhood is a sob story."

"Everyone's childhood is not! Some people have great childhoods."

"Like whom?"

"Lots of people. My childhood was happy. I was a berserk supergirl climbing on everything in sight, crawling round with my dogs on my back so they could ride me like I was their transport turtle."

"Mmm, yes, sounds like you."

Though Ben's father continued his rant, Ben and Marley rested for a moment in the sunny Gillingham morning. Light traffic made its way past the shops across the street. A group of starlings alighted on the church's tall roof. How many times had Ben wandered these streets with Annie, chatting with the shopkeepers, exploring back alleys, not a care in the world? Much less helicopter parenting in the sixties. More social trust. Ben's father was among the many who let their children roam free.

"I was raised to be a wife, if you must know," Marley said. Unusually sombre, she seemed to be looking into the past, too. *In all our years of partnership, have we never opened up about our younger years?* Ben's childhood had been too painful, his youth too embarrassing. He'd always taken Marley's silence on her past to mean she felt similarly about it. But hearing her share this piece of herself with him for the first time made him wish they'd spoken of it sooner. It might have deepened their connection; they might have become true friends rather than mere coworkers.

"Wear the right dresses, the right makeup," Marley continued. "Become the world expert in cooking and cleaning. Keep myself beautiful enough and conventional enough to snag a good man, be his domestic servant the rest of my life. Pop out five or six kids. Say goodbye to any hope of a career." She kicked a rock down the pavement. "I guess there are some women it worked for, but my mum wanted to force it on every woman. She's rolling in her grave that I never got hitched."

Ben's child self returned to the passenger seat and tried to connect the surviving pieces of his action figures back together. "My dad's rolling in his grave over a great many things, too."

"It's like, the more you pressure your kids to be a certain way, the more likely they'll do the opposite," Marley said. "Why does no one understand that?"

"I didn't do the opposite," said Ben. "The pressure does work sometimes."

Marley glanced at Ben with questioning eyes, vaguely sad. "You're worth more than was planned for your life, you know."

He met her gaze. Wisps of her white hair blew in the light wind. "Thanks," he said. "So are you."

"Stop crying," Graham demanded. He got in the car with Annie and slammed the door. Young Ben cried even harder.

"All right, enough of this," old Ben said. He strode around the Sunbeam, opened the door, grasped his younger self by the hand, and pulled him from the car.

It worked. The child stumbled into the street. His dad started the engine and drove off, ignorant that his child had been abducted.

Ben gripped the staff tightly and closed his eyes. When Marley saw what he was trying to do, she rushed over to him.

Rochester dissolved around them in bits and pieces. St Mark's flew apart brick by brick, and Regent's Park in London coalesced in its place. By the time the trees, the stage, the hundreds of seats in the Open Air Theatre and the people to fill them had dropped into place, Ben no longer felt the boy's hand in his own. When he looked, the boy was gone.

Marley patted him on the back. "It would be nice," she said with a grim smile.

Yet, in a way, a bit of Ben's younger self was still with him: he was back on stage, where he'd always loved to be, this time playing Gayev in Chekhov's *The Cherry Orchard*. A big part – he'd come a long way since Elizabeth in the Sunday school skit. The entire cast were teenagers. While still in secondary school, Ben had fallen in with a group of first-year theatre students at the university in Gillingham and talked them into letting him perform with them.

He'd practised months for this. Now he strutted across the stage with aplomb. His lines were precisely memorised, so he stayed in each moment, reacting, building his energy off the other performers. Intentions zinged from one person to another all around the stage in a game of emotional ping-pong. But subtle. It had to feel spontaneous, unrehearsed.

Ben had forgotten the thrill of losing oneself so completely in the moment that he could all but ignore an audience of hundreds. He'd forgotten he loved this so much. Not a thought in his mind about wealth or status. Just his character, his mates and their characters… and Sandra. She sat in the fifth row, watching. He hadn't known she was coming. His heart jolted as the memory surprised him with her presence all over again, like it was happening for the first time.

They'd just spoken about travel and dating during their closing conversation last night at the cinema, when Ben and Marley had fled from the ghost. And now she was here. She'd come all the way to London for him! That had to be a message, right? She fancied him. He couldn't bring himself to believe his good fortune.

When the performance finished, the actors lingered at the foot of the stage to chat with their friends and family. Sandra threw her arms around him in a tight embrace.

"Brilliant!" she said. "What a great show. You're so talented, Ben."

"Aw, cheers," he said. He searched for any companions who might've tagged along with her, but she was alone. "I can't believe you came."

"Of course I came. I've been wanting to see you in action for a while. But you're actually, legitimately good. Like, you don't just talk the talk. You can really act."

Ben's face grew hot. "I'm more than thirty years younger than the character, but I gave it my best shot."

"Well, I'd love to see more. You'll have to let me know when you do another."

"I will!" Ben said. He never would do another.

"To be honest," Sandra said, "I'm also here to meet my dad's mate from Birmingham tomorrow. He phoned my parents yesterday and offered me a job. They were up waiting for me at two a.m. to tell me the good news."

"Oh," Ben said, forcing a smile. "A job. In Birmingham?"

She hesitated. A fraction of a moment. But it was there. "Yes."

When Ben had imagined a future together with Sandra, he'd pictured moving in together. But he was still in school in Rochester. Could a long-distance relationship work? Ben had no car – his dad hadn't bought him one, and he didn't earn enough at the cinema to afford one himself. Would Sandra be willing to drive three hours every fortnight to see Ben? That seemed unfair. Could they stay in touch on the phone, with Ben moving to Birmingham himself as soon as he left school? What kind of job could he get there?

"That's brilliant," Ben said, doing his best to keep her from seeing the calculations he was frantically making. "What kind of job?"

"Administrative. In his textile company. It's good pay." She spoke with caution, tentativeness, like the question *And how will you and I stay connected?* lingered beneath her words, unspoken.

Their gazes locked on each other, and in her eyes, doubt hid beneath her outward excitement. He searched those eyes, trying to find her estimation of his worth reflected in them. This divine girl who meant everything to him.

"Uh, you want to grab a bite to eat?" Sandra asked.

"Definitely."

They strolled to a bistro a few streets away, where they dined and spoke of Sandra's new job. Ben sought any possible angle by which they could remain close, even if not physically.

He caught Marley, one table over, smirking at him.

"What?" he asked her.

"You're beaming," she said. "It's nice to see you enjoying yourself."

"It is embarrassing, you know, you seeing me like this. All gaga over a teenage crush."

"Yeah, I've been wondering about that. The boy I see here is about as different from the man I met as Lady Di is from me. So what changed?"

Ben grunted dismissively and turned back to Sandra, who was a much more pleasant conversationalist, even if she wasn't real.

"I mean it, you blighter," Marley pressed. "Why didn't you go into theatre? It doesn't make enough money or something?"

"Bah," Ben said. "There's already enough great art in the world. Everyone thinks they have something new to say about good versus evil, about romantic connections. But it's all been said. It's all daft. It only exists to mash certain reward buttons in our brains over and over again. I grew up a little and no longer wanted any part of it, that's all."

"But you loved it," Marley said. "You clearly loved it. I like this side of you and she does, too. Seems you had no incentive at all to go in a different direction. But you did."

Ben chuckled darkly. He tapped in to the staff's power and probed his memories. Had a certain memory actually taken place on Christmas? Yes, it had. One year after today.

With a regretful glance towards Sandra, Ben left her and walked to Marley. "You want to see incentive?" he asked, raising a beckoning hand towards her. "I'll show you incentive."

A question came to Marley's face, but she didn't speak it. She grasped his hand, and Ben took them away.

———◆———

Ben yanked the family telephone out of the wall and lobbed it up the stairs at his dad.

Graham ducked. The phone shot above him and crashed against a wall.

"And now you owe me for that, too!" he bellowed.

Ben stormed to the kitchen, unplugged the toaster, and stole it from its perch on the Formica countertop. Graham ducked, but Ben didn't throw the toaster. He marched right past his dad, back up the stairs.

"If you're kicking me out of the house, I'm taking this with me," Ben said, in tears.

"Damn, you really loved that toaster," Marley said.

"It's not about the toaster, Marley! That tyrant won't support me unless I go to stupid university to be a stupid banker like him."

"Damn, you're really a teenager right now," Marley said, eyes even wider.

It was true. Ben had a hard time separating his old self from his young self, especially right after transporting. He threw the toaster into a suitcase on the bed in his childhood room.

"He really did this on Christmas?" Marley asked.

"Ice cold, wasn't it?"

"Liquid nitrogen cold, more like."

Graham tramped up the stairs. "If this is what it takes for you to make something of your life, it's what needs to happen."

"All right," Marley said. "I've seen enough. I get it. Let's leg it."

But indignation burnt inside Ben as hot as a forge, as if melting his old and young selves and merging them into one. "You'll never see me again," he told his dad, stuffing clothes into his suitcase.

"Fine. You'll never see any money from me. Not a penny. I'll cut you out of the will. More for Annie. Maybe being skint for a spell and having to work your way up will teach you the hard way how the real world works."

Ben spun to face him. Kicking him out of the house was one thing, but *no* financial support at all? For a seventeen-year-old in the economic doldrums of the late seventies? Ben would have no hope of moving to Birmingham to be near to Sandra unless he got a job there. "Dad, have you seen the news lately? They're calling this the Winter of Discontent. A new strike every weekend, a new essential service failing every month. Sterling depreciates constantly. I won't be able to find work."

"Then I'm sure you'll be a compliant worker for whoever's eventually lucky enough to end up as your boss."

"I'll be my own boss."

"Sure you will."

Ben put his hands on his hips. He'd never – not once – stood up to his dad as stridently as in this moment. *But great threats bring out aspects of ourselves we don't know are there until we need them.*

He faced his father down. "I made playmaker on the football team, I've gone to every Chamber of Commerce meeting with you for the past three years, I stopped hanging about with my mates, who you called pushovers. I hated all of that, but I did it. To please you. I do everything I can to be perfect. But it's still not good enough. So tell me, Dad. What is?"

Graham Scrooge's eyes were carved into his skull like caves into the side of a mountain. Deep, shadowy, hard. They didn't move. He didn't speak. He just stared at Ben with that implacable gaze, waiting for Ben to jump through yet another unknowable hoop.

Well, Ben wouldn't jump this time. Graham would never accept his role in all this. Would never admit to being anything less than a flawless parent. Ben couldn't argue. It was why he'd never even tried until today. It was why – he realised only just now – the fanged monster who lived in his bedroom always came out to torment Ben whenever his dad had scolded him for being less than expected. At least the imaginary monster was something he could wrap his mind around and defend against.

"You'll never see me again," Ben repeated.

He couldn't remember his father's reaction to that. He only remembered stalking out of the house once he'd finished packing. But before he could do so, darkness enveloped the room.

Ben and Marley turned to the window in unison. The Ghost of Christmas Past was just finishing dissolving through the wall and window, blotting out the sunlight.

"Marley, over here," Ben said. They ran to each other and backed away from the ghost. Ben clutched the staff with such force that his grip might have cracked it.

The apparition's unseen head swivelled on its shoulders, inspecting Ben's dad as it passed him. Ben's dad watched his son leave, just as he had so long ago, as much cold fury in his eyes as Ben had ever seen.

All this happened in seconds. Then the ghost was on them.

The staff displayed the memories in Ben's mind seconds before the ghost would reach them. He didn't have time to think. He just went.

Ben and Marley had been hovering right above a black hole. One of the memories that drew Ben towards it with the force of life's defining moments. One of the memories he'd been determined from the beginning to avoid. Ben's dad had kicked him out that Christmas morning, and the black hole had happened later that night.

They were just too close. The emotions radiating from it were too strong.

It sucked them in.

And there she was, seated across from him at the Royal Crown pub, back home in Rochester to see her family for Christmas. And to see

Ben. Her cheeks rosy after walking in the cold air outside. Her eyes bright. Sandra was happier than he'd ever seen her. A vision.

And she was single again.

"It's a bit odd, really," she was saying while munching on some chips. Simon & Garfunkel's 'Bridge Over Troubled Water' played tinnily from a small radio at the bar. "The whole factory floor is open to the street through those huge windows. So people walk by and gawk at us while we're working. It's mental. Don't know why they built it that way."

"But you're happy?" Ben asked. "The job's a good fit for you?"

Sandra beamed at him. "They give me so much freedom. I feel like a real adult all of a sudden."

"You think you'll stay in it, then?"

"Rise through the ranks of administrators?" Her eyebrows raised as she considered. "Nah. Everyone bright is going abroad now. That's where the real money is. Did you hear Ronnie got a job at IBM?"

Ronnie? Ben thought. *The kid who picked his nose in class and once stuck a screwdriver into a live electric socket?*

"In New York?" Ben asked.

"Mmhmm. He moved to the States last month."

Ben leant back in his chair, marvelling. "Moving abroad. Huh."

"Vanishing like a ghost."

A ghost! Ben snapped out of his fugue. Where was it? Had it followed them? He spotted Marley at a table farther from the window, eavesdropping as usual.

"This is not sustainable," he told her. "That thing will catch you eventually."

Marley was bent over the top of the table, her fingers massaging her temples. "I know, I know. I'm thinking."

"I'm so sorry, Ben, about your dad," Sandra said, unknowingly interrupting.

Ben turned back to her. How had she learnt about that? Had he told her, earlier tonight, that he'd been kicked out of the house? *Foolish, foolish boy.*

"It is what it is," Ben told her. "I'll get through it."

His meal finished, Ben's hands had been resting on the table. Sandra took one of them in her own. Gooseflesh rose on his arm. "You can ring me any time, you know," she said. "For anything you need. You're better than him and I know you'll find a way to come out the other side of this."

"Thank you," he mumbled, not meeting her gaze.

"This might be a gift, in a way," Sandra said. "You get to be the architect of your own life now."

The architect of his own life... with only a suitcase to his name. The pub staff had kindly agreed to hold the suitcase – containing all his worldly possessions, including a toaster – at the front.

And here Sandra was, living independently halfway across the country, still a teenager yet already working in a mid-level position. What could Ben possibly hope to offer her?

Sandra pulled her hands away and put on her coat. "Well, I'm done. Walk me to my car?"

"Marley, come here," Ben said. "I'm taking us to another memory."

At her table, Marley looked up. "What, are you two finally going to shag?"

"I'm serious, Marley." He strode towards her table, but she backed straight through the chair and floated up to the ceiling before he reached her.

"Well now I have to see what happens next," she said, crossing her arms.

"This is *my* memory and *I* get to choose what you see and what you don't!"

"That seems like a silly rule. I never agreed to that."

Ben clenched his fists, one of them clutching the magic staff he now carried everywhere. He could leave Marley here. Abandon her, stranding her in this pub until the ghost happened across her. She was behaving full of herself for someone entirely at Ben's mercy.

Her playful smirk vanished when she saw the gleam in Ben's eye. "Ben, no. Don't—"

Suddenly, Ben was two minutes later, just outside the pub, walking away with Sandra beside him. He'd come back later for his suitcase.

Marley burst through the pub's doors and raced to catch up. "Oh, wicked funny. Gamble with my life, what a laugh."

"You're the one gambling with your life," Ben said. "I'm just along for the ride."

"I waited for you for two minutes! I thought you'd gone forever. Do you realise how terrifying that was just now?"

"Keep it in mind before trying to pick and choose memories. I have the staff. You don't."

"Well, isn't this a lovely microcosm of our entire relationship?" Marley said.

"It isn't a—"

They'd arrived without Ben noticing. Sandra's white Mini was parked ahead of them on the kerb beneath a streetlamp. The pavement was wet despite no recent rain or snow. The temperature bordered on freezing as dusk was settling into its final deep violet. Just like

Ben remembered. Sandra kept glancing at him with expectation in her eyes, like she was waiting eagerly for him to say something.

They'd walked in silence the whole time, unspoken thoughts racing through him. Nervousness that bordered on full-fledged fear. This brilliant, beautiful young woman was about to leave his life again. How long would it be before she returned home to visit? Another year? Surely she'd meet someone in Birmingham during that time. Or get a better job and move to the States.

This was Ben's last chance.

Sandra stopped by her car and turned to face him. The hopeful look on her face, the slightly uneven breath escaping her lips into the cold, had haunted Ben all his life. Seeing them again, seeing her, in this moment, in the flesh, felt like getting hit by a car. He dropped the staff. It clattered against the pavement.

He forgot the ghost. He forgot Marley. The only thing in the world that mattered was Sandra. How had his teenage self let all these years pass without telling her how he felt? How had the potential for a life with her come to hang by such a slender thread?

"It's good to see you again," she told him.

Ben's voice shook as he spoke. "Um, yes, it was fantastic to see you too."

She breathed in deeply, out slowly. She made no move to get into her car.

Ben smiled a goofy grin at her, but quickly lowered his gaze to the ground. Rowdy men sang a bawdy song from a passing car with its windows rolled down. It filled the seconds with a blessed, if fleeting distraction, and then they were alone in the early evening silence again.

"Is there anything else you want to say?" Sandra asked.

Ben tried to calm his own breathing. "There is. Uhm…" He dug deep within himself and mustered all the courage he found there. Finally, after years, he said it.

"I'm smitten with you," he said frankly, locking eyes with her. "I have been for years, and I'm so sorry I didn't say anything till now."

There. The truth was out. He scrutinised her face for a reaction. She looked… surprised, maybe?

Not pleasantly surprised. Just surprised.

Ben's chest seized up a bit. "You're kind, ambitious, so smart. Sharp as a tack. You're hilarious. And I know we live in different cities now, but of all the girls—" He stopped, corrected himself. "Women… of all the women I've ever known, you're the only one. The only one I've ever really wanted.

"And if you feel even an inkling of what I feel, maybe we can give long distance a chance. I'll find a way to get a job in Birmingham. I'll find a way. It might be rough at first, but if you take this chance on me, I will be so impossibly devoted to making this work. I—"

He was rambling. Denying Sandra her turn to speak. Or maybe delaying it for fear of what she'd say. Ben closed his mouth, and waited.

A vacuum of silence followed. Nothing rushed to fill it.

Sandra's mouth was open, frozen in the act of forming a word. The memory wasn't paused; Sandra just clearly didn't know what to say. She started to speak. Stopped again.

"It's fine if you… If you don't…" Ben said to fill the silence, though of course it wasn't fine at all.

"Ben," Sandra said. "You're so sweet. I mean really. Those were some of the sweetest things anyone has ever said to me. And I can't deny that... that I have felt some things for you..."

A white plume of air left Ben's mouth as he digested her words. Thrilling, hopeful words...

"But," Ben said, prompting her.

"But," Sandra confirmed. She hesitated. "I don't think so, Ben. I'm so sorry."

Utter panic. Sandra turned to enter her car. Ben grasped for the future that had just been snatched away from him.

"Sandra, I— What—" he stammered. "Why not?"

"It's best if we leave it at that," Sandra said, setting her handbag inside the car. "Again, I'm so sorry. I know this isn't what you wanted to hear."

"Is it the distance?" Ben asked. "Lots of people make it work these days."

"It's not the distance." She sat in the driver's seat. He was losing her.

"Have I changed in some way? Is there a character flaw or – Sandra, I can work on myself if you need me to." Ben's words sounded desperate to him even as he said them. Was that the reason Sandra was saying no?

"It's none of that, Ben. Please, let's just drop it." She shut the door and started the car.

Ben approached and rested his hand pleadingly on the window. "Please. I care so much about you. I-I just want an explanation. You've known me for years, you had to have suspected I fancied you. You said yourself you've had feelings for me. Please, Sandra. Why won't you date me?"

He saw, rather than heard, Sandra sigh deeply through the window. She leant over and rolled the window down.

They were still for a moment, she in her car that would take her to her future, Ben stuck on the pavement of his past.

"It's just that..." Sandra began. She again struggled for words.

"I'm boring?" Ben asked, trying to make a joke of it. "Ugly?"

Sandra chuckled politely. "Of course you're not boring or ugly." She closed her eyes, hung her head, brought it back up. Their eyes met each other's for the last time.

"I think it's wicked that you want to be an actor. But you do want to be an actor. And... Ben, there are things I want to do in my life. Places I want to go, milestones I want to meet. You can't fault a girl for that. And you're an absolutely lovely, attractive man. But you're also homeless, cut off from your family, you've got no ambition to leave your cinema job..."

She paused, as if even she knew the next words to leave her mouth would become the foundation for the rest of Ben's life, much deeper and stronger than anything his father had ever told him.

"You haven't got enough money, Ben."

The words hit him like a lightning bolt from a clear sky. Bizarre, unexpected. Deadly. Had Sandra truly spoken them? Worse, had she truly meant them? She'd voiced no such concern during the two years he'd known her.

Ben staggered back a step. Sandra frowned, her eyes downcast.

"I don't mean to be cruel," she continued. "I love being your friend, but... I only get one life to live, you know?"

And you don't want to live it with me.

"I'm sorry," Sandra finished. She rolled up her window.

Ben stood in the cold. Branches above him swayed in a light breeze. Sandra turned on her headlights, then pulled out into the street and out of Ben's life. The night continued around him as if nothing had happened. Christmas revellers cheered back at the pub. Carollers sang 'O Holy Night' somewhere nearby. A squirrel climbed the rubbish bin across the street and dived right in.

Ben's feet were still under him, connecting him to Planet Earth, but he felt numb, frozen, drifting off into space, never to return. He felt no different now than each time he'd replayed this memory in his own mind, weekly, for over five decades. He'd been worried that the visuals, the tactile experience, actually seeing and touching Sandra again would wound him even more deeply.

But it was the same. Devastation. Something precious and vital had been torn out of the fabric of the universe, and it would never be right again. He would phone Sandra, of course, in the days ahead. He'd write her letters. But she'd never pick up, never write back.

Eyes downcast, Ben's vision grew blurry. Then suddenly clear again, just in time for him to see the teardrops splatter against his shoes.

Marley stepped up beside him, her ghostly form radiating faint light. She, too, was watching Sandra drive away. Neither spoke until Sandra turned the corner beyond the pub and disappeared for good.

"Young love," Ben said, shaking his head, still in his seventeen-year-old body. "Painful lessons must be heeded if one is to have a better future."

"That didn't—" Marley said before cutting herself off to think for a moment. "I don't know. Something about that didn't add up. I could've sworn she was practically in love with you."

"You saw it with your own eyes," Ben said. "She led me on for so long, then left me in the dust. Incredible how someone can do such a thing to another human being."

"Yes," Marley said, eyeing Ben with an unreadable sentiment: sorrow, pity, but something more as well. "Incredible."

Penniless and truly alone, Ben didn't even know where he'd be spending the night. He picked up his staff and walked back to the pub to retrieve his suitcase.

Three Quid

One Christmas later, Ben awoke to his elderly neighbour banging on his flat's door.

"Ben!" Maude croaked in her permanently hoarse voice. "Phone for you."

He'd been dreaming – something pleasant about the summer trip his family had taken to Cornwall when he was only five or six, back when Ben's mum was still part of the family. Maude pounded on the door again, and the dream evaporated, and the significance of a phone call on Christmas Day dawned on him.

It was the call he'd been waiting for.

Ben shot upright in the sofa that also served as his bed. Trailing the bedsheet stuck to his foot, he strode to the door, unlocked and opened it. Maude was in her nightdress, and sleep had barely left her eyes. The phone's cord stretched all the way into her flat next door.

She handed Ben the phone with a slight frown. "Happy Christmas."

Ben mouthed *thank you* and took it from her. "Hello, this is Ben."

"Yes, Benjamin Scrooge?" said a deep male voice on the other end. "This is Peter Lees with Morgan Grenfell."

Yes! Finally, they've called me back. At Maude's number – Ben couldn't afford his own phone line, so it was the only number he could give them.

But Mr Lees sounded disapproving already. Had Maude not covered the receiver while she was clobbering his door?

"I'm in the office going through the CVs my assistant gave me. Yours is rather unimpressive, but he tells me you are by far the most persistent person he's ever met. I think sometimes resolve is more important than qualifications. Do you have time today for an interview?"

A smile as wide as the moon blossomed on Ben's face. "On Christmas?" Ben asked.

"I've nothing better to do today. Do you?"

Ben didn't.

A test of devotion, then. If Ben would interview on Christmas Day, he was advertising he would work on Christmases to come. And that was fine. For a living wage, he'd be willing to work every public holiday throughout his whole career.

"No, sir."

"Very good. I'll meet you in the foyer in two hours. I trust you know our location?"

"Of course."

"See you soon." Click.

"Maude, you're an angel," Ben said.

She grunted, took the phone back, and waddled back towards her flat.

Could Morgan Grenfell start him working fast enough? Ben's landlord had already deferred his rent for several months, and he was due to be evicted on January 1. But a job at Morgan Grenfell, even an entry-level job, might change the landlord's mind.

Ben's clothes were arranged in a pile on some chairs at the back of his lounge. He found his only dress shirt, his only tie, and some passable trousers. He didn't have a suit jacket. Hopefully it wouldn't reflect poorly on him.

Ben traversed his small lounge and microscopic kitchen – his entire two-room flat, given that the loo was a shared room outside – and scrubbed his teeth clean. He'd arrive an hour early to impress Mr Lees.

He was two streets away, halfway to the taxi rank, when he remembered he'd spent the last of his money last night on groceries, just before the shop had closed. He checked his wallet to be sure. Other than his ID, it was empty.

He ran back to his flat. The cab would be a quid for the Christmas charge, plus another £1.50 for the fare. But when he turned over his sofa cushions, he only found a few pence. He checked the box where he kept special belongings and coupons, but had no luck there either.

"Maude?" Ben asked, knocking on her door as politely as he could manage. "Could I borrow a few quid for the cab?"

No response. Ben knocked again. "Please. I'll pay you back double – triple – when I land the job."

He listened for any stirring inside, but either Maude was ignoring him, or was dead asleep. After getting ready, he had only an hour and fifteen minutes until the interview. No public buses came out here to the Docklands, and in this neighbourhood, no one would dare let Ben borrow their car.

Could he catch the Tube? He'd have to run all the way to Bow Road for that. It'd take an hour to get there, which would surely make him late.

And Ben would *not* be late. He had no choice but to take a cab.

Sod it, I couldn't have stashed away three measly quid?

Kirby Sandwiches, his workplace. They weren't open today, but Mr Kirby was having his whole extended family there to celebrate Christmas since his own ancient mews house was too small. Mr Kirby was a stickler, though. Would he help?

Ben tried one last time to get Maude's attention. "I'll sell you my groceries," he said. "Apples, bread, eggs..."

Nothing. Ben sprinted back down the stairs.

A sunny, cloudless, cold day. He momentarily forgot where to go. This was Canary Wharf, one of the financial centres of the world, was it not?

Not yet. All these flats and the vacant docks next to them would be torn down, and ten years from now, Ben's executive office would be built almost exactly here, forty floors above his head. Ben looked up at the spot, now just empty sky.

No time for sightseeing, though. Magic staff in hand, he sprinted through the Docklands, past rusty cranes and boarded-up pubs, one riddled with bullet holes. Marley accompanied him, but she didn't speak, and the urgency of Ben's mission immersed him so fully that he nearly forgot about her.

He covered his nose against a thick oily smell coming from a fenced-off area on the shore of the Thames. All Ben saw was industrial machinery, but big government signs warning of pollution hung from the fence every ten yards. This was the quickest route to his destination, though, so Ben took it.

After half a mile, he reached the sandwich shop. About two dozen people milled about inside, many of them kids playing with new toys. A Christmas tree had been erected near to the till, and wrapping paper littered the tables and floor. Muffled carols resounded from a cassette player.

Ben pulled against the front doors, but they were locked. A rambunctious child ran to the door to throw a handful of Lego pieces at him, and this caught Mr Kirby's attention. Chatting over food with his wife and some relatives, a scowl of petulant offence fell over his face when he saw Ben. He adjusted his glasses, quickly strode over, and unlocked the door. He only opened it a few inches. Just enough to talk through.

"This is my family Christmas celebration, Ben. Get out of here."

"I'm sorry, Mr Kirby. It's an emergency. I need a cab fare to take me to the City. Can you take it out of my next pay cheque?"

Alarmed, Mr Kirby left the building fully to address Ben face to face. He shut the door behind him. "Slow down, slow down. What emergency? Is someone hurt, lad?"

"What? No. It's a-a last-minute job interview. With Morgan Grenfell. I have to be there in less than an hour but I don't have the cab fare."

Kirby crossed his arms. "A job interview. So you're leaving us, then?"

Ben tried to brush his misstep aside. "No! Not right away. I'll—" What could he say to lower his boss's defences? "I'll work both jobs for a while."

"My arse you will. We'll be buggered here on Wednesdays and Thursdays without you."

Ben bent over, hands on his knees, thoroughly out of breath. "Please, sir. Just three quid. You can take it out of my next pay."

"You haven't earned it yet. Get out of here."

He turned his back to Ben and opened the door. Ben pressed a hand on Kirby's shoulder, maybe a bit too hard, because Kirby jumped inside in fright. In doing so, he thrust the door outwards into Ben's face.

"Did you just try to grab me?" Kirby said.

Ben clutched at his nose, blooming with pain. A trickle of warm blood fell on his fingers and mouth. "No, sir. I just... Can I borrow your car?"

Kirby pointedly locked the door. He waved the kids, who'd been gaping at the confrontation, back to their play with both hands.

Ben stooped with his head far out in front of his shirt and tie so no blood would fall on them. At least Kirby hadn't sacked him. He'd gone from cinema worker to dry cleaner to bricklayer to sandwich maker, with long spells of unemployment in between, and Kirby's was by far the most stable employment he'd had since the cinema.

But at Morgan Grenfell, he could change his life. Move to a safer neighbourhood, have food on the table every night. Meet someone nice, settle down and have kids, work his way up the corporate ladder, start his own small business on the side. The worth society placed on him would be tied to the true value he could add to the world, not to how often he made the sandwich or rang in the coupon the right way.

What tiny dreams I had, Ben the billionaire thought. Maybe Sandra had seen the truth of him after all.

He flagged down a passing cab and opened the back door, but out of politeness, he didn't get in yet. "I'm sorry," he said, squeezing his bleeding nose closed, "I can't pay, but I have a very urgent job interview that could change my life. It's less than half an hour away. Is there anything I can do for you that'd convince you to take me?"

The driver sat dead-eyed and slack-jawed, staring at him. "You been in a brawl?"

Ben tried bending his eyes inwards to look at his own nose. How bad was it? "No," he said. "I get nosebleeds."

"Well, I'll phone the rozzers for you. Have a happy Christmas." He pulled the cab forward. Ben had to leap out of the way to keep his foot from getting run over.

He spotted some passersby and explained the situation to them, too, but his nice clothes may as well have been rags for the way they looked at him.

He tried to slow his thudding heart. *Okay, think. I'm creative. I can find a way.* Could he hide in a car somehow? Sneak into someone's boot at a petrol station? *And end up in Scotland nine hours later? No, think, Ben, think!*

He reached for his iPhone to call an Uber before remembering neither of those existed yet. "Bah!"

He had no mates who could lend him a ride. Maybe in Rochester, but not here in London. Working or looking for work constantly, he'd lost touch with his theatre mates. Besides, he didn't have time to run back to Maude's and beg to use the phone again.

If only he had a skateboard or roller blades or...

A blue, classic-style bicycle, leaning against the outside of an Indian food shop. Seconds after he saw it, Ben was zooming down the A13 half as fast as a car. People were leaving the food shop behind him and pointing at him.

"Did you just steal someone's bike on Christmas?" Marley asked, drifting along beside him.

"Not the worst thing I've ever done," Ben said, focused on his route. "Do Indians even celebrate Christmas?"

"Yes!" Marley said. "Many, many Indians celebrate Christmas. And how do you even know the bike belonged to an Indian person?"

"You about to yell at me and call me a racist? That's so 2018, Marley."

"You're so 1980."

"I'll take that as a compliment!"

He zoomed down inclines and round corners, seeking shortcuts. Pedestrians jumped out of his way, shouting insults. Scarcely any trees grew in the Docklands, so when Ben started seeing chestnuts, he knew he was nearing Whitechapel. The City loomed ahead, but still quite far off.

From nowhere, it hit him. Sudden, wrenching pain in his stomach. A feeling of edginess and unwellness spreading through his body. He stopped his bike so he could be sick in a rubbish bin. Not much came out; he hadn't eaten this morning.

"What's this?" Marley asked. "You're ill now?"

"I was ill for years," Ben said, waving her away. "Don't worry, it'll pass." But a new pang of gastric pain lessened his certainty of that. He ran into a restaurant to urgently use the toilet.

"I'll wait out here, if you don't mind," Marley said.

No time for this, no time for this.

Six minutes passed before he could come out. He rushed towards the doors, but a young woman sitting at the bar stopped him.

"Ben?"

Dear God, it was Annie. He'd last seen her only a year ago, but she looked grown up! "Uh, hi," Ben said, startled by her appearance. Two mates sitting next to her waved hello as well. "What are you doing here?"

"Choir. We're performing in St Paul's this morning. What are you doing here?"

"I'm, uh..." He was feeling sick again, but couldn't afford another second.

Annie frowned, perhaps seeing he was struggling. "Do you need any help, Ben? Have you got a job?"

Almost, Annie, almost. Lord knew he'd applied to about a hundred jobs in faraway Birmingham to be near to Sandra, but not one of them had phoned him back. Morgan Grenfell was about his hundredth attempt in London as well. Perhaps the greatest benefit of landing a job there would be Sandra finally writing back to him.

"You know, Dad still gives me a nice allowance," Annie said. "I can sneak some to you under the table if you want."

"I..." The room spun a bit. Ben tried to blink away his dizziness. "I have to go." He patted a confused Annie on the shoulder and strode to the exit. "Tell Dad I'm fine!" he called back to her. "No problems here. On my way to an important interview, actually."

Annie looked concerned but said nothing. Back outside, Ben rushed to the bike, only to find a pasty, red-haired young man about his age, completely out of breath, inspecting it closely.

Ben backed away, but not before being seen.

"Is it you who snatched my bike back there?" the man said, moving menacingly towards him. He wasn't much bigger or more muscular than Ben, but Ben already had a bloody nose, and time was well past running short.

"See? What'd I say?" Marley said. "Never assume another person's ethnicity—"

"When you steal their bike. Got it."

Ben bolted in the opposite direction, towards the City. The man behind him hopped on his bike and gave chase.

"Bugger all," Ben said, ducking into an alley. He threaded a path through several back streets, sprinting the whole way. His stomach protested at the exertion. He clutched at the pain and groaned as he ran.

"What's the problem?" Marley asked. "Food poisoning?"

"Peptic ulcer."

"Say what?"

"I used to get them all the time." Ben puffed as he ran. "They barely knew what caused them in the eighties. I saw a dozen GPs and five specialists before even getting a diagnosis. Three years later!"

He had to stop to throw up again. Shortly after, they arrived back on a main road. No sign of the angry bicycle man. Ben continued running.

Three quid. All of this because he hadn't had three lousy quid. He should've applied for Supplementary Benefit months ago.

No. Absolutely no. I'll never let myself become one of those people.

If only he could transport even a tiny fraction of his fortune back in time to help himself now. Pocket change to his future self would feed this young man for several lifetimes.

Ben crossed a junction at Wormwood and Old Broad Street. *Almost there.* The four-storey, concave Morgan Grenfell building lay just ahead. Ben charged forward, sprinting faster than he'd run all morning. It couldn't have taken him more than an hour to get here, despite all the delays. He'd ace the interview. He'd regain control over his life.

As he ran the final steps to the entrance, a man in a business suit left the building and locked it behind him. A stylish streak of grey ran through his otherwise black hair. A luxurious saloon was waiting for him.

Ben ran to the door, tried it even though he'd seen the departing businessman lock it. Not knowing what else to do, he turned to the man.

"Excuse me, sir, is anyone in here? I'm Ben Scrooge. I have an interview."

The man furrowed his eyebrows, looked Ben up and down, lingering at what must have been blood drying beneath his nose. He checked his watch. "You're thirty-two minutes late."

"Oh," Ben said. "Mr Lees. I'm so sorry. I got—"

Ben abruptly bent over and vomited on the pavement. Lees cringed and looked away.

Ben wiped his mouth and pretended it hadn't happened. "Sir, I'm sure if you interview me, you'll see I'm the perfect man for the job."

Lees stared, dumbfounded. He turned and got in the saloon's back seat.

Ben grabbed the car door before Lees could close it. "Please. It's not my fault I was late. I was trying—"

"Everything is your fault, dear boy," Lees said. "Every single thing you do, or don't do, is your responsibility. That's the sort of man I was looking for. Not a man who blames his misfortunes on others."

Ben stammered, blubbered, unsure how to salvage this. "B-but... The cab fare. At my current job... I couldn't afford..."

"Negotiate your salary," Lees said, then scowled. "And clean yourself up, for Christ's sake."

He shut the door. The saloon drove off, leaving Ben alone with Marley on the empty street.

Half an hour. Half of a damned hour.

And now what? He was working practically around the clock to better his situation. What else did he have to do to convince people he was good enough?

As an old man, Ben liked to tell himself a story about how he'd made all the right choices in his life, and they'd led inevitably to his success. He'd forgotten until now how many mistakes he'd actually made.

He instinctually felt as Lees had: that his younger self was to blame for his own failures. But after this run, after the nausea, after every ridiculous trick he'd pulled out of his hat to get here on time... was that response too easy?

Amid repeated calls of "Officer, that kid stole my bike! That kid right there!" Ben glanced idly at some rubbish on the ground, blowing past in the breeze. One particular piece of paper got stuck in his vomit.

A ten-pound note someone had lost.

Grand Entrance

Ben still lived in the same flat the next Christmas. Next door, Maude was playing Queen loud enough to wake the angels. He spent half an hour watching *The Generation Game* on his twelve-inch telly and drinking six bottles of London Pride before remembering he was actually an old man, this was all in the past, and Marley was in the room with him. She stood apart from him, gazing through the small window at the car park below.

Why didn't she speak with him? Was this glimpse into Ben's past too depressing even for her? Was she disappointed his origin story revealed him to be someone lesser than the man she'd thought he was? Ben would've loved to indulge her – and himself – by reliving the same happy memories over and over, but then the ghost would quickly find them.

The early eighties were hard years for Ben. He spent night after night, Christmas after Christmas, like this. He often went without food so he could pay rent arrears, always narrowly avoiding eviction, yet still he gained weight. The loss of his sandwich job was, at last, the straw the broke the camel's back: Ben finally went on the dole, and got it weekly as long as he kept applying for work. It helped a bit. Especially since he couldn't get much work after the bicycle theft went on his criminal record – an early CCTV camera had caught him in the act.

He did get in to university, at the Polytechnic of the South Bank, but quit after three weeks. Walking and Tubing across town every other night was just too much. Ben would often pass out from extreme stomach pain. He woke up in the A&E a few times with no memory of how he'd got there. His student housing grant, small though it was, hurt when it vanished.

Illness shrank his world. Everything else in his life – relationships, ambitions, even his desperate need to scrounge enough money to live on – became secondary to his sickness, for a spell. He lived in constant, chronic pain. He'd spend days reading medical books at the library, trying to glean some morsel of information that might help him.

During one Christmas they visited, Ben was recovering from stomach surgery. He'd had three operations during his twenties, to treat the ulcers after medicines failed to cure them. When he tried to get off the sofa and could barely move without pain at the surgery site, he skipped the rest of that Christmas.

He hand-washed his dishes. He cooked all his food in the microwave, if at all, because the oven and the hob didn't work. Sometimes he could afford a launderette, more often he washed his clothes in a bucket in the shower. He made acquaintances at various jobs, but no friendships. Whenever a potential friend invited him out, he couldn't afford a restaurant or transportation, or was too sick.

Every so often, he saved up enough to afford the greatest luxury of all: a discounted ticket to a stage show. These were only available shortly before the performance began, so Ben sometimes waited hours – much of it sick in the theatre toilet – to snag one of them. Sometimes none were available and he had to walk miles back home. More often, he was rewarded with a comfy seat, dimmed lights, and actors who transported him to other places and times, where people had worries both far removed from and nearly identical to his own. Theatre was catharsis for Ben, even if he wasn't on stage. It let him feel like he wasn't alone, like other people struggled with the same shame and self-doubt as him. After the shows, he'd walk his miles home feeling he'd tenuously reconnected to humanity, and that was better than nothing.

As the years stretched on with anxiety and ulcers corroding his insides, self-doubt grew into self-loathing. He could only reassure himself for so long that if he made good choices and persisted with determination, he'd become happy. When the self-loathing became too much to bear, Ben redirected it outwards towards those around him. Towards the rest of the world.

He often fantasised about Sandra: about winning the lottery, running into her by happenstance, waiting through a teary apology for the awful things she'd said, and generously forgiving her before taking her on a romantic stroll through a country town under a starry night sky.

His fantasies about his dad were entirely different. He dreamt it was his father rather than he who'd lost his position in life. How would the mighty Graham Scrooge cope with living in this roach-infested dustbin on a few quid per day?

Ben relived these Christmases in a jumbled order so the ghost would have a harder time hunting them. He could have jumped to random Christmases to confuse the ghost even further, but he felt an inexplicable duty to his younger self to review these Christmases mostly chronologically. Like his life story wouldn't make sense unless he remembered every piece of context. The fires of ambition hadn't lit within this young man yet, but the tinder and kindling were in place. Even then, he'd known something had to change.

Marley cleared her throat out of the blue, and spoke hesitantly. "Can you… can you look at your younger self and see he's still worthy as a person, even stripped of all your wealth?"

Ben glanced away from the TV, at his reflection in the mirror tipped sideways on the floor. He made a true effort to answer Marley's question honestly and accurately, searching for anything in his younger self he could admire.

He admired the tinder. He admired the kindling. But he saw no fire. Not yet.

"No," Ben simply said, and Marley was quiet.

Nerves. A hum of tension vibrating from Ben's feet to his head. Most strident in his chest. Every inch of him on edge. His mind rehearsing a hundred different scenarios. His hands fidgeting with his tie.

He pulled a chair out for Helen, his first date in years. "Cheers," she said. "And happy Christmas. Not often you get a date on Christmas."

Helen was rocking a true eighties perm, huge blond waterfalls of hair flowing around her head. She wore a baggy, square-shouldered, button-up blouse and a black A-line skirt: an outfit that told Ben she was looking for a professional man.

Good. I can be professional.

As Ben took his place at the table opposite Helen, Marley settled into a third chair, smiling at the upscale bistro around them like a child who'd been handed an unexpected sweet. Tension visibly left her ghostly body. "Well, this is a pleasant change of scenery, innit?"

"Bah," Ben replied.

"You start going out more now? No more Christmases in the dumps? You seem agreeably absent of vomiting today – dear God, there's a sentence I never imagined I'd say to you."

Ben chewed on a response as Helen settled in, smiled at him, and surveyed the menu. "I finally got treated for an *H. pylori* infection. Got rid of the stomach stuff," he told Marley. "Would've been nice if someone had told me I could do that to cure it five years earlier."

"Still, that's brilliant for you. Say, this seared tuna looks delicious. Do you think I could actually taste it if I find it on someone's table?"

"So what do you do?" Helen asked from across the table.

Ben steeled himself. The question set off prickles on his younger self's skin. She'd asked the one outwardly innocuous getting-to-know-you question that Ben knew from experience hid a self-serving interrogation: how much money do you make, and therefore, what's your worth as a boyfriend, as a husband, as a human being? Seemingly unaware of Ben's edginess, Marley reclined to watch them as if reading a charming romance book.

"I work at an asset management firm in the City," Ben said.

Marley's eyes grew as wide as headlights. "No," she said. "Ben, noooo."

Ben was, in fact, a pizza delivery driver. But what were the odds he'd ever be called on to deliver pizza to Helen's flat? And what did he know? By the time he and Helen got serious, he'd likely have a job in the City after all.

Helen reacted neither positively nor negatively to Ben's supposed work. "That's nice. Do you enjoy it?" she said.

He placed a business card on the table and slid it across to her. "Quite a bit. Phone me there sometime. I'll get you a good deal."

Marley dragged her hands down across her face, contorting her features. "Ben, you made business cards for your fake job? What were you going to do if she phoned you?"

"The number doesn't work." Then, seriously, to Helen: "I'm paying for this meal, by the way."

Marley dropped her head into her hands. Helen's expression quickly shifted from confusion to gratitude. "Of course. Thank you."

The conversation died a ruthless death, and Helen turned back to the menu. "Lovely weather we're having," she said.

"Yes," Ben agreed, sipping from the water the waiter had poured when they first sat. "Plenty of good clouds lately."

She glanced up at him and chuckled. Had Ben just successfully told a joke? Unintentionally, but yes! He'd been so out of practice at chatting women up, he'd forgotten how.

"Did you go to university?" she asked.

"No, never. University's for pretentious toffs who think they're better than everyone else."

"Really? I study business at Imperial College and I don't feel like I'm better than anyone."

Ben tried to take a second sip of water only to realise he'd already drunk the whole glass. "Yes, well..." He searched for words.

He was still searching for words when Helen filled the awkward silence herself. "Do you have any pets?"

Marley interjected: "He has a rat that gnaws on his shoes sometimes."

"No pets," Ben said. "I prefer to spend my time and money on things like... this watch." He flashed his wristwatch at Helen. "Four hundred pounds, this."

It was fifty.

Helen, her polite smile waning into something much more doubtful, nodded. "It's a very nice watch."

Mercifully, the waiter arrived to take their orders. Ben reconsidered his approach. Helen had been asking him so many questions; he needed to express curiosity about her, too. Women wanted men who cared about them and their perspective, and here Ben was talking only about himself. He needed a more personable topic that would let Helen loosen up.

So as soon as the waiter left, Ben asked her, "So how do you feel about the Tories?"

Helen paused in the act of unfolding her dinner napkin across her lap. "Excuse me?" she asked.

"You know. The Conservative Party. Are they good or bad?"

"Uh..." Helen cautiously patted the napkin down. "How do *you* feel about the Tories, Ben?"

Ben barely followed politics at all; he'd only brought them up because other people liked to chat about them. "I think they're all right," Ben said. "Seem like the type of blokes you could go fishing with."

"The prime minister's a woman, not a bloke," Helen pointed out.

"That she is, yes." Ben nodded thoughtfully, as if this were a profound statement. "She's quite strong, I think. Very serious."

Ben stared off into space, desperate for something to keep the conversation flowing. He hoped she'd interpret this as him thinking deeply about some political issue or another.

"You really want to know what I think about the Tories?" Helen asked.

Eager to let himself off the hook, Ben nodded. "Absolutely."

"Well, them abolishing exchange controls has attracted a lot of international capital. The futures exchanges have decreased market volatility so much that they've absolutely revolutionised commodity trading. I do think we talk too much about equities and not as much as we should about whether integrating debt markets with the stock market is sustainable. Thatcher's quite the monetarist, though. I was worried about the increase in the value-added tax and its effect on the real exchange rate and unemployment, but in the long run, inflation is declining and business is booming, so at the moment I'm cautiously optimistic about the Tories." She threw Ben a curious smile. "What about you? What do you think about the plan to computerise trading and get rid of fixed commissions?"

Ben blinked a few times. Words failed him.

"Oh, Ben," Marley said. "I think *I'm* actually in love with this woman now."

Helen craned her head forward, waiting for a response. Ben made a mental note to be more honest in future classified ads he placed. "Brainy finance leader seeking stimulating conversation" may not quite have played to his strengths.

If nothing else, though, Ben could act. He buried his nerves and spoke with confidence.

"I think the returns from the residual investment markets are proving highly, highly liquid, but it's the fiduciary duty of the Thatcher government to use that collateral to amortise the, uh, derivatives before the next election," Ben said in a jumble of lingo his younger self was rather chuffed with. At this age, he'd had no idea what any of it meant, so he hadn't known it hadn't meant anything.

Helen stared. Marley cringed so deeply, her neck nearly sucked her chin into it.

"Do you even work in finance at all?" Helen asked.

"I'm a very successful man."

"Is this date a joke to you?"

Ben's heart raced but he kept his composure. "No. No, not at all."

Now Helen was cringing. He was losing her. Time to use the nuclear option. He'd spent years too afraid to tell Sandra he liked her, and his cowardice had ruined that for him. He'd never make the mistake of not being assertive enough again.

"In fact, I quite fancy you," he said. "I think you're completely beautiful."

Helen sank in her seat, rubbed the bridge of her nose. "Oh, dear."

Ben's cheeks heated up and probably turned red. *This whole thing was a mistake. I haven't developed myself enough to be dating yet.* Deep embarrassment at wasting Helen's time overtook him. He hoped she saw it on his face. He leant towards her.

"Look, Helen, I'm terribly sorry. I'm making a horrible fool of myself. I honestly don't think I'm ready for this. I don't blame you at all if you want to call the date off."

There. He'd moved Helen's hand onto the eject button; now he waited for her to press it and save them both from the exploding plane of this date. She sat still for a few moments, her arms crossed, staring at him. Then she leant in close. Very close, almost as if for a kiss. But biting hostility edged her low voice. "You don't get to apologise," she said. "You get to wallow in your smugness and privilege while the rest of us build a world with no place for men like you in it."

Marley snorted in wry bemusement – whether at Helen's barbed reply or at Ben's sorry situation, he didn't know. Helen scrambled to gather her handbag and get out the doors as fast as she could.

Ben rubbed his cheek as if she'd physically smacked him. "I'm going to be a billionaire someday!" he called after her as she left.

Marley grabbed him. "You didn't actually say that."

Ben sipped the melted dregs from his glass full of ice. "I didn't," he admitted. "Though I wonder if she'd have treated me differently if she knew that."

"You think *she* should have treated *you* differently?"

"She should've seen I just didn't know how women work yet – that was completely obvious – and ended the date more politely, at least."

"It's less about women and more like you didn't know how human beings in general work."

Ben glared at her. "I'm a whole literary genre, you know. Billionaire romance books. Have you heard of these? They're delightful." He stabbed his finger at the door through which Helen had left. "Thirty years from now, that woman will be curled up by her fireplace, flipping through the pages, fantasising about a man like me."

"About a retirement-aged arsehole?"

"About a rich alpha male into edgy sex, with hidden wounds deep in his past that make him sympathetic."

Marley looked like she had some strong words for Ben, but the waiter returned with the starter they'd ordered. Ben explained his date had left, and that he wouldn't be eating here after all – he needed to save every pound he could. Before the waiter left, Marley stole a stuffed mushroom from his platter and popped it into her mouth. "Bleh," she said. "Can barely taste it."

She threw her arms up in the air, lowered them to her side. "I'm sorry, Ben. I thought this would all be fun. An adventure through our past together. One last hurrah." She lowered her hand through the table and brought it back up again, as if trying to come to terms with her condition. "Maybe I'm doomed and that spirit will eventually catch us like you say, but I wanted... something more than what I had in life."

"Then pick a memory," Ben said. "I'll take you anywhere you want to go."

Marley shrugged, still chewing. "I don't know. You're the alpha male. You tell me."

Ben pulsed the staff and combed through his memories, trying to find one Marley might enjoy.

"I'm a billionaire, too," Marley said glumly. "Why are there no romance books about me?"

"Correction: you're not a billionaire, because you're dead."

"Lots of romance books about dead people, too. Vampires, ghosts, zombies..."

"Ah!" Ben exclaimed. "I got one. Ohhh, you'll love this."

"Necromancers, wights..."

Ben grabbed Marley's hand and focused on transporting them away. A quizzical groove settled on Marley's brow.

"Wait, are you actually into edgy sex?" she asked.

The room disintegrated around them.

There were two Christmases during the dark years that Ben actually enjoyed. On the first, he spent the whole day reading a finance textbook. He'd relived this Christmas with Marley's ghost a little while ago, out of order from the rest of his memories.

His abysmal date with Helen had spurred him to actually learn a thing or two about business so he could speak on the subject like someone who wasn't an idiot. That Christmas, he read Warren Buffett's annual shareholder letter from earlier that year. Before 1983, only companies and wealthy people had access to the stock market, but once regular people were able to invest, Ben saved up and purchased a single share of Berkshire Hathaway for £250. He read everything about Buffett he could get his hands on.

Ben eventually scrounged up enough money to buy a car: a used Austin Metro sporting eighteen-inch wheels and a green neon underglow. He just needed it to get him from A to B. The extra flourishes came courtesy of its previous owner.

By the time Ben's second not-as-horrible Christmas came round, he could easily get around the city. Annie offered to spend Christmas in London with him, but he didn't want her to see him like this: thirty kilos heavier, wearing eight-year-old clothes while working in dead-end jobs, barely making his monthly rent. So he declined her offer and chose a random pub in Shoreditch in which to drink his Christmas Eve away.

It wound up being the most important decision of his life.

A few dozen others filled the pub, mingling at the big wooden tables on tufted leather seats, or playing billiards in a corner. The smoke machine steadily puffing vapour into the room obscured the photos and sketches of patrons going back several hundred years covering almost every inch of the half-timbered walls. Fairy lights decorated a jukebox, where a young woman in neon clothes had just started '99 Red Balloons'. An ancient clock mounted behind the bar struck midnight.

Halfway drunk, Ben was trying to read *Iacocca: An Autobiography*, but a raucous group of traders kept hollering bawdy jokes at each other at one of the tables. Wearing suits that cost several times more than Ben's new car, the men all looked younger than him. A brave newswoman, out quite late, was trying to coax one of them to answer some questions about homelessness and unemployment in London in front of a camera.

"It doesn't matter, it doesn't matter!" one of his yuppie friends said, jumping between him and the camera, spilling some champagne. "Tell all those people to come to the City. You can make *so* much money here. There are toilet rolls here made of money. I'm not kidding." He drew his face right up to the camera and pointed into the lens. "Quit your manky job. Work in finance. Eat squid every night for dinner."

Ben turned back to his book and tried to tune them out. If there was money to be made in the City, he hadn't found it yet.

"Wait a minute," Marley said from the barstool next to him. "I recognise this place. I used to work here."

"You did. Look down."

"Look... huh?" Marley tilted her head downward. It took a few seconds for her to realise she was in her younger self's body, in her mid-twenties, with a buzz cut and a nose piercing. She yelped and jumped up out of it.

"Gracious Rhea, mother of Zeus," Marley whispered as her young memory, on autopilot, strode round to the far side of the bar. "It's me. And my student. I can't believe you remember her. I don't even recall her name. Did we meet tonight?" She gestured between herself and Ben to indicate the two of them.

Marley's younger self addressed a girl at the far end of the bar examining the alcohol licence displayed on the back wall. The girl was far too young to be in a bar this late – maybe fourteen or fifteen years old – but she scrawled notes on a notepad.

Ben smirked at Marley. "You were the best bartender I ever met."

"We met on Christmas Eve?"

"Technically yes, I suppose you'd been serving me drinks for hours by now."

"Aw, sod it, that means we're about to see your grand entrance into my life."

"Or is it your grand entrance into mine?"

Marley ignored the question, frowning at her mid-twenties self. "God, I look stocky."

"Oh, nonsense. Not at all," Ben said. "I was the unhealthy one. When I first saw you, I thought you were very well proportioned."

"Well proportioned?" Marley said, scowling. "What does that mean?"

Having spoken without thinking, Ben paused to think. It took him a moment to figure out how to make his words sound like something other than what they were.

"It means, uh, this memory was meant to be entertaining, not an excuse to judge oneself." Though Marley might have said the same of half of Ben's memories they'd visited so far.

"Sounds like *you're* judging me, too, Scrooge."

Ben held out his hand to gesture towards the young Marley, but words failed him.

The edges of the older Marley's mouth curved upwards in amusement. "You thought I had a nice bum, did you?"

Avoiding eye contact with her, Ben held his empty glass to his cheek, icing it to keep it from flushing. The "student" pointed out Ben's glass to Marley the bartender, who approached him.

"Try not to blush at me," ghost Marley said. "For a stick of a man, you have a pretty nice bum yourself."

Aghast, he stared at her. Never in their whole professional lives had she said such a thing.

Marley winked at him.

"You want another?" her young memory asked him.

Ben was too stunned to do anything other than let the memory take control. He let it pull him downstream, reliving it as it had happened.

"Sure," he said. Marley took his glass to refill it.

"How many pints of bitter do you give someone before you have to kick them out?" the student asked.

Marley cringed while laughing at the question. "Sorry," she said to Ben. He waved forgiveness, and Marley addressed the teenager. "It depends on the person. If I get a real piss artist who can barely walk any more, I cut him off."

"I solemnly pledge not to become said piss artist," Ben said as she returned the glass to him. "Is she training you to be a bartender?" he asked the fourteen-year-old. "You seem a bit young."

"This is Gillian," Marley said. Ben's memory must have filled in the blank, because he had no idea what her actual name had been. "I'm her supply teacher while her maths teacher's popping out a baby. Gillian wants to be a journalist and is doing a report on London's nightlife for another class. I told her come on, you have to see me juggle a million balls at my second job."

"On Christmas Eve?" Ben asked.

"It's not due till April," the girl said, "but I'm getting a head start." Marley shrugged.

He could have left it at that – graciously laughed, then returned to his bevvy. It was true that an initial attraction had pulled him towards Marley, but Ben seldom spoke to women he found attractive. On any other night, he'd have let the conversation die. But by this point he'd spent years pouring every ounce of himself into merely subsisting. He had no true friends. He was desperately lonely.

Half-intoxicated, he didn't see Marley as a romantic prospect at all. He just wanted someone to talk to.

"You like teaching?" he asked.

"God," she said. "It's all I've ever wanted to do. Soon as I get full-time, I'll be putting in my notice here."

"I thought you hated kids," Ben said to the ghostly woman seated next to him.

"I hate *little* kids," she said. "I like teenagers."

Ben redirected this info at young Marley. "Why do you like working with teenagers?" He'd asked her a similar question in real life.

Gillian spoke up: "Because the adult world hasn't poisoned us enough yet that we get hammered alone on Christmas Eve."

Marley the bartender lightly elbowed the girl's arm. "They tell it like it is, for one," she said. "Not as much tiptoeing around social rules and hierarchies. Just, 'You're a loser, mate,' and that's that."

Ben chuckled, and took the jabs in good spirit. "Billy no mates, guilty as charged. Maybe I should be a supply teacher. Seems like more fun."

"What do you do?" Marley asked him.

Ben didn't have the strength to tell her he was a caretaker at a prison. He cleared his throat. "I sit around my flat all day reading books about finance and business in the mistaken illusion I'll put the knowledge to good use someday," he said. On his days off, this was true.

"Ah."

Marley's polite smile told him his answer was entirely uninteresting, she'd heard the same story from ten other people here tonight, and she was about to leave to return to her duties. So Ben followed up with: "I think she's right about the poison of the adult world, though. It's the energy kids have that draws you in, innit? The optimism? The certainty that bugger all can go wrong, that life can be anything you make it?"

Marley leant against the back bar in front of a shelf of spirits to face Ben directly. "Yeah. I think, yeah," she said. "I still have that, and it's like everyone I know around me is losing that part of themselves."

"I know," Ben said. "It's so sad. How different would the world be if we could all keep the child inside of us?"

Marley's gaze went beyond the bar and its patrons, as if she were staring at her own thoughts. "Well, there'd probably be nuclear war," she said. "World run by children? Seems like a shite world to me."

"You know what I meant," Ben said.

"Do I?" Marley smirked at him. "I think that's really why I love it so much. You only get this narrow window of time when you can teach kids not to blow up the world when they grow up. It's important that teachers show their students how to *not* be kids."

"Hmm," Ben said, pondering this. He sipped from his pint glass as two businessmen sat next to him, one right in the middle of Marley's ghost.

"Blimey," she said, drifting backwards and away from him. "Send in the clowns."

Both men were in their mid-thirties and wore nondescript business suits. The thin man next to Ben had hair slicked back with enough product to drown a small town. The other man, stout and burly, removed his jacket, revealing braces beneath. He draped it across the bar.

Ben's blood pressure rose at the mere thought of dealing with these two again. They'd become a lot of trouble in about fifteen minutes.

"Barmaid," Slick Hair said. "Two Johnnie Walkers, neat."

New solemnity fell over the young Marley's face. Apparently, she recognised these men. "Oh," she said. "Hello again."

"Hey, it's the teacher!" Braces said. "You work here?"

"I, uh... No," Marley said, with a quick glance at Ben as if warning him to play along. She put an arm around a confused Gillian. "No, my mate here is just taking me on a tour. Nice pub, innit?"

The men appraised Gillian, who withered a bit beneath their unwanted gazes. "You're the barmaid?" Braces asked. "Are you twelve?"

"I'm—"

"She's eighteen," Marley said. "I'm sure you fellas are busy ringing in Christmas, but what do you say you give me a few more minutes to tell you more about my business? You can cut me off any time."

Slick Hair and Braces exchanged a cryptic glance. Slick Hair nodded, and Braces turned back to Marley. "What are you drinking? It's on us."

Marley gave a wavering laugh. She surveyed the pub, maybe looking for her supervisor. "I'll have a woo woo. Mind if I make it myself?" she said to Gillian.

Gillian looked as if she were reconsidering a career in journalism. "No. Please do."

Marley got to work on the cocktail and whiskies. Her older, ghostlier self had meandered to the stool on the other side of Ben from Slick Hair.

"What was this all about, again?" Ben asked her. "You'd tried to get financing from these blokes for..."

"For a technical college." Melancholy tinged her voice – due to a lost dream, or to the events that were about to unfold, Ben didn't ask. "Even back then, I knew the country needed more electricians and auto mechanics than it needed psychologists and graphic designers. I'd met these two sods at Morgan Grenfell last week."

Morgan Grenfell? Were these men colleagues of Mr Lees, perhaps?

The memory of Ben's failure at the most promising job interview of his life distracted him, let his younger self's thoughts take over again. Here was a nice woman he'd been striking up a friendship with, and now her attention had been diverted by wealthier men. *Typical.* Apparently, the universe wouldn't even give Ben the solace of a pleasant conversation on Christmas Eve.

He'd be alone on Christmas again. He tried to take consolation in Annie having escaped their dad – she lived in Manchester now and had built herself a good social support network. Graham was probably alone now, too, which was a darkly happy thought.

How had Ben got here, with nothing and no one to live for? How had his life come to this? It wasn't for lack of Ben trying to steer things in another direction.

More to the point: was this to be Ben's life forevermore? Merely trying to connect with others, trying to find meaning in the too-short life that was passing him by? Trying, trying, trying?

A boy yields. A man achieves.

His father's words came to him unbidden. Had Graham Scrooge been right after all? *Was* life truly a competition at its core? Survival of the fittest? Had civilisation painted a pleasant veneer over evolutionary struggles that had never fundamentally changed since their origins in prehistory?

If life was a competition, then Ben's failure to acknowledge this fact could be the main reason he was losing that competition.

Something broke inside of Ben. Some piece of an unspoken contract between him and the world. It had been bending far past what should have been its breaking point for quite some time. Tonight, it finally snapped.

It was time that Ben started competing. No more playing by the rules, no more playing fair. If life wanted him to play a contest for survival, he'd do far more than survive. He'd prosper. He would adopt more self-discipline than ever before, and he'd approach every job, every opportunity, every relationship by asking what was in it for him. He would paste that pleasant veneer of civilisation on his own face, but behind it, he would scheme to take everything he could for himself. Any future colleagues, subordinates, shareholders... he'd fleece them if he had to. He would build enough power and wealth for himself that no one would ever look down on him again. Not his dad, not Mr Lees, not women like Helen. At the top of society's hierarchy, Ben could set his own rules.

Ben would make himself as ruthless as he needed to be in order to win over all of them.

I will crawl out of this hole I fell into. I will climb all the way to the top.

In his twenties, Ben found in these thoughts a lifeline. Ben's older self, to his surprise, feared them and the youthful intensity with which they raged in his mind.

"Oof," said a man who plopped onto the barstool next to Ben – again, right in the middle of ghost Marley. She cursed and drifted forward so the top of the counter bisected her waist.

"Life, am I right?" the newcomer said. Tall and bearded, his extreme muscularity was evident even beneath his tweed jacket and glasses. His hair was neatly combed. He looked a strange cross between a professional weightlifter and a university professor.

What's this bloke want?

Ben had trouble remembering. He looked around to see if other bizarrely dressed people accompanied the man – maybe some mates or colleagues, so Ben could place him – but apparently he was alone.

"Life," Ben cautiously agreed. He raised his glass as if in a toast, then sipped.

Oblivious to the newcomer and to Ben's dark thoughts, young Marley strolled round the bar and sat beyond Slick Hair and Braces. A harder, more familiar side of her appeared as she talked business.

The happiness that had lit up her face when she'd discussed teaching with Ben vanished. Ben caught her ghost watching her, wearing a hint of dismay, or maybe regret.

Abandoned by her nightlife guide, Gillian discretely left, maybe to catch a cab home. The newcomer leant across the counter to search for the absent bartender. "Life," he said again. "A grand adventure. Who'll serve me a drink? I don't know. It's a mystery. I'm on the edge of my seat to see how it turns out."

Ben squinted at the man. His tone was a bit too cheeky to be sarcastic. "She ran to the loo," Ben said, covering for Marley. "I'm sure she'll be back soon."

"I'm sure she will." The strange man rested back onto his stool. "And what brings you here on this spectacular Christmas Eve?"

"I'm lonely," Ben said. "And I want to be alone."

"True, true," the man replied. "Christmas can do that. Don't worry, mate. I'll keep you company."

Had the fool not heard him? Ben readied himself to tell the man to bugger off, but Marley's ghost spoke first.

"A bit of a weirdo, this one," she said. "I'm glad you had the wherewithal to notice what was happening with me and the creepers in a few minutes, with the likes of this bloke competing for your attention."

But now that Marley mentioned it, in the real events corresponding to this memory, Ben had been exclusively focused on her and the bankers. Hadn't he? Had he had this conversation with the newcomer *at all*?

"I am a weirdo," the newcomer said straight to Marley's ghost. "But aren't we all? Once we've lived each moment, it slips out of our reach forever, so why waste it on being anything other than your truest self?"

"You can see me?" Marley whispered, backing away from him.

Ben tensed. If this newcomer wasn't a memory... "Who are you?" Ben demanded, even as he realised the man was ever so slightly transparent, see-through. "Why are you here?"

A tremendous grin spread across the man's beard, revealing flawless white teeth. "Actually, I came to see you." He reached a muscular arm forward and offered Ben a handshake. "I'm Ralph. I'm the Ghost of Christmas Eve Present. Have you two seen my staff?"

Ralph

"Well, that's the worst pickup line I've ever heard," said Marley.

Ben got to his feet and prepared to run, but this "Ralph" fellow just sat there, looking a bit disappointed at the refused handshake.

"We are, in fact, in a memory of the past," Marley continued. "What's a Ghost of the Present doing here?"

Ralph's grin returned as he swivelled, hand still outstretched, to Marley's ghost. "It really shouldn't surprise you. The present gets stuck in memories of the past all the time. Yes, technically I'm supposed to help capture you and haul you back to the underworld, but whatever. I really just want my staff back. So just, you know, give it. And I'll leave you to your drinks."

Ben snatched the twisted wood from where he'd set it on the floor, and brandished it defensively, waving the jade light at its top end in

Ralph's face. The Ghost of the Present wasn't nearly as terrifying as that of the Past. Ben could take him if he had to. "Get out of here, you. We're on holiday here."

At the sight of the staff, Ralph cringed and withdrew his hand. His jaw dropped. "Sweet baby Christ, did you kill the Past Ghost and take his staff?"

"What?"

"That's not *my* staff, mate."

"How'd you get here without a staff?" Marley questioned.

Ralph cleared his throat and spoke meekly, like his words embarrassed him. "I talked the Ghost of Imbolc Present into sending me to this memory. Based on what the other ghosts know about you, I guessed you'd come to this one eventually."

"You've been waiting for us in this crummy pub?"

"Mainly I've been listening to Roxy Music on the jukebox. But I've also been waiting for you, it's true. Now please, I'm stuck here for eternity without my staff, and the jukebox only has so many songs."

Marley's ghost crinkled her face at Ben, who shrugged and kept the staff aimed at Ralph. "Is it like when I lose my keys?" Marley asked. "Where did you last see it?"

Ralph scratched his beard. "Well, I was in Philadelphia, helping a child psychologist realise he was dead. I set my staff next to some kid's bed so I could talk to them, then when I turned round a minute later, it was gone."

"So the kid could see you, too?" Marley asked.

"That's not important, mates. Focus. Have you seen *any* other staffs besides the one you have here?"

"No," Ben said. "So bugger off."

"Well, the Ghost of Christmas Past has a staff," Marley said.

Ralph's face collapsed into an even more despondent grimace. "*He* stole my staff?" He gazed at Marley as if expecting a response. She took a cue from Ben and shrugged.

Ralph opened his palms and stared down at them, like an existential crisis had just fallen into his lap. "That smug, friendless arse stole my staff."

"Explains how he was able to come after us," Marley said.

Ralph glanced up at Ben. "That's *his* staff you have, right? I don't suppose I could have it? Maybe he'll trade with me, and I can get mine back? Don't worry, I'll take you two back to the present first, of course."

Ben stuck the staff right in Ralph's face, inches from his eyes. "We're. On. Holiday."

"Your 'holiday' is the only reason you're in danger, you know. We ghosts are usually restricted to doing good things. We can't harm you. But when you escape from Hell and cause an emergency manhunt—"

"Womanhunt," Marley corrected.

"Womanhunt," Ralph acknowledged. "We're allowed to hurt you. *He's* allowed to hurt you. To hurt the dead, at least. He's still restricted from harming the living."

"Then it'll be a thrill-seeking holiday," Marley said. "I'm always game for a thrill, aren't you, Ben?"

Ben raised a sceptical eyebrow at her.

"Years ago, when I snuck back to my old house and told my wife about my new powers," Ralph said, "she tried to talk me into a trip through time." He frowned, quirked his head. "Actually, first she said, 'Holy shit, you're a ghost', but once we got past all that, I told her she had to stay behind, it's too dangerous to break rules and cross the other ghosts. I'm not allowed to see her, anyways. Got in massive trouble for that visit."

Ben withdrew his staff and stood it at his side. "You're a person?" he said in astonishment. "Or, you were a person?"

"Generally ghosts are people, yes. I was a secondary school history teacher."

"Oh, that's nice," Marley said. "A fellow educationalist."

"I thought you were spirits," Ben said.

"Oh, we are. There's been a Ghost of Christmas Eve Present as long as there's been a Christmas Eve. I'm just the latest in a long line. Bought it from colon cancer in 1975 and decided the afterlife's too short, I might as well spend it spreading some Christmas cheer, eh?"

"Is that what you do?" Ben said dryly.

"Mostly they police life and death," Marley said, her wary eyes bearing down on Ralph. "Or serve as prison wardens for the dead."

"We do quite a lot more than that!" Ralph protested. "We're the Ghosts of Time. We salve old wounds. When you're rushing to and from work, we nudge you to stop and enjoy the summer breeze. We remind you of what once was and inspire you with what will be. We help build societies. Every year, we live the day we're responsible for over and over again until our work is done, all over the world. Okay, yes, it's true that each person has a specific number of seconds to live on the Earth, and we do help to ferry people to the next worlds – at least the Ghosts of the Past and Present do. But our mandate is bigger than that. And so is our power. So you'd best give me that staff if you don't want me to, uhm, beat you up?"

Ralph balled his hand into a fist and gritted his teeth, but he looked more like a queasy actor afraid to go out on stage than an all-powerful time ghost.

"You strike such fear into my heart," said Ben.

"Do I?" Ralph said with disappointment. "I'm sorry. I hate scaring people. I wouldn't really beat you up."

Ben cast Marley a glance that asked *What are we going to do with him?*

Marley inhaled deeply, which Ben found odd, seeing as she didn't breathe. "When you died, you didn't go to Heaven or Hell," she said to Ralph. "You found another path. How?"

And might I take that path myself? Ben heard her subtext.

Ralph sputtered for a moment before coming up with an answer. "It's not that simple. After they die, some people aren't ready yet to face all the people they hurt in life. One way to avoid that is by waiting until a spot as a time ghost opens up, then volunteering for the work. You serve until you finally come to terms with what you did. Until you're ready to atone and move on. I don't recommend it, though. Running away from your punishment prolongs it in the end."

Marley crossed her arms and leant back as if reclining in a seat, even though she rested on nothing but empty air. "You seem a nice enough guy. What did you do to deserve punishment?"

Ralph let out a nervous chuckle.

"Oi!" Ben's younger self shouted from behind him. Ben looked down to find the glowing ghost of an old man where his body should have been. Being caught up with Ralph, he'd let the memory slip past him, and it was playing out behind him.

Still, he waited for Ralph to answer, but the relieved ghost gestured towards the commotion, his expression asking Ben if he was going to intervene.

Ben re-entered his body to pause the memory again. But once inside his youthful brain again, the extreme urgency of helping the bartender with her situation overcame everything else. Forgetting about Ralph, he drunkenly tottered over to Slick Hair and Braces, to whom the young Marley appeared to be pitching her business idea.

Ben jabbed his finger into Slick Hair's chest, unbalancing him and spilling some of his whisky. "He put a roofie in your drink," Ben said to Marley.

His younger self had seen it a minute ago, in the corner of his vision. Marley had set her drink on the bar top and was so involved in her pitch that she didn't notice the man dropping a small pill in her drink when he stretched his arms. Now her animated spiel sputtered to a halt, and her wide eyes darted between Ben and Slick Hair.

"What are you blathering about, mate?" Slick Hair said. "You're pissed. Sit back down and mind your own."

"They're trying to drug you," Ben pressed on.

Marley picked up her pint glass and searched for the pill that had long since dissolved. Finding nothing suspicious, she lifted the drink to her lips and gulped down half of it in seconds. She sighed and smiled rebelliously at Ben.

"No they aren't," she said.

Oh dear God. Ben stared in awe as she smacked her glass back down on the bar top, spilling a little even though it was now half-full. *Just how badly does she want this funding?*

"They're not going to fund your…" – he searched for the word through the booze in his brain – "your thing. They're trying to drug you."

"And you're crashing our important business meeting," Slick Hair said. "Bugger off."

An important business meeting held in a pub, after midnight, on Christmas Eve? Not bloody likely.

"Then you drink it," Ben said. "If there's nothing in her drink, you drink the rest of it."

Slick hair chuckled. "I don't drink girly drinks." Braces stood, fists clenched, glaring at Ben.

They'd obviously done this before. Their excuses were too ready-made, too boilerplate. Another complaint from Ben and he was sure his face would be invited to an important business meeting with Braces' fist.

Past Braces, Marley was frowning now, fighting a battle behind her eyes: trying to cling to the hope that this wasn't really happening, that her college could still get funded, Ben guessed.

"You really won't take a sip of my drink?" she asked Slick Hair. "Just to prove him wrong?"

Slick Hair threw her an incredulous grin. "What, you actually believe this pisshead?"

In answer, Marley cleared her throat and held the pint glass out to him. She nodded at it, prompting Slick Hair to drink.

Slick Hair feigned offence and laughed at Marley like she was a child who'd accidentally told an offensive joke. "This must be the first time I've been accused of drugging a founder who wants my money."

"It's not your money," Ben said. "It's your bank's."

The room shifted, tilting sideways. Ben's head hit the floor before he even felt the pain from Braces' punch. It bit through his cheek into his teeth and gums. He flailed, but the alcohol in his system kept him from standing back up.

Everything happened as if in slow motion. Slick hair, still laughing, stood to leave and put on his coat. Braces turned to Marley, opening his mouth for what was sure to be a piercingly witty comment of his own. But Marley had a new pitch for him. She pitched her pint glass right at his face with all the force of a cricket bowler.

It missed. Sailed right across the room and shattered against a wall.

Braces stared at Marley in shock. She didn't let a moment pass. She swung her arm back and punched him in the face. A full-armed, perfectly aimed punch right into Braces' nose.

Old Marley's ghost ran to help Ben off the floor while young Marley readied herself for another attack. Ralph, immaterial though he was, leapt behind his barstool and cowered away from the re-enacted memory.

Braces fell back onto Slick Hair and both tumbled downwards, sweeping their arms out to try and stop their fall, sending beer and spirits flying from several pint glasses on the bar top.

Dozens of other patrons turned to watch the incipient pub brawl. One even dialled the police on a public phone near the entrance.

Young Marley leapt on top of the downed men and punched one of them again, but Braces flung her back.

Marley's ghost knelt beside Ben. "Come up out of your body. You're hurt."

Ben winced at the pain in his head, at the dizziness growing worse by the moment. He squinted at old Marley in front of him, and

141

young Marley fighting the men behind her. Was he imagining what he was seeing? He'd thought the memory had been moving slowly due to its vividness and intensity, but old Marley spoke and moved at a normal speed, while the brawl behind her slowed considerably.

When old Marley glanced at it, she noticed it too. "What's going on?"

Ben wasn't just perceiving the fight in slow motion – it was actually happening in slow motion.

His dizziness became unbearable. He felt as if gravity might yank him towards a wall or the ceiling. His head dropped the few inches to the floor. The scuffle stopped completely, Marley in a temporary position of strength, one hand grabbing Slick Hair's coat as he tried to flee, her other elbow pinning Braces to the floor. Frozen in place, all of them.

Ben rolled away from the fight, trying to shake the wobbly feeling out of his head. Everyone else in the pub was frozen, too.

Everyone, except for the black-cloaked phantom, staff in hand, drifting through the fog at the pub's entrance. It wound through the pubgoers with a serpentine movement, studying each face in the smoke machine's vapour. The crowd near to it was dense, watching the brawl from a safe distance, but the number of punters thinned closer to Ben and Marley's ghost.

"Stay still," Marley whispered to Ben. "Don't leave your body." She fled quickly into her younger self's body and vanished.

The Ghost of Christmas Past raised its hooded head towards the fight frozen in time. Had it seen Marley? Could it see Ben, or just the veneer of his younger self, inside which Ben was hiding? Did it have a way to know Ben was there, or would it see just another memory?

Without seeming to move its feet, it glided across the pub, directly towards Ben lying on the floor. He gazed at his staff where he'd left it behind the barstools, yards away. The ghost would certainly reach him before he managed to grab it.

He stayed frozen. It hovered above him. In the dim light, through the fog, he still couldn't see its face beneath its hood.

It leant closer. It reached a bony hand towards Ben's face. Towards his body, and Ben's spirit inside it.

"Don't kill me," said Ralph.

The ghost jerked its head upwards. Ralph was still crouched behind a stool, his body curled nearly into a foetal position. The phantom left Ben and drifted towards him. Towering above Ralph, it stopped so close to him that its robes grazed his forehead.

"They're here," said the phantom, its voice a deep rumble. "Where are they?"

Ralph's jaw shook as he tried to form words. He breathed raggedly in and out. Was he having a panic attack?

The phantom snatched Ralph by the neck so quickly it would have killed a human. It raised him above its head. Ralph coughed, gagged, struggled for air.

"Thrall," said the Ghost of Christmas Past, "have you aided them?"

"Don't—" Ralph choked. "Don't hurt me. I haven't" – More coughing – "h-helped them. I swear."

"Then tell me where they are."

Ralph gave a distinctly unconvincing shrug of ignorance. A grumble, almost a growl, rose from the phantom's throat. Still clutching Ralph with one hand, it raised its staff – the staff it had stolen from Ralph – in its other hand. The top of the staff pulsed with green light.

Dizziness twisted Ben's mind in a knot. He felt at the verge of falling from a great height despite already lying on the floor.

Things started moving backwards. The pub patrons. The fight. Every movement played in reverse. Braces reached out as if to catch Marley when in fact he'd flung her off him.

Marley, however, couldn't play along. The memory rewound, but she controlled her own body – apparently it didn't move automatically while she was in it. She tried to play along, falling on top of Braces and grappling with him, but she still looked like a woman moving forward in time, not backwards, so her movements were out of place. When Braces' head jolted in response to Marley's previous punch, she quickly moved her fist into position, slightly too late, then retracted it.

Fortunately, the phantom wasn't looking in her direction. Yet. But it scanned the crowd, neglecting to drop Ralph, searching for its prey.

The man at the public phone dialled in reverse, then paced backwards towards his mates. Beer droplets coalesced out of thin air and funnelled themselves back into pint glasses. Soon Ben would need to stand, to somehow fall upwards, in an inverse re-enactment of getting punched by Braces. He prepared himself.

But the phantom spotted Marley's implausible movements. She saw that it saw her. She poorly faked that first punch at Braces, then sighed, stepped backwards, and lifted her arms in a challenge to the ghost.

"You think you can take me, too?" she yelled at it. "Then come at me."

The ghost dropped Ralph, who heaved lungs' worth of air and rubbed his neck. It raced towards Marley, an old woman in a young body.

She raised her hand.

The pint glass she'd chucked at Braces reconstituted itself, shot backwards across the room in a beeline towards the woman who'd thrown it, and slammed into the back of the phantom's head. It stumbled at the impact. Marley had lined up her attack perfectly. The glass continued on its course straight into Marley's waiting hand. She lifted it high, then brought it down with all her might and shattered it again on the phantom. It fell, but immediately clutched the edge of the bar to pull itself back to its feet.

Marley reached a foot behind the stools and slid out the staff they'd been using. She kicked it towards Ben.

He grabbed it. A smorgasbord of memories appeared before him. Once again, he didn't have time to choose. The ghost was rising. Marley and Ralph were grabbing at Ben, shouting at him to get them out of there.

The ghost flew towards them, and as it reached them, Ben's staff lit up. A disorienting whirlwind engulfed them.

Ben found himself in his fortieth-floor office working on financial spreadsheets over Christmas. A festive page in his office calendar informed him this was Christmas 2002.

Caught up in the memory, he intended to keep working till he finished the spreadsheets, but Marley pulled him right out of his seat. Ralph screamed as the phantom appeared in their midst. Ben clutched his staff again.

Now he stood on the fourth floor of the house where he lived with Lauren, his third wife, near to the stairs they'd recently raced each other up. Rhys, still a child, played video games in an entertainment alcove nearby.

"Our family should be important enough that you make time for us, too," Lauren was saying.

The phantom appeared next to them. It was too close. When Ben transported Ralph and Marley – both disoriented, leaning on the railing – he was transporting the Ghost of Christmas Past, too.

It reached towards Ben.

He shoved it. Hard.

It fell over the railing, but instead of plummeting four floors, it grasped the edge of the top floor and held on.

"I don't understand why you have to be running around all the time," Lauren's memory continued, oblivious to all the action.

"Sorry, luv," Ben said. Then to Marley: "Out the window." He had to get far enough away from the phantom that it wouldn't get sucked in when he transported them. At least, that was his theory.

He led Marley out a dormer window onto his mansion's roof. It slanted enough that they'd fall if they weren't careful. What would happen then? Marley was already dead. But could Ben die in here? Fall and break his back?

London at night stretched to the south, its skyscrapers like Christmas ornaments on a sparkling tree. A third set of footsteps joined them.

"What are you doing with *us?*" Ben asked Ralph. "You're one of them. Go fight that thing and get it off our backs."

"Hell no, I'm not gonna fight him!" Ralph said, running beside them. "The Ghosts of the Past are bonkers powerful."

"And you're not?"

"No!"

"You should try anyways. It can't kill you if you're already dead." Ben tried to focus on transporting them away.

"Look," Ralph said. "There was a war. A huge war. The Ghosts of the Past against the Ghosts of the Future, and the Ghosts of the Past won. Now the Future Ghosts are in hiding, so the Past Ghosts have all the power. Yes, they can end my existence if they want. Not 'going back to Hell' dead. *Dead* dead."

A flutter of robes behind them. The phantom left the dormer window and sped after them, but they were running much slower.

"Does it have a weakness?" Marley asked. "Can we fight it or trap it somehow?"

Her question gave Ben an idea. He concentrated on his staff as they ran along the rooftop. He searched for a particular memory.

"No!" Ralph said. "It's invincible. We can knock it flat but it'll always jump right back up. You should turn yourselves in to it. It's less likely to hurt you that way. Probably."

The ghost had seemed quite intent on hurting Ben in his encounters with it so far. He wasn't about to test Ralph's theory.

Green light from the ghost's staff shone behind them as it neared.

"Hold on," Ben said, and blasted them all into a new memory.

A stormy night in the early 1960s. Ben's childhood bedroom, at two in the morning. He'd been trying to fall asleep for hours, but the thunder kept him up, as did the leafless tree branches scratching against his window. Years later, when he was honest with himself, the cause of his insomnia during these nights became obvious. This always happened after his dad yelled at him, spittle flying from his mouth because Ben forgot to take the dog out, or got a not-quite-perfect score on his homework.

Lightning cast long shadows across the room whenever it struck, but it never quite illuminated one of the far corners beyond the wardrobe, which remained a yawning gap of darkness. In his child's mind, the shadows rocked and swayed, each a spirit of its own whose cold fingers he might feel brushing against his leg in the night.

He cowered under his bed sheets, only his eyes poking out above them. Marley lay to his right, Ralph to his left, both of them under the sheets, too.

"What are we doing here?" Marley whispered. "This is terrifying."

As if to validate her fear, the Ghost of Christmas Past rose from beyond the foot of Ben's bed. Silent and menacing, its robes seemed to stretch and stretch until its head nearly touched the ceiling.

"This isn't the actual past, is it?" Ben asked, to be certain. "Just a memory?"

Neither Marley nor Ralph answered, so fixated were they on the phantom, so mortified by the vulnerability Ben had led them into. Ben pushed through the terror in his own young mind.

"When I was a lad," he whispered, "my father terrorised me. To cope with it, I imagined a monster who lived in the corner." He stared into that corner now, a threatening void behind the ghost. "It watched me at night, came out to murmur in my ear while I fell asleep. It wanted me to suffer. I wasn't welcome in my own house, and it was always ready to attack me, to force me out into the streets."

The phantom leant forward above them. Lightning struck, and Ben perceived the barest outline of a human face within its hood.

"That monster was all in your head, though," Marley said. "It wasn't real."

The phantom reached towards the bed. Slowly. Like it was savouring the moment. Its appendage reached not towards Marley, nor even towards Ralph. It reached straight for Ben.

"In my memory," Ben said, as two glowing red eyes opened in the corner, "the monster was real."

A six-limbed beast latched strong, sinewy arms onto the walls surrounding the dark corner. It looked for all the world like a giant ant, if ants were muscular mammals and had the heads of vampires. Enormous fangs protruded from its upper jaw. It growled a low snarl.

The Ghost of Christmas Past turned.

The monster pounced. Ben raised a leg and kicked the ghost's staff hard enough that it fell from its hand just as the creature attacked. Defenceless, the spirit buckled beneath the thing, which mauled it ferociously. It bit at its torso, clawed at its neck, the ghost thrashing against it, trying to force it away.

"Quickly," Ben said, and flung the sheets aside. They ran to the lounge. Lightning struck again, and the beast howled behind them. Ben led them out into the rain, into the street outside, then finally, relievingly, into a memory free of the Ghost of the Past.

A Novel Idea

Ben's piercing headache woke him, but promptly urged him back to sleep to avoid its pain. He rolled over and tried to ignore it. Whose sofa was this? Why wasn't he in his own bed in his crummy flat back in the Docklands?

He blinked. Let his eyes adjust to the Christmas-morning light.

Ecru silk curtains hung before immense, two-storey-tall arched windows lining a wall on the far side of the sitting room. Sunlight slanted through them to fall on plush furniture, marble floors, and various arrangements of flowers and plants – real or fake?

Ben sat up and tried to figure out where the hell he was. His headache faded in the shadow of a new pain: his cheek, where Braces had hit him last night.

Ah, that was it. That bartender had single-handedly taken on both businessmen, sending them fleeing for their lives, but she'd soon wilted, barely conscious, from the roofie they'd drugged her with.

She said she lived nearby, so Ben walked her halfway home, although he'd been so drunk by that point he had trouble remembering. She'd completely collapsed on the pavement somewhere, hadn't she? Ben had carried her, poorly, falling several times and bruising them both. He'd found her flat key in her handbag.

Then nothing. He remembered nothing after that.

"This kitchen is fully stocked," a man said, and whistled. Ben shielded his eyes from the sunlight and searched for the source of the voice. The flat's open-plan layout placed no boundary between the sitting room and the kitchen, so he soon located the Ghost of Christmas Eve Present rooting through Marley's fridge. "You want me to make some crepes? Smoked salmon? She's caviar in this fridge that costs three hundred pounds. And I'm talking mid-eighties currency!"

Ralph's oh-so-sunny presence brought Ben back to the – *hmph* – present.

"No, no, no," he said. "You don't get to lounge around with us. This is *my* memory. You go back where you came from."

As he spoke, he stood and stepped towards the kitchen. His foot bumped into the staff. It lay abandoned on an ornate rug in the middle of the room. Ben studied it for a moment. He furrowed his brow at Ralph.

"You were saying?" Ralph said.

Ben cleared his throat. "You could've taken this staff while I was sleeping."

Ralph grinned and stroked his beard. "Oh, could I have? Funny, I didn't think of it." He winked, then returned to the fridge.

Brilliant. Now we're saddled with a nosy spirit who wants to get involved in our lives. Ben's hangover was too fierce to let him protest.

A half-hearted, "Bah," was all he could manage as he probed at his injured cheek to test the extent of the damage. He found Marley's drinks cabinet and set out making himself a drink.

Tanqueray, Louis XIII, Glenfiddich from 1937, some French and Italian spirits Ben couldn't even identify, and many others. Marley had quite the collection. A film poster for *Educating Rita* decorated the inside of one of the drinks cabinet's doors, one for *The Prime of Miss Jean Brodie* the other. Ben had seen the stage play on which the former was based but knew nothing of the latter.

By his forties, Ben had learnt that drinking more alcohol didn't cure a hangover, but at this age he hadn't known that. His mind still fuzzy from sleep, he mixed himself an ungodly concoction of eight different spirits.

"I see you found the drinks cabinet," Marley said.

Ben shut one of its doors so he could see her. She stood at her bedroom door, still wearing what she'd worn last night, half her face creased from firm contact with a wrinkled pillowcase, looking like she'd be sick had she not already done so several times this morning.

Ben nodded at her. "Are you okay?"

Marley rubbed her neck and smacked her lips lightly, like she was trying to identify some strange taste in her mouth. "What happened last night?"

Ben wasn't sure where to begin, but thankfully Marley said, "After the fight, I mean."

"Oh. Uh, you fell asleep and I carried you here. Apparently I passed out on your sofa. Apologies. I'll be leaving." He gulped down half his drink while Marley shut some of the curtains.

"You didn't sexually assault me while I was sparked out, did you?" she asked.

"Dear God, no."

Marley grunted.

Ben set his drink down and sidled towards the front door. "Well, lovely meeting you. Nice place."

"Yeah, my dad's in oil," Marley said. "He pays for the flat, but my mum won't let him pay for anything else."

"Ah," Ben said. "Well, I'm very sorry about your cancer."

Marley grimaced in confusion. "My cancer?"

"Your hair." Buzzed nearly to the scalp, as she'd worn it until the mid-nineties.

Marley patted her head as if checking whether something was wrong with it. "I don't have cancer. My hair is a statement."

"Oh," Ben said, still moving away from her, trying to salvage what decorum he could. "Keep stating it, then."

"And back when this happened in real life," Marley said, "you tried to take a bottle of Hennessy as payment for carrying me home."

Ben stopped in his tracks. "I did not!"

Marley's ghost floated up above her body, which paused in mid-memory. "Yes you did, you cheap bastard. You can't do a single kind thing for another human being without expecting compensation."

"Clearly, if that had happened, I'd be carrying a bottle of Hennessy right now." He held out his empty hands for Marley's inspection.

"Your memory must be deficient, old man."

"My memory is flawless."

"Or maybe your memory doesn't want to admit to you that you're the kind of person who stole a bottle of Hennessy."

At a loss, Ben turned towards the strange man in the tweed jacket, who was still in the kitchen, munching on some avocado toast he'd made himself three decades before anyone else would be eating it.

In mid-bite, Ralph reopened his mouth and set the teeth-marked toast back on his plate. "I mean, when you remember the past, you're never really *remembering* it," he said. "You're recreating it in your present mind. Sometimes things get added, or changed, or lost."

"Like a bottle of Hennessy," Marley said smugly.

Ralph shrugged and took a bite of his toast.

Defeated, Ben trudged back to the spirits cabinet and snatched the bottle of Hennessy. "Happy now?"

"No, you thief. Give it back," Marley said.

Ben grunted. "Let's just… let the memory play out. If that phantom finds us, I don't want it to recognise we're here. Which means you" – he pointed at Ralph – "need to leave."

Gob full of toast, Ralph replied, "I can't go anywhere without a staff. You have the staff. I'm stuck with you."

"Fine, then at least hide."

Ralph haphazardly glanced around the kitchen. Finding no hiding spot readily available, he squatted so his eyes barely peeked above the kitchen island's countertop.

Ben had half a mind to bop him on the head with the staff and send him to another memory, trapping him there. But Marley sank back down into her younger self's body, so Ben gave himself over to the memory, too.

"Ridiculous," Marley said. She plodded to a cheval mirror in a corner of the room. Some makeup from her left eye had got smudged all over her cheek. She tried to wipe it off with her shirt. "I work my bum off to prepare the best pitch and business plan ever made by a human being, and what does the world see me as? A pair of boobs."

Ben stopped his progression towards the exit. He'd feel strangely guilty leaving her like this, despite not knowing her and having no obligations to her. Could he cheer her up somehow?

"Are you going to report those blokes?"

A slight scowl was all the response she gave. Ben took it as a "no".

"I think approximately half of all employees at the big investment banks are sociopaths," he offered. "Those two were particularly despicable."

"Half of all *people* are sociopaths, if you ask me," Marley said, studying her bedraggled face in the mirror.

Ben glanced at the bottle of cognac in his hands. He paced back to the drinks cabinet, set it back down, and took another sip from the drink he'd mixed.

"More than half," Marley's young memory continued. "It's like you have this kernel of love and passion in you – this thing you *have* to do to live your truest life and make the world a better place – and everyone just sees it as a tool they can use to manipulate you."

"Or as a handicap that will stain you forever."

"Exactly. So much short-sightedness. Selfishness. They think the only people who deserve anything good in life are the people who already have it."

Ben glimpsed his own reflection in the mirrored back wall of the drinks cabinet. As bad as Marley looked after last night, he looked worse. "And they judge you for your ugliness."

"And boldness," Marley said. "And showing even the slightest sign of vulnerability. Which, of course, this whole conversation is vulnerability, but what do I care? You're nobody. I'll never see you again."

"Right," said Ben. "We can be honest with each other that the world is shit."

"That people are shit."

"And that if that's the game all those arrogant, avaricious faultfinders want to play," Ben said, "then maybe we might as well suck it all up—"

"—and beat them at their own game," both Ben and Marley said together.

Silence. Slowly, cautiously, Marley turned from her cheval mirror, and Ben from the mirror in the drinks cabinet. They faced each other from across the room.

Marley stepped towards him. "Who are you?" she asked.

"My name's Ben." He set down his empty glass.

The intriguing woman circled round him, as if sizing him up. "Hi Ben. I'm Marley."

Ben stepped away from the spirits cabinet and let himself be circled. "You're a bartender *and* a supply teacher?"

"I'm an entrepreneur working as a bartender and a supply teacher until the world realises what it's been missing and gives me a bunch of money to build a good company. What do you do, Ben? You said something about reading finance books?"

"I'm... an investor. An inspiring investor."

"*Aspiring* investor?"

"Yes. That. I invest other people's money."

"You dolt, I forgot you said that!" Marley said, channelling the ghost inside her.

"Oh, what was I supposed to say? That I'm a caretaker at a prison and haven't touched anyone else's capital since my dad gave me pocket money as a teenager? You'd have run me right out of your flat."

She glanced down at his grimy trousers and his shirt, which was a size too large. "Clearly you invest other people's money rather than your own," her younger self said as she let the memory resume.

"I've had a bad week, okay? I'm wearing the type of clothing one wears to a pub on Christmas Eve."

Marley stopped circling him. Her arms had been crossed; now she lowered them to her sides. "Thank you for... whatever it was you did last night. Taking a fist to the face, I guess."

Ben touched his sore cheek, reflexively covering it from her view. "Thank you for beating those blokes up."

"Pleasure. I probably lost my job over it." She dropped her gaze and plodded towards the tall windows. "'I told you so,' my mum will say, endlessly. 'You're not cut out to be on your own. No one will take a single woman seriously. You need a man. You need me dictating everything you do forever.'"

Marley staggered, held her arms out for balance, then rested against a side table. She groaned and placed a hand on her head.

"Do you need some food?" Ben asked. "Tea?"

Marley inhaled deeply and pointedly stood. "What I need," she said as she resumed her march to the windows, "is..."

She didn't finish the thought. At the only window she hadn't drawn curtains over, she squinted down at London's streets, three floors below. "Peons," she muttered. "In their boxes. So eager to put other people in boxes of their own. They should all just vanish. Gone from the Earth."

Ben cringed. "I thought you said you wanted to make the world a better place."

Marley said nothing. Just stared menacingly downwards.

"Let me make you some food," Ben said.

He went to the fridge. Ralph was sitting on the floor behind the kitchen island, munching the last of his breakfast. He raised a glass of orange juice to salute Ben.

"My water and electric bills are due next week," Marley mumbled by the window. "Car's almost out of petrol. My dad will give me money if I ask for it, but the money comes with conditions, see? Not from him so much. From my mum. It's not proper for a woman to chase a career in business, if you haven't heard."

"How do you take your eggs?" Ben said, setting a frying pan on the hob, and trying to figure out why he wanted to ingratiate himself to this bitter person. *I should leave and go home. Am I really so lonely that I'd latch on to the first morsel of connection another human being grants me?*

Well, yes. I am.

"I don't suppose you could lend me any money?" Marley asked him. "Invest in an up-and-coming entrepreneur? I'm good in a fist fight."

If you need money, sell some of your fancy furniture, Ben almost said. But he said nothing and let that be his answer. He wanted no more questions about his imaginary investment company.

"Scrambled," Marley said when Ben didn't respond. He began cracking eggs into a bowl. "What do you do when you need money fast?" she asked him.

Oof. How to answer that one? When Ben needed money, he walked to work instead of taking the Tube. Even on Supplementary Benefit he barely ate so he could save on groceries. At this point in his life he worked sixteen hours a day. But of course, he couldn't admit these to Marley without outing himself as a loser.

"When's your next pay cheque come in?" Ben asked.

"From the pub, mid-January. And school's out, so no work from the education authority till after break." She leant against the wall next to the window and brought her hands to her face, covering it. "It sure would be nice if you could get your pay cheque sooner."

Ben grunted agreement. "Especially when you don't qualify for a credit card." Realising his words were a bit too personally implicating, he added, "Like half of those... those peons down there."

"I could stay out from under my mum's thumb," Marley said.

Ben recalled when three quid for a cab might have changed the course of his life. "I'd gladly pay a lot later so I could get my money now."

An egg, half-cracked in his hand, oozed onto the countertop as a thought occurred to him. An idea that ping-ponged around his brain. Marley was still there, sliding her hands down her face. And the hubbub of the streets outside was still there, the windows muffling it before it reached the flat. The mundaneness of a world that was about to change forever.

Incredible, to re-experience the genesis of this. An old man in this young man's body, he cradled the idea, this small flame that might be quickly extinguished and forgotten. He clung to it far more possessively than he had when the thought had first occurred to him. He almost hadn't said anything, so insignificant was the idea to him then.

How precious it was now.

"You know, I think a lot of people would pay to get their pay cheque sooner," he said. The flame hopped from Ben's mind into Marley's. The train of their lives switched onto a new track.

Marley's face grew pinched, quizzical. Her pupils slid from one corner of her eyes to the other as her mind worked. "How much would they pay?" she asked.

Finally noticing the eggshell in his hands, the goo inside having fully leaked onto the counter, Ben discarded it, turned on the hob, and started cracking more eggs. "I mean, I'd pay interest of two, three hundred per cent," Ben said. He actually wouldn't, but he wanted to put the idea in her head.

Marley scoffed. "Bollocks. No one would pay that much."

"Unsecured short-term loans? That's risky. Risk means high fees. Why not go as high as seven hundred per cent? Maybe a thousand? There's plenty of demand."

Marley placed her hands on her hips. "So how would it work? You make little shops people go into, they give proof of income and a bank account, and you give them their next pay cheque before they get it?"

"'Cheque into cash' we could call it," Ben said, whisking the eggs. "The loan is due when they get the cheque."

"Whoa, whoa, whoa, whoa, whoa," Ralph said. He stood slowly with his hands in a "timeout" gesture. "Hang on. You're telling me that you two *invented* payday loans?"

Ben paused in mid-whisk. He looked to Marley for an answer, only to find Marley was looking to him for an answer.

"*Ben* invented payday loans," said Marley.

"It was your idea," Ben said cordially, to give her credit.

"You're the one who turned it into a business."

"It took two for that tango, my dear."

"I feel like I'm witnessing a crime," Ralph said, mouth agape.

Ben dumped the eggs into the frying pan. Marley left the window to approach him, and they let their younger selves continue their conversation. "So people take out a loan for a few days and pay it back. Maybe we'd make money at that if we get a million customers, but there's no way it's profitable until then, even if we charge high interest rates."

"Think bigger, Marley!" Ben said. As the liquid eggs congealed, he scraped them off the bottom of the pan and flipped them over. "People who pay the loan back right away aren't our customers. Our customers are people who *can't* pay back right away. We'll market specifically to people in financial trouble, set up shops in poor neighbourhoods. When the loan comes due, they'll need to take out another loan to pay it off. So it's a cycle, you see? They keep borrowing, and the fees keep piling up."

"Is that legal?"

"It's not *illegal.*"

Marley leant over the frying pan to sniff at the eggs. "Overdraft fees," she said. "Rollover fees, transaction fees, default fees."

Ben grinned. "Fees to fill an Olympic swimming pool. A lake."

"A universe!" Marley said.

"Uni—? I was going to go with 'ocean' next, but if you want to escalate all the way to a universe of fees, I'm sure we can make that happen, too. You could get out from under your parents, and I could—" He could what? Escape poverty? Show his father up? "I could help you," he said. He scooped the scrambled eggs onto a plate, added a fork, and presented Marley her fry-up.

Marley withdrew a step, crossed her arms, bit her tongue. "Just to be clear, you're proposing I start a business together with the bloke who goes drinking alone late at night on Christmas Eve?"

Still smiling, Ben held the plate out farther, extending his arm to its full reach.

"Where would we get the start-up funds?" Marley asked. "Your investments? What do you even invest in?"

Ben kept his expression neutral while frantically searching for a plausible answer. "I invest in what I know," he said.

"Ah, a disciple of Warren Buffett," Marley said. "He says that, doesn't he?"

A genuine grin bloomed on Ben's face. "You know Warren Buffett? He's brilliant. But my investment business is, uhm, small. Compared to his. I don't make enough to invest in something new. What about your dad? Would he—"

"No. Don't even say it."

"Then we'll need a loan. Or an investor."

Marley rested her head against the fridge. She blew air out through tight lips. "I don't know."

"You have to admit it's a good idea."

"But I have my technical college idea, and I'm putting everything I've got into that right now. And I know bugger all about you. You could be a serial killer."

"A serial killer who just made you scrambled eggs. Education is bust right now. Finance is where the money's at. The City is booming."

Marley lackadaisically ran a hand through her short hair, seemed to pick one hair at random, and plucked it from her scalp. She looked at it briefly then flicked it away.

"I can see the college is important to you," Ben said. "But think of it this way. What's more likely to show your parents you can be your own person? Managing a college you barely got off the ground? Or being a powerful woman leading the charge into the man's world of finance?"

She yanked out another hair. She raised her eyes to Ben.

The memory played on, but Marley's ghost rose up from her body. She made no snarky observations, but instead just hung there, watching. Had the decision been so difficult for her that she didn't want to re-experience making it?

"Did you ever create that college?" Ralph asked. He was sitting on the countertop no farther from Ben and Marley than they stood from each other. Given that he wasn't part of the memory, they'd been ignoring his presence.

Marley's younger self took the plate of eggs and started eating.

"No," her ghost said. "No, I never did."

The Pitch

Ultimately, after months of begging, Marley did convince her dad to lend them enough funds to live on while they honed their business plan and pitch. She called it a pittance, but to Ben it was a small fortune, even if they'd have to pay it back. Overnight, he rejoined the middle class, and promptly set about refashioning his image. He might not yet have been the type of man he wanted to be, but he could at least look like he was.

He splurged on a charcoal-grey three-piece suit of worsted Italian wool, and complemented it with polished black Oxfords, a Chesterfield overcoat, a business watch, pocket squares, argyle socks, aviator sunglasses, and even an ascot. This last piece he soon abandoned after realising it made him look like a fop.

He bought a navy blazer for casual events and a Stresemann jacket and formal trousers for upscale ones. For the first time in his life, he had clothing items tailored to fit his body.

Soon those items needed retailoring. Leaving his caretaking job had freed enough of Ben's time that he took up weightlifting, and as the months passed and his diet changed, the extra kilos he'd carried melted away. He would watch his body changing in the gym mirror and exult in the alpha male he was becoming.

His older self was grateful he never worked out on Christmas, to save himself the embarrassment of Marley's ghost seeing him lust at his own body in a mirror while whispering the word "alpha".

Still, he couldn't blame his younger self. As far as he'd been aware, there was no other role in society for which people would value him. He'd felt he needed to be an "alpha" just to be seen as a person, so naturally, that was what he tried to become.

He joined a golf club, a fitness club, and a gentlemen's club – ostensibly to meet the type of people who could provide Marley and him funding, but at a deeper level, he wanted to prove to himself that he could stand his ground in a higher rung of London's social scene.

Apparently, some of the clubs were starting to accept women as members. The other men complained about this, but Ben enjoyed the exposure to upper-class women. He forced himself out of his comfort zone, and chatted with them on the golf course, in the smoking room, at the poolside. He never made a pass at any of them, though. It was still too early for that; now was a time for learning. Through trial and error, he grasped what topics to avoid, how to master the punchline of a joke, how to present himself as a relatively polished, modern man.

You haven't got enough money, Ben.

Sandra's final words remained lodged like a splinter in his soul. He made no effort to remove the splinter, to dull its ongoing pain, or even to grow scar tissue around it. He kept those words, that fresh wound at the front of his mind daily. It motivated him. It reminded him of the nobody lurking just beneath his skin. A single misstep now and the world would gaze through the veneer he was carefully crafting and see that nobody once more.

For so long, it had been difficult for Ben to even conceive of any path for his future other than the one he'd been on. But now, with the cheque into cash business plan and enough money to fake a measure of status, he saw that he was *not* less than other people. His father and Sandra be damned. In fact, other people were less than him: the vain upper-crusters lording their wealth over everyone, and the poor sods with no self-control spending half of every pay cheque on football pools. He'd broken free of the boxes Marley had spoken of. The fools he passed on the street were still stuck on inflexible tracks, as if life were a train with one possible origin and one possible destination, with no opportunities to switch tracks.

But Ben had found an opportunity to do so, and by God he was seizing it! Through sheer force of will, he'd wrested the reins of his destiny from cruel fate, and now he could chart his own course, surpassing everyone who'd looked down on him. He still felt schadenfreude, for instance, over Morgan Grenfell's downfall in the Guinness share-trading fraud in '86. *I'll start my own sort of bank with Marley and make far more money than you old sods*, he thought to the dead investment bank.

By late summer, Ben and Marley had a pitch lined up every week, but most potential investors saw their proposition as too risky. By the time their older selves caught up with them again the next Christmas, they were getting desperate, and needed a new hook to get an investor to finally commit.

"Five interviews and a pitch on Christmas Day," Ben greeted Marley as she opened her flat's door for him at six in the morning. The sun hadn't risen yet, so all the lights were on. "I don't know how you do it."

"Ben," Marley said, a hint of surprise in her voice, "you look nice."

The most recent ingredient in Ben's new look was his new haircut: a short back and sides, faded, with a side part.

Marley also looked fantastic, in a deep red power suit with square shoulders and giant lapel Ben had never seen her wear before. Her nose piercing was gone. She only wore makeup on pitch days like today, and Ben was briefly mesmerised by how the colour of her lips precisely matched her clothing.

When he didn't respond after a few moments, Marley said, "I sleep about three hours every night. That's how I do it."

Ben could relate; he'd been sleeping about four hours each night.

Marley tilted her head towards the sitting room behind her. "The first bloke's already here. I've been trying to chat and get his thoughts on the business. He doesn't seem to have a personality."

"Remember," Ben whispered, entering the flat. "We need to project power and success. We need to attract the best employees. We don't want bottom-tier loafers."

"Of course, of course," Marley whispered back. "We only want the top-tier loafers."

Ralph plodded beside them, his face still sunken with dismay at what he was seeing. "I'm reminded of the Roman moneylenders in the forum back when London was Londinium," said the dead history teacher. "Recording every scam on a wax tablet. Fraud and theft at every table."

"Oh, go preach a sermon to someone who wants to hear it," Marley said. Then her younger self, louder: "Mr Bhat, this is Ben Scrooge, our CEO."

Wearing a suit expensive enough to put Ben's to shame, posture straight as a torture rack, a young man of Indian descent stood from a lone chair in the centre of the room. He gripped Ben's hand like he wanted to crush it, and shook vigorously. "Suresh Bhat," he said, brows furrowed, face intense. "Thank you for the interview."

Ben smiled and hoped the bones in his hand didn't break. "A pleasure," he said. When he finally freed his hand, he and Marley sat on the sofa across from their interviewee.

Marley took out a notepad and pen. "Well. Mr Bhat, shall we begin?"

"It's already over," Suresh said. "You've already hired me."

Marley mouthed a word, but no sound came out. She glanced quizzically at Ben.

"Why don't you tell us a bit about yourself first?" Ben prompted. "And what you know about the role you're applying for."

Suresh sighed as if being inconvenienced. He further straightened his already-straight tie. "You need a results-driven marketing expert to take your firm to the next level. I am the world expert in marketing. I graduated first in my class at the Institute of Management Ahmedabad, which is the best university in India. I worked for Rolls-Royce for five years, during which time I single-handedly doubled their share price, won a Marketing Society Award for brand communication, and was invited to the CEO's house for dinner three times. I speak five languages, I excel at maths, and I won the gold medal in darts at the Los Angeles Olympics. If you hire me on your team, your company will quickly reach the stratosphere."

Silence followed. Ben and Marley stared at Suresh, and dust motes drifted between them. He stared them down with utter self-assuredness.

Ben cleared his throat. "Well, your English is quite good."

Marley coughed pointedly.

"Cheers," Suresh said, poorly suppressing a scowl. "I'm rather impressed with your English, too."

"And why do you want to work with us?" Marley said, cutting in before Ben offered a prejudiced retort.

Because three-fourths of his CV is faked, Ben almost said.

Suresh answered: "I see this as an opportunity to get in on the ground floor of the next big idea. The next company at the top of the *Times* 1000. When both of you retire, I will have your jobs."

"That's nice," Marley said, "but we don't even know if we'll be success—"

Now Ben coughed pointedly. He made a fist and mouthed *power* to her. If she didn't demonstrate that this team would triumph to even a candidate like Suresh, they'd never interest any future candidates who were actually good.

Marley looked unsure, and even a bit sad, for a moment. She inhaled, deepened her voice, and rose to meet Suresh's level of confidence. "With great risk comes great reward. In ten years, you'll be CEO, and we'll have moved on to… I don't know… prime minister, film star, or something. If we hire you. What do you think about that?"

From his place on the floor, where he'd been sitting cross-legged watching them, Ralph chimed in. "I think all three of the people in this interview need years upon years of intensive therapy with a good mental health professional. That's what I think."

"Bah! You're still here?" Ben said. "You're completely ruining the moment. This was when our lives really got exciting. A part of my life I actually want to re-experience without interruption, okay?"

Ralph leant back and forth, perhaps stretching his back, perhaps weighing Ben's demand. "Are you sure you don't want a conscience on your shoulder? Suggesting how you can learn from your past... how you made other people feel... exploring the moral dimensions of—"

Ben activated the staff he was still holding, located the present, and tapped Ralph on the head. He vanished in a puff of white light. Smug, Ben reclined back on the sofa.

"I guess that answers that," said Marley. "Where'd you send him?"

"Back to the future," Ben said. "So, Suresh. Marley's explained our business model to you?"

"Genius," Suresh said. "It is pure genius."

"Yes. Well, imagine we hire you as our marketing bloke. Operations are in full swing. We're lending small sums to the have-nots while we plunder the gold mine of interest payments. How would you sell our business to the world?"

For once, Suresh didn't have a ready response. "Hmm," was all he said. He lowered his gaze to the rug, folded his hands in his lap, and stayed as still as a boulder for several seconds. Ben leant in to try and see whether he was thinking or stumped, but when Ben started speaking, Suresh held up a finger, silently demanding he wait.

Marley leant forward, too. They could almost smell what was cooking in Suresh's mind. Their mouths almost watered.

Finally, Suresh raised his head, and the boulder rolled. "I... see..." He reached his arm forward, palm open, as if a great vision was appearing before him. "Employees," he said. "On street corners.

With huge plastic signs. Spinning them, over and over. Dancing with the signs. Nearly making love to the signs. 'Get cash now!' each sign will read. Giant plastic arrows pointing the way to our illustrious shops."

Ben mimicked the twirling motion Suresh was making with his arm. "Employees... spinning..."

"Oh, that's rubbish," Marley said, falling back onto the sofa. "It'd be indescribably annoying. No customers would be drawn in by that."

"Maybe not in the UK," Suresh said. "But wait until you export your business to America, eh? They will love the sign spinners there. And a mascot! We need a friendly, furry mascot so people think we are helping them instead of defrauding them."

"We could put it in cartoon advertisements," Ben suggested, warming to Suresh. "And a fun little jingle plays whenever the mascot comes out. Cute little cats at Christmastime, or something."

Suresh nodded with enthusiasm. "Maybe they are playing darts."

Marley made a gagging noise. "Why not have toy shops inside the loan shops that give out sweets and balloons to kids while we take their parents' money?"

Suresh's face lit at the suggestion, but Ben spoke first. "That too!"

"That was a joke." Marley waved Ben away, but didn't leave the sofa. "Why not a traditional ad campaign? 'We help you get back on your feet', or something like that?"

"Why do that," Suresh said, "when you can pay the Tube fee for the entire London metro area? Do it on New Year's Eve. You will be a legend. They will never forget you."

"That's a good idea, too," Ben admitted, eyeing Marley in the hope she'd acclimatise to Suresh's marketing vision.

"Suresh," Marley said. Her hands pivoted on her wrists as if trying to conjure the right words. "What do you value in life? What kind of person do you want to be?"

"Winning," Suresh said immediately. "I value winning, and I want to be a winner."

Ben tried to read Marley's reaction to that answer, but she kept a good poker face.

"Imagine it's Christmas Eve," she continued. "You and your wife were expected at your grandmother's hundredth birthday party two hours ago. She phones from the emergency ward to tell you she's having a baby – your wife, not your grandmum. You didn't even know she was pregnant. As soon as you hang up, the phone rings again, and it's me. And I tell you there's an emergency at the business, and you must drop every single thing you're doing and speed through every traffic signal to get to the office, because the business needs you. More than your wife or your family need you.

"Tell me, Suresh. What would you do?"

A monstrous grin slowly smeared itself across Suresh's face. He leant towards Marley, resting his elbows on his knees. "I would get into my car and run every traffic signal," he said. "The baby drama and my grandmother's birthday... they could wait. Even if my house were on fire, I would come in to work. Because the business needs me."

When they finally closed the door on Suresh, Ben and Marley both let out a breath. She raised an eyebrow at him. He leant his back on the door and appraised his shrewd business partner.

"He's a complete sociopath," Marley said.

"Complete sociopath," Ben agreed.

"He's perfect."

"Absolutely perfect in every way. I don't even need to see the other candidates. Let's hire him."

"Yes, let's."

"Can you pull onto the pavement and drive past these cars?" Marley asked their cab driver later that afternoon. Their pitch was set for four o'clock, so they'd practised all day, but were now stuck in congestion on Euston Road.

"There's a huge accident near King's Cross," the driver said. "Streets are clogged a mile in every direction."

"We have time," Ben said, wiping some sweat from his forehead before checking his watch. "We'll make it." His chest felt like it was full of ants and his hands kept jittering. He always got like this before a pitch. "How do I look?"

Marley appraised him impassively, then looked back out the window, as if staring at the congestion hard enough would make it go away. "You look like you're ready to invade the Falkland Islands." Then, to the driver: "Come on, you must know some good side streets."

The driver shook his head. "Transit strike over the whole festive season. Shortcuts are all clogged, too. I was a half hour late taking my five-year-old to his mum's this morning."

"Well, no one who's reproduced has a right to complain about traffic," Marley quipped.

The driver said nothing to that. He turned up the volume on the radio. Queen's 'I Want to Break Free'.

Ben flipped through the documents in his lap. "Shall we go over the pitch again?" he asked.

"No, Ben, we've got it good enough. I want to get Suresh's feedback, but that's all." Not only had Suresh accepted the position, he'd agreed to meet them outside the office where they were presenting for a last-minute pitch critique.

Marley craned her neck to examine the business plan Ben was rifling through. "Ben, the whole thing's marked up in red ink."

"Mmhmm. My sister was kind enough to give us notes. I haven't had time to look through them all yet."

"You have a sister?"

Ben perked up and squinted at her. "I've never told you about Annie?"

"No."

Ben frowned and returned to Annie's notes, jotting his own thoughts next to hers in blue ink.

"How can you even read the text with her scribbles all over it?" Marley asked.

"They're actually quite helpful."

Marley slouched back in her seat and crossed her arms. She stared straight ahead, at the back of the seat in front of her.

After a few seconds of pointed silence, Ben set his papers aside and turned towards his disgruntled associate. "What is it?" he asked. Marley glanced sidelong at him, her frown telling him he'd done something wrong. "Go on, out with it."

She sighed like the act of breathing in and out could transport her to another place, a happier time.

"I can't put my life on hold forever," she said softly.

The meaning of her words didn't register to Ben at first, but when it did, ice seemed to creep through his veins. His partnership with Marley was his one shot. This was his chance to become somebody whose life was worth a damn. She'd poured her soul – long hours of discussion and compromise – into this business plan; he'd been sure she was in this with him for the long haul. If she was thinking of quitting...

She watched out the window as they crept past buildings and pedestrians. Her comment had left Ben so flustered that he couldn't think straight enough to try and win her back. Instead, he said nothing, set the documents back on his lap, and studied, studied, studied.

They arrived at a nondescript office building in Mayfair with fourteen minutes to spare. Suresh was already there, still dressed to the nines.

"Why are you doing pitches on Christmas Day?" he asked as Ben shoved his papers back in his briefcase to protect them from the barest misting of rain that had begun to fall.

"The highest-up blokes are all on holiday," Marley said. "The few left at the office are the ones with no families, who do nothing but work, who have nothing better to do today than hear our pitch. Any other day they wouldn't even take our calls. But today they'll meet."

Suresh smacked his hands together. "Cunning. You do what you must to get ahead. I like it. So where should we practice?"

The building's foyer was small, with two doors, a lift, and a plastic plant, but it was empty, so they performed for Suresh there. Marley went first, detailing the history of small loans, and an overview of their company and its services, then Ben gave a market analysis and financial projections.

They asked Suresh what he thought. His hand wafted in the air, as if guiding a delicate aroma to his nose. As he did so, the lift doors opened, and an old man in braces and a dress shirt, but with no coat, emerged. Ben's heart leapt. It was time.

"Bolder," Suresh said, pointing at Ben and Marley. And that was all the feedback he had time to give them.

"Mr Scrooge and Ms Jacobs?" the man in the lift said in a raspy, sluggish voice.

Ben and Marley forced themselves to grin. "Indeed we are," Marley said. She shook his hand, and Ben followed, heart racing. Could he even pitch in this state? Nerves threatening to climb out of his skin? What if he tripped over his words, answered a question wrong, and Marley finally saw through him? Saw that he was less a clever co-conspirator and more a hapless also-ran?

"I'm Rod Talbot. So... you two are really so desperate that you'd pitch to us on Christmas?"

Well. The bloke they were pitching to certainly saw through them. Ben pursed his lips and looked to Marley for guidance.

"They're not desperate," Suresh said from behind them. "They're dedicated."

Talbot frowned in confusion at Suresh. "There are three of you?"

"Oh, he's—" Ben started.

"Yes, there are three of us," Suresh said. He reached out and shook Talbot's hand, too. "I'm chief marketing officer."

Talbot accepted the newcomer with a shrug and, oddly, a burp. "Well, we're ready for you. Come on up."

With no way to tactfully abandon Suresh, Ben and Marley got in the lift with him and Talbot. The doors shut. Talbot pressed a button. The ancient lift's whir was thankfully loud enough that Ben didn't feel the need to make friendly chit-chat.

Nevertheless, Talbot said after a moment, "I don't understand *pitches*." He spoke the word like he was trying to spit out a rotten sunflower seed. "It used to be that if you wanted money, you asked your father or your uncle for it. Why don't you kids just do that?" He burped again.

All of them – even Suresh – traded glances. Ben's colleagues had no more idea how to answer than he did. Ben made something up in his mind: *It's not about what you're offering us. It's about what we're offering you. Investment in return for equity.* Did that sound like something a real businessman would say? Regardless, before Ben could say it, a scowl formed at the edge of Talbot's mouth, and he said, "Well, since you're here, I suppose we have to listen."

Though Ben was fighting to resist panic, Marley just looked tired, and ready to get out of here. He was losing her. Maybe he'd already lost her.

The doors opened and Talbot plodded into a poorly lit cave of an office, the curtains drawn, several ceiling tiles missing, stacks of paper scattered atop the stained carpet in one corner. "That's Doherty, that's Blackburn," Talbot said, pointing to two additional men in their seventies reclining in plush office chairs. Doherty, stubble-faced and barely awake, gazed lazily forward but didn't seem to notice them enter. Smoking a cigar, Blackburn appraised them with a dour frown. The desk in front of them was built for one person, but notepads for all three men were arrayed atop it.

Ah, the early days of venture capital. Before most people even knew it by that name.

"Claret?" Talbot asked. He stopped at a drinks cabinet full of enough bottles to rival Marley's collection at her flat. Most of them were nearly empty. A wine glass sat on the desk before Blackburn, a scotch glass before Doherty.

Talbot burped yet again, and a clearer picture of who exactly they were pitching to developed in Ben's mind. "Please," he said, and Talbot poured Ben a glass.

Marley grimaced at him. Ben upturned his hands, nonverbally asking what the hell else he was supposed to do but accept a drink.

"All right," Talbot said, handing Ben the glass of wine, then shuffling to his seat beside his colleagues, "let's hear it."

Without so much as a glance at Ben, Marley took her place before the old-timey moneymen. A single recessed light above her shone down harshly, like they were interrogating her in a police station. Ben went over his part of the pitch yet again in his head as he stood with Suresh behind her.

"Gentlemen," she said. "Thank you for taking this meeting with us. I'm Marley Jacobs, and these are my associates, Ben Scrooge and Suresh Bhat. We have a vision. A vision we believe can provide real value to—"

"Excuse me," Talbot interrupted. "What is this?"

Marley's eyes darted around her, as if searching for the source of Talbot's displeasure. "What's... what?" she asked him.

"We want to hear from the CEO," Talbot said. "If a company is pitching, it should be the leader who speaks."

"Oh," Marley said, politely smiling, "we're both the leaders, in practice. You'll hear from Ben. We split the speaking time in half, so he'll give the second part of the pitch."

Talbot removed his glasses, polished them on his shirt. "Luv, we're not against business leaders with gentle and nurturing dispositions. Sometimes businesses need that. But is that really the foot your team wants to put forward right now?"

Ben actually vocalised a soft "Ugh" at Talbot's request. Marley quirked her head, and her jaw dropped a bit. Ben knew that look – she was about to chew through Talbot's neck and decapitate him. So Ben stepped forward. "Apologies," he said. "Give us a moment to conference." He put an arm around Marley and led her out of the light to huddle with Suresh.

"Unbelievable," Marley whispered.

"He doesn't want a woman pitching to him," Ben whispered back. "In this day and age. You know what? You should give the full pitch, Marley, even my part. Tell him you're the CEO. Shatter the glass ceiling and ram the shards of it right up Talbot's—"

"I am the world expert at business pitches," Suresh chimed in. "I'd be more than happy to step up and do your part."

"You?" Ben said with derision, "Who's heard the pitch precisely once?"

"Ben, please," Marley chided. "You are my partner in this. You're a genius and I'm in your debt for coming up with this cheque into cash thing. Yes, Talbot is a sexist bastard and I'd love to squeeze him for all the money I can get. But that's not going to happen. This pitch is already in the rubbish bin. Either we acknowledge that and leave, or Suresh takes my place right now so we can at least save face."

"We don't want anyone to take your place," Talbot called from behind them. "We want to hear from the CEO."

Ben exhaled through tight lips. How many of their whispers had Talbot heard?

Suresh placed a hand on Ben's shoulder. "It is up to you, my friend," he said.

Ben locked eyes with Marley, saw disappointment. He'd failed her. His whole idea for this business had failed her. She was done with it.

His hand shaking, nearly spilling the claret he was still holding, Ben raised the glass to his mouth.

He gulped down the whole thing. He turned. Set the glass down and held the business plan in both hands. Stepped into the light.

In front of him, Talbot's arms were folded. Blackburn checked his cigar, which had burnt almost to its end. Eyes now fully closed, Doherty may have been asleep.

Ben cleared his throat. Turned to the part of the business plan Marley was supposed to pitch. "Uhm, the cheque-cashing business started during the Great Depression," he began. His older self, sitting quiet inside him, sneered at the tepid opening. But this was the early days of business pitches, and the idea that one's first words should be gripping hadn't caught on yet. "With banks defunct, workers needed something – ahem, somewhere – to cash their cheques. When banks reopened, most of them wanted nothing to do with people who were living pay cheque to pay cheque. And they still don't. But we see this as an opportunity. We believe..."

He trailed off. The eyes of the men he was pitching to were already glazing over. His voice was unsteady, which made him more nervous, which made his voice more unsteady, in a vicious feedback loop. Ben didn't belong here, in this world of self-important networking, of hustling from before dawn till long after dark, of people who thought they were better than him.

He'd lost his place in the pitch. He glanced down at the business plan in his hands, past Annie's notes in red ink, trying to orient himself. At the bottom of the second page, the only blue ink on the page drew Ben's eyes. Words he must have written in the cab on the way here, though he had no memory of doing so.

A man achieves.

Ben stared at the words, Graham's words, reaching out from the past, tickling his brain like a spider's legs. He stared at them long and heavily. Let them permeate his fretful thoughts. Let them replace them.

How could he reach these obstinate men, whose world was so foreign to him? They were rich while he was poor, old while he was young.

There is one thing we have in common, though...

Calm descended on Ben. His hands stopped shaking. He twisted his torso to see Marley behind him. Her gaze had been turned down to the floor, but at Ben's attention, she looked up at him. The fingers on her right hand were fidgeting with each other, as they always did when she found herself somewhere she didn't want to be. She looked defeated.

I'm an actor, Ben thought to himself, *and this is nothing but a play.*

He tossed the business plan aside; it thwacked against the carpet. Ben did his best to ignore his pounding heart, and turned back to the men.

"What did your fathers want for you?" Ben asked them.

Talbot's eyes went wide. Blackburn lowered his cigar.

"What did your fathers want for you?" Ben repeated. "If they were anything like my father, they wanted you to be strong. To master the world around you. To protect. To provide." *To dominate.* He gestured to the men before him, inviting them to answer. Blackburn remained a scowling enigma, but Talbot reluctantly nodded agreement.

"My old man was... a joy," Ben said. "A humble but jovial man. Responsible. Worked hard as a grocer for thirty years to give his children a better life." Ben stepped towards his targets and paused for dramatic emphasis. "But then our home burnt down when I was ten years old. A bad electrical socket sparked during a gas leak. Then, due to a paperwork error, our buildings insurance wouldn't cover us. So my dad found himself in need of a loan. Problem was, with his income, and no collateral, no one would give him a loan. Even a small one. Even one the size of a single pay cheque."

Ben placed his hands behind his back, strode to the left, and circled slowly round to the right so he'd pass near the small committee. "A man must be strong. Protect. Provide. But my father couldn't do any of these. So my mum left us." Of course, her actual reason for leaving had been more sympathetic: Ben's dad was a vile, ego-driven despot. "But my virtuous old man, he didn't give up. Even when we had to live in council housing, he went to work every day to support us. Some days..." Ben tapped into his inner thespian and managed to shed a rather convincing tear. "Some days we didn't eat. We could have used a small loan on those days, too."

Ben passed Talbot, tilted forward in his seat, rapt by Ben's story. Doherty's eyes were open and he was actually paying attention. "My father passed his work ethic on to me, and I stand before you now knowing it hasn't been easy to be a man lately." Ben glimpsed a rip in the curtain behind Blackburn, a leaking, rusty air vent nearby. "You've all felt it, too, I'm sure. Money doesn't go as far. The economy's been rough, and I know the Iron Lady's trying to turn it round, but no matter at what income level, men have been made weaker than we were in the good old days. We even hear political types say how they're building a future with no place for us in it – don't tell me you haven't heard it. Every man has.

"Mr Talbot, you mentioned that if you wanted funding, you'd ask your father for it, but I'm sure at one point or another he said no. I want you to remember how that felt. When you needed to protect, to provide, to be a man. And you were denied it. You were told you weren't enough of a man. Mr Talbot, *that* is the feeling I want to stop every man in Britain from ever having to feel again."

He backed away from them, towards the light where he'd started. "I want to give us all a lifeline. A tiny boost to our bank accounts, whenever we need it. The security that my dad, and millions of potential customers just like him, could use, knowing they can get their next pay cheque *now*. Yes, I intend for this business to generate a massive financial return, but we also exist to help people."

Ben momentarily brought his hands together and bowed his head as if in prayer. "My dad, rest his noble soul, passed away in a road accident six months ago. I invite you to join us in keeping his memory alive and giving some dignity back to the working men of this country.

"Now, let's discuss market, strategy, and business model."

He delved right back into the thick of the original pitch – including the part about the astronomical interest rates – blending it with his improvised credo to manliness. His heart was still working overtime, his brain juggling five ideas at once, synthesising them, vocalising them. He was a virtuoso performing his first great composition.

Marley watched, slack-jawed. Ben expected her ghost to call him out on his colossal fabrications, but she stayed quiet. Maybe she was getting a kick out of reliving this part of their career, too.

When Ben was done, each of the three old men looked at his peers. Unspoken thoughts passed between them. Talbot inhaled several times longer than a normal breath, then said, "This business. Is it ethical?"

Ben arched his eyebrows. "Ethical?" He thought he'd allayed any such fears in the pitch. "It's not illegal. We've checked all that. There's no liability for you."

Talbot grunted. "You seem a bit… How can I put this delicately? You seem a bit American."

"American?"

"Yes, God, don't get us started on the Yanks. It used to be you looked for financing partners who'd help shepherd your business and offer solid advice. It was a gentleman's work. Now the Yanks have come in and it's all money, money, money."

Anxiety climbed Ben's throat once more. Maybe he'd come on too strong when he'd discussed financing and profits. "Well, the purpose of a business is to make money," he said.

"Granted. But the Yanks take it up ten notches. What used to be cultured rivalry is now ruthless warfare. Rig the game, take what you want, et cetera. Do you have any experience in finance or business, Mr Scrooge?"

They'd left their bios out of the pitch precisely to hide that they didn't. Talbot lifted his hands behind his head and leant back, waiting for an answer.

"Mr Bhat here worked for Rolls-Royce for five years," Ben said, content not to know whether it was true. "He doubled their share price. Ms Jacobs gained exposure to the petrol business through her father. And I... well, I'll let my pitch stand as evidence of the quality of leader I'll be."

Talbot tapped his finger against the desk, apparently in thought. Blackburn took out another cigar and lit it. "It's a risk," Blackburn said just before his first puff. "I assume you're here because you couldn't get a traditional bank loan?"

Before Ben could answer, Talbot said, "It's an interesting idea, though, and I'd consider funding you, Mr Scrooge. *If* you agree to step aside as CEO. Let a more seasoned professional take the reins, with you in a supporting role."

No one they'd pitched to had ever asked Ben to do such a thing. He had no response prepared. Every second he waited to answer, Talbot's assertion that he wasn't good enough to lead would weigh on him more, and his jitters would grow, and Talbot would see his weakness. So before that could happen, Ben simply gathered his papers off the floor and said, "Me stepping aside is out of the question. Thank you for your time, gentlemen."

He turned and walked back to the lift. Marley scurried after him as fast as propriety would allow, horror on her face. But before she could protest at Ben's sudden departure, Talbot stopped their exit with a loud clearing of his throat.

They turned to him. Talbot sipped from his wine glass. Burped.

"Stay a minute longer," he said. "Maybe we can work something out."

The jubilant trio left the building with plans to celebrate at a pub. Ecstatic though Ben was, he told Marley and Suresh he'd meet them there. First, he had another mission.

He hailed a cab and rode to an antique toy shop he passed all the time on his way to Marley's flat. Bright pink and yellow boxes from decades past adorned the windows: stuffed animals, dolls, cars and trains, a rocking horse, a pinball machine, several marionettes.

Ben entered and found the glass display case he'd been eyeing for months, on the left side of the showroom beneath the giant toy windmill. Inside rested action figures of Brains, Scott Tracy, and his fighter jet identical to those that Ben's dad had crushed when he'd been a kid. And many more. The whole Tracy family, Tin-Tin, the Hood, and even Aloysius.

"Can I help you sir?" a clerk asked, stepping up beside him.

"Yes," Ben said. "These Thunderbirds action figures. I'd like to buy them all."

Rocket Lord

Son,

I hear from Annie that you are doing well for yourself. Occasionally I find a small article about you in the paper. I show these to everyone at church and they are very proud of you.

But I think you can do better. This business partner of yours, Marley Jacobs, comes from a Catholic family. Even worse, it's undignified for you to portray her as your equal, as you've done in two interviews I've read. Frankly, sharing the spotlight with a woman makes you and your business seem unserious. I could understand the optics if she was attractive, but she is not good-looking. You should make yourself independent. Do not let her run your professional life for you.

I hope you are staying physically fit. If there is a woman in your life, I would like to hear about her. There are some business opportunities we should discuss if you would like to give me a ring. <u>Real</u> business opportunities, that I could help finance, that have nothing to do with this crank you've fallen in with.

Your father,
Graham Scrooge

Ben reread the letter, then read it a third time. He folded it and handed it back to Annie, seated on the sofa across from him in the middle of Marley's sitting room. Annie gingerly accepted it.

"You don't want to keep it?" Annie asked. Now well into her twenties, she looked younger than her age, and much thinner than normal. She'd been visiting him in London for Christmas.

"Shred it," Ben said. "Burn it. Flush it down the toilet. I don't want anything from him in my life."

She took the letter from him. Even her hand appeared gaunt next to his. She wore blue jeans and a red-and-green blouse, while he sported a full white-tie suit.

"Thank you for reading it, at least," she said. "I've discharged my duty."

"I don't understand why you feel like you owe him anything."

Annie folded the letter and tucked it into her pocket. "He seems lonely. I feel bad for him."

"Of course he's lonely. He drove everyone in his life away." These words stung Ben's older self, eavesdropping from within. As if they'd been directed at him instead of at his father. At this age, Ben had fantasised about his dad finally exercising some humility. Dropping his defences, coming to Ben and asking for a relationship, listening to how he'd hurt Ben and accepting some responsibility. Such catharsis was the stuff of dreams, not memory. *But why not do that exact thing with my own son, when I return? Could he want it from me as much as I wanted it from my old man?*

"Still," Annie said, "it's a kindness. My good deed for Christmas, right?"

Ben appraised the stick figure on the plush sofa before him, looking for all the world like a limp fish on dry land. A curious sense of guilt had crept up on him during Annie's visit; after Ben left his childhood home, she'd had to live there alone with Graham – his psychological abuses, his endless judgement. What had that been like for Annie?

It wasn't Ben's fault. His dad had kicked him out, after all. But still, he couldn't help the nagging feeling that he should've been more of a brother to her.

"Annie," he said carefully, "are you well? How's baby Frieda doing?"

Brief eye contact before Annie averted her gaze. The slow climb and fall of her shoulders barely counted as a shrug.

"I'm okay," she said.

"You seem... I don't know. You've been off."

Following her shrug came a smile that barely counted as a smile. "It's hard sometimes," she said. She lapsed into silence.

"What's hard sometimes?" Ben prompted.

Her shoulders hunched and she seemed to withdraw, like she sat in the hot seat on a gameshow and she didn't know the answer.

"Scott called me worthless," she whispered, barely saying the words. "Now that he's left, he reminds me of... And I can't..."

"Oh, Annie." Ben crossed to sit beside her. He put his arm around her.

So their childhood *had* scarred her, too. She carried emotional bruises not so different from Ben's.

"It's okay, it's okay," Annie said. "You don't have to comfort me."

"Is there anything I can do?"

"No." All the melancholy left her face, replaced by false cheer. "You look after yourself, Ben. I'll be fine."

"Please. I can't stand to think you're sad all the time. There must be something I can help with."

The façade of happiness left her again. She glanced around the room, like she didn't know how to ask for help but perhaps she could find the words hiding behind Marley's furniture.

"I suppose a bit of money would be nice," she finally admitted. "If you can spare it."

Unfortunately, he couldn't spare it. Not at this moment. Fast Quid, the cheque to cash company Ben and Marley had founded, was suffering default rates of fifty per cent in both of the shops they'd opened so far. They were trying to learn ahead of time who wouldn't pay their loans back, so they could reject them.

But still, a good portion of the microloans the company was making were, unknown to investors, loans to Ben and Marley themselves. Sure, they had to pay much of their personal salaries back into the company as interest, but at least on paper it looked like the company was making some money.

The truth, though, was that if nothing changed, they'd be bankrupt in two months.

"You have a lot of friends in Manchester," Ben said to Annie. "And your ex-husband. He ought to lend you money to apologise for what he called you."

Annie opened her mouth to answer, but before she could speak, Marley called out from her bedroom. "Okay, downstairs! Let's go!"

In seconds, Ben's heart was beating twice as fast. Talking with his sister, he'd nearly forgotten the guillotine about to fall on his head. "Is there any other way we can get more funding?" he asked Marley as she swept into the sitting room in a sparkling purple dress with puffy sleeves. She wore so much makeup she was scarcely recognisable.

"This party is the best chance we'll get," Marley said, gathering her handbag from the countertop. "Remember, I'm targeting Kathleen Shaw, you're targeting Charles Bortley. If they won't agree to fund us, I don't know who will."

"Bah," Ben said. "You're sure you don't just want to ask Talbot for more money?"

"And reveal we're a sinking ship? Besides, it's an excuse to go to a fancy party and drink fancy drinks like the fancy fancies we are, eh?"

"Bah," Ben muttered again. He hated parties.

Annie followed them downstairs. Ben's younger self paid her no mind, but his older self dwelt on their aborted conversation, yearning to return to it.

"Ben," Marley said as she slid into the passenger seat of his Jaguar, parked at the kerb. "Can we go to a different memory, please? I don't know that I want to relive Bortley's party."

"Ah, she speaks at last," Ben said, strapping in to the driver's seat and rolling down the window. He spoke distractedly, glancing frequently back at his sister. "Rubbish. This party is one of my best memories." And he badly needed something to lift his spirits after the troubled thoughts Annie's presence had stirred in him. Maybe later he'd return here, replay this memory with Annie a few more times.

His little sister waved to him from the pavement. "Thanks for spending some time with me, Ben. It was good to see you."

Ben waved back and started the car. "Happy Christmas. I'll see you about." Ben's mind had moved on to other things as he drove Marley towards the fundraising opportunity of the season. But with the benefit of hindsight, the old man turned the young man's head to watch Annie, his precious, magnificent sister, recede into the London evening.

It was the last time he saw her alive.

The Bortley estate sprawled over sixty acres of woodland, landscaped gardens, and lawns at Wentworth. The mansion itself was a Beaux Arts fortress the size of a small stadium. Ben and Marley had to queue in their car for ten minutes just to reach the valet. They spotted stables, badminton courts, a helipad, and three swimming pools from the avenue leading into the property. In the carriage circle at the entrance glowed an immense fountain that shot water higher than the mansion itself. This building – lit from below, with red-and-green fireworks detonating overhead – practically bellowed to Ben *You do not belong here.*

He rolled his eyes at how intimidated his younger self was. Back in the present, he could finance a more spectacular party if he really wanted to. His wealth was greater now than Bortley's had ever been, even adjusted for inflation.

"Splendid, innit?" said Marley, grinning out the window as the fireworks lit her face. "I could live in a night like this my whole life." And then a moment later: "This is miserable. You're sure you don't want to skip this memory?"

Well, at least it'd be easy to tell which version of her was speaking to him: the young or the old.

The valet scowled at Ben's £30,000 Jaguar like he'd ridden in on a donkey, but accepted his keys. Marley laughed at this and whispered excitedly to Ben, "We're the new rich."

"We're not rich," Ben shot back. "Not yet."

"Ahem," Marley said when they reached the foot of the steps leading to the entry portico.

Ben chuckled and offered her his arm. "Milady." Marley took it, and they ascended together towards the words *HAPPY CHRISTMAS 1989!* spelt out in fairy lights above the tall wooden doors. Faint violin music bled outwards into the night.

"Do you think we'll be safe here?" Marley asked, peering at the shadows behind the immaculately trimmed bushes they were passing beside the steps. "From the Ghost of Christmas Past? It's fishy we haven't seen it in a while."

"Maybe it gave up," Ben said.

"Or maybe it's doing what Ralph did, hiding in a specific memory it knows we'll visit eventually. Waiting to spring a trap. Ben, what if *this* is that memory?"

"I'll keep an eye on you. If I see it, I'll run right to you and take us away."

"Assuming it doesn't get to me first."

What could Ben say to that? No memory would be truly safe, and the phantom might be waiting in any of them. *But what other options do we have? Where else can we hide?* Ralph had been no help, and Marley had no clue how to permanently escape the phantom. He'd asked her several times if she wanted to just hide in a closet, but she always said no, this was her afterlife, and she wanted to really live it. *Well, Marley, this is what living it looks like.*

Knowing nothing of the spirit world and how to interface with it, Ben could only hope living through more of his memories might spark an idea that would let him save Marley. But at the very least, he could try to enjoy them while he thought through the problem.

A giant chandelier hung over the entry foyer. Renaissance murals of scenes from Norse and biblical antiquity adorned nearly every wall.

But normality ended there. As Ben and Marley entered, a rambunctious group of men in tailcoats ran after two medium-sized pigs, squealing as they stampeded through the foyer. Several of the men held wads of cash, and were cheering the pigs on.

"Are they racing pigs?" Marley asked.

Half the men at the party seemed to be missing their trousers, and a few women wore only undergarments. A cased opening led from the foyer to a large room containing a bar and an entire, full-sized carousel, currently spinning, ridden by a dozen people in various stages of undress. A poster stand advertised *Red Dawn* showing on repeat, all night long, in the building's fifty-seat cinema.

"There's Kathleen Shaw," Marley said. She nodded towards a middle-aged woman in a green evening gown who'd just jumped out of the pigs' way. In fact, a number of the women present didn't appear to be here merely as men's dates – a new sight in the world of London finance, where few women had worked until recently. A few, like Ms Shaw, seemed to have actually brought men as their dates.

"She started her talent acquisition company just as Thatcher opened the City up to the world and it needed new expertise," Marley explained. "She's utterly brilliant and I want to have her babies."

"I'll settle for having her money, if you can pitch her on us," Ben said. "Hey, look who it is."

Also dressed in white tie, Suresh nearly backed into them with a hefty VHS camcorder on his shoulder. Its red light was on; Suresh was rolling.

"Suresh!" Marley said. "What are you doing here?"

He jumped with a start and stopped recording. His eyes grew wide and he said nothing, like they'd caught him burning their money.

"Are you okay?" Marley asked.

Suresh blinked. "What are you doing here?"

"Uh, it's a party with rich people and we want their money."

Suresh frantically looked around him, as if for an escape route, but a mask of confidence soon slid down to hide the fear that had just radiated from him. "Excellent," he said. "I have not told you before now, but one of my hobbies is videography. I'm friends with Mrs Bortley, and I politely agreed to videotape the party for her."

Ben grunted his annoyance. "You *know* Mrs Bortley and you never thought to mention—"

Marley elbowed Ben in the side. "That's lovely," she said. "If you see her, please say some good things about us."

Suresh's cheeks had grown flush. He backed away into the crowd without another word, leaving Marley waving goodbye, and Ben frowning, perplexed.

"What just happened?" he asked.

"Suresh doesn't really know the Bortleys," Marley explained. "I think they hired him, and he's embarrassed we caught him doing something as lowly as videography work on the side."

Ben wrinkled his brow at this new information. He tried for the hundredth time to discern whether Suresh was a shameless faker or just cagey about his personal life.

"Well, you have fun finding Bortley. I'm going in." Marley beelined for Kathleen Shaw.

"Good luck," Ben called after her. He sidled over to the bar, next to a man wearing a T-shirt featuring an American flag above the words *JACK WELCH IS THE REASON FOR THE SEASON*, and ordered a glass of wine possibly more expensive than his car, but free to the guests here.

Ben was far from being a social creature. But he'd studied for this. The mingling upper-crusters surrounding him were not a nightmare come to life; they were the same ordinary humans he spoke with at his clubs. He was no longer the foolish boy who'd been ignorant of their arcane lingo, of the refined mannerisms that would signal his membership among them. They were objects. Ben had the tools he needed to tinker with them, to engineer their thoughts and desires, to use these esteemed magnates and socialites to make himself one of them.

At least, this was what he told himself to soothe his anxiety while the pig racers had another jaunt through the room.

He found Bortley, whom he recognised by his ostentatious handlebar moustache, smoking a pipe and conversing with two other men in a lounge. Of average build, the sixty-four-year-old wore his hair trimmed in an undercut and carried himself with the posture of a man utterly self-assured. Lamentably, the rumours about him wearing a monocle and, absurdly, a cape, appeared to be true. The black cape hanging from his collar to the floor suggested a villain from a children's cartoon.

Eccentric though Bortley might be, he was a pillar of Britain's upper crust, a man of the age, and he had the funding Fast Quid needed. Ben picked a random book off the bookshelf next to the men and loitered there, pretending to read.

"Are you mad?" a short man who bore a permanent expression of disinterest was saying. "Liberalising the economy has been Thatcher's greatest achievement. The City is meritocratic now. No more dunces from the petty nobility running everything. There's opportunity now for anyone willing to put in the work."

Bortley made a *tsk, tsk, tsk* sound, then spoke in the prissiest received pronunciation Ben had ever heard. "You would have that perspective, Gilbert, wouldn't you?"

The third man, younger than the other two and scarcely older than Ben, had been nodding agreement with Gilbert, but at Bortley's words, he shook his head and spoke opposition. "It's true. Ever since Black Monday, who knows whether Thatcher knows what she's doing? Mass privatisation, computerising the Stock Exchange. What would our grandfathers think?"

"Absolutely, Stokes. It's the passing of an age," Bortley mused, swirling his wine. "A man's word means nothing now. You have to sign a contract. And completely sober, mind you. We've lost the gentlemanly greatness we once had. Business used to be about family. Now it's about chasing the next big thing."

Okay, Ben thought. *Bortley doesn't sound so different from Talbot, and I've dealt with him. I can do this.* He had leant in to the family angle when he'd pitched to Talbot. Maybe it would work again here. He moved closer, waiting for a chance to seamlessly insert himself into their discourse.

"And insider dealing is illegal now," the young man, Stokes, said.

Gilbert didn't object. He bowed his head in sad acceptance.

"And so is slipping my MP a few pounds under the table for a favour or two," Stokes added.

Gilbert bowed his head even farther, and Bortley groaned as if in physical pain. "And Britain isn't even British any more. Foreign capital has grasped us all firmly by the crown jewels."

"No, no, no," Gilbert said, perking up. "You're being hypocritical."

"How so?"

"Well, who hates globalisation the most? The Brits, the French, and the Yanks. Our nation first, the rest of you sod off. But aren't those countries the three thugs who colonised the world and started globalisation to begin with? Now we don't have the horse's reins any more, we want to shoot the horse."

Bortley pursed his lips like something indescribably bitter had landed on his tongue. "The great horse of empire was..." His mouth worked as he searched for words. Gilbert graced him with a subtly smug smile. He'd caught Bortley off guard.

Two steps, and Ben stood in their circle. "Is it possible for all nations to build their economies at once?" he asked, dropping a touch of Bortley's accent into his own voice to sound more sophisticated. "Perhaps Britain need not decline while other nations ascend. Perhaps we can still be the greatest."

His synthesis of Bortley's argument with Gilbert's won him looks of admiration from both men.

"If only Thatcher didn't feel the need to tear everything down first," said Bortley.

"And you are?" Gilbert asked Ben pointedly.

"Ben. Ben Scrooge. I'm in lending. What do you do?"

"Oh, our business is similar, then. I'm in genocide insurance."

Ben tried to pass the words over his tongue. "Geno... what?"

"Governments take out a policy, then if there's a genocide in their country, we disburse their benefits."

The business model didn't compute well in Ben's mind. He winced, trying to process it. "But wouldn't that give those governments an incentive to—"

"I'm Nathan Gilbert. This is Bortley."

"*Lord* Bortley," corrected the moustachioed man.

No one bothered to introduce Stokes, who simply nodded, said, "Hear, hear," and drank some wine.

"Lending, you say?" said Bortley, adjusting his monocle. "What type of lending?"

And so Ben explained himself as the men tried to ascertain his social status. In this place – in an ever greater share of the places Ben found himself these days – it seemed to be everything worth knowing about a person.

Dogs sniffing each other's arseholes.

And yet, Ben wanted it. He wanted them to scrutinise him and find him sufficient. *Nouveau riche*, maybe, but well on his way to true affluence. No matter whether Ben was in his early thirties or his late sixties, the teenager he'd once been always seemed to stalk his psyche like the cloaked phantom, always two steps behind. Full of wonder and good will, yet hopelessly, devastatingly naïve.

These men didn't seem to have that ghost inside them. They hadn't once been another type of person, like Ben had been, whom time had hardened. No, they'd been *raised* to see the world this way, to evaluate every person they met for weakness, for opportunity. Had they ever known anything else, even in childhood? Did they, too, carry gremlins in their brains, warping every interaction into a struggle for status, whispering every second *You're not enough, you're not enough, YOU'RE NOT ENOUGH?*

Ben had worked his whole life to be like these men. Had to unlearn so many of that naïve teenager's foolish habits. Had to be painstakingly assiduous, had to hit just the right string of luck. His younger self, at this party, was still caught up in it. His older self, now that he'd achieved everything these men had and more, including their calcified sense of superiority, for the first time felt a new, uncomfortable emotion surrounding the whole edifice on which he'd built his life and sense of self.

Doubt.

His younger self walked a fine line, giving enough specifics to whet Bortley's appetite for investment, but leaving enough out that Fast Quid didn't seem as rickety as it was. He didn't want to test his luck, so he left the ask itself for later.

"Sounds like you're a busy man, Mr Scrooge," said Gilbert.

"I pour my heart and soul into the business, yes. I confess I've been working fourteen-hour days lately."

"I feel your pain. I typically work fifteen-hour days."

"And I twenty-five hour days," said Bortley, with a smirk. "What sods have any time for time any more? Mr Scrooge, have you seen the ice room yet?"

Ben probed his self-education on the upper class to recall what exactly an ice room was. Coming up empty, he said, "I haven't."

"Oh, do follow me. You'll quite like it."

Ben left his book on a console table. Gilbert trotted after them, and Stokes, a bit drunk, shambled in the rear. Two rooms over, they entered, essentially, Antarctica. Bortley opened a thick aluminium door, and inside lay a freezing blue wonderland. Pillars and arches of ice supported an ice dome over their heads. Twelve-foot ice sculptures encircled the room, mostly depicting the muscular bodies of warriors in the classical style, though Ben did spot one winged woman, spear raised to strike, charging forth on the back of a horse. A Valkyrie?

The rounded walls held evenly spaced windows into other rooms of the mansion. Between the windows, more paintings hung behind protective cases, which a handful of other party guests were browsing.

"I keep my most prized art in here," Bortley explained as Ben marvelled at the room. "In climate-controlled cases, of course." Ben's feet crunched on artificial snow. Beneath a statue of Atlas hefting his orb nearby, a man lay flat on his back making a snow angel.

How much did this room *cost*? If Bortley had this kind of money to burn – or rather, to freeze – Marley had chosen the right man to ask for funding.

Ben stopped to examine an ice luge down which a steady stream of water flowed. A display of glasses for spirits rested further down the same table. When Ben drew close to puzzle out whether the liquid was actually water, Bortley prompted him to fill a glass. He did, and sipped. Vodka.

Stokes, shivering, huddled close to Bortley for warmth. Bortley stepped away, but Stokes approached again and this time wrapped his arms around him. Bortley sighed in apparent tolerance as Ben examined a painting.

"This is *Mother Mary with the Holy Child Jesus Christ*," Bortley said. "One of Hitler's best paintings."

In an effort not to spit out a mouthful of vodka, Ben sucked part of it down the wrong pipe and erupted in a coughing fit. Stokes patted him on the back as if burping a baby. "Are you all right, chap?"

"I'm sorry," Ben said to Bortley. "Did you say 'Hitler'?"

"He was a great painter, didn't you know? Impossible to get a hold of most of his work. The Western governments keep much of it in vaults, claiming it's propaganda."

Ben studied the painting more closely, but nothing seemed special about it. Just a generic picture of Mary and a blond, blue-eyed Baby Jesus.

"He didn't have much talent," Gilbert said, echoing Ben's thoughts.

"I think it's quite good," Ben said, taking satisfaction from Bortley's ensuing smile. "Better than most of this abstract rubbish you see in museums these days."

"We've lost so much good taste," Bortley agreed. "The world used to admire real artists with actual style. Vera Lynn and Errol Flynn. Mae West and Jean Harlow. These days we're left with Madonna and Prince and those 'Hungry Like the Wolf' buffoons and all the other partly nude teenagers bleating into a microphone like a sonic flogging and calling it song."

"Hear, hear," said Stokes.

Gilbert grunted and gestured to the clothed and unclothed party guests cavorting beyond the windows around them: a bacchanalia of drunken revelry. "At least you still have good taste, Bortley."

Bortley's eyes narrowed. "Your wife certainly thought so."

Gilbert's face became stone, and Ben took a step back from whatever animosity was passing between him and Bortley. But both men were glancing sidelong at Ben's discomfort, and after a second, they both erupted in laughter.

"Relax, old sport," Bortley said to Ben.

"Oh," Ben said, trying to decipher the odd joke he hadn't understood. "Dressing-room banter, I see."

"No, I actually did sleep with his wife," Bortley said. "It's our pastime, seducing each other's wives. All of us at the Garrick Club."

"None of the women much like it," Gilbert chimed in. "Are you married, Ben?"

Ben took a brief, deep gulp of vodka and exhaled past the burn in his throat. "Uh, no. Eligible bachelor here."

"Oh, how I'd love to be your age again," Bortley said. "A ravenous beast, prowling the night for flesh. No divorce to worry me."

"That's me," Ben said, a sheepish waver in his voice that he tried to suppress. "A prowler."

That this was a lie troubled the old Ben whose memory this was. By this point in his life, he'd had at least two successful dates, taking women he met in the course of his business out to Le Caprice and a

West End show. Only two. He'd thanked each woman for an evening out, dropped her off at her flat, and that was the end of it.

He caught women's eyes now. It puzzled him that although his core person was almost exactly the same as it had been before he started the business, he now interested *many* more women. Yet he hadn't connected with anyone. He hadn't even slept with anyone. He hadn't had the time. Or so his younger self had told himself.

His older self, who'd had three wives, and had woken up in bed next to women he barely knew more times than he could count, felt oddly dirty even taking part in this conversation, as a version of himself much less accustomed to manipulating them.

When had he become such a lecher, like Bortley and Gilbert? He'd felt intense envy all through his twenties at seeing successful men in their thirties scoop up women with ease when he couldn't get a single date. Why had it taken him so long to take advantage of his own success? If a part of him that longed for closeness, for true companionship, had lingered into his adulthood, and was here even now at the infamous Bortley party, what had eventually extinguished it? Or if it hadn't been extinguished, where had it gone? He'd felt that longing once, so strongly.

You haven't got enough money, Ben.

He downed the last of his vodka. "I'm sorry about your divorce," he said to Bortley.

"Oh, it's no real bother. When your old BMW starts to show some wear, you upgrade to a Ferrari." He peered over his shoulder at Stokes, who'd started giving him a back massage through his suit without asking. "Stokes?" he asked in confusion.

Stokes raised his eyebrows. "Oh, me? I don't much like women at all."

"We know," said Gilbert. "If you're giving back rubs, there's plenty of lads here who might like one."

"I shall go forth and explore, then. Unless..."

Stokes's inquisitive gaze landed on Ben, and Ben waved *no thanks*. But he welcomed the chance to evacuate. "But Mr Stokes, do you mind if I follow you until you find someone? I'd love to see more of this wonderful party Lord Bortley has put on."

"Please," Stokes said, and Bortley crooned a bit at the flattery.

After enduring some parting banter about the many attractive women at the party, Ben and Stokes left the cold men in the cold room and wandered through a dance studio, a small bowling alley, and some type of brewery, all filled with well-dressed, and in some cases partially dressed, guests. Stokes rhapsodised about the estate and Bortley himself, buttering up the man as if he were still with them. In a grand ballroom, a cover band was performing U2's 'I Still Haven't Found What I'm Looking For' on a stage beneath a full suite of concert lights, in front of a sea of banquet tables. As no pig races or orgies were in sight, this seemed the place calmer guests had found to rest from the rest of the party. Hundreds of them chatted at the tables most distant from the stage and the throng that was crowded around it, and among them, alone at her own table, Ben spotted Marley. He excused himself from Stokes and made his way to her.

"Ben!" she greeted him. "How'd it go with Lord Bortley?"

He sat next to her. "Unclear. He's... he's a bit odd. I'll circle back round to him later. What's this?"

Marley was dipping a small stick of cardstock into her wine glass. "Oh, it's a chemistry test." She lifted it, shook it off, and examined the coloured patch on its end. "Negative! The bloke who's been flirting with me is *not* trying to roofie me. He must be a winner."

"I admire your high standards." He most certainly did not feel any jealousy whatsoever that someone had been flirting with Marley, and to prove this to himself, he added, "Where's he gone off to? I'll leave you as soon as he returns, if you like."

Marley beamed at him, the warm light from the distant stage soft on her face. Coloured fairy lights twinkled lazily on the wall behind her.

"What is it?" Ben asked, smiling himself.

"Nothing. I'm just glad you're my partner. My business partner."

Ben exhaled a delighted laugh through his nose. But his gaze had lingered on hers too long. He turned to the stage. "Good music. Sounds just like the real…" He squinted and leant forward, as if this would help him see the stage any better. "Dear lord, is that actually Bono?"

Marley plucked out a piece of her hair. "Somehow I don't think they knew they were signing up to play at a bachelor party for Satan."

The monstrosity of Bortley's wealth display was starting to smother Ben, so he shook his head and cleared it from his mind. "How'd it go with Ms Shaw?"

Marley's smile inverted. After dithering for a few seconds, she lifted the wine glass to her mouth and imbibed its entire contents in a series of quick gulps. "She told me she'd fund my college," she said, almost too softly for Ben to hear.

He pretended not to hear her anyway. "I'm sorry?"

She raised her voice above the music. "She hates Fast Quid but she'll fund my college."

Ben's heart dropped in his chest. He studied her, but she kept her gaze forward, on the stage.

"I'm not gonna do it," she said at last. "Of course I'm not gonna do it. We have a good thing going." But it was clear on her face that the decision was eating her up inside. "And Fast Quid gives me much more earning potential. Leaving it to start a whole new business would look weak to my parents."

Ben had nothing to say. He wasn't about to cut her loose, to offer her a path out of their partnership, when he'd be so much worse off without her help. But his older self ached for not having done so. She'd have been so much happier building her career apart from him. Offering her that would've been the right thing to do.

His younger self wanted to change the subject. He searched the room for Stokes, or Suresh, or even whoever had been hitting on Marley – maybe returning to finish an earlier conversation. His attention finally settled on the floral arrangement at the table's centre, identical to those at every other table. Red, pink, white, and yellow carnations, fresh and redolent.

"Are these..." he started, before reconsidering whether he really wanted to ask the question. "Marley, are these flowers in the shape of a swastika?"

Marley diverted her attention from the band to the carnations. "Nooo," she said. "I mean, it's a Hindu symbol, too, right? 'Good luck' or something? I'm sure that's how it's meant."

"Is Lord Bortley Hindu?"

Marley frowned at the unlikeliness of this. Maybe she was right. Or maybe the floral arrangement was just a strange mistake. On the other hand, maybe someone had *really* tricked Bono into playing this concert.

"This is all a bit much," Ben said. When Marley nodded agreement, he added, "Bortley and his mates spent the whole conversation either trying to one-up each other or prattling about all the women they'd like to sleep with."

"About par for the course, innit?"

Ben leant back and sunk his hands in his pockets. "You don't find it a bit off-putting?"

She shrugged. "Why would I?"

U2 finished their song and Ben applauded with the scattered crowd. They started 'With or Without You' – one of Ben's favourites.

It might have been that he'd had a bit too much to drink, or that the wild turns his life had taken were finally getting to him, or even that he'd got caught up in the music. Even looking back from the vantage point of the future, Ben couldn't explain why or how he'd opened up to Marley at this moment. She'd only ever been his plucky business partner. But she was also the closest thing he had to a real friend.

"I'm not sure I like the type of person I'm becoming," he said.

Marley jerked her head from the band to Ben in apparent surprise. "What? You think you'll become Lord Bortley?" When he didn't react to her quip, her smirk disappeared. "If you're feeling guilty about being horny, don't give in to the double standard. We tell men the only socially acceptable way you can feel human connection is through sex, then we turn around, smack you, and say, 'Bad man!' for wanting sex."

"No, it's not that," Ben said. Well, not only that. It was the fawning obsequiousness in Stokes and even in Gilbert, despite his apparent rivalry with Bortley. Like Bortley was the sun and they the planets orbiting him. What would it be like to always have to wonder whether your friends were really your friends? Whether anyone in your life would still be there if your achievements and wealth all vanished?

Ben had told himself he'd started Fast Quid – and created this new, industrious version of himself – to earn financial security. He hadn't achieved it yet, but he'd come light-years from where he began. So why did he still feel just as insecure as he had when he'd started?

Cautiously, unsure whether it was safe to lower the mask of his overambitious alter ego in front of Marley, he peeked around its outer edge at her. "I feel like if I don't work myself into the ground and earn enough money, I'll never be good enough for other people. But I feel like if I do, I'll become the very type of person who tells other people they aren't good enough and ensnares them in the same place I am. It's… it's a horrible catch-22."

Marley studied him for a long moment. Her gaze shone against his face, as warm as the stage lights.

"I know that when I feel the need to distinguish myself by, I don't know, getting a tattoo of Sting on my arse, or moving to Mongolia and marrying a sheep herder," she said, "when I feel that, it means part of my brain got stuck back in childhood. When I was vulnerable, when I needed to act out in every way I could to stop my parents from putting me in the boxes they'd designed for my life. And that part of my brain protected me." She reached a hand towards him, but stopped just before she touched him, as if she were wary of a hob's heat. "You're not in that vulnerable place you used to be in any more. But maybe a part of your brain is still working on overdrive, protecting a man who no longer needs protection."

And suffocating me, Ben thought. Marley's words landed on him like rain on a man dying of thirst. He couldn't have said it better in a thousand years.

"What should I do?" he asked her, his voice barely a whisper above the music. "How can I escape this?"

Marley took a measured inhalation. Her downcast eyes fluttered about. She shook her head slowly, like she didn't know the answer to Ben's questions but was offering him the best answer she could come up with.

"The part of your brain that wants to protect you," she said, meeting his eyes again. "Keep reminding it that it did its job. The fight is over, and you won. Bugger what anyone else says you should value, and figure out what you really value."

Ben soaked up her answer. What did he truly value? When he was honest with himself, he didn't actually know. Was there a void of values at his core? After deep introspection to discern what he really valued, would the answer still just be "money"? Or were his real values so incipient, so undeveloped, that he couldn't see them even though they were there?

He valued his life, of course. He valued...

The stage lights lit in a new configuration, now shining green, now shining violet. The change sparkled in Marley's eyes.

"Maybe we should do it together," she said. "Slow down a tad, once we get funding. I start work an hour before you and keep going an hour after you leave, so believe me, I need to reorient my life, too."

All at once, Ben's mask went back up. He pulled away from her hand, which had been lingering above his tail coat, nearly touching his arm. "You don't think I contribute as much to Fast Quid as you do?"

Marley withdrew her hand and crossed her arms. "That's not what I said."

"You said you work more than me. Like I'm not doing enough."

Marley's stare was withering. Ben braced to receive a piece of her mind.

But instead, Marley dropped her gaze. "Oh," she said, properly chastised. "I'm so sorry. I was wrong to imply that. You do as much work as I do and more."

Worms seemed to gnaw at Ben's insides as he shut down every thought he'd just been thinking, every feeling he'd just felt. "I thought so. Now. I should be getting back to Bortley."

"Ben!" Marley yelled. Her voice carried far over the music, but no one turned their head. Ben jolted at her outburst. She was standing now, hands on her hips, staring him down. "Is that really how you remember this conversation ending?"

Cowering in his chair, Ben squeaked out a response. "Yes?"

"Ben, we had a huge row. You'd opened up to me, and I accidentally said something that triggered you, then we both closed up and blew up at each other."

"I take it I'm now speaking with the older, deader you?"

Marley huffed, turned completely around, and back. "Next you said something to justify your salary being higher than mine even though you work less, and I was so sodding livid, and this was *right* after I told you I'd passed up a chance to leave Fast Quid for another job I would have loved, and not only did you dismiss me, but you filed this memory away with me as a meek, submissive doormat so you could feel rosy about bullying me?"

Ben grasped for words. "I liked – I appreciated your guidance. I don't know why I remember it the way I do. I just wanted a friend who wouldn't scorn me."

"I just wanted some acknowledgement! I slaved away at our business for you. For us. We were a team, and you took all the credit. You always took all the credit." A tear fell across her reddened face. "And do you know the saddest part, Ben? We had this conversation thirty-something years ago. You had my affection, you had my support. You had everything you needed to help you to *grow*." She wiped away the tear, steeled her expression to rid it of emotion. "And you didn't grow a damned bit."

Marley turned her back to him, and this time she didn't look back. She couldn't leave, not in her memory's body. It had stayed here, while Ben had left.

So he left to fetch another drink. How drunk could he get in a memory? He'd noticed glasses of booze were essentially bottomless here. No matter how much he drank, they always refilled to the level they'd been at in his memory. He'd originally gotten obscenely drunk during this party. Could he get even more hammered now, if he kept drinking and drinking and drinking, even more than he had in real life?

His insides twisted. His young self peeved that Marley thought him less than her. His old self flustered by her sudden anger at him, confused by his faulty memory, fuming at the universe for its stubborn insistence that the arrow of time run always forward, so that by the time he knew how best to live a moment, the moment had passed.

Ben made his way outside, hunting his prey. He'd give Bortley a pitch to rival a Churchill speech. Even a twentieth of the budget of this single party could catapult Fast Quid into financial sustainability, and Ben into a life where no one would ever talk to him like Marley just had again.

A Christmas wonderland had been set up in the grass field behind the mansion. Fake snow, coloured lights everywhere, a giant tree, and carnival elements, including an elf-themed tilt-a-whirl, a Ferris wheel, and a funhouse conspicuously named "Lebensraum". A faraway string quartet played Christmas carols, and someone nearby was playing 'Stand by Me' on a ukulele.

All this with not a child in sight to enjoy the whimsy. Every party guest was an adult. This seemed a bit sad, but when a nude woman drove past a moment later, saluting Ben from atop an army tank, he reconsidered the wisdom of not inviting kids.

He stopped at a bar on a balcony by the house, ordered another glass of wine, drank it, ordered another. If he didn't remember the specifics of his argument with Marley, he sure as hell remembered this bitter afterglow.

Why shouldn't I build myself into a great man? With enough wealth and power, who cares if my personal relationships shatter? I can buy new ones.

A million pounds, that's it. If I can get a million pounds of personal wealth, I'll be safe. Safe from criticism. From condescension. I'll be free.

And if the effort turned him into an alcoholic old man who cared nothing for others, and who couldn't enjoy the fruits of success because his mind was always stuck in the better days of the past... Well, at least he'd be safe. Safe at least from all threats outside his own body.

I'm at a party, I'm at a party, Ben reminded himself. Maybe thinking the words would help him pull his mind back into itself, or at least ignore his anger for a while. *I should try to have a good time.*

When the string quartet finished 'It's the Most Wonderful Time of the Year', all that was left was the ukulele music, performed by a sixtyish-year-old man in white-tie attire, standing near Ben on the balcony.

When he finished his song, Ben clapped. "You bring much-needed groundedness to this garish spectacle. Bravo."

The man chuckled and set his ukulele back into its case on the ground. "It's quite a party, isn't it?" he said in a flat American accent. "I was in London on business and they invited me to what they described as 'a small soiree'. It's a giant, weird, and creepy soiree if you ask me."

Ben laughed. Set his elbows on the balustrade and looked out at the carnival. His older self tensed at what he recalled from this exchange.

"What brings you here?" the ukulele player asked, closing his instrument's case.

At the farthest edge of the carnival, several zebras and giraffes meandered in a small enclosure. Guests queued up for photos with them, but the animals looked cold and miserable.

"I'm trying to find a way to own the world," Ben said.

The other man didn't react. He latched up the ukulele case, then set his own elbows on the balustrade, mirroring Ben. He adjusted his glasses. "That's a tall order," he said. "If Emperor Trajan and Queen Victoria couldn't do it, I don't know who could."

"I could," Ben asserted. "If I can get my business to turn a profit, it's only a few more steps until I own the world."

The ukulele player flashed a grin. "Ah, that's it, is it? Tell me what ails you. I'm more than happy to advise on vision, customer relations, team building, employee satisfaction..."

"No, bugger all that," Ben said. He gulped down more wine, tapped a finger against the man's chest. "The purpose of a business is to make money, you know."

The man looked down at where Ben had tapped him, revealing a head of thinning hair. "Hmm," he said, then pursed his lips and stared at the sky, as if in concentration. "I think the purpose of a business is to create value for all its stakeholders – everyone involved in it. Its customers and suppliers, the communities it operates in. Foremost its employees."

"And what would you know about that, huh? The ukulele player."

"Oh, a thing or two," he said. "I have a lot of friends who've turned their companies into profit vacuum cleaners for themselves and their shareholders, damn whatever their other stakeholders need."

"And be honest with me," Ben said. "Did it make them happy?"

"Oh yes," the man said immediately, "absolutely blissful. The companies usually fail, though, and of ones that haven't, their owners are some of the most spiritually empty people I know."

Ben snorted dismissal, and cursed the universe again. When all he wanted was companionable chit-chat to help him through a difficult night, *of course* it would send him a moraliser.

"I'll put it to you this way," said the American. "Think about a person you profoundly respect."

Ben scanned the outdoor crowd for Marley. Maybe she'd wandered away from the ballroom and was now basking in some posh man's attentions on the Ferris wheel. In fact, he hoped she was. He hoped he hadn't hurt her too badly.

"Okay, fine," Ben said. "A person I respect. Got it."

"Great. Now tell me what about this person made you pick them."

Ben held an image of Marley in his mind. Her face, her eyes. Her ingenuity, her stalwart self-assurance and her determination to chart her own course through life. Her carefree guffaws when Ben made a crude joke. Her suppressed passion for education.

"Did you pick this person because they were rich?" the ukulele player asked. The suggestion was so jarring that it derailed Ben's thoughts. "Did you pick them because of their luxury house, clothes, car? Did you pick them because they're sexy? Because they won awards or have a lot of admirers?"

Ben grasped the point the man was making. It was simple, almost trite... yet surprisingly confounding to him.

"Interesting," the man said, aligning his glasses again, "the difference between what we admire in other people, and what we think other people admire in us."

With a sigh, he picked up his instrument in its case. After surveying the extravagant back garden one last time, he patted Ben on his back. "You don't have to own the world," he said. His footfalls faded behind Ben as he made his way back into the mansion. The string quartet started 'Jingle Bells'.

Ben rubbed his face, and graced the universe with a sarcastic laugh for its efforts. Marley had asked him to reconsider what he valued, and immediately afterwards some philosophical musician had given him these words of wisdom out of the blue. Distractions from his goal, surely. He had to keep moving. If he stopped to assess what he was working towards, it was possible that the reflection would change his goals, and thus that he'd never achieve them.

I chose my goals for a reason, Ben reminded himself. *Wealth is safety. If I forget that, I'll fall right back where I started.*

Someone was rushing up the steps from the back garden towards Ben. Stokes?

"Mint!" the young man exclaimed when he reached him. He clapped Ben on his shoulders. "Absolutely cracking. What was it like, talking to him?"

"To whom?" Ben asked, utterly confused.

"The Oracle of Omaha," Stokes said. "The chap you were just with."

"I'm sorry, who? The Yank?"

"Yes, man. Warren Buffett. I've been too nervous to start a conversation with him the entire evening, and here you are, marching right up to him for a chat. Brilliant, man."

Stokes kept talking, but his words didn't reach Ben's ears. The world dulled around him, the colours of its many fairy lights blurring together.

Warren Buffett?

The man whose investment advice Ben had been following for years despite having no money to invest? The wealth-building genius whose annual shareholder letters electrified Ben's initiative to get out there and earn? That unassuming American ukulele player had been *him?*

"I understand if you want to keep mum about it," Stokes was saying. "If he gave me any prime advice, I mightn't want to share it, either."

Ben was stupefied. He couldn't talk, couldn't move.

Stokes shifted from foot to foot, rubbed his hands together. "Say, Lord Bortley is about to start a tour of his residence's private wings. The parts most people never get to see. What do you say we join him?"

Warren Buffett? That was really him? Ben had assumed the world was growing cloudy due to his shock at meeting his idol. But his younger self's mind was fading away from him. The entire world around him grew dark. He reached his arms out to steady himself.

"Bortley's quite handsome for an older fellow, you know. Do you think he'd ever..." Stokes said, his voice now a muffled drone.

Everything faded completely to black.

Suddenly, Ben was in Bortley's library some time later, sipping even more wine from a newly full glass.

What the hell just happened? He hadn't passed out, had he? If he had, wouldn't he remember waking up?

He leant against a stepladder, but it was on a track. It rolled away from him and he almost fell. He stabilised, spilling only a bit of wine.

He stood among a group of six other men, including Stokes and Gilbert. Bortley hefted a thick book and tossed it to one of his friends, who barely caught it. "That's my Gutenberg Bible," said Bortley. "Pass it around. You'll also see first editions here of *Ulysses* and *The Wealth of Nations.*"

A tour. That was what Stokes had said. Ben must be on Bortley's tour of his house. His wooziness lingered, but he meandered among the shelves with the other men, feigning interest.

"That one is quite a provocative text," Bortley said from right behind him. Ben hadn't even realised what he was looking at: a whole shelf full of various styles and editions of *Mein Kampf.*

"Oh!" Ben said in alarm, then contained himself. "Yes. Provocative."

"You've read it?" Bortley asked.

"Have I read—" He almost said no. Remembering his mission, he said, "I've read it twice, actually."

"Really?" said Bortley, a fond smile burgeoning on his face. "What did you think?"

Ben racked his inebriated brain for something positive to say about the book. Thankfully, Bortley saved him the effort when he grabbed one of the oldest copies, removed it from a slipcase decorated with an embossed golden bird, and opened it to the title page.

"Oh dear God," Ben said, "it's signed."

"Autographed copies are quite rare. Exorbitantly expensive." Bortley presented the book to Ben. "But I have five of them. Please, keep this one. It's yours. Consider it an invitation to future philosophical discussions."

Cringing, Ben reached his hand towards the book, suffered an automatic recoil, inched his fingers forward again as he tried to stifle his repulsion, then finally snatched the book and stuffed it under his armpit, so it wouldn't be touching his skin.

"I'm... so grateful, Lord Bortley. What a gift."

Bortley snatched the book back. "I was joking. Dear God, man, you really think I'd give something so priceless away?" Only when he slipped *Mein Kampf* back into its slipcase and onto the shelf did Ben wonder how much money he could have sold it for.

He set his wine on a bookshelf and tried to force himself to focus. *How can I sneak a pitch for funding in, then run far, far away? Blitzkrieg then retreat.*

"This way, gentlemen," Bortley said. His cape swished as he led them into a gargantuan room, nearly the size of the ballroom where U2 was playing. This one was empty of people, though, and full of marble pillars running its entire length. Gilded friezes adorned the ceiling, and at the far end, atop a short set of red-carpeted steps, stood a tall-backed chair that seemed to be made of pure gold. Velvet curtains hung from ceiling to floor behind it.

Stokes whistled, while Gilbert squinted as if to better make out the impressive chair. "What's this room?" Gilbert asked. "It's going to be an art gallery, maybe?"

"Oh, this is my throne room," Bortley said, barely turning to address Gilbert as he strode across the polished stone floor.

Gilbert stopped and scowled as the rest of the men walked past him. Ben, at the group's rear, struggling to walk straight, stopped beside him to catch his bearings.

"A throne room?" Gilbert asked Ben in utter confusion. Louder, to Bortley, he called, "What's it for?"

"It's a throne room. What do you think it's for?" Bortley shot back. "Come now, come. You must see my dressing room."

His dressing room was three times the size of Ben's old Docklands flat: an ovular sanctuary of recessed lights, faceted mirrors, and swirls and whorls carved into wooden partitions. Bortley pressed a button next to a slightly pixelated computer screen set into the wall. The room whirred to life as suits, trousers, and every hanging item in his wardrobe slid along the conveyer where they hung.

The group of men oohed and ahhed and clapped.

"An automated garment machine, designed bespoke for this room alone," Bortley bragged.

"So you're against using robots for manufacturing and in the Stock Exchange, but you'll use them in your own dressing room?" Gilbert said.

Bortley swatted at the snipe like it was a fly as his clothing glided past behind him. "I'm not a Luddite, Gilbert. I do, sometimes, enjoy change. All this fretting about automation taking people's jobs is an unfounded panic on the part of people who fear competition."

The conveyer lurched, stopped. Bortley's suits swayed. He lifted one off the rack. Ben tried to mouth something complimentary, but his vision was darkening again, and nausea was roiling his stomach.

God help me if I puke all over Bortley's best suits. The memory of throwing up on the pavement in front of Peter Lees at Morgan Grenfell still stung. He really should have waited until after his pitch to Bortley to drown himself in alcohol.

Bortley switched out the suit jacket he wore for another that looked identical. He threw the group a mischievous grin. "Now, gentlemen. Would you like to see my rocket?"

The men murmured among themselves while Ben tried to parse Bortley's question. What did he mean by "rocket"? Ben's older self knew perfectly well, and his younger self soon found out. His vision went black again – these were wine-driven gaps in his memories, he now suspected – and when it returned, he was still with the tour group, but in a completely different part of the mansion. Some sort of raised viewing platform, in yet another expansive room. But whereas the ballroom and the throne room had been wide, this room was tall. It smelt like a mix between a petrol station and a wine cellar, though there was no wine in sight, other than the newly full glass of it that had somehow found its way into Ben's hands. The walls, floor, and distant ceiling were all dull metal. An immense transparent barrier bisected the room, separating the raised platform from... what the hell was that thing?

Ben tried to be sceptical of his wine-soaked brain, but when the image before him didn't flicker and become something more reasonable, he had to believe his eyes. Bortley did indeed have a rocket. Not a small hobbyist's rocket, but a fourteen-metre-tall behemoth that wouldn't have been out of place at NASA. A black-and-white chequered pattern adorned the four fins at its base, elongating to rectangles at its midsection and finally tapering to a black nosecone. It appeared to stand mostly on its own, supported only by a small metal platform the height of a person beneath its base.

'Let it Snow' chimed merrily from speakers in the walls as the men in the tour group sipped their spirits and stared upwards in admiration and awe.

Bortley giggled. "You'll never guess where this rocket came from," he teased the group.

"Did it come from the Nazis?" Ben said dryly.

Bortley gaped at Ben in seemingly genuine amazement. "What a guess, Ben! Yes, it came from the Nazis. Their taste in rocketry was as impeccable as their taste in art. This one doesn't even need a water deluge system. You know they were the first community to put an object in space? People think it was *Sputnik*, but no. It was a rocket just like this one. Quite advanced, those Nazis."

"Does it still have explosives in it?" Marley asked.

Ben turned his head, and in his current uncoordinated state, his whole body followed until his back was turned to the rocket. There was Marley, dawdling in the group along with a few other additions – including Suresh, devotedly taping everything with his camcorder.

"Oh yes," Bortley answered her. "It's still armed. My men maintain it. Dietrich!"

As a bespectacled eighty-year-old man limped up from the operations pit to the viewing platform to answer Bortley's call, Ben crept next to his cofounder. Marley looked… rough. Her mouth and eyelids hung slack, and she had to make a visible effort to focus on Ben when he whispered to her. "What are you doing here?"

Marley breathed in deeply, like answering him required her to lift a heavy weight. "Saw you walking by. Looked like" – she hiccupped – "looked like fun."

"Dear lord, you look as drunk as I feel."

"I'm fine." With a wavering hand, she tried to steal Ben's wine glass. He moved it to his other hand, out of her reach. "Have you asked the rich bloke for his money yet so we can leave?"

"Working on it."

At the front of the group, Bortley conferred quietly with Dietrich, then beamed at the tour group. "Gentlemen, what do you say we fire this banger up?"

The group, until now wickedly playful, abruptly lost their gaiety. Everyone in it took a step or two back towards the exit behind them.

"Not to launch it," Bortley assured them. "The roof doesn't even open. Whitehall doesn't know I have this, so I'm not about to launch it right over their heads. No, I'll just turn it on for a spell. Enliven the night with the fires of its bowels." Dietrich trundled back down into the pit and started flipping switches. The lights dimmed, save for some show lights illuminating the huge forty-five-year-old antique, because of course Bortley flaunted the rocket to visitors often enough to install show lights.

"You keep it fuelled?" Gilbert asked.

"Von Braun designed it to run on distilled potato alcohol," Bortley confirmed. "I buy it directly from Egypt."

Marley disgorged a farting noise from her lips. "Just like the Nazis to use ethanol instead of proper petrol," she said.

Bortley didn't seem to mind the newcomers to the tour. At Marley's comment, a sagely smile graced his face. "You know," he said, "the Nazis weren't wrong about everything."

The rocket rumbled. As the men craned their necks to get the best view, Marley leant over to Ben's ear. "I truly, deeply feel that we should leave."

A deafening boom shot through their ears, to which they promptly pressed their fingers. Beyond the see-through safety barrier, bright white light flashed beneath the rocket, sputtering and cascading over the metal floor.

"*Mehr, mehr!*" Dietrich called from the pit, his fist raised. "*Heißer! Stärker!*"

Exhaust smoke quickly filled the half of the room beyond the barrier, but giant fans pulled it away, so the rocket stayed visible. Most of the tour group had ducked as if for cover, though the raised platform they stood on offered none. "It's loud now," Bortley shouted, barely audible, "but it travels faster than sound. If this came right at you, you'd be dead before you heard a peep."

Everyone stared at the thundering giant, lost in awe. "It's so…" Gilbert started, then searched for a word. "… manly," he finished.

The circle of writhing flame beneath the rocket grew, licking the edge of the barrier. A few men backed away again, but Bortley gestured for them not to worry. Stokes disregarded him, discreetly opening the door when he wasn't watching, then promptly ran for his life.

The rocket's burn grew no further, though, and the group settled more comfortably into their spectator role as the sputtering flames continued. But far ahead of them, a person was climbing up over the edge of the pit. Ben barely caught sight of her at the edge of his peripheral vision. Marley! She was stumbling towards a safety door set into the barrier between the viewing room and the rocket.

Oh, hell.

Ben shoved past Gilbert and another man and sprinted down into the trench. He ran past switches, indicator lights, and computers born in the 1960s – and Dietrich, still cheering the rocket on. He ascended a short ladder where Marley had climbed. She was already at the safety door, trying to pull it open, so he sprinted towards her, tripped, fell, then stood and sprinted the rest of the way. This close, the rocket's roar was an all-consuming earthquake from just beyond the thermal glass. And despite that glass, enough heat seeped through to drench Ben's dress shirt in sweat.

With an ear-splitting *thud*, an immense crack opened in the concrete slab beneath the rocket's exhaust plume.

"Marley!" Ben barked. "Get back!"

She threw him a blithe grin, yanked on the door again. "I want to ride the rocket," she shouted above the noise.

Back at the viewing platform, Bortley's cape was flapping as he jumped up and down, waving his arms and shouting something inaudible. *Don't go in the room with the inferno on the floor, probably.* Head-sized chunks of concrete were starting to pelt the transparent barrier wall, leaving spider-web dents in the ballistic glass.

"Ben!" Marley called. Her eyes were lucid, caustic, the intelligence of sobriety back behind them. "Is this really how you remember it?"

It must be old ghostly Marley speaking, then. Ben had to temper the urgency driving him. This was all just a memory, after all. He'd been dragging the magic staff around this whole time, and he could pause everything with barely a thought.

The rocket rumbled. "You shouldn't have had so much to drink," Ben said.

Behind Marley, the clamps holding down the rocket shattered within seconds of each other. It levitated off its platform at a slight angle. Dietrich, who'd been running to intercept Marley and Ben, ran back to his controls, but it was too late. The Nazi rocket rose, the flames beneath it elongating into an elegant glowing ray. Bortley clutched his head in his hands as the prized possession lifted to the ceiling. The sound of it punching a hole in the roof couldn't be heard above the roar of the rocket itself, but Ben jumped as the roof pieces crashed to the floor and ricocheted into the transparent barrier. A dozen huge cracks, like human-sized bullet strikes, peppered its length. Ben looked helplessly through the new skylight at the rocket slanting, arcing north-east, right towards downtown London.

Colour had drained from Bortley's face. Marley was her inebriated self again, startled on the floor and looking around in confusion. Her ghost, though, hovered overhead, gazing down on the wild scene with what looked like sorrow.

Is this really how you remember it? she'd asked.

It was how Ben remembered it. Was his memory wrong? And if so, what had really happened?

STAVE XI

Masks

Bortley did not give Ben and Marley any funding. Mr Gilbert, however, found the whole episode so hilarious, and took enough delight in Bortley's humiliation, that he invested just enough to keep Fast Quid afloat until it became profitable. Over the next two years, they scaled it to twenty-eight shops across the UK, large enough that it needed a board of directors. They invited Gilbert, Talbot, and other key investors to join the board. Ben got them to pass a resolution attaching far more votes to the shares he owned than to anyone else's shares. He needed neither their advice nor their oversight, and he wouldn't have them controlling him.

By the time Ben and Marley caught up with his memories of Christmas 1991, their younger selves were spending the big day moving into fancy new offices in One Canada Square.

Ben zipped his Barbour jacket shut against the morning chill as he directed the removals men unloading the lorry. While they worked, the Pixies performed 'Where Is My Mind?' from a ghetto blaster they'd set up on the pavement.

My God. We actually called those things "ghetto blasters".

When Marley rolled up a small sack truck of her own and started loading it with boxes, Ben drew close and whispered, "You're not a bartender any more. Don't you think this work is beneath the chief of operations?"

"Oh," Marley said after a moment, like she needed to digest words that were foreign to her. "Sorry, I hadn't realised. Uh…" She searched for the nearest removals man. "You. Could you please get these boxes, too? Thank you."

"You needn't say 'please' or 'thank you', either," Ben said.

Marley rolled her eyes. "Hey, blighter," she said to the approaching removals man. "Box. Upstairs. Now." A fire of fear lit beneath the man, and he hustled to wheel the sack truck away. "Was that more to your liking, Scrooge?"

He rubbed the bridge of his nose, but didn't respond.

"You skipped a Christmas, you know," Marley said. "What happened to Christmas of 1990? Bad memories there?"

"No, 1992 was the really terrible one. I skipped one because we've been going in order for a while now. Hopefully that thing chasing you has given up, but if it hasn't, a bit of unpredictability won't hurt."

"And wait a minute." Alarm in her eyes, she clutched Ben's arm and gazed up at the sky. "What happened to the rocket? I don't actually remember. Did it hit anyone?"

Ben tried to recall. He'd asked Gilbert about it once. Hadn't the authorities searched for it but never found it? "It must've run out of fuel mid-flight. It's probably still out there in the woods somewhere."

This was fortunate for Bortley, who'd died in 2009 still as wealthy and hedonistic as ever. Word was, he'd had his bed and his doctors moved to a concert hall and had hired a full orchestra to serenade him as he drifted off this mortal coil.

A storm that had been building all morning soon broke, so they went up to the fortieth floor to direct the work inside. Later, they took lunch in the empty office that was to be Marley's. With takeaway sandwiches resting on the windowsill, they gazed out together on sheets of rain lazily falling on London. The drizzle was thick enough that it obscured all the cars and pedestrians. The City was shrouded, its skyscrapers giants in a fog, the Thames a watery superhighway leading into gloom.

And now, at long last, Ben stood above it all. He was safe. In the midst of climbing house prices, he'd bought a two-storey, three-hundred-square-metre detached house, all his own. An entire room was devoted to nothing but billiards and other games. He'd complemented the home's chic furnishings with a brand new Silver Spur in his garage. He had private health insurance, a burgeoning art collection, and four or five MPs who felt they owed him favours.

In fact, nearly everyone he met sought to appease him. Suddenly, the normal rules of the world didn't apply to Ben. He could get away with more. He'd stopped at the pictures last weekend and been struck that the deference, the servility with which he'd once been required to treat patrons, was now directed at him. He truly had become... better. Better than his former self. Better than other people.

And yet, he couldn't shake the feeling that he still teetered at the edge of personal disaster. He was only a few years separated from working a dead-end job, after all, and the fragile future could easily collapse into the squalid past after a few bad decisions. He had to guard his diet like an anorexic, his mind screaming at him to eat a decent meal now, while he still had enough money for one in his bank account. Worry gnawed at his chest constantly, hunching his shoulders in defiance of all the workouts he'd been doing. To keep it at bay, at least partially, he thrust himself into his work, labouring nights and weekends, teasing apart the British finance system piece by piece to find new ways to make money from making money, sleeping four hours per night long after the need for doing so had evaporated. He had permanent bags beneath his eyes by his early thirties.

A small, weak part of Ben – both the young memory and the old man eavesdropping inside him – looked down on rainy streets far below, trying not to be wowed by the panorama, as if he could will his admiration of this view to be anything other than the pathetic gawking of a poor man, newly rich. *If only I could speed up time itself,* his younger self thought, *so I could reach an era of my life when I'll be even more secure.* When the shame of poverty would be even further in his past.

How long would the fear haunt him? Until he was a billionaire? For the rest of his life? Could he do nothing to lessen it?

Someone was watching him from outside. Eyes in the mists. Twenty yards from the window, a young girl was floating in midair. No older than ten, she appraised Ben with critical eyes. The wind flung her hair about and sent billows through her long, loose dress, which would have been white in sunny weather but was now a drab grey.

In one hand, she held a staff. Multiple thin strands of wood wound tightly around each other until, at the level of her head, they diverged, veering away from each other in varied directions so that the top of the staff looked like the bottom of a broomstick.

Ben blinked at the witch-like apparition, and she was gone. A ghostly girl replaced with rain and howling wind.

"This actually feels great," Marley said. She'd been arranging a line of cocaine on the windowsill; she hadn't been looking out the window. "The Christmas when our success was freshest, most invigorating. I wonder how many times we can relive this memory without one of the ghosts coming after us here."

"'One of' the ghosts?" asked Ben. "Ralph's no threat, so I assume you mean there are more of them. How many?"

"Three for every day. Past, present, and future. But I bet all of them for every day are fuming about my escape."

Past, present, and... Ben glanced out the window again, searching for the girl in the wind. No sign of her still. "How comforting," he muttered.

Marley snorted her line of coke, crinkled her nose, then cheered. "Woo! Blow was so much better in 1991. You want some?"

Before Ben could answer, a meek voice interrupted. "Excuse me. Ms Jacobs? Mr Scrooge?"

One of the removal workers stood at the office door. A short man in company uniform. Marley rubbed a bit of cocaine off her nose. "Yes?" she asked.

The man had trouble making eye contact. He kept looking at the floor or the ceiling or the rain beyond the windows. "I'm sorry to pester you. I saw on some of the boxes that you're both with Fast Quid, and I just wanted to ask, because, uhm..." His voice quavered with nerves. "You see, I've been trying to pay off my Fast Quid loans for months, but they just keep growing. I've paid three times what the original loan was. So I'm just wondering if, maybe, you could put in a word with your bosses to see if they'll let Iain Cartwright off the hook?"

Ah yes, Ben remembered this. Iain Cartwright, the first of many. A throng of grocery clerks, caretakers, and waiters throughout Ben and Marley's lives, materialising without warning, begging for debt forgiveness, culminating in the scumbag who'd infiltrated Marley's office the day before her ghostly return. That one had been unique in style, but not substance.

But here, now, the first time this had happened, their younger selves didn't know quite what to say. "What are you—" Ben started. "I mean, how did—"

Marley, perhaps with Ben's admonition for her to act more like a COO fresh in her mind, took the lead. "We *are* the bosses, mate," she said to the man. "You borrowed the money. You accepted the terms. You pay what you owe or we'll have you up."

Marley paid no attention to the man's reaction. Instead she looked to Ben expectantly, as if seeking his approval. He had no idea if she'd given the proper response, but she'd given it and she was his business partner, so he felt he needed to back her up.

"What she said."

The removals man stammered something soft and incomprehensible. His breathing quickened. But he was too small a man to stand up for himself. He left the room with no further comment or complaint.

Ben let out a breath he'd been holding. "Well, that was awkward."

"I know," Marley said. "I didn't like that."

"We'll need to hire security," Ben said. "Keep people like that out."

Marley nodded uncomfortable assent. Behind her, her older ghost had removed herself from her body again. While her younger self returned to her lunch, her ghost watched the removal worker plod down the hall, downcast.

◆

Something intangible was different about Suresh when he stepped into Ben's slowly materialising office later that afternoon – the office that would remain his for decades, big by the standards of the 2020s, positively profligate for the 1990s. His stride was lighter, the tension he always seemed to carry gone. He sat across from Ben's desk, smiled, and set a single piece of paper in front of him.

Ben set down the glass of brandy he'd been drinking and picked up the letter. It was Suresh's resignation. Before speaking a word, Ben ran through a quick analysis of the business's connections with Suresh. Could they afford to lose him? How could Ben stop the value Suresh brought to the company from being erased? How quickly could he be replaced?

He'd considered all this before, about everyone high up in Fast Quid. Everyone in his life, really, were either assets or liabilities now. But Ben constantly sharpened his own mind and business acumen against Suresh's. How would he stay at the top of his game without him?

"We'll double your pay," Ben said. "You name the benefits you want and we'll provide them. You're too valuable, Suresh. I can't accept this."

"You can, Mr Scrooge," Suresh said politely.

Ben studied him, trying to pinpoint the difference in him.

Faced with Ben's silence, Suresh added, "I plan to spend more time with my family. Be a father to my children and an ally to my wife."

"You need more time off. Got it."

"No, it's not that. I'm sorry. I've proved what I needed to prove, and now it's time for me to move on. I have an organisation I've been wanting to start."

Ben spat air and scoffed. "Come on. You've come so far and earned so much."

"It is enough for me," Suresh said simply.

"You're someone now, and you're going to turn yourself back into nothing?"

That got under Suresh's skin. He sat up straight and furrowed his brow. Grabbed his knees. But regained his composure before he let himself say anything careless. He breathed in deeply, exhaled slowly.

"I no longer accept that view of the world," he said.

Ben stood, strode round his desk, and sat on it. A power move, placing his eyeline above Suresh's. "As long as I've known you," Ben said, "you've been Mr Competitive, jockeying with me over every little decision. Always optimising, always striving, always driven. I know you, Suresh. And whatever it is you think you're doing…" – he waved the resignation letter in his face – "this isn't you."

Suresh crossed his arms, leant back in his seat. "Then tell me, Ben, please. What *is* me? Since you know me so well."

"You're cut-throat. You're a social climber, like me."

"My wife wouldn't say that. My kids wouldn't either. Neither would my close friends. That was a mask I put on the moment I stepped into my interview, because I had to be seen that way. But I take that mask off every night when I leave work. I have been thinking, and I would very much like to live for the rest of my life with it off."

Ben waved his words away as if Suresh were a gibbering baby. "Suresh, I think you're confused. This *is* the life you want. Otherwise, you wouldn't have worked so damned hard to achieve it."

"No..."

Suresh struggled to come up with words, but Ben pressed on. "If that's not the case, why are you so competitive?"

"Why are you?" Suresh asked.

The room grew so silent that all the air seemed to have been sucked from it. Defiance glimmered beneath the professional face Suresh was showing – another mask? – but a fatigued melancholy soon replaced it. Suresh's head sagged on his neck. He opened his mouth, said the beginning of a word... and still he paused. He pursed his lips as if to keep the words down. Finally, he shook his head, and spoke so softly that Ben had to lean forward to hear him.

"My parents sent me to this country and said don't come back until you have an advanced degree, or a hundred crore. You see, my family are from the high caste – supposedly we abolished caste forty years ago, but people still act like it's real – so I am expected to be a certain type of person. I needed to compete in the way that's expected of any high-status man. Without this, I could not marry. Even then, most women were inaccessible to me because they are of lesser castes."

"Sounds miserable," Ben interjected. "I'd hate to live in a society like that."

"Hmm," was all the reply Suresh gave, as he glanced around the office. "So you see what was in my mind after my family sent me here. Growing up, my whole public life must be a performance, so I carried that to London. I was not allowed to make any mistakes. I had to become someone I was not.

"But stepping away from your culture lets you see it more plainly. Here in London, I'm not Brahmin or Maratha or Puneri. Here, I am only Indian. A Dalit, who is our lowest caste, is seen the same as me. They are not untouchable here, unless I decide to make them that way in my head. But many British see us both as undesirable.

"So at the end of this journey, my question to myself was: why does moving from the top of a hierarchy to the bottom expose the foolishness of hierarchies so clearly in one's mind, but moving from the bottom to the top makes the hierarchy seem great, even when every day you walk by the beggars it creates on the street?"

Ben didn't have to think long to answer that question. "Everyone's just self-interested, Suresh. If they're at the bottom, nothing seems fair. If they're at the top, everything seems fair. No one has any objectivity."

Suresh's newfound smile returned to his face. He rose to his feet, and now Ben was looking up at him. He patted Ben on his shoulder. "We should try," he said. He turned to leave.

The best employee Ben and Marley had ever had, and they'd lost him so early. Ben had had no contact with Suresh in the intervening years. He didn't even know if he was still alive. He longed to reach back through time, reach out past his ignorance of Suresh's growing discontent, and offer the man something more. Different expectations, maybe. He saw now that Suresh could have been a light in his life. *We could have been friends.*

Marley's ghost, sitting next to Ben on his desk, wore a sad look. She felt the same way.

Instead, the business had launched from the promising start Suresh had helped give it to truly staggering heights, lifting Ben and Marley onto magazine covers, their names household names among the financial elite, while no one ever heard of Suresh. Payday lending had gone from a daydream to a global economic powerhouse with more shops than there were McDonald's restaurants, most of them regulated beyond belief. When they became illegal in a county or state, Ben moved them online. They were a licence to print money. If Suresh had known the gold mine he was walking away from, would he still have done so?

"You're back on top of the hierarchy again," Ben repeated to Suresh, echoing his older self's thoughts in one last attempt to persuade him. "Why leave now?"

Suresh stopped at the door, thought for a second. "I want to learn who I truly am if I have no one to be better than," he said. He walked out of the room, and out of Ben and Marley's lives.

Both Ben and – he was sure – Marley knew what was coming next, but neither spoke of it. It had lingered as an unacknowledged secret between them; they'd never discussed it since the night it happened, and Ben had never mentioned it to anyone else. He had reservations about literally revisiting the memory, and he couldn't say what kept him from avoiding it. Curiosity, to see if his memory matched Marley's? A masochistic drive to re-experience every single up and down – and embarrassment – of his roller coaster life, so he could study how he'd become who he was?

Ben had been taking flying lessons. He'd secured a loan to buy a TBM 700, which he occasionally took for joyrides in wide circles around London, above Essex, Kent, Surrey. Marley had waited until he'd got his licence before she deemed it safe to fly with him. Tonight was her first night in the plane.

"Spectacular," she said into her headset, the glittering immensity of Greater London outside her window. This was long before the Eye, the Shard, and their mates had ruined London's skyline, so the City looked more continental: everything low, unplanned, organic. A lake of light amid the surrounding countryside, it beckoned with promise.

"You can see it better in the back," Ben said. He unstrapped his seatbelt and stood.

"What? Ben, sit back down!"

"It has autopilot. It's perfectly safe."

"Okay, so at the time I believed you, but was this actually safe?"

Ben considered, crinkling his nose at the answer he quickly reached. "Not in an early nineties plane, it wasn't. I actually can't believe we did this."

Marley huffed, but left her seat and followed him. "Look at us, living on the edge, baby you and baby me."

They settled at a window in the cabin, facing the opulent city. From this height, the Thames was a serpent ribbed by bridges, the M25 an uneven nebula birthed outwards from the supernova at the city centre.

The City slid by, slow and dreamlike under the stars. The engine buzzed dimly beyond their headsets.

"This has been fun, you know," Marley said. "In spite of the pitfalls. Seeing you grow up. Seeing us start the business again. Even if it is my last hurrah, I'm glad I came back to see you."

Ben gently squeezed her arm. "I hope it's not your last hurrah."

She placed her hand on his, sighed a deep sigh. "Well, we still have plenty of Christmases left to visit, at least." Her voice was shaking a bit. In anticipation? "Pardon. My younger self wants to say something." Anxiety drained from her face, replaced by the contented delight Ben remembered so well from this night. Ben's headset amplified her voice. "We made it, Ben. You and me."

"Quite the team," he said, trying to ignore London's lights reflecting in her eyes. "Tell me, what do you think about these new quarterly reporting requirements? Are we really going to hire a whole bureaucracy to generate all these reports?"

"Ben," she said, smiling as she slid a hand onto his cheek, "leave the business out of this for a minute, hmm?"

But Ben kept blabbering like a fool. "I worry it'll allow our shareholders a window into the company they can use to dissect me. We'll need to hire PR people, I think."

"Ben," Marley repeated, her hand still on his face. He started saying something else, but she repeated a third time, "Ben."

Finally, he looked at her. Gazing up at him. His business partner. A good, reliable worker. Nothing else. Nothing more. She wasn't indescribably charming and disarming, she was just his colleague.

But some strange magnetism he couldn't resist was pulling his face towards hers.

Slowly, softly, Ben and Marley's lips touched. He shivered, as if an electric shock had run through his body.

I don't want this. I don't want this. This isn't what our relationship is supposed to be.

But these denials didn't keep him from running his hand over her cheek, of locking their lips more tightly together. Her skin soft under his touch.

They pulled away. Just a few inches. Each's eyes studying the other's. Both then and now, Ben couldn't speak. Her breath was still brushing his lips. He couldn't think. He was sure his younger self was about to say something stupid, so he headed him off.

"I'd forgotten this happened," Ben lied.

Marley exhaled a tremulous breath. "Apparently not."

"I remember wondering the next day if it had happened. We'd been drinking."

"We hadn't been drinking."

Ben's heart both leapt and broke to stand at this crossroads again, to see another path through life reopened before him – a path he hadn't taken. Did Marley feel the same way? What would their lives have been if they'd gone down that road?

Too late now, he told himself. Or was that the same denial his younger self had used as a shield? As a crutch?

"It's okay to be vulnerable," Marley's younger incarnation said, her words reaching across the years. "You can let your guard down, and I won't hurt you."

He basked in her words. A welcome salve, but a salve placed on a bullet wound that went far too deep for them to affect. London and their lives drifted past.

Okay, fine. Let me at least be honest with myself.

He cared about Marley, deeply. His affection for her had grown from the instant he'd met her; like a frog in hot water, he hadn't realised when it started to boil. Now a crisis faced him. If they became romantically entangled, and it didn't work out, the business might unravel along with it. The source of Ben's security and prosperity, traded for a woman's affection – and Ben knew not to trust women, even a woman as dedicated as Marley. She might abandon him suddenly, as Sandra had.

And what would other people think? His associates, his employees, his father? That he'd become ensnared in her get-rich-quick scheme so thoroughly that now he was sleeping with her? That he'd settled for the woman who was close instead of a woman he could have reached if he spent a few more years climbing higher?

"I can't..." Ben began, words catching in his throat. "Whatever this is, whatever you want me to be, I can't be that for you," he said.

Her hand still resting on his cheek, she ran her fingertips over his stubble with a tenderness that threatened to consume him.

"Why not?" Marley asked, her voice a whisper in the headset. "We could be..."

"You're not an appropriate romantic partner for me," Ben said, tearing his gaze away from her to face out the window. He didn't want to see her reaction.

No sound but the hum of the engines, and then, "What do you mean by that?"

What did he mean? She wasn't socially graceful enough to run in the truly elite circles Ben aspired to join? She didn't have the conventional physicality of the trophy wife Ben thought he deserved? Or did he need to see other people as stepping stones so he wouldn't feel stepped upon, and this opportunism extended even to Marley? Or was it all these, and more?

"This is a painful memory for me," Marley said, her voice cracking. "What is it like for you?"

It was a confusing hell, calling back into question decisions Ben had tried desperately to convince himself he'd been sure about. Marley's affection for him was a precious, glimmering flame in a cold, cruel world. Had he really imagined he needed to trade it for status, then done so easily? Would he really have lost anything by acting on his feelings for her?

Would he have become a better man?

"Are you in there?" a deep, gravelly voice breathed next to them.

Ben's rational mind caught him just before he glanced to the side, which would've given him away. He saw enough of the phantom in his peripheral vision. Its staff glowed green above their heads.

Marley and Ben stared at each other, locked in place one moment by old emotional wounds, newly fresh, the next by sheer panic.

The Ghost of Christmas Past manoeuvred between them, studying their faces. It turned to Ben first, and he stayed utterly still, locking his fear deep so it wouldn't show on his face. It turned to Marley, and Ben had a second to think.

So the ghost *had* chosen a memory it was sure they'd visit, and lurked in wait. But why this one? How had the ghost known of Marley and Ben's history, or that this night would be so meaningful to both of them? Had it interrogated her in the afterlife?

He needed to let the memory play out if they had any hope of convincing the ghost they weren't here. What had he said next? Had they talked longer, or had he returned to the cockpit? In the terror of the moment, Ben couldn't remember.

The phantom turned back to Ben, its hood concealing its face in darkness. Unseen eyes looked at him keenly.

For how long could they stay hidden inside their younger selves' bodies? Could it reach Marley's spirit, sequestered in there? Surely Ralph or Marley would've told him about this cheat if it was a way to stay safe indefinitely. But if the ghost could reach in and grab her... why didn't it?

No sooner had he thought this than the spirit reached out a bony hand... towards Ben.

It was long past time to run a test.

But they had nowhere to run. The plane was tiny, and with the ghost so near, it would tag along anywhere Ben transported them. And it wasn't as if he could jump out of the plane.

Ben stopped his racing thoughts, considered for a moment. *Could* he jump out of the plane?

"Marley," Ben said, keeping his voice even. "I have to tell you something, and I want you to listen to me very carefully."

The spirit paused, its hand frozen halfway to Ben. Ben's words could have fit right into his and Marley's previous conversation. Hypothetically, the ghost had no way of knowing they didn't.

"Okay," Marley said, her breathing a little too quick.

Ben readied himself, built up some nerve. Found the staff he'd originally stolen from this unearthly being on the floor, and gripped it. If he was wrong, he was about to get Marley killed. But he wasn't wrong.

"Run for the cockpit," Ben said. He immediately jumped to the other side of the plane, unlatched the door and lifted it. Freezing air pummelled him as the plane hurtled through the sky. Directly below, the dark Surrey countryside yawned like a void.

He checked behind him. Marley had dived into the cockpit and was huddled in the passenger seat.

The ghost ignored her. It flew straight at Ben.

He had no time to think through the implications that the ghost was there for him, not for her. Ben leapt out of the plane.

Rushing air pulled his headset off into the darkness. The roar of the atmosphere he was falling through quickly replaced the buzz of the plane. Its shrinking lights and London's golden exuberance supplied his only frames of reference. All else was black.

Ben was no expert skydiver, but he'd skydived before. It scared the piss out of him – Marley was the one who enjoyed it – but he could at least keep himself from spinning out and losing consciousness. He hoped he could do the manoeuvre he planned, especially while clutching this staff for dear life. Its presence in his hand jeopardised his arch position, destabilising his fall.

Focus... focus...

His life was in no real danger from the fall, he hoped. When he and Marley had first arrived in his memories, back at their post-pitch celebration with Suresh, he'd tried fleeing from the pub only to find it back in front of him, because he had no memory of anything other than the pub. Thus, his reasoning went, he had no memory of jumping out of his aeroplane, so the memory would naturally lead him right back to...

There it was, maybe a thousand yards beneath him, its tail light blinking. Ben's Socata rising from the darkness. He was falling right towards it, and so was the ghost above him. The green light of its staff was... right on top of him!

Something yanked on Ben's staff, nearly wresting it from his grasp. In the darkness, he saw nothing but the light of the two staffs, until the phantom drew its hood near to the jade light at the top of Ben's. Its cloak fluttered wildly as it fell with him. It reached a hand around the green light and smothered it.

Ben panicked. Had it just disabled his means of escape? The light was completely gone. But no. The ghost removed its hand and the light immediately returned. Only now the light was a flaming, cardinal red.

As soon as the phantom let go, Ben spun his body and brandished the staff like a cricket bat to strike the thing in its midsection as hard as he could. It grunted, and tumbled away into the night.

It took Ben several seconds to reorient his body after that stunt. The new red light at the top of his staff distracted him, and he almost missed grabbing hold of the plane as he passed. The plane wasn't in freefall like Ben was – in real life, he'd never have had the skill nor the muscle to re-enter a plane like this, falling from above it. But memory is memory, and Ben easily grabbed the open door and slipped back into the plane, closer to where the recollection wanted to play itself out.

"Ben!" Marley called, climbing out of the cockpit to reach him. He reached out his arms to hug her in relief, but she shouted: "It's right behind you!"

Ben spun. A green light outside the door grew rapidly brighter: the thing's staff as it approached.

Was there enough distance between them and the phantom that it wouldn't be able to follow? Even if not, Ben had no time. He sprang towards Marley, embraced her, and transported them to the nearest other memory.

He realised immediately that this had been a terrible mistake.

A Man Who Achieves

No light escapes from a black hole. The memory in which Ben now found himself had warped any light he found elsewhere in his life, compressing the enormity of his years on the Earth into a single dark decision – the imploded star of the man he might have been had this night never happened. It gripped him like an overwhelming colossus of gravity. He tried to visualise other memories and use the staff to escape, but the scene before him wouldn't let him close his eyes, wouldn't let him pause or fast-forward. His feet shambled inexorably down the hospital halls. He greeted the ward staff, straining to break free from the memory, but it pulled him with implacable force, distending his mind as he fell deeper into it.

"What's the matter?" Marley's ghost asked, muffled, far away. "Where are we?"

The Ghost of Christmas Past hadn't appeared. They were free of it, for a spell. *But Marley must not be allowed to see this. I cannot let her know this about me.*

The defining event of Ben's life had played out late at night, in a small hospital room in Rochester. He hadn't been there before nor since, and he'd buried the memory deep inside himself, but it was still so crisp, vivid. The stench of disinfectant and vomit and vaguely sweet decay. White linoleum, green wallpaper. Blinds swaying gently in too-cold air conditioning. A token Christmas tree half a yard tall on a desk by the bed.

He spoke with the nurse about his father's condition, then willed his feet to turn back towards the exit. They wouldn't comply. Instead, they compelled him to the bed. Ben often wondered whether he, and all people, were just clumps of atoms playing out their scripts. It seemed he had no choice now but to act out his.

In his hand he held a briefcase. He set it and the staff on the floor beside his father's bed. He pulled up a chair and sat. The nurse left and shut the door behind her.

"Oh, Ben," Marley said.

Graham Scrooge had lost about a third of his body weight. His muscles were sinew, not a bit of fat on them. He hadn't shaved in weeks. Cords snaked into his arms and beneath his bedsheets, a thin tube of oxygen up to a nasal cannula at his nostrils. Crackling breaths escaped his lungs with difficulty, and irregular-shaped, dark red splotches covered his skin wherever it was visible: his arms, his face. Illness aside, Ben's father was older than he remembered, his face more wrinkled, and his hair, which had been black when Ben had last seen him, now mostly grey.

Graham opened his eyes. They were unfocused, looking at nothing in particular, and the mere effort of keeping his eyelids up seemed to tax him.

"Ben?" he said, his voice a wheezing murmur.

Ben kept resisting the powerful memory, but his lips moved without his consent, speaking words he'd first spoken in 1992.

"Are you in pain?" Ben asked.

Beeping monitors combined with his father's crepitant breath to form sickly music. At first, Ben thought he hadn't heard him, but seconds later, he said, "They say I... I don't have long now."

"They're going to give you lots of meds," Ben said. "You won't feel any pain."

He marvelled at this once-imposing man, hollowed to a husk. The power that had made Ben feel so insignificant in childhood and beyond had dwindled so much that he was actually able to feel sorry for him.

Each of us has a certain amount of time with health and vigour, and those give us the power to act, to affect things. But that influence eventually fades. Eventually, I and everyone who dies a slow death will have time at the end of our lives – and apparently afterwards – to evaluate what we did with the time we had.

How far away was Ben's own life from that time of reflection? How would he feel about his life once he'd got there?

"What is it like to die?" Ben asked Marley's ghost on a whim. He hadn't asked this with the intention of evading the memory, but evade it, it did. Graham said nothing while Marley was speaking.

"Well, the anticipation is terrifying. Especially when it's sudden, like my heart attack. Knowing you're leaving the world when there's so much left you need to say and do." She wiped her eyes. Ben hadn't seen a tear forming. Could ghosts cry? "The transition itself isn't so bad, though. One moment you're here, the next... you're somewhere else."

No health conditions threatened Ben's life, yet he was already terrified in anticipation of his own death. At his age, it became a statistical possibility no matter one's current health. Perhaps this fear was one factor behind his workaholism. Immersing himself in the present and the near future kept him from thinking too deeply about the farther future.

"Tell me a happy story, lad. What were you doing..." Graham took an effortful inhalation – "last Christmas?"

Ben had half a mind to keep speaking with Marley to avoid this final conversation with his dad, but he couldn't do so forever. So he turned back.

"I, uh, went for a romantic plane ride around London," Ben said. He paid no attention to Marley's reaction to this description of last Christmas.

"Hmm," Graham muttered. His lips moved like he was chewing. "That was my last real Christmas. I learnt about this AIDS bollocks a few days after." His glazy eyes focused a bit. He tilted his head to get a better look at Ben. "The magazines are talking about a cure. And medicine to keep you alive. You don't suppose..." – a weak cough – "they have any of that here at the hospital?"

"I don't think it exists yet, Dad."

"Hmm." Graham closed his eyes. "Maybe we can just ask the virus to go away."

Despite himself, Ben actually patted his dad's arm to comfort him. "I don't think viruses can be reasoned with," he said. "They're following the behaviour instilled in them by evolution, competing with other germs and with your immune system."

Graham chuckled, and it turned into a crackling cough. "Competing so fiercely they don't realise they're destroying the very thing they're competing for... heh."

Ben pulled his hand away, picked up his briefcase.

"I'm not a queer," Graham blurted. "Don't you let anyone ever talk about your old man like I was a queer."

Ben paused, the briefcase halfway to his lap. He didn't know what to say to that, so he said, "Sure, Dad."

"There's a good lad." Graham's jaw made that chewing motion again. "Annie gonna come and say goodbye?"

Anxiety so strong in his chest that he felt his ribs might break, Ben rested his arms on his briefcase. Both then and now, it dared him to open it, and he feared the dare. This had seemed quite amusing in the planning stage, but actually going through with it? Surely his all-powerful father, dying though he was, would learn what Ben had done and find some way to get revenge.

Nonsense, Ben tried to reassure himself. *I have the power now.*

"Annie doesn't have enough money for a plane or train ticket," Ben said. "And she doesn't have a car right now. But she told me she spoke with you this morning. Is that right?"

"Oh." Graham's eyes defocused again, staring at the ceiling. "Oh, yes, we did talk. She said... She said goodbye. Will I never see my daughter again?"

Ben didn't answer. He unclasped his briefcase and opened it on his lap. Inside rested a pen and some papers attached to a clipboard.

"What's this?" Marley asked, peeking over his shoulder.

How could he possibly answer that question? "This..." Ben started. He removed the briefcase's contents, gripped them in his hands like a grenade with its pin about to be pulled. "This is the worst thing I've ever done."

Ben held the clipboard for Graham to see. "Dad, the hospital needs you to sign some papers."

"Oh?"

"Yes, this just gives them the authority to release your body to me, if the worst should happen."

"There's paperwork for that?"

"I'm sorry. They've asked me to have you sign it."

Graham grunted, tried to push himself up in his bed, failed.

"Here, I can hold it for you. You have to sign in three places."

Ben's father clutched the pen and got to work on his first signature. Halting and slow though he was, the signature was perfect, easily recognisable as Graham's.

"Have I made enough of a mark... on the world?" Graham asked.

Where had that thought come from? From marking the paper? Ben flipped to the next signature page. "You wanted to make a mark?" he asked politely, not caring about the answer.

Graham signed his name a second time. His voice was a weak mumble, difficult to understand. "I think I did make a mark, in you. In the kids I raised. Even if I die, maybe my life will echo, through you." He smiled the wan smile of a dying man trying to convince himself of his own immortality.

But in a way, wasn't Graham right? Hadn't Ben given power to his dad's ideas even in Ben's own old age? Didn't he often wonder what his father would have thought of various decisions he made?

Each action Ben took would then pass a little bit of his father into all those affected by it, diffusing Graham's ethos across London, the UK, eventually the world.

And who had influenced Graham? Through Graham, the ideas of anyone who'd influenced him were impacting the world still. This chain of influence stretching back through the generations, newly visible to Ben, awed him. *The past has so, so much power over the future.*

Ben turned to the last page. One last signature. Graham signed, and in so doing, he unknowingly signed his entire estate over to Ben. His investments, his house, his car. With the stroke of a pen, Ben took him for everything he had.

Marley seemed to realise this as she skimmed the pages Ben had flipped to. She raised a hand to her mouth in shock.

Having finally avenged his childhood self, Ben tucked the papers back into the briefcase. He clasped it shut. "Thank you, Dad."

"What about Annie?" Marley asked. "She needed that money. Badly, from the sounds of it. What about little Frieda?"

Indeed, in Graham's real will, he'd left everything to Annie. But Ben's hatred for his father burnt far stronger than his love for her. *She'll find her way, like I did,* Ben's younger self thought, excusing his theft. A cold void gaped within his older self's soul: a wound he'd inflicted upon himself, an injury he deserved to carry.

Annie would complete suicide in a few short months. Frieda would be left motherless, off to be raised by a dad who didn't want her.

Would this have been different if Ben hadn't stolen Annie's inheritance? Perhaps not. Ben hadn't spoken much to Annie in the years prior to her death. Perhaps she'd been depressed enough that their dad's money would've done nothing to improve her condition.

But perhaps her material problems had been a great source of mental stress. Perhaps, if Ben hadn't done this, she would have lived.

Marley was shaking her head, backing away from Ben, from the bed, from what she'd just witnessed. "You didn't need that money," she whispered.

Ben sat with his shame. With the memory of his younger self feeling proud that now he was the big man, his father small.

"Well, Dad, I've got to be off. Good seeing you again. Take care."

Ben grabbed his briefcase and staff and stood to leave, but he stopped when Graham didn't respond. "Dad, did you hear me? I'm leaving."

Graham's eyes were still open, glazy, unfocused. Unmoving. The crackling from his lungs had stopped.

Ben looked closer. A chill took him. He'd got to Graham just in time.

An alarm sounded on one of Graham's monitors. Marley pressed her back against the far wall, shaking her head. The nurse rushed back in, checked her patient, called for help. Soon a whole swarm of hospital workers had gathered around Graham's bed, trying to revive him. He hadn't signed a DNR order.

Ben felt nothing. No joy, no sorrow. Even the satisfaction of revenge drained away now that his father had suddenly, actually died. *When a man who caused so much misery passes from this world, what should I feel? Gladness that he can never harm anyone else? Disappointment at his waste of his years?*

A soft glow bloomed on the deathbed. Light that didn't touch the room around it, leaving the nurses' faces and the room's walls illuminated only by the overhead lights. The glow seemed to light up the air itself.

A transparent apparition rose from the bed. Graham, bending at the hip to sit up, but Ben could see right through him. Eyes wide, his father's ghost lifted a hand and examined it. He turned back to look at his body lying lifeless on the bed.

Ben stared, utterly confused. *What am I seeing? Graham's soul leaving his body?* Ben had no memory of that – how could he?

And yet, it was happening. Ben was seeing now what he hadn't seen the first time this had happened. Graham's ghost, aged yet healthy, pivoted his head to take in the whole room. His gaze stopped to rest on Ben. His eyes narrowed.

"Lad?"

Ben froze. This was not part of his memory. *What's happening?*

Graham's ghost looked past Ben, to the room's far corner. "Is that that Marley whore you're always traipsing around with? Why do you both look so old?"

Ben patted his chest to check that his spirit was still inside his younger self's physical body. How could Graham see him? The real, future Ben? How could he see Marley?

Before Ben could bring words to his lips, a large, dark shape osmosed through the window from the night outside. Its cloak spilt to the floor. Ben's hand tight around his staff, he stepped back towards Marley.

"I don't get it," he said to her. "How'd it find us so fast this time?"

Ben's dad could see it, too. He crept backwards, spider-walking along the bed until he reached the headboard and could go no farther. The phantom glided, clicking its staff against the ground every few moments, as if mimicking steps.

The nurses' activity around Graham slowed. One of them announced the time of death. Graham looked up at the spirit, the very image of the Grim Reaper. It reached out its emaciated hand towards him, palm sideways. As if asking Graham to take its hand. It ignored Ben and Marley entirely.

Ben puzzled over what he was seeing. "I don't think it did find us," Marley whispered to him. "I think maybe we're seeing the Ghost of Christmas Past... in its past."

"What? That's absurd. How?"

"I don't know," Marley said. Ben prepared his mind to jump them into a new memory now that this one had played itself out. The light at the top of his staff was crimson now. The phantom had tinkered with it, just briefly. But it had done something important to it.

"No," Graham said to the spirit. "I'm not ready yet. I've got decades ahead of me. You're not taking me. Not tonight."

With the swift reflex of a predator, the spirit lurched forward and grabbed Graham's throat. He choked. It examined his face. Its robes drifted around it as if gravity were a minor rule by which they were only occasionally bound.

A terrifying thought pried into Ben's mind: could he save his father? All these years after the man's death, had the universe presented him a chance to atone for his life's worst decision? He'd used his staff offensively against Ralph, transporting him away to another time. Thus far, he hadn't had the nerve to try this against the Ghost of Christmas Past.

But do I want to save him? And what would it mean if I do? Would Graham's spirit then roam with Ben and Marley through Ben's memories, another soul snatched from the clutches of the afterlife? Waiting around with them until, inevitably, the phantom caught them?

Ben willed his feet forward. He brandished the staff like a weapon.

"Ben, what are you doing?" Marley said.

"You there," Ben called out. "Spirit."

It turned its hidden gaze on Ben. The light at the top of its staff was also red, and Ben saw now that they were indeed the exact same staff, gnarled and disfigured. Ben's was the future version of the same object.

"Help me, lad," Graham croaked. "Get this sod off me."

Ben readied the staff, but before he could strike, one of the nurses approached him cautiously. "Excuse me sir, what are you doing? I'm so sorry for your loss. Do you need some kind of help?"

Ben kept his gaze on the phantom, lest it lunge at him, and tried to organise his confused mind. "What do you mean?" he asked the nurse.

"I'm just wondering what you're doing with this piece of wood," the nurse said of the staff.

This interaction, too, had certainly not happened in Ben's memory.

A hand came to rest on Ben's shoulder. "Not now, Marley. Stay away from the ghost. I don't want it to..."

His voice trailed off as a second hand came to rest on his other shoulder. As the red light of a *third* staff hovered above his head.

Ben swallowed. He looked up. The Ghost of Christmas Past, on the bed assaulting Graham, also stood right behind Ben. Towering above him.

There were two of them.

Ben's mind reeled. Both versions of the phantom appraised each other. The one on the bed nodded to the one behind Ben. It lifted

Graham's spirit by the neck, flew to the window, and carried Ben's father away.

Without thinking, and fearing for his life, Ben queued up his memories and aimed for the earliest one, Christmas at age three or four, as far back as he could go, irrationally trying to put some distance between the phantom and Marley, as if it couldn't come back for her here at any time. As if it were there for her at all.

The light at the top of his staff pulsed, and so did the light above the phantom's staff. By the time Ben realised it was trying to transport him somewhere, too, he'd already initiated his own journey into the past. The hospital walls exploded outwards, the bed fell sideways into nothingness. Ben's destination vanished from his mind as he and the spirit hurtled through memory. Flashes of events Ben had never lived through whizzed past him. Impossible memories of what looked like the Trinity Test, Napoleon's defeat at Waterloo, the fall of Constantinople.

Onward they travelled, further and further back...

Christmas Past

en landed hard on his chest in a pile of rotting leaves. It knocked the wind out of him. He scrambled to right himself, to fill his lungs with air, to get his bearings.

He sat at the edge of a forest. Dusk was ebbing over the horizon. The silhouette of some kind of house lurked in the evening gloom, but darkness obscured its details. Loud voices trilled inside. A dirt road led, presumably, to civilisation, but nowhere else in the vast landscape surrounding him were there signs of people.

Where am I? When *am I?*

He was certainly in no memory of his own. Had the phantom taken him to one of *its* memories? If so, why? And what the hell had just happened in the hospital ward?

Ben searched the ground for his staff, but the instant he found it a bony hand snatched it up. The phantom billowed up from the leaves, its robes seeming to inflate around it. It now carried two staffs: Ralph's and its own.

I have no way to get out of here.

It had caught him, utterly. He couldn't run, couldn't hide, had no chance of defeating it in physical combat. Could he somehow reason with it? He didn't know a thing about it.

The phantom raised its arms in a V-shape above its hood, a staff clutched in each hand as if to strike Ben. Ben had no time to ponder the end, to ponder death, only time to flinch away and brace himself for the blow.

The blow didn't come. He reopened his eyes. The phantom hadn't moved. It hovered in the same menacing posture, about to strike.

But it didn't. After a few more moments, it slowly lowered its staffs. A sigh drifted out from within its hood. A low-pitched, raspy breath.

The spirit turned. It hovered out of the woods, towards the house, away from Ben.

It's letting me live?

But of course, it would. Hadn't Ralph said the spirits couldn't harm a living person? As far as Ben knew, his body was still alive in the present, unconscious in the bedroom while his soul took a trip through his memories. Or perhaps his security had found him by now and transported him to hospital. Did time work the same way in memories? He'd been reliving them for, subjectively, weeks.

Stay safe, Marley. I'll find a way back to that hospital room. You won't stay trapped in that horrible memory for long.

Lost in the phantom's memories, he wasn't about to go wandering around. Whatever its plans for him, he had to face it. He plodded through the leaves, across a field of wild grass. The phantom was silhouetted against the setting sun, an ominous scarecrow. Ben stopped right next to it. He listened for its breath but heard none. It made no motion to acknowledge Ben's presence. It simply gazed at the house, and thus so did Ben.

A woman walked the premises lighting torches and lamps, so Ben could soon make out details. The house was made of stone and plaster, a modest structure with an attached courtyard enclosed by a stone fence. People laughing and chatting in a language Ben didn't recognise filled both the courtyard and the house. The women wore long tunics while the men wore short tunics and trousers. All were bundled against the cold in thick cloaks, but spirits seemed high. A musician dodged a band of running children as he played lively music on a strange-looking double flute, and circular tables positioned about the courtyard held food of which everyone freely partook. A spear-throwing contest was taking place at the edge of the grounds. Off to one side of the courtyard, several people were kneeling in prayer at a shrine.

"What is this?" Ben dared to ask.

The phantom stirred but did not look at him. "Christmas," it replied.

"Christmas?" Ben asked sceptically. "Where's the tree? Where's baby Christ in the manger?" But as soon as he'd said this, a pair of women presented a small object of some kind to a third woman – a Christmas gift? – who lifted her hands and grinned in surprise.

"Oh, I get it," Ben said. "I was trying to take you to one of my earliest memories at the same time you were trying to take me somewhere else. Our plans got jumbled, and we ended up going to one of *your* earliest memories. Is that right?"

The phantom said nothing for a long moment, then muttered, "The earliest memory of the part of me that is spirit, that is immortal. Yes."

Ben eyed him sideways. "And part of you is human? A soul like Ralph who chose this service to avoid punishment in the afterlife?"

The phantom gripped its staffs tightly, its hands winding tighter, choking the wood as if it were alive. Abruptly, it flung both staffs aside, well away from Ben's reach. Over the course of a dozen heartbeats, it turned its head to him. Chill wind ballooned its hood. The fabric undulated, and it raised its hand as if to hold it in place. Instead, it lifted the fabric back, and pulled it all the way over its all-too-human head.

Ben took in the phantom's parched eyes, its purple, rotting flesh. The thin wisps of white hair falling in patches from what was left of its scalp.

He turned back to the house. Nodded to himself. Accepted it. *Well, who else's face did I expect to see beneath that hood?*

"Why did you choose to become a ghost of time?" Ben asked. "To come back and terrorise me?"

"It's not unheard of," his father said from hoarse, dead vocal cords, his voice deeper than it had been in life. "Dead people who want revenge and volunteer for the service just so we can reach you mortals again."

Ben huffed derisively. "Surely someone is supposed to police you. Otherwise every petty hateful dead person would volunteer, and every ghost there is would be out for blood."

"Ah, but that's why I became a Ghost of the *Past*, lad. We hold all the power. Long as I don't draw too much attention to myself, I can get away with things the Present and Future Ghosts can't."

"And still it took you over thirty years, didn't it?" Ben said. "Thirty-some years to build up enough trust that finally, when someone close to me died, none of the other ghosts would be watching when you let Marley escape from Hell. So you could follow her to Earth and get to me."

Graham chuckled, smoothed his billowing cloak with both frail hands, but he didn't respond. Ben took that to mean he'd guessed correctly.

"I must know, lad, did you love me?" Graham asked out of nowhere.

Or perhaps not out of nowhere. His father had had decades to reflect on what he'd done wrong in life. To wonder about every human connection he'd ever had, about whether anyone truly loved or cared about him. Maybe death had softened him to the point that he could now relate to Ben as a human being rather than as the hard bloke he'd always tried to present as.

Still, Ben couldn't possibly honour Graham's question with an answer. One's love for an emotionally abusive parent is complicated, if it exists at all.

Graham nodded at Ben's lack of response, and turned his attention back to the celebration eighty yards away. "*Dies Natalis Solis Invicti*," he said. Ben hadn't known him to speak Latin during life. It must have been a perk of inheriting the spirit of the Ghost of Christmas Past. "Sometime around year four hundred of the common era, somewhere in Italy. Christians would later change this festival of the sun god into their own celebration. But even now, this is Christmas. One of the first."

"Rome?" Ben asked. "This is the ancient Roman Empire?"

Someone shouted at the fringe of the party. A man, pointing right at Ben and his father. He called over to the spear throwers, waving them to him.

"We'd best get into the woods," Graham said, retrieving both staffs from the grass.

Ben's gaze darted back and forth between the Romans and his dad. "They can see us, even though we're spirits? Or... wait a minute, we're actually here? This isn't a memory. We've..." The phantom that was his father floated swiftly over the grass, back into the trees.

"We've travelled through time," Ben said, trying to process it. As the Roman men gathered around the one who'd spotted Ben, he ran to catch up with Graham. He couldn't run well. The night was freezing cold, and Ben wore nothing but his usual pyjamas. His knees ached fiercely. Amid his flurry of thoughts when he'd arrived here, minutes ago, he'd wondered why he had a physical body in a place and time he had no memory of. In all the other memories, he'd been a spirit that could optionally choose to inhabit his younger self's body.

Here, he had no younger self. Here, he was old again, in his real body.

This is real. This is happening. I've leapt into the distant past.

That must have been what Graham had done to his staff when he'd changed its light from green to red. He'd changed it from a memory travel device into a true time travel device. Which meant...

"The hospital!" Ben said, reaching the phantom and jogging next to him. "That wasn't a memory, either. That was real. We were really in the past."

Graham said nothing. He continued relentlessly deeper into the thick woods.

Dominoes kept falling in Ben's head. "You saw us, me and Marley," he said. "Just after you died, before the previous phantom took you away. You heard me talk about the Ghost of Christmas Past. That's how you knew to become him when the opportunity arose."

Ben stopped running, stopped walking, halted completely as the full weight of this realisation hit him. *It was me who gave him the idea. From the moment of his death, he knew exactly how he could get back to me.*

The phantom was approaching a tall bluff overlooking a valley. A nearly full moon lit rivers of fog as they drifted among forested hillocks. Snowcapped peaks dominated the distance. There were no human settlements as far as the eye could see.

Ben collapsed onto the ground next to him. "Give me a staff. If they truly let us travel through time, with the red light, let me go back, please. Let me fix my mistakes."

Graham made a *tsk, tsk, tsk* noise and shook his head. "That isn't a power meant for human hands. Even I can't change things. Believe me, I've tried. The past may be more real than memory, but it's much less malleable."

Ben's voice threatened to dissolve into sobbing, but he wouldn't let it. Not in front of his father. "What did you try to change?" he asked. "Annie? Did you try to save Annie?"

"I tried to stop you from stealing all my money on my deathbed. I suppose that counts as trying to save Annie."

"Where is she now? Have you seen her, in the afterlife?"

Graham hung his head, which looked terribly eerie on a dead man's thin neck, like his head might actually fall off. "No, lad. I can only hope she's in a better place than us."

"Than you, you mean," Ben snapped. "I'm not dead yet."

"Yet," Graham said.

"You intend to kill your son, is that it? Is that why you've returned?"

Graham crouched and examined Ben at his level. The cold bit into Ben's skin. He wrapped his arms around his torso.

His father didn't seem to feel or even notice the cold. "Such bitterness, boy. Tell me, where did I go wrong with you? You know and I know that I never laid a hand on you, so don't tell me I did. The opposite, actually. I gave you all the tools you needed to succeed in life."

"'You're not good enough, you're too weak, you're more like a girl than a man,'" Ben said with pointed enmity. "Those were your 'tools'? Every hour of every day for my entire childhood?"

"It's how my old man raised me."

"So? Why would anyone pass that on to their own kid?"

Graham pulled back and considered this – perhaps a brief moment of true introspection. A moment later, the same obstinate defensiveness that always took him during arguments reasserted itself. He pursed his lips and seemed to speak as much to convince himself as to convince Ben. "It kept me tough. Helped me survive. It did the same for you."

"But at what cost? It hurt, Dad. It still hurts."

"I wanted you to have a better life than I did! And it worked, lad. It worked. Look at all you've achieved. Do you really give a shit if you got your feelings hurt a little along the way?"

Well then. So much for any hope of death having softened Graham. Ben stood in spite of the cold. In life, he'd stood head-to-head with his father, even as a young man. As the Ghost of Christmas Past, Graham was much taller. Ben felt like a child again, like the monster in his bedroom had manifested in real life.

"I'm not you," Ben said. "I won't be on my deathbed, wondering if I've made a mark for the sake of making a mark. Wondering if I've climbed high enough in the hierarchy." Even as he said this, he knew it was a lie. "You have no power over me any more."

Graham snorted. "You still think about me all the time, don't you? I'm always in the back of your mind."

Ben swallowed a biting retort. "I... You..." He couldn't bring himself to deny Graham's claim.

"Yes, it was the same with me and my old man. He's with me still. Not in the flesh, like me with you. Hell, I can go back to the birth of Christ or the age of the dinosaurs, long before the ghost in me was even born, but I still spend half my time just watching my pops, working myself into a rage over him. Or watching you, ungrateful git you turned out to be."

All right, that's enough. Whatever Graham's own internal turmoil, he'd made himself unreachable. Ben couldn't help him. There was no hope for reconciliation. *Time to go on the offensive.*

"And how would your old man feel about your git of a son achieving astronomically more success in life than you did?"

The phantom dropped its staffs and lunged at him. Clutched his throat as its predecessor had clutched Graham's on his deathbed. Lifted him, gagging, towards the moon.

"You did *not* achieve more than me! You mooched off a woman, you narcissistic joke. You got a lucky business idea in a lucky economic environment, and it's caused nothing but pain and despair. I built a real life and supported my kids with the sweat on my back. You cheated and got away with it."

"And that makes you a real man and me a sissy, does it?" Ben rasped.

"Damn right. I had half a mind to pull that bitch back to Hell after all, after what she allowed you to become."

"You mean after she empowered me to be happy and successful in a way you couldn't control? After she replaced you in my life?"

Graham tightened his grip on Ben's throat, not quite tight enough to cut circulation. He tugged at the phantom's massive hands, choking.

"You can't harm me," Ben sputtered. "It's against the rules. Spirits can't hurt the living."

"I see no one here to stop me, lad. Those rules were set by other spirits; they aren't divine law." A smile full of decomposing teeth spread across Graham's face. "Seems I can make a mark on the world yet."

He threw Ben to the ground. Ben gasped and clutched his neck. Firelight shone harshly in his face, which made no sense. He squinted. It wasn't a fire at all. It was the phantom's staff, lying in the grass not three yards away.

Graham hovered to the edge of the precipice, a wraith haunting the pastoral landscape. He gazed up at the moon. "I don't know much about time," he said. "I do know that it fights me when I try to change it. When I try to make sure you never got rich, you never met that woman. You never left my house. Not till you were ready to be a man in the world. And show me some respect." He reached a cloaked arm towards the horizon, as if beckoning forth the *autostrade* and wine fields and a glorious future. "I can only change little things. Where you put an item or what I ate for breakfast. But what if there were two of us, playacting our parts, trying to change the way things turned out? Would the timeline be so stubborn then?" He spun to face Ben. "So now you're going to come back with me. Relive—"

He caught Ben in mid-scramble. Ben grabbed one of the staffs – Ralph's, it turned out – and tried to focus on the memory he needed. If the staff could transport him to other times prior to his life, he couldn't tell. Perhaps his mortal mind was confined to travel only among the Christmases he'd lived.

Graham's smirk vanished. He charged him. Ben narrowed his attention to a pinpoint. *The hospital, the hospital.* The black hole should've been easy to concentrate on, but the distraction of his enraged father was too much. He reached him and clutched his arm with crushing force. "Drop it."

Ben held fast and tried to focus on the right memory. Graham grabbed his own staff of deformed wood off the ground.

"You haven't had enough dashing about? Lad, I'm off my usual leads until Marley goes back to the underworld. I've got all the time in the world."

Ben found the memory. He catapulted himself across time. The moon fell into the stars, the mountains flattened.

His father's dying hospital room coalesced around him.

Around *them.* The phantom still clenched his arm, past the point of bruising, almost to breaking. Ben gritted his teeth against the pain.

"I would let you change the past, too," Graham said. "Give yourself that girl you liked back when." He ran his hand over the top of Ben's staff, changing the light there from red back to green. Restricting him from true time travel, back to the realm of memory. Graham's voice grew deeper, quivering with a suppressed fury Ben had no desire to see loosed. "You want to abandon me again?" It was an accusation, maybe a threat, not a plea.

Marley, in ghostly form, bellowed a war cry and brought a chair down on the ghost's head. The phantom crumpled, let go of Ben.

"Run!" Ben said. Marley dashed out of the room just behind him. Porters jumped out of their way as he triggered the staff. It glowed brighter, and the ceiling split open. Hospital rooms collapsed into oblivion beside them.

"I'll keep hunting you!" Graham called down the hallway. "I'll never stop!"

An upscale office party from their late middle years: 2015? 2016? Ben couldn't tell. He couldn't take it all in, he was so panicked. Gleaming ornaments spun round him. Men in suits, women in red-and-green dresses. Several women in suits and even a bearded person in a dress, because this was the 2010s. Wine glasses. Christmas trees lit from beneath. A band. A spectacular view of London at night from high above it.

Ben collapsed next to a fireplace, and Marley with him. She was a ghost in a younger body again, only this body wasn't quite so young.

"What happened? Are you okay?"

"That—" Ben's throat caught. He massaged it, tried to clear it. "That thing is my dad."

"What?"

"The Past Ghost. This is all about me, not you."

"Yes, I know, you've been telling me that since I was thirty, but could you be more specific?"

Ben inhaled deeply, exhaled deliberately. His thudding heart started to slow. The Christmas party steadied around him until he stopped feeling as if the wrong step would fling him centuries into the past.

He closed his eyes. "Sometime after my father died, he became the Ghost of Christmas Past. He freed you on purpose, to create an emergency that would let him get to me. Now he wants to take me back with him to try and rewrite our past."

Marley digested this. With each passing second, she looked nearer to being sick. She raised both hands to her face, massaged her eyes.

Now that Ben knew the full nature of their predicament, his analytical mind ought to have been running wild with potential solutions, creative ways out. But he was too stunned. His dad was still around, to this day, pulling strings. Immortal, supposedly. *Could he be killed, if it came to that? How do you kill a ghost?*

It was all Ben could do to stay present, grounded in the here and now with Marley, watching three people standing in a semicircle above them. Apparently, Ben and Marley had arrived at midnight, in mid-conversation. Anika, a twenty-two-year-old fashion model, was resplendent in her red dress: Ben's date for the night. And Brian, a rather good-looking doctor, lingered close to Marley.

"I'd forgot you dated that bloke," Ben said. "For what, two years?"

Marley blew a dismissive puff through her lips. "A boy toy. Eight months."

"Hmm. Felt like longer."

Frieda, the last member of the group, looked just like Annie had at her age. A bit older than Anika, which Ben had felt odd about, even at the time. She'd needed a career boost, so her Uncle Ben had invited her here to network.

Ben motioned towards the group. "Do you want to..."

A faint scowl crossed Marley's face. "Do I want to what? Join the party?"

"We should try to blend in. It'll give us time to escape if my dad finds us again."

"Ben, we need to plan. Really think about how we get out of this."

Just now, Ben couldn't think. "I don't know that there is any getting out of this." Without even glancing at Marley's reaction to his words, he left his physical body and drifted towards the giant window. His slightly younger self sprang into action behind him, bragging about Frieda to his guests. He'd felt so guilty about Annie, he'd have done anything for her daughter.

When Marley joined the conversation behind him, warning Frieda that if she entered the business world she needed to be tough and ruthless, to keep her emotions in check, to own every room she was in or the men would walk all over her – "No offence, Ben" – he knew her spirit had also left the memory of her body.

Ben stopped at the window. London below him. Reflections of the Christmas party behind him. Marley's ghost stepping up beside him.

They stood in silence for a long while. The band started up with Duran Duran's 'Ordinary World'. Ben loved that song. It was sad, but it made him feel comfortable, at home. Took him back to a better time in his life that he now knew may have been only a nostalgic fantasy.

"You realise," Marley said, "I never came to another office Christmas party after this. This was our last Christmas together before I died."

Ben glanced back towards himself and Marley in their fifties, drinking and laughing with Frieda and their dates. Both Anika and Brian wore thoroughly fake grins, and even Frieda looked bewildered as Marley went off on some tangent that had Ben guffawing. Such was how these events always played out. No one really understood Ben and Marley but Ben and Marley.

At least they had these times together. These fleeting moments between terror-stricken defences of their business assets and stressful all-nighters that kept the gears of the place turning, when they'd shared laughter and companionship. When they'd given each other joy. A thousand moments like this passed every year, underappreciated by the two people who lived them. But they'd happened nonetheless.

Life hadn't all been bad.

"What a world we built," Ben said, resting a transparent hand on the window. Beyond it, the City glistened in its Christmas splendour.

"Ben," Marley said. She swallowed. Her voice touched her next words as carefully as if they were broken glass. "I think I'm done. I think I'm ready to move on."

Ben gave his best impression of confusion and asked, "What do you mean?" although he knew very well what she meant.

"Send me back to the present," Marley said. "We'll find a spirit to take me back."

Ben stammered for a bit before he got out, "You can't give up", even though he, too, felt like doing so. But giving up meant he and Marley would be separated again, forever. That was even more unthinkable than continuing to face the phantom. "We've made it this far. You were right; let's think. There's got to be another way."

She vigorously shook her head. "If I go back to the underworld, the emergency among the spirits will end. Your dad will lose his authority to hurt me. To chase you through your memories. You'll be a human again and he'll be a ghost again, invisible."

"And when I die in ten or twenty years?" Ben asked. "Will he be waiting for me?"

Marley's eyes fluttered closed and she took a deep, annoyed breath in. "I don't know, but in truth, Ben, that's in the future. And in the present, I don't think I want to accompany you through the past any more."

Ben studied her face, searching for a morsel of affection, or ambivalence, or pity. Anything he could latch onto to get her to stay. But her face was hard as a stone.

"Is this about what I did with my father's will? If so, I'm extremely regretful of—"

"It's about that and so much more, Ben. It's about this." She extended her arm behind them to take in the party. "I was supposed to work in education. I was supposed to be an innovator. That was my life path. And then you came along and all I used my career for was to steal part of millions of people's pay cheques. And I own that decision. If I'd really wanted to build my college, I would've. I had the money. But still, you and I—" Her face constricted, as if words that had been trapped in her throat for a long time were straining to get out, and she was fighting to stop them. "We did a bad thing," she finally said. "*This*, our business, is the worst thing we've ever done. Maybe it took me seeing what you did to your dad and Annie to admit it to myself. But I should" – her voice cracked; she looked away – "I should never have got involved with you."

Marley's admission washed over Ben like a bath of acid. He jolted and shivered. His blood boiled as if she'd physically attacked him. "We..." he started, his voice shaking with whatever strange emotion he was feeling. Aggrievement? Resentment? Desperation not to lose Marley, who'd never voiced anything so accusatory before?

She'd rather go back to *Hell* than stay with Ben? Did she mean that?

"We give poor people another option," he said. "We don't steal from them. We provide needed capital that helps them withstand life's financial bumps. Helps them meet their basic needs."

"Maybe sometimes," Marley said. "But mostly we just price gouge them then set the debt collectors on them, don't we?"

"Then why do they keep coming to us for more? If they didn't value our services, we'd go out of business."

"They're our customers because they have no choice, Ben. Unless their choice is to not eat. To have their power shut off. We took baby steps, and we each had our own needs that the business met, so we didn't realise the type of people we let ourselves become."

What in damnation did she mean by *that*? Ben had worked tirelessly his whole life. In what universe did that make him a bad person? And to the extent that he *had* harmed others, well, maybe they'd deserved it. If Ben stole from society now, it was only fair, after all that society had stolen from him during his young adulthood.

He stepped forward. Marley stepped back. He stalked towards his business partner, defences sky high. "Do you really believe that if only I'd made different choices in life, none of this would've happened? If not me, another man would have followed the same path, and he'd be standing here now in my place. Everyone – *everyone* – has always told me my worth is tied to my job, my possessions, how much money I have. And here you are hauling me up for responding rationally to the way the entire world expects me to be. The world we live in *demands* that men like me exist, Marley. I'm not the bad guy. The lot of you" – he pointed at Marley, and his finger briefly wandered towards the party, before veering away and aiming recrimination at London itself – "you're the bad guys. All I'm doing is responding to you."

Marley's gaze had softened whereas Ben's had only grown harsher. A weaker man might perceive her eyes now as sympathetic. Eyes with tears forming at their edges. But he'd heard her charges. He knew now what she really thought of him. He wrapped her accusations around his mind like a sheet of ice, thickening by the second, to armour himself against her.

Pensive, Marley laid a gentle hand on Ben's chest. She locked eyes with him, spoke deliberately. "I have loved you for thirty-five years. Unrequited. But I cared so deeply about you, and I couldn't imagine living my life without you, so I stayed. Always hoping you'd grow out of your fears."

Against Ben's better judgement, the ice in his mind began to melt. Marley had said the words he'd longed to hear for every one of those thirty-five years, despite never admitting that longing to himself. It had not been as unrequited as Marley assumed. Not nearly.

"I see a better man in you. I always have," Marley said. "A man you could've become if you'd had the courage to accept your flaws and grow past them. If you'd had the curiosity to explore all the ways you're worthy that have nothing to do with how you measure up on all the benchmarks." She raised her hand and touched his cheek as lightly as falling snow. "If you'd focused on the things that really matter in life.

"I wish like mad I'd prioritised those things more than I did. But you, Ben. You still have time. You can still become the man I wish you'd been. But only if I give myself up."

Ben set his staff against the window and took her hand in both of his. "Please, Marley. Stay. You make me a better person."

"I think you make me a worse person." She said this with frank sincerity, her eyes on his, unflinching. Only her voice faltered a bit. It drove a stake through Ben's heart.

"I died before I ever really lived," she continued. "Even if we could find a way out of this, would resurrecting myself change anything? I'd still have built my life the way I did. Around opposition to my mum's ancient social roles. Around the expectations imposed on children of successful parents. I was the bleedin' COO of an FTSE 100 company. Why was I so unhappy? I was finally a powerful woman, the type of woman other women want to be. I took all the right advice. I 'leant in'. I tried to be assertive, aggressive. I tried to be…" Her words tapered off as her mind seemed to grasp for a description of her loss.

"A man?" Ben finished her sentence.

Marley's gaze, which had wandered, darted back to Ben. Disgust lodged there, but also doubt. She shook her head as if to clear a disturbing thought, and turned to the huge window next to them, again gazing down over the City. "I hope the future's brighter for you, for everyone," she said. "But my time has passed. Send me back to the present. I'll find the biggest, brightest public event and stand right in the middle of it, so any passing spirit will see me."

"Marley…"

"I know I'm hurting you by leaving, and I'm so sorry. But I've made up my mind."

"Bah!" Ben spun on his heels, paced away, circled back round. "I won't let you kill yourself."

"I'm already dead." She picked up the staff from where Ben had set it, and held it out to him. "Please. This has been quite an adventure. But there was always only one way this was going to end."

Ben stood motionless. He'd stolen so much from Marley; if this was truly what she wanted, guilt alone would be enough to force him to respect her wishes. But her loss would devastate him all over again. Would he spend even more weeks mourning her? Long into his future, at his death and beyond, would he regret letting her go?

Would she be waiting for him after he died?

Ben reached for the staff, every inch a struggle to move his trembling hand forward. He wrapped his ghostly hand gently around Marley's, but she pulled away, leaving the staff with him. She shook her arms out as if readying for a round of exercise. She exhaled sharply. "All right, back to the future. Do it."

Ben couldn't. Not when he'd never see her again. After she'd died, he'd obsessed over not getting a proper goodbye, fantasised about what he'd have said to her if he'd known she was about to leave him forever. And now they were parting on these terms?

"Do it," Marley repeated. "I'm so, so sorry."

He stretched the glowing green tip of the staff towards her, but hesitated, frantically racking his brain for a path that would let them both survive. Could they talk Ralph into helping them flee to another time where they could live out their days? Could they fight Ben's father somehow, defeat him?

Could he find a way to earn Marley's forgiveness?

"Do it!"

Ben yelled, found the present day in his mind, and touched the staff to Marley's shoulder. It pulsed green.

Marley disappeared. From the office, from Ben's life. Emptiness in her place.

Ben took several moments to process the weight of what he'd done. The party was winding down, the band packing its instruments. Ben stood frozen, barely past the precipice of a life-changing choice. Too far to go back.

He let his arm fall to his side. Numbness took him, save for the morass of regret that churned inside him. Had he had a single relationship in his life that hadn't ended with deep remorse? Would he ever?

Ben stepped through the window, outside the fortieth floor. Strange how difficult he'd once found it to walk through solid objects as a spirit. His time spent in memory must have let him acclimatise to the capability.

Marley was dead. Her absence like a missing limb. A fissure had once again been gouged out of Ben's future, and nothing would ever be the same.

A lone red fox prowled the street beneath him. As he drifted down to earth, the sparkling behemoth of Canary Wharf rising to meet him, he browsed his memories for an emotional escape. He could follow Marley back to the present, plead with her more, watch her be taken back to her death. But what would be the point of that? No, better to crawl into a hole somewhere and sulk.

He visited six memories, trying each one out, grateful for the contemporary thoughts that drowned out his sorrow over Marley, for a minute at least, each time he jumped into a new one. Upon reaching a seventh memory, he was surprised to find an infant in his arms.

Baby Rhys, born a month ago, sleeping soundly. Sometime in the 2000s – Ben couldn't remember his son's own birth year. A shimmering glow from the fireplace cast warm light onto Lauren, reading a book across from Ben in a snug on their mansion's ground floor.

A thousand business opportunities from the time flooded his attention. Fast Quid was growing into a true multinational corporation, Ben's wealth ballooning beyond his wildest dreams. He hadn't a care in the world for his new family. They were a trinket, a toy. Something to say he possessed, when it suited him to do so. His climb up the *Sunday Times* Rich List was what truly mattered.

Rhys's small chest rose and fell with each tiny breath. Ben, with the wisdom of hindsight, could spend hours here watching him now. Why did his older self feel such heartrending love for Rhys while his younger self had barely cared? *How precious, this time I threw away.*

This tiny being's future life paths were infinite, as Ben's had been once. And Graham's before him. "You can become anything," Ben's older self whispered to his son. *You could even become me. Carry my legacy into the future. Have children of your own who can do the same.*

Had Graham once thought the same about Ben? Was that all most fathers thought their sons were good for, or was Ben's family a unique beast? *How dare I desire it? How dare I even think to impose my identity and plans onto another boy's life?*

As Ben had aged, and as the knowledge that he wouldn't be around forever had sunk in, Rhys's importance to him had grown. Hence Rhys's complaints of a childhood of neglect, followed by intense pressure during young adulthood.

If only Ben could go back and impress upon his younger self that Rhys, not Fast Quid, would become the legacy that mattered more to him. If only he could tell himself he'd better devote time to raising him right.

Raising him right. To become me, or to become his own person? Marley should have been his mum. She'd know what to do. And there, again, were thoughts of her, bursting unwelcome into the forefront of his mind.

He'd had enough of all this. The major problem of retreating into memory to escape one's regrets, he was finding, was that memories are private. Without Marley to share them with, the interpersonal interaction and companionship he needed to solve the problems inside himself were gone. Ben was in his own little world.

And still in danger, he couldn't forget. His dad could find him here.

Nothing was left for him in these past Christmases. He'd relived all the memories he cared to relive.

The fire briefly blew across the carpet before extinguishing itself. An invisible force pulled Lauren and her sofa, the Christmas tree, a shelf of liquor bottles away. Ben tried to hold on to baby Rhys, but the infant vanished in his arms.

The lights turned off. The world went dark. Ben no longer felt his comfortable recliner beneath him. In its place was the hardness of his bedroom floor.

Of the present.

STAVE XIV

Presents

Ben opened his eyes. The transition had been seamless and he felt fully awake, not sleepy in the slightest. He was still on the floor where he'd lain when he and Marley had first fled the ghost, back into his memories. There was his fireplace, his chandelier, his canopy bed.

Marley's fireplace, Marley's chandelier, Marley's canopy bed.

There was her grandfather clock, reading 11:59pm. Hadn't Marley shown up at one o'clock? Either Ben had returned earlier than when he'd left for his trip down memory lane, or this was a different night, and his empty shell of a body had been sitting here for weeks. He didn't feel hungry or thirsty. Had no time passed at all? Ben and Marley had visited more than half of the Christmases in his life.

And there was his laptop on the nightstand – this being the only item here that felt truly *his*. The rest, he felt, still belonged to Marley, as this had been her flat.

Was she here? He saw no sign of her, nor of his father. Perhaps he'd already picked up Marley and they'd both left the world of the living.

Ben stood and opened the curtains. The fog from earlier had cleared, so he could see the City clearly: the Gherkin, 22 Bishopsgate, and the Shard across the river. Fairy lights and décor still adorned the flats across the street.

No time has passed. Incredible.

Had his trip to the past with Marley been real? Mere seconds ago he'd been in a memory, but maybe reliving his memories had been a vivid dream. A bizarre dream, that had seemed to last weeks, and that had begun when Ben took a drunken nap on his bedroom floor? It would be immensely comforting to know none of it was real and he could return immediately to his normal life.

Was there a way for him to know for sure?

One particular old video might help. Ben examined the wooden doors by which the phantom had entered. They were double-locked – he'd locked them with his own hands – and the bolts were undisturbed. Now he unlocked them, flung them open, and tromped down the grand staircase. No hellfire on it now. Its wood was flawless, unburnt.

In one of the boxes he'd packed personally, Ben kept collections of old keepsakes. But had it been brought here yet, or was it still at Lauren's house?

BANG!

He was about twenty paces away from the cabinet when the noise burst from the direction of the kitchen. It sounded like a large pot or pan falling from the pot rack. Ben tensed, but relaxed when he heard a pathetic, "Ow!"

He marched into the kitchen. Into a bizarrely changed kitchen. New greenery hung from the walls and ceiling: crisp ivy, holly, mistletoe, and vines. Grapevines, from the looks of them, with plump grapes glistening. Radiant light seemed to come from nowhere and everywhere, overpowering Ben's comparatively puny kitchen lights.

In the centre of it all, nursing a minor head wound next to the open refrigerator, bearded, bespectacled, and jolly as ever, was Ralph. No longer in his tweed jacket, he was clothed in a simple deep green robe, bordered with white fleece. It hung loosely on him; huge muscles bulged underneath. His feet were also bare, and above his glasses he wore a holly wreath set here and there with shining icicles. Girded round his middle was an antique scabbard, but no sword was in it, and the ancient sheath was eaten up with rust. And, of course, he was a ghost – Ben could see right through him.

So... it was *all real.*

Ben groaned at the cracked tile on the floor and the dented pan lying next to it. "What are you still doing here?"

The spirit perked up, noticing Ben's presence. "Ben! My troubled mate. You're back!" The refrigerator door stood open. The hob and the oven were on, and food in various states of preparation littered Ben's countertops.

"Are you cooking?"

"Uh, are you *not* cooking? It's Christmas! You celebrate with food."

"I typically celebrate by reviewing my profit and loss accounts. And not at midnight. What are you doing in my flat?"

Ralph popped a piece of roast potato into his mouth, which garbled his words. "I still need my staff, if that's okay."

If that's okay? Really, how did such a physically and metaphysically powerful man become such a wimp? But his point about the staff was valid. Where was it? Ben hadn't given it a second thought.

"It might still be in my bedroom. If you can refrain from judging my morals or stealing my food, you're welcome to it."

"Ben, I—" Ralph seemed to swallow umbrage and turn it into self-scrutiny. He spoke with humility. "I'm sorry I judged you. That's not my role. My role is to guide you."

Oh, enough of this. Ben had better things to do. He spun and paced towards the stairs. "If I phone the police on you, will they be able to see you?"

"Uhm... no?" Ralph said, unconvincingly.

In the lounge on the second floor, Ben removed two old boxes from a cabinet and pried open the one stacked beneath them. There he found his collection of old VHS tapes. Thinking of the video had ignited his curiosity. Although Ralph's presence confirmed that his journey with Marley's ghost had actually happened, a much more significant question lay just beneath that one: *how many* of his memories had actually happened? Marley had constantly disagreed with his recollections. Things hadn't happened that way, she seemed to have said every other memory.

Ben found the tape he was looking for, labelled "Bortley party 1989". Suresh had kindly given him a copy when Ben had demanded it in exchange for a pay raise. Now where was that damned VHS player? He still owned one, but had the removals men hooked it up when he'd moved in?

They had! There it was, beside the projector in his small home cinema. Ben inserted the tape, hit fast-forward, and booted up the projector.

"I found the staff!" Ralph called from far away, his tinny voice resounding down the staircase. "You left it in the bedroom."

"Then goodbye," Ben called back. "And good riddance," he muttered.

After a minute, the VCR clicked, ending its fast-forward. He rewound a little ways and pressed play.

The past sprang to life before him. A bit blurry on the ancient VHS, but nonetheless real. After his recent trip, he felt he could walk right through the projector screen back into Bortley's ridiculous launch bay. On the tape, recorded by Suresh, a group of men gathered on the platform to watch the rocket while the old man blathered on about how great it was. Ben spotted Marley among the group, but where was...

There Ben was. In the distance, climbing over the edge of a trough then stumbling towards the rocket. Spilling wine everywhere – from a bottle, not a glass. Marley noticed him before anyone else did and immediately charged after him.

Ben stared at the video in shock. The scene played out, the rocket ignited, Ben tried to wrest open the safety door, and Marley stopped him just in time.

Marley stopped *him.*

All these years, his memory had been wrong. He'd been too drunk to form proper memories. Or maybe he'd been so embarrassed that his brain had warped the memory into something safer. Something that fit his image of himself. Ben certainly wasn't the type of person who'd get hammered and accidentally cause the destruction of someone else's property.

But the hard evidence before him didn't lie. He had been exactly that type of person. Marley, by contrast, looked stone-cold sober.

Ben paused the video as the rocket left its launchpad. His trust in his own mind collapsed like a house of cards. If this key memory was incorrect...

Which of Ben's other key memories were also wrong?

A twinge of emotional pain fluxed through his heart. He knew exactly which other key memory was wrong. He always had. But he'd buried it so deep – whether intentionally or unintentionally, he didn't know – that fiction had won out over fact, and the model of the world that underpinned all of Ben's actions didn't have to be challenged.

The fear of what additional houses of cards might collapse if he peered into that darkness pulled his mind away in every other possible direction. But Ben knew better now. He looked at his own pain.

Ralph, in his absurd stripper Santa garb, plodded down the last of the stairs and came up behind Ben. "I'll regenerate the nosh I took before I leave. But, uh, I have some absolutely delectable mince pies in the oven. Do you want me to leave them baking, or turn the oven off?"

Ben squeezed his eyes shut. Steeled himself. "Ralph," he said softly, "would you mind if I borrow your staff one last time?"

Ralph rocked back and forth on his feet. "I mean, it's really not okay for a human to have a time staff. I'd get in huge trouble if anyone found out."

"Just two minutes. I need to see—" Ben stopped, and briefly fought with himself over whether he wanted to continue down this path. "I need to *experience* a particular memory again. I need to experience the truth."

Backlit by the kitchen, Ralph's head dipped. He sighed twice. Vigorously shook his head. "I'm here to help you, Ben," he said. "I'll do what I can."

"Thank you," Ben said, and rose to join the ghost.

"But!" Ralph held his staff out as if blocking Ben's way. "I have to escort you. And after two minutes, I'll pull us back out. Or if we encounter any other spirits. And then that's it. No more memory travel."

"Deal," Ben said, and rested a hand on the staff. Once more, the timeline of his life opened within his mind, from blurry early childhood to crisp recent Christmases. He dreaded this. He let his attention lazily drift towards the memory in question instead of seeking it outright. A black hole beckoned for him to return.

He fell back into the past, to a time before he knew or cared about hierarchies and how to climb them. Ben was young again, just seventeen. The totality of his life's ambitions at this point were to become Sandra's boyfriend. They'd just left the Royal Crown pub in Rochester, where she was visiting for Christmas. She was an absolute vision walking next to him in her winter coat, with her rosy cheeks and expectant eyes. And she was about to leave him forever, gone off to her adult job in Birmingham, or maybe abroad to the United States.

They reached Sandra's car, parked on the kerb beneath a streetlamp. She turned to face him, the purple light of dusk glowing softly on her face. Ben shivered, more from nerves than the cold. He didn't feel like an old man in a memory. He felt like this was his last chance to express his feelings to the girl he loved.

"It's good to see you again," Sandra said. Her breathing was patchy; she was nervous too. Nervous, but expectant; eager for something.

Every neuron in Ben's brain told him to flee to the present. He forced himself to stay. His voice shook as he spoke. "Um, yes, it was fantastic to see you too."

She breathed in deeply, out slowly. She made no move to get into her car.

Ben smiled a goofy grin at her, but quickly lowered his gaze to the ground.

"Is there anything else you want to say?" Sandra asked.

"Uhm..." Ben dug deep within himself and mustered all the courage he found there.

He found none. He hadn't been prepared for this. Who was Ben to think he could make a move on this goddess? Ben was nothing, he had nothing but himself, and that wasn't good enough for Sandra. The stakes were simply too high for him to risk telling her how he felt. What if he said the wrong thing, alienated her forever? This was all happening so fast and he didn't want to ruin things.

A vacuum of silence grew between them. Neither filled it. Until finally...

"No," Ben murmured, a fake smile plastered on his face. "No, nothing else to say."

Sandra opened her mouth, but it froze in the act of forming a word. The expectation in her eyes dissolved into disappointment.

"Oh," Sandra said. "Okay. If you're sure."

I have to tell her. I have to say something. But I don't want to seem desperate. But she's the only good thing in my life right now, and what will be left if she turns me down?

Sandra opened the door and sat in her car. Ben did nothing to stop her. He stood there with his hands folded in front of him, too petrified to act.

She wants better things for her life than what I can give her. But maybe she'll come back next year and I'll be good enough for her by then. But I can't leave it like this. I have to say something!

She started her car. Shut the door. Gazed up at him through the closed window.

"Have a happy Christmas, Sandra," Ben said. He gave her a little wave. *She only gets to live one life; why should I be so arrogant as to presume she'd want to spend it with me?*

Sandra returned the gesture. "Take care, Ben." Her voice was a paper-thin mask of courtesy covering something deep and sorrowful just beneath. Still, he said nothing about his feelings for her.

Their eyes met each other's for the last time. She turned on her headlights, shifted the gear lever, and eased her Mini out into the street.

He stood in the cold. Branches above him swayed in a light breeze. The night continued around him as if his world hadn't just fallen apart. Christmas revellers cheered back at the pub. Carollers sang 'O Holy Night' somewhere nearby. A squirrel climbed the rubbish bin across the street and dived right in. Ben's feet were still under him, connecting him to Planet Earth, but he felt numb, frozen, drifting off into space, never to return.

And she'd never said it.

You haven't got enough money, Ben.

The words that had lodged themselves in the core of Ben's soul. The words that in many ways had defined his life.

She'd never said them.

So much of what he'd done in his adult life, he'd done to make Sandra regret her decision. He'd thought she'd gutted him, and it was this fuel that motivated him: the idea he could become so wildly successful, leave Sandra so far behind, that she'd have to haul a heavy burden of regret through her life, knowing it was all her fault for rejecting Ben all those years ago. He'd wanted to do to her what she'd done to him.

But the rejection hadn't been her decision. It had been his. If she thought about Ben at all, she probably wondered why *he* rejected *her*.

In this moment, he certainly felt as if she'd spurned him. The experience seemed to clutch his heart and yank it into the pavement. Something precious and vital had been torn from the fabric of the universe, and it would never be right again.

You haven't got enough money, Ben.

The words *felt* true. Like she'd actually said them. And deep down, he'd known the truth all along, though he'd smothered it for so long that the lie had become the memory. *Surely she must have been thinking it!* went his excuse, whenever the true memory resurfaced. *Surely that was why she never phoned me again, why my calls and letters went unanswered.*

And so the lie lingered. But where had it come from? Whenever he replayed this night in his mind – and he'd done so on a weekly basis for many years – those words rang out, vivid and piercing. He'd made them into a motto of sorts. Had they been a coping mechanism to help him make sense of what had happened, to reassure himself that if he worked hard enough he could become happy after all?

Or had they ultimately, at their most foundational level, come from his father? Not that Graham had implanted the false memory in his mind. But Graham had planted the seeds of low self-esteem that had grown into a vine around Ben's throat, and that vine had choked off any admission of his feelings he might have tried to express to Sandra.

Ultimately, the miasma of Ben's feelings of inadequacy had coalesced in this particular time and place to drive away the girl he loved. He could have told her how he felt, she'd have admitted she felt the same, and Ben might have lived a completely different life.

A gentle hand rested on Ben's shoulder. Eyes downcast, his vision grew blurry. Then suddenly clear again, just in time for him to see teardrops splatter against his shoes.

"Did you find what you were looking for?" Ralph asked softly. The pavement and street around Ben faded into carpet. The billboard across the street grew nearer, morphing into the screen of his home cinema.

"I did," Ben said, wiping his eyes. The skin around those eyes sagged with wrinkles. He ran a hand through his hair, and found it thin.

"I'm so sorry," Ralph said. "That seemed quite sad for you. I hope you can have some compassion towards yourself."

"Ha. I'm enough of a narcissist already, I think."

"Having a high opinion of yourself and compassion *towards* yourself are two different things," Ralph said.

"Yes. Well..." Ben turned off the projector and ejected the VHS tape. "It's in the past. Thank you." He plodded to the cabinet.

Ralph hovered behind him, his levitating feet hidden behind his Christmas robe. "You were young. It was a learning experience," he said.

"Yes, it was. And I learnt the wrong thing."

"It's a pitfall of being human, really. In our twenties, we get fixated on one way of thinking about the world and our place in it. We assume it'll stay the best, most correct way to view the world for the rest of our lives. Then, when the world changes, and a better way of thinking about it comes along, we shoot it down because it contradicts that sacred thing we learnt as a twenty-four-year-old."

"You say this from experience?" Ben asked as he packed the VHS tape back up.

Ralph snorted. "My worldview was, 'Life is terrifying. Go read a book.' Took me till I was dead to want to relate to other people, and then it was too late."

"Sounds like my son and his video games," Ben said. "He needs a mental update, too."

"We do update ourselves. We do grow. I'm sure you act differently in romantic situations now."

The poor man probably thought he was comforting Ben rather than digging a deeper hole of despair. *Yes, Ralph. My adult self is forward with women, to a fault.*

"And I'm sure Sandra does, as well," Ralph finished.

Ben paused in the middle of stacking a box. He turned to Ralph. Was that a subtle, mischievous smirk on the spirit's face?

It didn't matter if Ralph was manipulating him; he didn't care. The idea exploded in his mind and arrested all his attention. "You're the Ghost of Christmas Eve Present," Ben said. "This is your domain. Could you take me to her, in spirit form? To Sandra, as she is now?"

The question sounded horrible to Ben as it left his lips. A jilted almost-lover using the spirit world to spy on a woman who'd spurned him decades ago?

But no, that wasn't why he'd asked. Certainly, he was curious. He'd searched for Sandra on social media countless times over the years, always unsuccessfully. Those searches had once been made out of anger – he'd been checking to see if she was as well-off as him. The bitterness eventually faded to pure curiosity, and now Ben felt something else. Something new.

He actually wanted to make sure she was okay.

Nonsense. I haven't seen her since I was a teenager. But after reliving most of his life's Christmases, life's true brevity was a knife at his back. The wellbeing of people he'd cared about over the years was suddenly important to him.

Ralph somehow read Ben's conflicted feelings, and said nothing critical of his request. He made a show of rubbing his beard in thought. "I could do that," he said as if he hadn't been the one to give Ben the idea. "But she won't be able to see us and we can't interact with her. And if the Ghost of Christmas Past finds us, we'll have to run."

"My dad's still looking for me? Even with Marley gone and me back in the present?"

Ralph wrinkled his face. "Your dad?"

"Long story. The Ghost of Christmas Past is my dad."

Ralph wrinkled his face further, to the point that it looked like a bearded prune. "I can see where you get your problems from. But who knows? He's not allowed to hurt you while you're still alive. But if they haven't caught your friend and taken her back to Hell yet, the emergency rules still apply. If she's still on the loose, he can go wherever he wants, even in the present. He could harass us."

Or kidnap me back to the past, to try and change the present.

So Ralph didn't know if the other spirits had nabbed Marley yet. Ben had half a mind to try and find her...

No. No, he wanted Marley as far from his mind as possible. *She made her choice*, he told himself. Dwelling on it would only hurt him further – despite the part of his mind that desperately wanted him to dwell on it, that didn't care what choice Marley had made. "You can't just give my dad a good drubbing if he shows up?"

"You mean *me* beat *him* up? No!"

"This is the present," Ben said. "You have all the power here, not him."

Ralph's headshake was so quick it seemed involuntary, like rotten food had touched his tongue. "That's not how it works. We ghosts draw our power from human decisions. If you're thinking about the past when you make a decision – any decision – a Ghost of the Past gets that power. If you're thinking about a specific memory of the past, the ghost for that day gets the power. Not to mention we Present Ghosts allied with the Past Ghosts in their war because – I don't know. It was before my time. I guess we thought the future is scary and you can learn a lot from the past, or something. So now they're our bosses."

"Do people really spend so much time making decisions based on the past?" Ben asked. "I'd have thought most people decide based on the future."

"You'd hope!" Ralph said, plopping down on a recliner. His staff scraped some paint off Ben's wall, but Ralph didn't seem to notice. He casually ran his hand over the top of it, extinguishing its light.

"Humans think about the future all the time, but they're usually still *deciding* based on the past.

"The arrow of time, you see, is a fundamental imbalance built into the fabric of the universe. We know precious little about the present, even less about the future. Until we learn to make decisions based on that little bit of knowledge, the past will remain far more powerful. Your dad, or any other Ghost of the Past, could fight off Present and Future Ghosts for days. Immortal, impervious. My stamina would wane in minutes. He'd snuff me right out."

"Ghosts... can kill each other?" Ben asked. "Aren't you already dead?"

"Like I said," Ralph replied, "there's a difference between 'going back to Hell' dead and '*dead* dead'. In one, you're in the afterlife, in the other, you're nowhere. Gone. Poof. There is no *you* any more."

None of this scared Ben. His dad couldn't possibly find them. It had been hard enough for him to find Ben and Marley in a finite timespan of memories. Now, if he and Ralph avoided places Ben frequented – mainly home and work – the chances his dad would locate them in the entire expanse of the UK seemed miniscule.

"You won't be punished for helping me, will you?" Ben asked.

"On the contrary. I'd get in trouble for helping Marley, but helping living people is my job."

"Well, it's nice that some ghosts actually do their jobs. Are we leaving or not?"

Ralph's smirk came back and grew slowly larger. "Lie down. I don't want you to hit your head." He readied his staff.

"Are the mince pies still in the oven?"

Ralph snapped his fingers. "They'll be waiting in your fridge. Please do let me know what you think. Even reheated, they're—"

"Ralph."

The spirit took a moment to reset his focus. "Right."

Ready for anything, Ben lay supine. The instant his head hit the carpet, Ralph tapped him with the staff, and he shot up out of his body, through the ceiling, above the flat, higher, higher. He was moving so fast, he was essentially falling upwards, but he heard no rush of air. Soon the sounds of honking cars and ambient Christmas music faded. All was quiet. London receded below him.

Ralph flew alongside Ben, rocketing upwards with him.

"I'm still in my pyjamas," Ben called to him, bending his neck to glimpse his own see-through body, still clothed in now-immaterial nightwear.

"Wouldn't you know," Ralph replied, "I am too!" His Christmas robes whipped as he arced sideways into a new trajectory, guffawing with a deep, hearty laugh.

Did I avoid getting kidnapped by one maniac only to let myself be kidnapped by another? The ground was a mile away now. Without the safety of an aeroplane or a parachute, Ben was completely at Ralph's mercy. This wasn't a memory – this was the actual London. If Ralph got too far away, could Ben fall? He wasn't moving under his own power.

But he needn't have worried. Some unseen force soon pulled him alongside Ralph again as they zoomed above London and away from it, far faster than a plane.

"Where are we going?" Ben asked.

"Birmingham!"

"She still lives in Birmingham? After all these years?"

"You still live in London. Why is it strange?"

It was strange because he'd imagined Sandra in a better place than he was. Somewhere outside the UK, and not necessarily a real place. Sandraville. A paradise high on a mountain where she sneered down at him.

The image was too childish to voice to Ralph.

They flew above rolling hills and streams that reflected shimmering moonlight, then swept down through clouds towards the "City of a Thousand Trades". Ralph landed first, next to a lamppost in front of a semi-detached house in suburbia. White fairy lights lined its eaves.

Ben touched down a moment later. He couldn't feel the pavement through his spirit feet, but they walked on it solidly nonetheless. Somehow he didn't even trip.

"I took us back to last night, around eight o'clock," Ralph said.

"Christmas Eve?"

"Yes. I am a Ghost of Christmas Eve. It is where I tend to hang about."

"Well, it's nice to know the spirit world runs on Greenwich Time. It really is better than all the other times."

A car pulled in to the driveway. Ben's heartbeat quickened. His mind went right back to that pavement near to the pub in Rochester in the late seventies. Sandra behind her car window, likely as heartbroken as Ben just because he couldn't muster the self-assurance to tell her he fancied her.

The car parked. The doors opened. A man got out of the passenger's seat, a bit wobbly on his feet.

There she was. Shutting the driver's side door and coming round the car.

"Those were quite some lights, huh?" she asked the man.

"I liked the house with the Krampus the best," he said, and hiccupped.

Sandra laughed. Her voice had flattened over the years. Age had affected her face in all the normal ways.

Did she ever have children? If so, they'd likely be middle-aged by now. Sandra was in her sixties, the same as Ben.

He wanted to ask her so many things. Had she ever made it to Santorini? Did she still hate horror films? Where had her career taken her after her early admin job at the textile company?

Most importantly, what did she think of him? She'd been invisible to him, but Ben was a public figure. Surely she'd read about him in the news and formed opinions.

As Sandra opened the house's front door and turned on the lights inside, Ben moved to follow her, but Ralph held him back with a firm shoulder grip.

"Sorry," he said. "Any other house and I'd let you go inside, but I don't think it'd be right... with her."

Ben pulled against him anyway, hard enough to protest but not enough to break loose. So this was all he'd get. Just a glimpse of Sandra's life.

His ridiculous fantasies of her sneering at him from her mountaintop, or of returning to him apologetic, shattered. She'd moved on long ago and made her own life. A normal life, from all appearances. She seemed happy. Did she fixate on her last meeting with Ben as a toxic motivating force, as he had? Seeing her now, Ben doubted it.

She'd been an eighteen-year-old girl, trying like anyone else to find her way in life. He'd built her into a deity passing ultimate judgement on him, but she'd been just an eighteen-year-old girl.

You haven't got enough money, Ben.

His father's words. His own words. Not Sandra's.

A tear slid down Ben's cheek. He wiped it away.

So spirits can *cry.*

"Oh, Ben," Ralph said.

"It's enraging," Ben said, "to learn that the present could be so different if I'd made different decisions." Maybe someone else would've started Fast Quid, or a company like it. Maybe the world demanded that men like Ben exist. But Ben didn't have to be one of them.

Sandra glanced out at the neighbourhood as she shut the door. Ben was looking beyond her, though, at the man who could've been him.

"It's never too late to try and fix a bad decision," Ralph said. "Ring her up, have a chat, become friends again, if she wants. They're a nice couple. I've spent some time with them. If I can say so, Ben, you need more authentic people who it's safe to be vulnerable around in your life."

Ben ran a hand over his face, through his hair. "The one person I know who matched that description just walked out of my life forever." Marley's exit loomed like a tsunami above Sandra's long-ago exit, even though Ben had just relived it. "She had no interest in deferring to my needs."

Ralph plucked a pink *Camellia* flower from a shrub beside the driveway. He twirled the stem in his hand. "Well, did you consider her perspective? Her feelings?"

"Oh, I think she just needed me to be her punching bag so she could feel better about her own situation."

Ralph waved his flower back and forth. "Don't write her narrative without her pen, now. Be curious. What do you really think she needed?"

"I don't know. I suppose for me to take some responsibility for my supposed misdeeds? She wanted me to try becoming a better man, whatever that means. And I think I made clear I don't feel I need to do that."

"Why not?"

"Bah, it's too late now."

"Come on, Ben. Indulge me. Why not?" Ralph idly spun the flower. As he did so, it wilted. Its petals drooped, faded to brown, fell to the ground, and dissolved into dust. All he was left holding was a dry stem. Ben stared at it, mesmerised by its near-instant decay.

"If I own up," he said, "if I try becoming a better man, it means admitting I was flawed in the first place. And admitting that opens me up to attack."

"From whom?"

From my father, Ben nearly said. But honestly, who wouldn't attack him? If Ben conceded his own shortcomings and sought to make amends, his ex-wife Lauren would dig her claws in, his son Rhys would just laugh at him. His employees would see a weak leader. Frieda would never talk to her uncle again after learning why her mum had really offed herself. And what would Sandra have thought? Or Talbot, or Bortley, or any of the many men Ben had counted as rivals throughout his life?

Ben had always thought that once he grew older, all the people from previous generations who looked down on him would be dead, and he'd finally be free of their captious gazes. But now that he was old, he knew this for a lie. His hypercritical forerunners were all still here, as memories in his own mind, watching him still, and frowning. Could he ever be free of them? Could he ever rid himself of the driving fear of what they'd think if they saw the *real* Ben, the Ben beneath the masks he wore to earn their respect?

And Marley. Marley...

She would still care about me if I admitted my mistakes. She'd love me in spite of them.

He'd been such a fool for letting her go: when they were young, when they were old, when they were ghosts in his memories, and all the times in between. Why had Ben let the imagined judgements of people far in his past carry more weight than the judgements of the woman who loved him now?

A smile bloomed on Ralph's face. All at once, dust gathered on the ground and coalesced into *Camellia* petals. "It looks like you're realising it wouldn't be as bad as you think it'd be," he said. The petals rose and reconnected to the stem. They unwilted, brown becoming pink, and soon formed a lush flower once again. "Maybe Sandra and her husband would like the new you. Again, you don't have to use me and my powers to see them."

Ben chuckled at the idea, which seemed sillier even than jumping through memories and time. "If only I did have your powers, Ralph. I'd fixate on everything I've done wrong. I'd obsess, I'd fetishise. I'd go back and try to optimise every decision, change things in my favour."

Exactly like my father.

"You'd give yourself a life where you get everything you want?" Ralph asked.

"I'd give myself a life where I never hurt anyone."

"Hmm," Ralph said. He eyed the ground beneath him, tapped it idly with his staff a few times. "You know, as a history teacher, I appreciate the value of learning from the past. But when we make the wrongs of the past into a core part of ourselves, we give them *more* power over the present and future, not less. All of history works like this. We see horrors in our past and we try to relegislate them, like we can make it so they never happened. This usually causes even more pain moving forward, and many people call that new pain 'justice'.

"But the horrors did happen. We can't save the past. Not even with time travel. It happened and it can't be undone. But we can save the present, and the future. That's justice."

Ben wiped his nose on his pyjama sleeve. What he wouldn't give at the moment for a spirit tissue. "Life isn't meant to be regretted, I suppose," he said. "Life is meant to be lived."

Ralph elbowed him lightly. "That's the spirit. There's hope for you yet, Ben." He leant down and tucked the *Camellia* flower atop the broken stem it had come from. When he withdrew his hand, the flower was reattached to the plant as if he'd never plucked it.

They turned away from the house and walked into the street. Sandra was okay, at least outwardly, and that was what Ben had come here to check. If he wanted to check whether she was *really* okay, he'd need to reach out.

Would that be healthy? He'd have to think about that. Perhaps it would be better to let her go. For good this time.

"There's someone else I'd like to see," Ben mentioned. "Would you take me there?"

"Ha! He's gotten a taste and now I'm the chauffeur. Possibly I can take you there. Who?"

Ben said the name, and seconds later, they were soaring high above England again.

They crossed above the Houses of Parliament and Big Ben, heading east and slowing down. Pleasure craft threaded lazily through light-lined bridges in the Thames. Giant Christmas trees at several points in the city sparkled with multicoloured brilliance, outdone only by electronic billboards in Piccadilly Circus.

"You see the streets around St Paul's?" Ralph said.

Ben gazed down at the great domed church, but saw nothing remarkable about the streets.

"The streets are wider in that part of London because of the Great Fire," Ralph explained. "When they rebuilt, they put the buildings farther apart so future fires wouldn't spread as quickly."

Knowing this, Ben looked again. He'd been to the area countless times on foot and never noticed it. But from the air, the streets there were clearly wider. In the parts of London that hadn't burnt, streets still held their old medieval widths.

"Remarkable that something that happened in 1666 is still so visible today," Ralph said. "I love this city."

Ben watched him for a few moments, this happy man with his staff, beaming down at his town. Spirits like him kept watch over humanity? If it was true, it would reassure Ben for as long as he lived. Less so spirits like his father. Ben may not have given a damn about the ghosts, but this one... he'd been lucky to meet this one.

"Tell me," Ben said, "When a history teacher gets a chance to become a ghost, why does he choose to be a Ghost of the Present instead of a Ghost of the Past?"

"Ha. Well, history teachers know enough about history that we don't want to go back to it."

"Funny. But really."

Ralph's grin slowly died while Ben waited for an answer. Canary Wharf slid past beneath them, and Ben glimpsed Fast Quid's headquarters inside One Canada Square. The overnight staff would be negotiating with partners in Asia, even on Christmas Eve. Working public holidays was in every employee's contract. Gave the business a competitive edge.

"My parents didn't let me play outside," Ralph said. "Didn't let me see other kids, schooled me at home. They were fearful people, and I inherited that fear. It was hard for me to trust. I told you I died of colon cancer, right?"

Ben nodded as best he could while horizontal in midair. "I empathise. I've had digestive problems, too."

"Well, mine was curable. My doctor said so. But I was so…" He winced as something unpleasant crossed his mind. "I was so scared. Afraid of my doctors, of the medical system. I didn't want to believe I was sick. Didn't want to admit my own mortality, relatively young as I was. So I hid it."

"You hid your cancer? Even from you family?"

"And from myself. I hid in my history books. The past is set in stone: terrible, but safe. The future is unknown, and therefore far more terrifying. So I worked until the week I died. Left behind a disabled wife and two children. So it was cowardice that sent me to Hell."

Cowardice? To Ben, that didn't seem like a good reason to punish someone so severely.

"So when the previous Ghost of Christmas Eve Present moved on and new souls could volunteer, I did," Ralph said. "I did it so I could see my family again. Watch them grow. I'm not allowed to interact with them, but I visit them whenever I can. It'll be nice if we can be a family again someday, when they pass on."

"Ralph," Ben said. "Who makes the rules about who is punished in the afterlife? Who decides each person's ultimate fate?"

The robed spirit took a deep breath of night air. He looked above at the stars, down again at the city. "All the people we've hurt," he said. "And all the people we've helped. Ah, here we are."

Before Ben had time to process Ralph's answer, they descended to a freestanding house in Kent, just outside the metro area. Climbing roses ascended walls of stained stone façade to wrap around French windows that once had been white but were yellowing with age. Both culinary and decorative plants, interspersed with the occasional weed, grew in the front garden. A few bricks were missing from the chimney rising from the roof. Several cars were parked out front.

It was a big house, an old house. A house belonging to someone with enough money to buy it but not enough money for the upkeep. A small shrine to Ganesh sat beside a fountain at the garden's centre. Reflections of the house's ample fairy lights sparkled in the water.

Another light source flashed. An ambulance, silent, parked at the nearest house, about fifty yards away. Paramedics were scrambling to pull equipment out of the back.

"What's that all about?" Ben asked as they touched down.

Ralph studied the scene as the medics rushed to the front door. "I'm not sure. It doesn't concern us, though. This is the house we want."

Ben strode past poinsettias lining the path to the door. "Will you let me go inside this time?"

Ralph gestured forward. "After you, fellow traveller."

They passed over an entry mat that Ralph classified as "rangoli", then through the wreath and the front door, as if they were made of air. Ralph identified the beat of the music inside, too: Keherwa, accompanying a peppy version of 'Jingle Bells' in Hindi.

Suresh's huge family were having a Christmas Eve party. Dozens of people from Ben's age and older down to young children, all wearing their Christmas best. Ties and vests, blazers, Christmas-print jumper dresses.

Lanterns in the shape of stars hung from the ceiling, each speckled with small holes through which light cast drifting highlights on the walls and the revellers. An immense Christmas tree laden with lights and ornaments climbed until the star at its top nearly touched the vaulted ceiling. Candles flickered on shelves and countertops, out of the children's reach.

"Ah! No, Vivaan," said a young mother, patting her child on the back. About six years old, he'd been caught just as he started tearing open the wrapping paper on a present under the tree. "Christmas Baba hasn't brought your presents yet. That's for someone else."

"But Nani said I could open one present tonight," Vivaan objected.

"Then we'd better ask her where your presents are."

"I have a present for you," said a well-dressed man who came up beside her. Her romantic partner?

He pointed to a joist above them, where a sprig of mistletoe was hung. The woman laughed, embraced him, kissed him deeply.

Definitely her romantic partner. Vivaan stuck his tongue out in an imitation gag.

Ben and Ralph moved deeper into the house and stopped at a truly extravagant spread of various foods arrayed on the kitchen island. Ben could smell it even though he was a ghost, and it made his mouth water even though he'd never once in his life eaten Indian cuisine.

"Ooh," Ralph said, rubbing his hands together. "Quite the Maharashtrian spread. I see varan bhaat and chapati bhaji. And for dessert it looks like gulab jamun and puran poli."

Ben glanced sidelong at him. "Proud you can name all the Indian food?"

"I interned in Mumbai when I was young. Fell in love with the culture."

"Looks like there are about a billion varieties of curry. It smells delicious. Can we actually eat this?"

"I can, because I have special afterlife powers. But sorry, mate, you're just a disembodied spirit. If you tried, it'd taste like nothing. Also it's not polite to steal people's food."

"Says you, the great fridge raider?"

Ben spotted Suresh, sitting alone on a sofa in a corner, drinking from a bottle of something called Rooh Afza. He'd grown a short grey beard, wore glasses, and age had etched lines into his face. From what Ben recalled, Suresh had never got along with his birth family. The family here tonight must be his partner's, or their children and grandchildren, or simply friends.

Ben approached his old employee, wishing he'd been invited here to catch up in person. He'd have to ring Suresh and set up a get-together.

An old woman in a goofy reindeer hat stopped in front of Suresh to do a little dance. He laughed.

"I don't have those moves any more, Savita," he said.

"Oh, come on," Savita said, plopping down next to Suresh and leaning on him. "Your granddaughter's been looking for you to play carrom. Your son is here from California for the first time in years. Your wife wants to dance. Why are you over here sulking?"

"I'm not sulking," Suresh said. When Savita pursed her lips and raised her eyebrows, Suresh's defences held for a moment, but his shoulders soon drooped, and a deep exhalation escaped him. "I found out yesterday that Bennett is pulling his funding."

Savita tilted her head to the side. "Oh no, I'm so sorry. Why didn't you tell me?"

Suresh shrugged. "I didn't want to ruin Christmas."

So he *was* still in the game. He'd seemed dead set on leaving the worlds of finance and marketing for good. What business venture *had* he been spending his life on? How profitable was it? Could Ben get involved, help him with his funding problem?

"I tried telling him we can save a life for every four thousand pounds," Suresh went on, "that thousands of people who'd have died from malaria are still walking this Earth thanks to his donations alone. I told him the Malaria Consortium is one of the most effective charities in the world. But he didn't care. He wanted to redirect his donations to the endowment at his alma mater. Now we have to fill the funding gap."

Savita cradled his cheek in her hand. "I know you worked hard to nourish that relationship, my love. What can I do for you?"

Suresh leant into her hand, pressed his own against it. "This is good," he said. "But I'm not the one who needs the help. These are people's *lives*, Savita. Many of them, the world has given them nothing but their lives, then malaria takes even that."

Savita said some comforting words and Suresh responded warmly, but Ben scarcely listened. He couldn't get over how Suresh had changed. That frightened boy who'd worn a mask of hypercompetitiveness was now so comfortable in his own skin that it was unthinkable he'd ever been otherwise. And Ben hadn't seen Suresh since the nineties. He'd been a whole different man all these years.

"Incredible," Ben said.

Ralph patted Ben on the back. "Some people find themselves at the bottom of a hierarchy and resolve to climb to the top. Other people find themselves at the bottom of a hierarchy and resolve to help the people whose lives it has crushed."

And some people are content to wallow at the bottom, Ben thought of Ralph. Out loud, he grunted and said, "And do tell, oh wise one, which type of person am I?"

He expected a tart rejoinder, but Ralph just gave an equivocal little head tilt, thought for a moment, smiled, and said, "To be determined."

Ralph meandered towards some kind of singing game in the next room, leaving Ben to ponder his words. If, in Ben's sixties, anything was left "to be determined" about the type of man he was, he couldn't conceive of what it could be.

He wandered. This whole extended family seemed to genuinely like each other. They played games, sang, danced, and the two spirits watched. The music and the lights lulled Ben into a sense of mirth. He laughed at the family's jokes and beamed when Vivaan and some other kids were finally allowed to open one present each.

This is how Christmas should be spent. Not in the office.

If only Ben had a family like this, instead of a trio of ex-wives and a son who hated him. He'd always blamed them for not giving him the type of happy family he wanted. *But it wasn't all their fault, was it? Or even mostly their fault?* Why did Ben suddenly feel so responsible for shortcomings he hadn't recognised until tonight? For that matter, why did he suddenly feel so carefree about other shortcomings he'd worried about all his life? Here was Suresh, who'd given up status-seeking like a pernicious addiction decades ago and had achieved far less than Ben… but his was a different kind of achievement. A better kind, Ben was learning.

Ralph looked greatly pleased to find Ben enjoying the convivial atmosphere. So much so that Ben was sure he'd agree to stay until the guests left. But after an hour, Ralph pulled him aside and said it was time to return to Ben's flat.

They left through the front door and drifted past the fountain, into the street. The ambulance was still parked at the distant neighbour's house, its lights still flashing. But something else had joined the ambulance: what at first looked to be a river of faint light passing through the air around the house. Ben strained to discern what he was seeing. People?

No. Ghosts.

Other spirits, as transparent as Ben and Ralph.

"Hide," Ralph said in a raised whisper. "Hide!"

They crouched together behind a shrub. Ben manoeuvred his head until he found a line of sight between some leaves. Yes, those were spirits. But not empowered ones, like Ralph or Graham. Every one of them wore chains like Marley when he'd first seen her. A few were linked together; none were free. They made confused noises audible even from a distance. Incoherent sounds of lamentation and regret, wailings of inexpressible sorrow and self-accusation. They wandered in restless haste.

"Who are they?" Ben asked.

310

"The dead," Ralph replied. "Coming to welcome a new recruit to their ranks."

"To frighten the newly dead person?"

Ralph scowled at Ben as if he'd thrown a fresh meal in the rubbish. "To try and *help* the dead person make the transition. Do you assume the worst of everyone, Ben?"

"Well, they're frightening *me*." One spirit in particular, an old man in a white waistcoat, dragged a monstrous iron safe attached to his ankle. Ben actually knew the man, Howard something-or-other, from a series of meetings years ago, when Fast Quid had acquired another payday lending company.

"They don't mean to frighten," Ralph said. "They're heartbroken. They wish desperately to interfere, for good, in human matters, but they've lost that power forever."

The spirits' mournful dirge burrowed into Ben's ears like a worm. "They can leave the underworld?" he asked.

"Only for this. And they're watched extremely closely. Hence, why we're hiding. Ah. There she is."

Two new spirits exited through the walls of the house where the ambulance was parked: a frail man in pyjamas, and a middle-aged woman wearing a crown of holly that mirrored Ralph's, and holding a staff. Ben glanced at Ralph for confirmation, and he nodded.

"The Ghost of Christmas Present. Looks like she's been pulling extra duty in my absence. I'd rather not get scolded by her. And she'd certainly have questions for you about Marley."

"Don't multiple people die every second?" Ben asked. "Yet the ghost is focusing on just this one man? Not to mention you said escorting the dead is only *one* of your responsibilities as ghosts?"

"Well, we can be in multiple places at once. We're like time-travelling Santa Clauses."

Ben rubbed his temples. "Please don't tell me he's real."

"Shh. You're ruining the show."

The river of spirits reached for the newly dead man, jostling each other, but afraid to cross some invisible barrier separating them from him and the time ghost. She appraised the miserable throng, then raised her eyes upwards and raised her staff. The light at its top pulsed a vivid yellow-white.

A new light dawned above them. Gossamer folds of energy unfolded in the night, billowing from an undefined light source towards the ghost of the recently departed. The frail man's spirit ascended towards the light. The myriad dead beneath him silenced and stilled to watch him go.

"What's this now? Heaven?" Ben asked. "He's off to Heaven?"

"I wouldn't call it 'Heaven'," Ralph said. "Not in the way the world religions understand it. But yes, he's off to a better place."

"You're telling me," Ben said, wresting his attention away from the spectacle and fixing it on Ralph, "that you could use your magic staff to open a portal to Heaven at any damn time you want?"

"Not for me! Much as I'd love to go myself. I can only open a portal like that for other dead people."

"Other dead people... like Marley?" Ben grabbed Ralph by the collar of his robe and drew their faces together. "You could've sent her to Heaven?"

"Keep your voice down!" Ralph glanced through the shrub. The frail man was in the process of vanishing into the light as the Ghost of Christmas Present, and the many dead, watched on. "You may have heard this somewhere before," Ralph said, "but you have to be a good person to get into Heaven, you dunce!"

"Marley *was* a good person."

Ralph lowered his glasses to eye Ben with withering scepticism. "I would say she single-handedly pilfered the livelihoods of millions of people and plunged them and their families into poverty, but your hands were also part of that equation."

"I seem to recall you promising to stop judging me," Ben said.

"I'd be happy to do so as soon as you stop clutching me like you're going to beat me up."

Ben glanced down at his fists, back up at Ralph. He let him go.

Ralph breathed deeply and brushed himself off.

Gears turned in Ben's mind. "Marley's had a change of heart," he said, walking through his thought process out loud. "She thinks Fast Quid is wrong now. It's not, by the way. But if thinking so is the first step on the road to a better afterlife, maybe with enough time Marley will get there. From what I've heard, they've got all the time they want in the afterlife to change for the better. But Marley won't have that time, because my dad is there, and he'll keep using her to try and get to me. So..."

He was grasping at straws. But the existence of some sort of Heaven and the knowledge of a way to get there was new knowledge and seemed important. *There must be a way I can use it.*

"Is there a way we can get Marley more time?" Ben asked. "Time in which my dad can't interfere with her? Time to think through her life, change herself? I know there's a brilliantly good woman in her. I've seen that side of her so often."

And I'm the man who most helped her smother it.

Ralph puffed up his cheeks and let the air – or not-air, or ghost air, or something – escape lazily through his lips. The light above the neighbours' house had vanished. The river of the dead was receding beneath the earth. "*If* the other spirits haven't caught her yet," Ralph said. "And *if* you're right that she's well on her way to becoming a truly good person… there is one place she could hide where your dad couldn't reach her. It's possible she could stay there until she grows enough that she can go to a better afterlife."

"Where is this place?"

Ralph stared at Ben with fear. He slid a hand over his face. "I can't—" Words caught in his throat. He grimaced. Shook his head vigorously. Finally, he reopened his eyes and appraised Ben with a resolute gaze. "When did you last see her?"

"In a memory," Ben said. "I used your staff to send her to the present."

"Okay," Ralph said. "As I am the Ghost of Christmas Eve Present, the staff would've interpreted your command as sending her to Christmas Eve. If you didn't specify the time, she could have arrived at any time of day or night on Christmas Eve, between midnight and 11:59 the next night."

Ben's heart jumped. *I might yet save her after all.* "So we have to find her."

Ralph watched the distant Ghost of Christmas Present as she glanced around the empty rural landscape, then rocketed into the sky. He swallowed. "We have to find her."

"And bring her where?"

Ralph tightened his grip on his staff. "The future."

The Night Before Christmas

Marley had said she'd go to a large public gathering to attract the ghosts' attention, but there were dozens of those on Christmas Eve. The services at St Paul's and Westminster Abbey, Winter Wonderland in Hyde Park, and the concert at the Royal Albert Hall were just the beginning. Ralph and Ben relived the entire day of Christmas Eve twice, knowing that the ghosts seeking to capture Marley could do the same. When the ice skating rink at Somerset House closed on their third replay of Christmas Eve and they still hadn't found her at any of the huge events, Ben thought beyond the obvious.

Maybe Marley had changed her mind. Maybe she'd gone somewhere familiar to sulk. He made a suggestion to Ralph and they started on their way. While leaving the crowd, Ben spotted the looming phantom, staff in hand, prowling among the ice skaters. Hunting.

"Can you teleport us out of here?" Ben asked.

"Uh, teleport?" Ralph asked quizzically.

"With your staff. Like I did in the memories?"

"Oh. Right. We can't do that in the real world. We can fly, but then he'd see us."

"So what do we do?"

"Walk briskly."

Disturbing though the sight of his father in the present was, it gave Ben hope. Graham hadn't found Marley yet either, and neither had any other ghost.

What would his father do if he found her? Surely not return her to Hell. Even if doing so was his responsibility, it would rescind the emergency of an escaped soul, and he'd lose the ability to go after Ben. At least until Ben eventually died and passed into the afterlife himself.

Ben and Ralph stopped at Marley's friends' houses, though none of them could be called a true friend. Business acquaintances, if anything. As extroverted as Marley was, she didn't get close to people. Except for Ben.

"If and when we find her," Ralph said as they approached the next flat, "we'll need to take her to the Ghost of Christmas Yet to Come. She's in hiding from the Ghosts of the Past, but I've spotted her twice this year around Parliament, of all places. I think she's holed up right under all our noses. Perhaps she's trying to influence the MPs on the sly."

"And she'll be willing to help us?"

"I don't know. I'm assuming that if your dad wants to harm you both so much, she'll want to protect you."

"He's her enemy?" Ben asked as they ascended from a busy street to the third-floor flat. "Because he's a Ghost of the Past?"

"Eh, it's more like she's *his* enemy. The Future Ghosts would make friends if the Past Ghosts weren't such plonkers."

"Which is why we'll be safe in the future," Ben guessed. "Because she'd defend her territory if he came after us there?"

Ralph chuckled. "She's even less power than I do, mate. No, the Past Ghosts won't go into the future because of... I don't know. It has something to do with probabilities and light cones and quantum uncertainty. They're inherently unsafe in the future. The Future Ghost can explain it all when you meet her."

Marley had grown fond of Ben's niece, Frieda, during the years before her death. She'd even lunched with her on a few occasions. Perhaps searching her Mayfair flat was a move of desperation, but Ben quickly checked the bedroom where her two kids were playing, and the kitchen where Frieda and her Algerian husband, Haddad, were cooking a meal together, both still in business attire from the workday. No sign of Marley. She could have stopped by earlier or later, but Ben didn't have time to sit around in each location she might visit, reliving Christmas Eve over and over again.

He was about to retreat with Ralph through the windows when Haddad said behind him, "You invited *him* to dinner? Greedy old Uncle Tightwad?"

Ben halted his exit, turned to appraise the couple. Haddad was stirring a stew in a *couscoussier*; Frieda was chopping carrots. "He's so detached and lonely," she said. "Don't you think that's part of why he is the way he is? Maybe no one reaches out to him, so the only group he feels comfortable around are other men like him, who just reinforce his view of the world. But if he at least comes to dinner..."

Haddad rested his spoon on the countertop and crossed his arms. "After he asked you to commit £412 million worth of fraud? Luv, you can't fix a man like that."

Spirit though Ben was, he felt his skin flush. He longed for his body back so he could give Haddad a piece of his mind.

"It's a first step, okay? I just want to show Uncle Ben he can have other types of relationships with other types of people."

Shaking his head, Haddad brought out measuring spoons and slipped some spices into the stew. "You ask me, we should let him wallow in the life he's built for himself. It's the punishment he deserves."

Ben wrinkled his nose at the comment. Was Haddad's assumption that he was miserable a coping mechanism, letting the young man feel there was some justice in the world? Many normies felt this way, but in Ben's experience, reality was quite the contrary. Some of the worst people he'd ever met had also been some of the happiest.

"You know I have this job thanks to Uncle Ben," Frieda said. She slid the chopped carrots into the stew. "And you still think he should be punished?"

"It's legalised theft, what that whole company does. Doesn't the average borrower eventually pay back like three times what they borrowed? The business model is pure callousness."

"Everyone is callous!" Ben said, as if Haddad could hear him. "Everyone is selfish, untrustworthy."

He caught Ralph watching him, shoulders slouched, hands hidden in his robe like Ben might leap forward and attack him. Somehow,

Ralph seeing Ben's only living family talk about him like this was as embarrassing as anything Marley had seen of his past.

"Bah!"

Focus, Ben, focus. He could get sucked into his own psychodrama and float here all night listening to Frieda and Haddad gab about him. But Marley needed him. He flew outside and Ralph followed, not saying a word.

After another unsuccessful night, they relived the day again. Ben searched again through his office, watched himself attend the AI demonstration and the audit meeting with Frieda. After the creep who'd snuck into Marley's office confronted him, Rob blabbered his apologies. Ben took a closer look at his assistant.

Rob hadn't worked for the company long, but he'd been Marley's assistant, too. The dual role was a holdover from when Fast Quid had been a much smaller company. CEO and COO had never found a need to hire separate assistants since their roles were so intertwined – Ben and Marley had done nearly everything together.

Well, he'd searched everywhere else. When Rob left early, carrying a small suitcase, Ben followed him home. Shortly outside One Canada Square, he took an escalator underground. Announcements droned from the loudspeakers, trains rumbled, brakes squealed.

Their Tube journey wound circuitously beneath London, ending on the Victoria line at Finsbury Park. As dusk approached, they followed Ben's assistant to Tollington.

Rob Cratchit, they soon discovered, lived in a positively decrepit social housing unit: five storeys of mildew-covered brick, rusty grates protecting the windows on the lower floors. The wall on one of the upper flats had collapsed, leaving the interior exposed. Orange plastic mesh fencing surrounded the fallen pile of detritus on the ground far below. Strange plants grew in odd places up each side of the building – nature, even here in the city, reclaiming that which humans had disused.

Dead trees on each side of the entryway held vigil over the building's corpse. A rubbish bag had spilt on the ground there, so Rob stepped over some greasy takeout trays and aluminium cans as he approached the door, where thin lines of illegible, artless graffiti marked that someone or other had been there.

Rob's small flat was on the fourth floor. The inside matched the outside. It reeked of mould, likely due to the torn-up wall in the entrance hallway, where rubber plumbing tape sealed a pipe that had apparently burst. The carpet was soaked all the way to the lounge. Rob's breath fogged in the freezing air as he trod over it and set his messenger bag and suitcase on a fold-out table.

"Tim," Rob called. "Come here. I bought you something." He bent to pick up an ornament that had fallen from a modest Christmas tree, and hung it back in place.

Ben took in the dismal environs. Rob, with his sharp vests and his flawlessly coifed hair, lived like this? Surely Ben paid him better.

A pale boy, eight or nine, shuffled in from one of the back rooms. Small red spots and occasional bruises dotted the skin of his stick-thin limbs. His feet never quite lifted off the floor as he dragged them forward. His eyelids drooped with fatigue, and the lymph node on one side of his neck bulged like a hand inside his skin was pressing its thumb forcefully outwards.

Rob held up the suitcase for Tim to see. "I bought you this. For spring term. It rolls, so you won't have to carry your books around."

Sick though Tim clearly was, a delighted grin burst onto his face. His teeth were crooked, yellow. One was black. From whatever disease ailed him? Or had Rob simply not had time to get him dental care?

"I can go back to school?" Tim asked.

"Doctors say yes, based on your new bloods," Rob said.

Tim's arms shook as he lifted them, and after a short struggle, he wrapped them around Rob. The boy closed his eyes and rested his head against Rob's sternum. "Thanks a million, Dad."

"What illness does he have?" Ben asked Ralph. "Does Rob have a partner? A family? Anyone to help him?" The few pictures on the walls showed only the father and son, no one else.

"I'm sorry, I don't know," Ralph said.

Rob removed some pre-cooked rice and beans from the refrigerator and heated them in a microwave. He made one bowl for himself and another for his son, then sat at the fold-out table and dug in. Tim picked at his food, but ate none of it.

"Were you working at Fast Quid or at the restaurant today?" Tim asked.

"Fast Quid," Rob said. "The restaurant's only on weekends now, remember. You need to eat your supper now, come on."

The boy ended his charade and set his spoon on the table. He gazed at his bowl like he wanted to want to eat. "I'm sorry, I'm just not hungry," he said.

"It doesn't matter. Your body needs food, especially now."

"Aren't we going to the match?"

"As soon as you finish your bowl, we'll go to the match."

"But we'll be late."

Rob became a statue with a firm stare. Tim sighed his discontent and picked his spoon back up. He dipped it into the bowl, scooped up a modest serving, and put it in his mouth. Rob smiled at him. "Are you sure you're game for the match?" he asked.

Tim nodded vigorously, swallowed. "You don't need to baby me, Dad."

Rob dropped his spoon into his bowl and plopped his hands on the table. "Tim, that's not fair. I love you, and I..." Rob's voice cracked. "I'm terrified. Do you understand?"

With effort, Tim excavated another spoonful of rice and beans. "I'm sorry you're scared."

Rob finished his meal and retired to the sofa. His whole face sagged; only forty, he looked at least ten years older. He kept eyeing the rolling suitcase.

When he pulled out his phone, Ben peered over his shoulder as he searched the internet for "five-year survival rate leukaemia stage four."

Incredible, the hidden worlds that course beneath external appearances. Ever since Rob had started at Fast Quid, Ben had seen him as he saw every employee: as an asset, a tool. Was that how other people had seen Ben, back when he'd been struggling?

Somewhere along the way, I started to see things and people from my father's point of view.

Rob scrolled through various financial websites: first his bank account, then the Universal Credit website, and finally the early wage access app that Ben's business had rolled out for its workers a few years ago. It was an internal, employee-only version of Fast Quid's business model, with slightly better terms. For a small fee, they could access their pay early, which was exactly what Rob was doing now. Paying to be paid. So he could afford a suitcase and a football match for his dying kid at Christmas.

A football match. A special one, on Christmas Eve, Arsenal versus Manchester United. A big public event that, even more so than annual Christmas events, would draw the attention of anyone in the area.

Including spirits.

"She's at the match," Ben said.

"Huh?" asked Ralph, who'd been studying the pictures of Rob and Tim on the walls.

"The football match. It's the biggest thing we haven't checked yet. The spirits might've overlooked it because it has nothing to do with Christmas. Marley mightn't have realised that. She might be there."

The flight was short. Emirates Stadium shined like a beacon in the night, soaking Londoners into it like a gleaming sponge. Ralph rounded its cantilever roof and alighted down in the car park – so as not to attract Graham's attention if he was lurking about inside, Ben guessed – where stragglers ran from their cars to make it to kick-off in time.

"Should we split up to cover more ground?" Ralph asked.

"No," Ben said. "I want you with me in case my dad shows up."

"In which case I will promptly run away, leaving you to fend for yourself."

"Not if I run away faster."

"I'm the one with the staff, mate. I can fly."

Concealing themselves in the crowd, they checked the pitch first. The seats surrounding it were filled to the upper tier. As the players rushed out through their tunnels, the throng of fans stood and roared.

The sound system resounded with 'North London Forever' and their singing voices echoed it.

After a childhood crammed with football training from a father who'd planned for his son to be a sports star, Ben had lost all interest in football. Whenever he entered a place like this, it brought back the powerless feeling of those formative years.

"She could be anywhere!" Ben called above the song. "You'd think she'd choose the pitch. Just stand right out in the middle of it."

"Maybe she was here earlier," Ralph called back. "Or maybe she hasn't arrived yet."

They roamed the terraces, then checked the turnstile entry area, several restaurants, and even the gift shop. "Bah!" Ben yelled when yet another search turned up empty. They'd stopped in the middle of a concourse, sparsely populated while most people were watching the match. A supporter whose body and clothes were covered in red, blue, and gold paint bolted past them towards the loo. "She needs me. And I'm not there for her. She was always there for me."

Ralph kept scanning the area futilely, like Marley would actually show up. *I should've come with her,* Ben thought. *I should've dealt better with my anger. I shouldn't have sent her away.* He should have done a lot of things regarding this woman whom he was belatedly realising meant everything to him.

"Thank you," Ben said to Ralph, scanning the concourse beside him. "Thank you for helping me."

Ralph smiled bleakly, and Ben read his own feelings in Ralph's face: they'd hit another dead end. "Pleasure's all mine, mate."

He spotted Rob and Tim outside, through a giant glass wall. Son was leaning on father, plodding towards an entrance. While still a good distance from it, Tim stopped in place. Ben worried he might be having a medical issue, but he soon found his feet again and struggled forward, oblivious to the spirits watching him.

Inside the stadium, the audience erupted in a cheer. Someone had scored a goal.

"Ralph," Ben said, tasting an unfamiliar interest in the wellbeing of someone he'd never met and didn't know. A painful sweetness. "Do you know if Tim will live? Do you have the power to see that far?"

"I can't go into the future," Ralph said, a bit too quickly. He looked down at his sandaled feet, pointedly avoiding eye contact.

"But you know," Ben said, reading him.

"I mean, I only have vague senses of other times. Little more than premonitions. It's not—"

"Tell me what you see."

Ralph met his eyes. His mouth was tense, shaking a bit, as if the words were a weight on his lips. "I see a vacant seat at Rob's table," he said slowly. "A suitcase full of schoolbooks without an owner, carefully preserved. I see Rob in a spiral of depression, unable to work."

The knowledge doused Ben like a bath of ice. He'd have never known. Rob would have turned in his resignation one day, Ben would've rehired immediately, and Ben would've continued ignorant of the man's personal crises.

But now he knew. And, much to his chagrin, he cared.

"Ben..." Ralph said.

"What, now you're going to tell me my number's almost up, too?"

"Ben, look."

He followed Ralph's gaze, glancing upwards just in time to see the ghost of an old woman pass in front of the moon and over the edge of the stadium. She carried no staff. Not one of the time spirits.

Marley.

Ralph raised his staff. They shot sideways rather than upwards, which surprised Ben at first. But it was a smart move. If they'd gone upwards, they'd have spent twenty seconds manoeuvring over the cantilever roof to get a good view while staying hidden from prying eyes. By going sideways, they stayed at ground level, blending in with the crowd as well as they could, and would quickly get a good view of the whole stadium as soon as they entered the arena.

They passed through a locker room, a shower, a staging area for the players. At the far end of that staging area, gazing out onto the pitch, floated Graham. A tall phantom, draped in black, hood drawn.

Ralph changed their trajectory, darting sideways and slightly upwards, through the ceiling, into the seats, surrounded by Arsenal fans. He found one of the rare empty seats and hunkered down into it, terror on his face. Supporters shouted. Arsenal pressed an advantage on the pitch.

My dad had the same idea we did. In the middle of the stadium, right above the players, Marley descended in full view of everyone with spirit eyes to see.

Ben rushed towards her, but he'd barely moved before Ralph caught his arm. "No! Ben, no."

Ben struggled against him. "Marley!" he shouted. Ralph wrapped a firm hand around his mouth and dragged him down into the seat so he was practically sitting on Ralph's lap. Ben bellowed into Ralph's hand and yanked against his arms, but the ghost held him down.

Arsenal scored, and 'Kernkraft 400' pounded over the sound system. Marley settled onto the pitch. Ben couldn't read her face from this distance. Was she dejected? Determined? If only he could communicate that he'd found a way to save her so she'd run for her life and stop this pointless suicide.

But after his father didn't show himself, even after Marley had waited there a minute, Ben stopped trying to break free.

"It's a trap," Ralph said, and let go of Ben, who quickly stood. "You see that, right? He doesn't care about her. He wants you. And if you show yourself, he'll snatch you right up."

"So *you* distract him!" Ben said. "I'll run and get her attention while he's dealing with you."

"He's not the only one, you know. There'll be other time spirits here, too. From other days. Who also have emergency authority to interact with humans. Knowing someone escaped from Hell, knowing their own sentences will be lighter if they help to enforce the rules."

Ben knelt to face him eye to eye. "Ralph, you know the way you feel about your family? I feel that way about Marley. Have you considered that the best way for us to see our loved ones again may be to stand up and do something for once?"

"I haven't a clue what you're on about. I do things quite often."

"Ralph…" How could Ben convey to the diffident schoolteacher what Marley meant to him? Ralph already knew their history. But he couldn't feel it in the way someone who'd lived it felt it. He couldn't know Marley was the one good thing, the one bright point in Ben's entire life that he could look back on and be genuinely proud of. Marley's companionship, her affection, her loyalty, her dogged altruism towards a man as unlikable as Ben – she was the only thing in his life that really mattered. He'd do anything for her.

But Ralph didn't understand that. With wide eyes glued on the pitch, he did nothing but cower deeper into his seat.

So Ben grabbed Ralph's staff and ran.

He bolted down the steps and heard a faint, "Stop!" from Ralph behind him, but the ghost didn't want to draw attention to himself, so he could do nothing to stop Ben now. He raced right through the barrier at the foot of the stands.

Hybrid turf brushed against his bare feet as his legs surged. "Marley!" he called. She loitered in the centre spot, waiting for doom.

Ben dared a glance behind him. Doom was on its way. His father's robes fluttered as he darted onto the pitch much faster than Ben. His shroud cloaked his face in darkness. One hand held his gnarled staff, the other reached forward, ready to grasp its quarry. His feet never touched the ground. Ben's didn't need to, either, but he felt faster running than floating.

Across the pitch, an Arsenal player intercepted the ball in mid-pass. A thunder of shouting supporters rumbled from all sides. They stood, waved flags, leapt up and down.

Ben ran for his life, and Marley's life, across the pitch in his pyjamas. A kick, and the ball zipped right through Ben's head. Arsenal and Man United players dashed round and through him towards the ever-shifting action.

Marley noticed him. A brief *Oh no you didn't* look gave way to sheer terror when she also saw the Ghost of Christmas Past barrelling forward, yards behind him.

Ben grabbed her. He gripped the staff.

He hadn't known how much of the time ghosts' power rested in the staffs, and how much rested in the ghosts themselves. But this gamble paid off.

They soared upwards. Just as Ben hoped: in the present, he could use the staff to fly. Marley yelped and held him tight. They rocketed through the sky, past the stadium's roof, towards London proper.

"Ha!" Ben said as they left his dad in the dust. "Now Dasher, now Dancer, now Prancer and Vixen!"

"I told you to let me go," Marley called over the rushing wind.

Jubilant at the rescue, Ben laughed. "On Comet, on Cupid, on Donner and Blitzen!"

"On my last legs, that's what I am."

"Marley, you took the best parts of me, the parts everyone else in my life ridiculed for being weak, and you made sure they survived all these years. Well, those parts of me are coming back in full force, and when I die, I'll be seeing you again."

"Are you on drugs?" Marley asked. "Ghost drugs?"

"I'm taking you to the future. My dad won't follow you there. You'll have time to think through your life and become the kind of person who goes somewhere nice when they die."

Silence, then: "Definitely drugs."

"Ralph thinks it'll work. We just have to find the Future Ghost."

"Oh, that's all, eh? Find the Future Ghost. Okay." But she smiled when she said this, and that was gratitude enough for Ben. He'd done the right thing. If there was even a small chance she could escape her fate, she wanted to try it. And maybe it wasn't too much for Ben to hope this rescue would atone, just a bit, for his self-centredness towards Marley over the decades.

The Palace of Westminster slept in the distance, lit from below. Ralph said he'd last seen the Ghost of Christmas Yet to Come there. Ben arced towards it.

No sooner had he done so than Graham rammed him from the side. He felt no pain in his spirit form, just a sharp jolt that sent him and Marley careening. Ben stopped their spin, looked frantically around for his father. His cloak matched the night sky perfectly. He could've been anywhere around them.

Ben cursed himself. His half-baked theft of Ralph's staff had been foolhardy, after all. Graham, of course, had a magic staff too, and could thus chase them into the sky.

"Ben, go. Go." Marley's arms constricted around him.

Go where? It was a cloudless night. The sky offered nowhere to hide.

He tried focusing on Ralph's staff, harnessing its power once again. But its light was dead – Ralph had extinguished it back at Marley's flat, probably to disincentivise Ben from filching it. Ben didn't know how to turn it back on. He and Marley couldn't escape into memory.

But he did feel a muted timeline. Not the expanse of a life full of memories, but the simple hours of a single calendar day. Today. Christmas Eve, the day Ralph was assigned to oversee.

Ben focused on the very end of the day and jumped them forward, the same way he'd jumped from one memory to another. Some lights blinked on or off in the city below, and a few rainclouds blinked into existence above, but jumping to 11:59pm seemed to have little other effect. Ben angled them downwards and started a descent.

Graham rammed them again, a lightning-fast phantom from the dark. This time, his aim was true. He impacted Ben directly in the arm holding the staff. Ben yelped as the force wrenched the stick loose. He watched helplessly as it tumbled to the earth. Their means of staying airborne lost, Ben and Marley soon followed.

Had Graham been waiting for them here for hours, biding his time until they reappeared? Or had he followed them directly from earlier in the evening to midnight? Ben had little time to wonder. His spirit plummeted with Marley's. They struck the pavement just west of St Paul's Cathedral.

London

The night was still. The streets were empty. Ben and Marley stood, got their bearings. The back alley where they'd fallen led to an inner-city residential district, five-storey flats looming above them. The wet ground smeared the reflection of a traffic signal at the end of the alley that blinked red, then green, with no cars around to appreciate its Christmas spirit.

A phantom's black robes billowed as it descended from on high before Ben or Marley could even say a word to each other. Graham landed a short distance from them. His staff clacked against the cobblestones.

Ben stepped forward to shield Marley from him, but Marley apparently had the same idea, and they bumped shoulders in their rush to defend each other. Marley chuckled a plaintive laugh.

The alley's walls hemmed them in from both sides. Staffless, they couldn't flee. They could run, but he'd catch them in seconds. Ben fought back panic.

"Ben," Marley whispered. Her eyes were wet, grim. Resigned. "Ben," she repeated, a lifetime of unsaid words summarised in one.

Ben took her transparent hands in his own. The cold gnawed at him. "I… I wanted better for you."

"If only we'd known what we know now," Marley said, "when we were young."

"Enough!" the hooded phantom called as it approached.

Ben let go of her hands. He turned to face his father. "Is there anything I can say or do that will convince you to leave us alone?" he asked.

Graham strode forward and spoke in that unnaturally deep voice: his father's, but more than his father's. "It won't be as bad as you think, lad," he said. "Changing history. I'll leave my payday loan empire to you when I die, don't worry."

Ben swallowed past a new lump in his throat. So that's what this was about? Jealousy? *He wants to steal my idea.*

If Marley was right – if Fast Quid had harmed people under Ben's leadership – how much worse would it become under Graham's? How would the course of Ben's life have changed if he'd never got out from under Graham's thumb? *I'd still be broke, no career and no friends, feeling sorry for myself, drinking every night away like I did in my twenties.* Graham wanted to reassert himself as dictator of Ben's life. Any promise of future benevolence in such a world was certainly a lie.

"And what if the past truly can't be changed, like the other ghosts say?" Ben asked.

Graham withdrew his hood to reveal his decaying face. For the first time in Ben's life, his father looked hopeful, like something good might be made of his future. Black teeth glistened behind his smile. "It *will* work. It must." He drifted closer. "I can undo all the hurt between us, lad. Make it so it never happened. Make you into the man I always hoped to raise, after all. You'll be tough! Important!"

Indignation boiled within Ben, but he strained to be outwardly empathetic. "Dad, I understand that you needed to be tough when you were growing up, and that it was a helpful coping mechanism. But now it's causing the very problems that made it needed in the first place."

"I want you and me to have lived better lives, lad. That's all."

"Well, I want to keep the life I lived. My life is far from perfect, but it's *my* life. It matters."

"And mine won't!" Graham yelled, despite his nearness to Ben. Oddly, he shrank away at his own outburst, hunching his shoulders a bit, as if ashamed. "Not if I don't make something of myself. Son, this is my last shot."

Ben considered, for a fraction of a second, using this rare moment of vulnerability to try to persuade Graham. *Use your last shot to connect with your son instead of outdoing him,* he might have said. Or maybe, *If you're able to change history, change it into something that's better for all of us.* These would have been the safe replies if Ben wanted to maximise the chances he and Marley would come out of this alive, or at least not fully dead.

But the bitterness that had made a home in Ben ever since the day Graham had kicked him out of the house, and had only grown since he'd learnt in ancient Rome what Graham was trying to do, was too great. The bitterness found Ben's voice, and spoke his reply without him even having to think.

"You had your shot," Ben said. "And you failed, you weak, enfeebled, effeminate layabout."

Marley's eyes went wide. She covered her mouth with her hands and shook her head fiercely, as if she could retroactively dissuade Ben from saying what he'd said.

Graham remained stoic. A throaty growl rumbled from his gullet. He extended his long arms to point his staff at Ben. A fiery crimson light bloomed at its pinnacle. The light of time, and travel through it.

"You could have made yourself so much better," Graham said.

Ben held his gaze. "You could have made yourself better, too."

"You ready, lad?"

"I'll run, if you take him," Marley said, stepping between Ben and his father's staff. "I'll hide. You'll spend ages finding me."

Graham laughed. A guttural, gagging sound. "I've got ages, luv. You spoilt my son. I won't let you off easy, trust me." He tapped Marley lightly with the staff, and her body was wrenched to the side as if hit by a car. She struck a brick wall and crumpled to the ground, groaning.

Ben moved to help her, but Graham lowered the staff to bar his way. "I sacrificed everything for you, lad. Most ungrateful goddamned son in history – and I've seen history. I slaved for you only to be forgotten. Abandoned." Graham drew his face close enough to Ben's that the stench of decay on his breath crept up his ghostly nostrils and down into his revolted stomach. "Owed," Graham finished, a fleck of his spittle landing on Ben's cheek.

"History," said a small voice behind Ben. He turned to see a figure behind him, silhouetted against the dome of St Paul's, a holly wreath crowning his head. His sandals shuffled over the cobblestones. "You don't seem to know much about history, for a Ghost of the Past."

Ben's father glared at the newcomer as he stepped into the light. Between the football match and now, Ralph had had hours to search for his staff that Ben had dropped, and apparently he'd found it. He clutched it firmly in his right hand.

Ralph was shaking. He approached as if each step might land on hot coals. The sight of him seemed to spur Marley to recover faster. She climbed to her feet.

"This is family business," Graham said to Ralph. "Get out of here."

"Family," Ralph repeated. His eyes lingered on Ben's as he said, "I'd do a lot for my family, too."

"Ralph," Marley said with a wary voice, "are you feeling okay?"

"I'm feeling..." Though Ralph's pace was measured, his feet never stopped moving as he drew close to Ben. He uncurled the fingers of his free hand, flexing it, then curled them into a fist. "I'm feeling powerful. Like someone back at that stadium made a decision robustly based in the present." He closed his eyes. Deflated his lungs in a long, slow exhale. Clearly quivering beneath a flood of fear. Nevertheless, Ralph stepped between Ben and his father.

"Ralph, take us back into my memories," Ben whispered, although his father was close enough to hear. "We have your staff. We can hide."

Ralph's voice quavered. "Enough hiding," he said.

Graham met his associate's eyes. A surprised, amused stare. "Scared out of your bones," he said. "Do you know who I am, little man?"

"Part of you is the ghost of a man I've barely met," Ralph said. "But part of you is the ghost of an idea: that the past should dominate the future." Ralph stepped forward. Ben stared in astonishment as Graham, the powerful Ghost of Christmas Past, stepped back. "It's a bad idea," Ralph continued. "We should learn from the past, we should use it. But we won't let it chain us down any more."

Ralph ran his hand over the top of his staff. A red light flared beneath it.

Graham seemed to realise he was ceding ground. He rallied and floated forward, closing the distance between him and Ralph. "Ghost of the Present, you have no power, next to me. You have no authority over me. You have no spine, no balls, no chance in hell of even dying like a real man."

Ralph stilled, seemed to centre himself. "I don't need any of that," he said to Graham with a twinkle in his eye. "I have London."

With the speed of a martial artist and the grace of a dancer, Ralph swept his staff in a wide arc between Graham and himself. At the spot on the ground where the staff pointed at any given moment, a gout of lava erupted from beneath the cobblestones, unleashing an intense ammonia smell that burnt Ben's nose and wet his eyes. A molten line of flaming earth separated them from Graham.

"Quickly!" Ralph said, and fled towards the other end of the alley.

Ben and Marley ran after him, each checking to make sure the other was following.

"What the hell was that?" Marley asked.

"Magma from London during the Hadean aeon, just after the planet formed," Ralph explained. Behind them, the phantom ascended alongside waves of heat, magma lighting it with a hellish glow as it hovered quickly forward, giving chase overhead like an avenging angel. Ralph, Ben, and Marley rounded a corner into a deserted street, running as fast as they could. "And here," Ralph continued like the world's most frantic tour guide, "we have the Old Bailey, where an IRA car bomb detonated in 1973."

They'd already passed the baroque building when he said this. Just as the phantom approached it, Ralph aimed his staff at the kerb behind them, and an ancient green Ford Cortina appeared there. It immediately burst apart in an ear-splitting explosion. Fire enveloped the street all the way up to the phantom. The ground shook and windows splintered all down the street. Even without a corporeal form, Ben felt the change in pressure.

Ralph waved his staff again, and the explosion vanished. Back into the past? The street was dark again, but broken glass was still falling through Ben and Marley's immaterial bodies.

A bottom-lit statue of Lady Justice stood atop the court building, her sword raised high and her scales balanced. A smaller figure clad in white robes flitted briefly behind her, watching the chase, but vanished before Ben could get a better glimpse. They ran onward.

The explosion had stalled Graham, perhaps disorienting him, but a minute later he was on them again, flying two storeys above street level. Ralph's eyes darted back and forth as he ran, as if searching for something in his own head. He raised his staff, and a sizzling streak of lightning flashed down from the heavens and struck the dome of St Paul's Cathedral. Still in mid-strike, it vanished when Ralph pointed his staff away from it.

"Oops, don't want that," he said, his eyes flitting about. He aimed his staff at the blank glass-and-limestone façade of the building they were passing. It disappeared in an instant, and in its place stood rickety wattle-and-daub dwellings with steep thatched roofs. People dressed in rags jumped out of the trio's way as they zipped past. Whether they were seeing Ben, Marley, and Ralph as ghosts or as physical time travellers was Ben's guess. One man was doubled over in a coughing fit, large bumps covering his body, his arms splotchy with alternating patches of light skin and marks as black as coal. The bubonic plague?

"Oops, *really* don't want that," Ralph said, extinguishing the scene as he moved his staff away. "Ah, here we go."

He aimed his staff at, of all places, a Fast Quid shop that happened to inhabit the bottom floor of a concrete building, its large Christmas tree inviting customers, prey. A three-storey timber structure topped with clay tiles on a sheer roof took its place. Flames wound through it and smoke billowed from the windows. It wasn't engulfed, not yet, but the whole structure would clearly go up soon.

"Now this is what I want," Ralph shouted over the fire's roar. He kicked in the front door beneath a hanging "Apothecarie" sign. "The Great Fire of London! Don't worry. I can see which areas will burn and which won't. I think."

Ben and Marley baulked. But Graham, cloak flapping, was coming up fast behind them. They had no choice.

Ralph led them through the seventeenth-century shop full of jars, bottles, and pots. They crossed away from a corner that was starting to blaze and raced up the stairs to a living space on the second floor. The place had empty square holes instead of windows, so air rushed in from all sides to feed the fire. Smoke grew thick enough that Ben couldn't see – it would surely kill them if they weren't spirits. The extreme heat was constricting enough as it was. He darted straight upwards through the ceiling, and the smoke cleared a bit on the third floor.

Ralph and Marley soon joined him, and Ralph searched the bedroom: a bed, a chest, a clothes press... a door. Flames licked the room's outer edges, intensifying by the second, as Ralph flung the doors open onto a balcony overhanging the street.

A thundering crash stole their attention. Graham broke through a burning timber beam that had fallen into the stairwell. A second fell in his way, but he simply passed through this one as a ghost.

"This way!" Ralph said. He took a running jump and leapt over the edge of the extended balcony onto another across the street. Beneath him, the street alternated between the seventeenth and twenty-first centuries depending on where his staff was pointing. One moment cobblestones, rats, diamond-patterned window panes, and darkness, the next a Costa Coffee limned with fairy lights.

Ben and Marley bolted forward, hopped onto the short balustrade, and jumped across the street to join Ralph. He waved his staff and erased the burning building, momentarily hiding Graham inside the offices above Fast Quid, and the trio inside a law firm above Costa Coffee. They raced down a flight of modern, less precarious stairs towards the exit, their feet barely touching the steps.

"Ralph, I've never seen this side of you," Ben said as they descended. "You're so brave."

"I'm so terrified I just peed my trousers!"

"Ghosts can pee?"

"I thought you ghosts weren't capable of changing the past," Marley said. "Aren't you changing the past by doing all this?"

"I'm not changing anything," Ralph said. "I'm just borrowing a bit of the past, then sending it back. Besides, who's to say there wasn't always a burning building that was transferred to the future for a minute, and I just helped it along?"

A security alarm triggered when they burst back out into the streets, squealing their location for half the City to hear. "We're still a ways from Westminster," Ralph said. "Keep up."

He zipped past closed pubs, street lamps, traffic signals, and Christmas displays, and now his feet didn't touch the ground at all.

"I think I saw her back there, at the Criminal Court," Ben said. "The Ghost of Christmas Yet to Come. She may be watching—"

A *centuria* of Roman soldiers sprang into existence around them. The instantaneousness of it startled the trio, forced them to stop in case they needed to defend themselves. The soldiers were stunned, too. A flurry of helmets, armour, red tunics, and sandals whirled round Ben. They panicked, staring at modern London above them, calling out to each other in Vulgar Latin.

In the middle of the street, one soldier raised his javelin to spear Marley. Too shocked to duck aside, she just stood there, and flinched when he impaled her before Ben could intervene. The javelin went straight through her. The confused soldier retracted the weapon, and tried again.

Graham stalked through the crowd of troops, his own staff raised as if to spear someone. "You fight dirty!" he shouted over the startled men. "I can match that."

A centurion shouted orders to his men, who gathered themselves into a testudo formation, shields facing outwards like a giant shell protecting the men inside, ready to defend themselves against the spirits.

Ralph zapped them all back into the past. He snapped his staff at Graham and threw him into the middle of a fight to the death between a group of Neanderthals and a cave bear.

Ben didn't stick around to see how the hominins or the bear would react to their new situation. He sped away, and Ralph and Marley followed. As Graham receded into the distance, he raised his staff towards the sky.

They turned into Fleet Street then down another back alley, and Ben was hopeful they'd lost his father. But a clunking, trainlike noise descended on the City.

"What is that?" Ben asked. Marley pointed upwards.

An immense hydrogen Zeppelin hung in the sky directly above them, blotting out the moon. Light from modern London reflected in the sleek curves of its canvas.

"Is that German?" Marley asked.

Ben and Ralph had no time to answer her before explosions rocked the street. Thunderclaps as loud as the car bomb had been, one after the other. A streetside birch split into fragments of fractured wood. The roof of a Vodafone shop blew up, raining debris.

"Let's go," Ben said. "Bombs can't hurt us. We're ghosts."

Ralph backed beneath a flower shop's awning as if it would protect him from the air raid. "They can't hurt us," he said, "but they can hurt other Londoners. If he's willing to go this far…"

Indeed, windows all down the street were lighting up. Although the City wasn't a residential area, enough people lived here that real-life bombs being dropped *would* cause casualties. A woman in a fourth-floor flat craned her head out her window, staring up at the Zeppelin.

"We can't let him hold the city hostage just so we'll give up," Ben said.

"Can't we?" Ralph asked, his features grim. "If we keep running, people will die."

Marley put an eager hand on each of their shoulders. "The London Smog of 1952. Ben and I weren't quite born yet, but I heard stories about it growing up."

Ben didn't understand why she was bringing this up, But Ralph seemed to. He nodded at her and lifted his staff.

Its red light pulsed. Visibility plummeted instantly. Ben could still see Marley and Ralph, but nothing beyond them, save for blurry lights in the fog.

No, not fog, Ben discovered when a passerby on the street started hacking. Whoever it was, they tried inhaling more deeply, but subsequent breaths only made their coughing worse.

"Air pollution," Marley explained. "Now the Zeppelin can't see the city."

When the coughing subsided for a few moments, Ben listened. The clunking of the blimp continued far above... but no more bombs fell. "Did they stop because they can't see their targets, or because they've noticed the Shard and are wondering what the hell it is?" he asked, grasping for a bit of levity.

"Shh!" Ralph said. He pulled Ben deeper into the smog. Marley gripped Ben's shoulders from behind.

They followed the wall of another alley. Chill, windless air hovered in all directions, an incorporeal menace to match the spectres wandering through it. They didn't speak. Ralph made no alterations to time or to the physical world. The clunking of the Zeppelin ebbed and quiet returned to the night.

Quiet, except the faint fluttering of robes.

"Sissy boy," Graham rasped in the darkness. Ben's skin, ethereal though it was, broke into gooseflesh. "Siiiissy boy..." The voice came from a different direction each time the phantom spoke. Ben could see nothing; he relied solely on Ralph to aim his feet. Ralph glanced back, his face grim.

"Come out, lad. There's no need to fear. I'll create a glorious new present for us. You won't have to be a sensitive little baby any more. I'll forge you like steel in a furnace." The swish of a staff through air. A thump against a wooden pallet that clattered to the ground. Close to Ben and his friends. "All you have to do is fall in line behind your old man and I'll put the both of us on top. I'll protect you. I'll destroy your enemies. No more softness. No more submission. No one will be able to touch you. Isn't that what you've always wanted?"

Ralph picked up his pace, leaving the safety of the wall and drifting directly away from Graham's voice. Ben and Marley held tight, keeping their human train intact as they drifted.

"And you," Graham continued. "Present Ghost. You're forbidden from dipping into the past. You weaker spirits love rules so much, and you want them to apply to stronger men who are above them. But you yourself have just broken a cardinal rule. Hypocrite."

Ralph made a twirling motion with his staff and pointed it upwards. Machine-gun fire resounded from above. Ben searched for its source, but all he saw was smog.

A *woosh* as the phantom moved quickly. Perhaps to go investigate? Ralph floated forward, waved the staff again, and the trio emerged into clear air. A wall of smog remained in place behind them, bisecting buildings and obscuring everything inside it.

Above them, British biplanes were circling the Zeppelin, raking it with bullets. Searchlights lit the great airship from below so the pilots could see it clearly.

All at once, it burst. Its canvas ruptured down the middle and a great fireball surged from its innards. The clouds surrounding it ignited with dim red light. A rumble like thunder split the heavens.

"Come on," Ralph called to Ben, who had stopped to gawk at the spectacle. Ben followed, but couldn't tear his eyes from the falling, burning Zeppelin. When it was mere yards above the tops of buildings, Ralph thrust his staff towards it, and the nose-diving wreck vanished into the past.

They were near the Thames now, heading west along its banks. The London Eye, a deep blue ring, was coming into view on the left.

The street around them shimmered. Chic buildings with modern façades evaporated, replaced by old brick ones with chimneys. Across the river, coal smoke was pouring out the top of the Tate Modern. The putrid stench of sewage assaulted Ben's nose. Mudflats stretching out into the river replaced its modern embankments.

Graham hadn't been distracted by the Zeppelin's destruction for long. He soared behind them again, his twisted staff outstretched, changing reality ahead. They altered course to avoid a new building that had popped up before them, and had to do so again mere seconds later.

"This smell is disgusting," Ralph said. "Sewer river, ugh!" He jabbed his staff back towards Graham, who was closing in fast a few metres behind them. A tall wattle-and-daub structure appeared next to him. Just as he passed, a woman with black teeth came to an upstairs window and shouted, "Gardyloo!" She threw a bucket of night soil downwards. Had Graham seen it coming, he could've let it fall right through his ghostly body, but Ralph had timed it perfectly.

As Graham lifted his staff to strike them, the nightsoil plopped down on him with a *splat*, covering the Ghost of Christmas Past in poo.

That finally stopped him. He spiralled sideways and crashed into the Thames with a glorious splash.

"Your own medicine!" Ralph shouted back at him. "Ha!"

Marley howled celebratory laughter, but Ben wasn't so optimistic. "He'll be back," he said. "We need cover. Something like the smog, but that we can see in. Can you put us in the middle of a crowd?"

Ralph pulled a couple of hundred suffragettes into the present, marching along the riverfront. The trio quickly passed through the bewildered women. Ralph sent them back. "No," he said, "too small. There was a huge suffragette march but we're too far away from where it was held."

"We need something bigger," Ben agreed.

Ralph thought a moment more. He smiled. "I think I know the thing."

Ralph sped up, his feet leaving the ground again, and Ben and Marley followed his lead. He hoisted his staff above him, and a radiant blast of red light beamed outwards.

Ben got the crowd he'd asked for. Tens of thousands of people appeared around them, clogging the streets as they danced, sang, revelled. Women wore utilitarian, square-shouldered blouses and knee-length skirts, while many of the men wore military uniforms. Papers fluttered like confetti from upper-storey windows. Union Jacks flew from the front of every shop, and from the top of a passing coupe into which a dozen young people were crammed.

Still running, Ben tried to make sense of the turbulent scene, and finally placed it when he saw a discarded newspaper on the ground, its headline reading *VICTORY! Prime Minister Announces End of War with Germany.*

They stayed at street level and flew along the Thames, passing bonfires, children jumping in fountains, and a gramophone playing Vera Lynn's 'The White Cliffs of Dover' to the streets. Ralph kept the arm holding his staff taut, straining as if the act of holding such a large piece of the past within the present was taxing him. The people in the crowd didn't seem to notice the modern buildings around them. Too lost in their celebrations, Ben assumed.

A burst overhead lit the streets in vivid amber. Ben glanced up to see the fireworks, but instead found that the corner of a hotel's top floor, next to the Victoria Embankment Gardens, had blown up. The explosion flared outwards. Shattered glass fell towards the crowd below. People screamed, ran.

Ralph sent them back to 1945 before anyone could get hurt. In place of their ruckus, the buzz of a million hornets vibrated through the night. A second bomb exploded in the gardens, many times more powerful than the small Zeppelin ones. A fountain of earth erupted from the blast.

Moonlight glinted off a squadron of aeroplanes high above them. "Damn, shouldn't have gone with World War II. Gave him the idea to invite the Luftwaffe."

A bomb exploded right in their path. They instinctively veered round it despite being ghosts that no explosion could harm. "Stay close!" Ralph called, raising his staff and bringing RAF fighters into the present as well. Vapour trails and machine-gun fire lit up the sky as the Battle of Britain reappeared over London.

Ben searched for his father, and soon found him: a phantom flying low over the Thames, darkness against darkness, like the fighter planes above. As they sped past firefighters from the Blitz spraying a bombed building, the bells of 'Westminster Quarters' resounded ahead of them. Big Ben, tolling the hour. They were close to the Houses of Parliament, and hopefully to the Ghost of Christmas Yet to Come.

But if Ralph was right that the Ghosts of the Past had much more power than the other ghosts, would she intervene? Or would she wait to approach them, for her own safety, until they'd found a way to deal with Graham?

Several wooden longships with dragon-headed keels popped into existence alongside the Thames. Warriors in mail and helmets surged over the river's embankment, brandishing spears, axes, shields. They could only have been Vikings.

They glanced upwards in confusion as they discovered the city they thought they were attacking was rather different than the one they'd planned to attack, but at this point, Ralph, Ben, and Marley were past being stalled by historical visitations. They sped right through the Vikings, round the corner towards the Palace of Westminster. Graham, apparently deciding enough was enough, dive-bombed towards the trio.

Ralph reached upwards, his staff conjuring forth an object hurtling much faster than Graham. "You want to invite the Nazis?" he yelled defiantly. "Fine, I'll give you the Nazis."

More than a third of a century after Ben had accidentally launched Bortley's V-2 rocket, Ralph plucked it out of history. It tore down from the sky in an instant and hit the junction at Westminster Bridge just as Graham was flying above it.

Asphalt fractured like glass. Within a second, a pillar of fire and earth shot into the sky, taller than Big Ben beside it. Little Ben's ghostly ears popped as the explosion ripped the street around him asunder. The apocalyptic roar would've deafened an embodied human. The Palace of Westminster's tall gothic windows shattered. Traffic signs zipped through the air like spears.

Ralph wasted no time. As debris pattered back to earth, he shouted to the old buildings around them, "Ghost of the Future! Help us! These souls seek refuge in times yet to come!"

Thick clods of dirt and asphalt fell like oversized raindrops. Ben leapt aside as a traffic signal fell from the heavens, right on top of him – had he been in his physical body, he'd have been struck. Detritus in the roadway burnt all the way down to Westminster Abbey. A cloud of dense dust drifted between the buildings. Somewhere inside that cloud was Ben's father, surely recuperating from the disorienting strike.

"Please!" Ralph repeated. "People with so much potential are going to die if you don't help us."

Potential? Why did Ralph think Ben had potential? He was an old man, his life mostly behind him.

A few cars that had been crossing the bridge were getting in each other's way as they all tried simultaneous U-turns. One man even hopped out of his car to flee on foot. Ben and Marley waited, scanning the blemished national landmarks for signs of the ghost. "Ha," Marley said. "Look at that."

Ben followed her gaze to an old church a short ways down the street. Gravestones ornamented the small lawn around it. Ben had stood among them, not long ago, and given a eulogy. Marley had paid a small fortune to be buried there.

"Fitting, that we'd end up back here," she said.

Ben preferred to see their presence here as a coincidence rather than an omen. He squeezed her shoulder. "We'll make it," he said.

His words seemed to do nothing to hearten Marley, though. And why would they? Ben's body was hypothetically safe back in his flat, while Marley's rotted beneath the earth. If Ben escaped his father, he'd live; if Marley escaped, she'd still be dead.

It's deeply unfair, death. So tragically, profoundly unfair.

Finally, the figure of a young girl emerged in front of Big Ben's great clock, high above them. Her silhouette carried a staff of twirling branches, splaying out at the top towards innumerable different futures.

Ben shared a smile with Marley. She took his hand in reassurance as the ghost began to descend.

Graham slammed into Ralph at high speed. Ben and Marley jumped back as the two spirits tumbled like a snowball.

Ralph detached himself, but Graham reared back and struck him in the head with his staff. Ralph cried out in pain. He half flew, half careened up towards Big Ben. Marley moved to help him, but Ben held her back.

"There's nothing we can do," he said. "Let's get to the Future Ghost."

"Ralph has helped us so much. We can't leave him."

But Graham was racing towards them. Ben pulled her towards the base of the massive clock.

Ralph held out his staff. Wind gathered around it, whipping at his robes. The top of the staff pulsed, not with its normal red glow, but with a brilliant flash of red light that briefly lit the streets as brightly as if the sun were setting.

What could only be described as waves of time washed over Ben and Marley. Marley's face appeared old, then young, then middle-aged, then that of a toddler, then a rotting skull. Ben lifted his own hand and found that it, too, was only bones. Another wave hit them, and Ben's hand returned to its normal self.

Ralph careened down towards Graham in a perfect reverse of his previous tumble upwards. Graham started running backwards. When the two spirits reconnected, Ralph's head knocked Graham's staff back behind the phantom's head.

He's rewinding their fight. Like my VHS player would.

Both spirits came together again, and they rolled rapidly towards Ben. Just as they reached him, Graham's staff pulsed red. He disengaged from Ralph and tried to grab Ben. Ben jumped away just in time, but Graham's bony fingers curled around Marley's torso. He snatched her away as he zoomed across the street.

Ralph followed, attacking him. Their clothes and limbs moved awkwardly, in slow movements punctuated by sudden jerks.

They're still moving backwards through time. Somehow, they'd already had this fight backward, and Ben was now seeing it played forward. He ran to help Marley, but the fight moved too fast for him to keep track of, the spirits practically bouncing off buildings and street, Marley caught in the middle of their battle.

A car came round Parliament Square. Its driver stopped in the street and gaped as Ralph and Graham hit each other repeatedly with crimson staffs, as if trying to send each other into the past. Marley got away from Graham and tried to flee back to Ben, but as she did so, Graham's staff let out another one of those blinding blasts of light. Marley's ghost rapidly shifted among various ages again.

Behind her, London itself shifted, now the squat stone dwellings of Roman Londinium, now bombed-out husks from the Blitz, now grand Renaissance structures from Elizabethan London.

Reality settled back to the present. The car in Parliament Square was speeding away. The spirits moved in forward motion again. Graham seized a bewildered Marley. Extreme strain pulled at Ralph's face. Beyond exhaustion, he kept battering away at his foe, but Graham seemed not to have exerted himself at all. One hand still clutching Marley, he effortlessly caught Ralph's staff in his other hand as Ralph brought it down for another hit.

Ralph's straight, almost regal staff lost its glossy finish. Its cylindrical shaft grew outwards, rewinding through time, until bark covered it. Finally, branches and leaves burst into existence, and the staff became a thin tree too heavy for Ralph to hold. It tipped over and fell in the street.

Graham whirled around Marley and gave Ralph one last, powerful strike with his staff.

Ralph went down. His head hit the pavement. His eyes closed. He stopped moving.

Ben glanced up at the Future Ghost. She still stood there, at the bottom of the clock face, making no move to intervene. Hood down, Ben's undead father drifted over burning debris, towing Marley, stalking towards Ben.

Ben had never truly experienced the terror of impending death. Much of his life had been spent on a hedonic treadmill of parties and profit maximisation designed in large part to avoid thinking about his own death. But now, with a premature afterlife of servitude to his father looming over him, his failure to prepare left him paralysed.

There was so much left to do, so many people he'd meant to get back in touch with, but hadn't. He was left naked, vulnerable, before the relentless onslaught of mortality – and maybe of an alternate, Graham-centric version of his life he'd be terrified to have lived.

Soft light blossomed above the roadway. Gently undulating coils of energy unfurled above Ralph, who stirred and tried to mumble something. Far above Ben, the Ghost of Christmas Yet to Come was pointing her staff at the defeated spirit, and it glowed yellow-white. Even Graham stopped for a moment to watch. Ralph and his staff levitated towards the new light source.

Ben took a small bit of consolation, at least, in this. What had changed, that Ralph could now enter a better afterlife? He'd told Ben that the time ghosts served until they came to terms with some suffering they'd caused and were ready to atone. Had Ralph's selfless defence of Ben and Marley earned him this deliverance? Had he, oddly enough, done it for his family? Had Graham's obsession with changing the past shown Ralph the futility of pining for living people with whom he was forbidden to interact? Maybe Ralph had delved deep into his motivations and he'd let his family go. Maybe he'd sought to save Ben and Marley from suffering as he had. Or maybe Ralph had simply wanted to become the type of person who would help others even at great risk to himself.

Ben would never know.

Distant though Ralph was, his eyes met Ben's as he disappeared. The apparition of his body, already transparent, faded further as it met the light. The light itself soon dimmed to nothing, and Ralph was gone.

Ben's feet left the ground. He felt for a moment like he was falling and flailed to catch himself, but no, he was levitating just as Ralph had. Only now no heavenly sunshine was beaming down. From the top of Big Ben, the Future Ghost was now aiming her staff in Ben's direction. Pulling him up? The storeys flew by, faster even than Graham could fly.

Marley, too, succumbed to antigravity. She was pulled up feet first, but Graham held tight to her arms and kept her from joining Ben in the air. "Ben!" she called, craning her neck to look up at him. It was a plea for connection, for Ben to see her in her fear. Neither of them could control the forces that were pulling them apart.

"You always find a way, don't you, lad?" Graham called as Ben rose ever higher. "You think I won't use my leverage over you?"

Graham slowly – dramatically, even, as if to make a point – extended the arm that held his staff. He aimed it at the asphalt, and the light at the top pulsed *black*. A new, vivid absence of light that pulled illumination from the surrounding street lamps and buildings into itself, and extinguished it.

A new gateway opened in the street. A portal to an inferno. Flames shot up as if alive, bursting at their chance to escape their confines. The rush of scorching air formed currents around the fire, and painted the space above it in the wavering lines of a mirage.

Graham held Marley over the flames.

The Ghost of Christmas Yet to Come caught Ben by his pyjamas at the top of Big Ben. He rocked to a stop but paid her no mind. "Dad, no!"

"You think I won't?" Graham yelled. Marley clutched his arm, pulled at it, tried to climb up it back towards safety. But he didn't budge.

"I know you will!" Ben called. "And I'm begging you to please, please show some mercy. This is the woman I love, Dad."

"Then get down here *now*."

Ben strained against the Future Ghost. "What are you doing? Go rescue her," he said to her, getting his first good look at her as she held him by his collar in the soft light of the great clock. About ten years old, she wore a white tunic, a simple rope binding it at her waist. Her unkempt hair was white and thin as if with age. Her face, too, bore a hardness, a gravity that no child's face should bear. She studied him with sorrowful, detached eyes, like the world had fallen apart, and tonight's events were only a small part of it. Like her saving him now would have no effect on an even greater tragedy.

The spirit flickered, blinking out of existence for a fraction of a second during which Ben started to fall. She reappeared, holding him. In another split second, her eyes skewed far to the left, her torso far to the right, and so on down her body, in what looked like an analogue version of a digital video glitch. An instant later, she was back, her normal self.

Ben did a double take. Graham actually flinched. He took a single step back, but that was enough of a tell for Ben. *Why is he afraid of the Future Ghost?* Ben had thought the Past Ghosts had immense power over the Future Ghosts.

"Last warning, lad. I never really needed her. All I had to do was wait for you to die. The only reason I've been chasing you across time is because I'm an impatient man."

Ben couldn't read the spite in his father's eyes. He'd never been able to. Did Graham despise his son for not living up to his impossible definitions of manliness and success? Or was it more personal? Did he still feel betrayed that Ben, as a young man, had been willing to turn his back on him and try to build a better life on his own? Or was

Graham just a bitter man to his core, ready to lash out and destroy anything he couldn't control, because someone had once told him he had to control others in order to be valued himself?

Regardless, real, deep pain simmered behind Graham's gaze, plain for Ben to see even from afar. Perhaps Graham's own father or society itself had put him there, but the shovel was now firmly in Graham's hands, and for as long as Ben had known him, he'd used it only to bury himself deeper.

"I'll find another way to get to you," Graham said to his son.

"No," Ben said, and wrenched away from the Future Ghost's grip on him. He sped down the side of the clock tower toward Graham. *I can reach her. I can take her away.* His father looked surprised, like he hadn't expected such a bold move from Ben. The surprise quickly morphed into a hateful little smile.

He dropped Marley.

Her eyes met Ben's, pleading, terrified. She screamed as she fell into the flames. Ben bellowed, wailed as she vanished back into the underworld. He reached towards her as if he could touch her if only he strained hard enough.

With a swift swipe of Graham's staff, the gateway to Hell disappeared, cutting off Marley's scream. He stood in the middle of Bridge Street, hand in a fist at his side, the fire in his gaze burning ever hotter for his act of spite.

What a thing to do. What a vengeful, pointless thing to do.

Graham had indeed given up his leverage. With Marley back in Hell, the "emergency" that had been declared upon her escape would be rescinded, and Graham would lose his free rein to prowl the present, to interact with Ben.

He'd condemned Marley's soul just to spite his son. Just because he knew how devastatingly it would hurt him. *If he couldn't use her to kidnap me, at least he could use her to cause me pain.*

And it worked. Grief was a mountain above him, unscalable, unfathomable. He continued his charge downward, his own safety be damned. He would claw at the asphalt where the portal had been to try and find some way to reach Marley.

For now Marley would not find safety by hiding in the future. Marley would not reach Heaven. Marley would likely be chained more tightly, watched more acutely than before to ensure she wouldn't mount another escape.

Ben would never see her again, unless he went to Hell himself. He'd had this chance to save her, and he'd failed, and that failure would forever drag on him like chains.

A second after she was gone, Graham gave pursuit a shot, and zoomed upwards to meet Ben in the air.

The Future Ghost was behind Ben again, yanking at his collar, scowling. Her staff pulsed red. London fluctuated around them. Graham, zooming towards them, disappeared. The damage from the explosion in the street vanished. They were in another time, but Ben had no hope his mind would ever fully leave the seconds when Marley had fallen helplessly away from him, or the weeks they'd spent together in his memories, wishing in vain that their time together would last.

A Memory of the Future

The spirit tucked a hand beneath each of Ben's armpits and carried him, limp, emotionally numb, down towards London. He could scarcely move, or think. The cars below all looked sleeker, extra skyscrapers dominated the city centre, and the air around them was swarming with a hundred thousand drones, but the significance of these observations was lost on Ben. Whenever they were, they landed in council housing from the 1970s, another dingy tower block untouched by time, except insofar as it was gradually decaying. Not unlike Rob's flat. But Ben didn't know these people: two adults and their children, huddled together in the cold on an upper floor. He couldn't guess why the spirit had taken him here.

She said nothing, but vaguely frowned whenever he looked at her, like she couldn't understand what Ralph had seen in him, yet was saddled with him out of fondness for or debt to the departed

Ghost of the Present. Or was Ben just projecting criticism onto her because he expected to be criticised?

When she let him go, he fell to his hands and knees on the stained carpet. He stayed petrified, utterly lost. Marley's death erased any curiosity he might have had about the time to which they'd travelled. What future could there possibly be for him, knowing he'd almost saved her? How could he live with himself?

"Take me back," Ben muttered.

The spirit stood impassive in the mouth of the hallway blocking Ben's exit, one hand on her staff.

"Take me back," Ben repeated, louder. "I don't need a place to hide any more. I don't wish to see the future. Take me back to my flat and let me be."

The old, familiar tightness in his chest constricted again. He'd always seen it as a problem with his body, but enough of that compressing feeling must have come from his spirit that it could still affect him now: anxiety that had started out of desperation for control over his own life, and that continued to take bites out of him each time he risked losing that agency.

The ghost remained silent. She made no move or gesture, or acknowledgement of Ben.

He lifted his head to face her. "Ghost of Christmas Future, I demand that you take me back."

"I am not the Ghost of Christmas Future," she said, her voice deep for a child's, forceful and imperious even in its quietness. "I am the Ghost of Christmas Futures."

Ben braced a hand against the stand that held the TV. He got to his feet, two heads taller than this girl who, he was starting to wonder, might be more captor than guardian. "What's your story?" he asked her, assessing her unadorned tunic. "You were a child labourer who died in a factory? Or maybe you were a human sacrifice made by the druids?"

"In most timelines, I die on the sixth of March, 2207."

A shiver ran through Ben. Her answer had caught him off guard. In his rush to get Marley to safety, what strange new realm, with strange new rules, had he wandered into?

"And what did you do to deserve the underworld?" Ben asked, wondering what sin a child could possibly commit that would sentence her to doom.

"I murdered two people," the girl said. And Ben had his answer.

He backed deeper into the lounge, away from the spirit. She watched him, vigilant. Ben couldn't shake the sense that beneath her stillness, all her muscles were tensed, ready to spring into action and tear him apart.

Let her do so. Let me be erased. Ben sat on the floor under the weight of Marley's second death. It was hitting him harder than her first had, now that he knew whom and what he'd lost.

He stayed there for hours. So did the family, only rising when one of them needed to run through the freezing cold to use the loo. Didn't the parents have jobs? Weren't there leisure activities they could enjoy together, even in the severe cold?

Marley dominated his thoughts. He kept replaying her death, wondering what he should have done differently. How could she be gone forever when she'd just been talking with him, touching him? Tangible. A ghost, yes, and not truly alive. But the fact that mere seconds could decide a person's eternal fate left Ben in disbelief.

"Well, it's brilliant news," the woman on the sofa said. She'd been holding a mobile phone so the whole family could see it. Now she retracted it and scrolled through a webpage. "Will there be a pause in their debt collections?"

"It's a multinational corporation," said the man sitting next to her. Worry marred his face. One of his kids nuzzled up next to him and he slid an arm around him. "They don't stop debt collections just because their CEO died."

Ben froze. The dread he'd been feeling squeezed his chest even tighter.

"Maybe they'll be more forgiving now, though?" the woman said. "New policies that give us longer to get the money? Maybe even a bit of debt forgiveness?"

"Maybe. At least we can sleep tonight with lighter hearts, knowing that man isn't in charge any more."

The man rubbed the stubble on his cheeks, and Ben recognised him. Older now, but this was the same man who'd snuck past security and ambushed Ben in Marley's office, upset by the lengths Fast Quid had gone to collect his debt. *Under terms he agreed to!* a part of Ben's mind pointed out, pre-emptively objecting to any pity Ben might feel. But he was too shocked to feel anything else – both by the knowledge of his own death, and the knowledge that this man was still in debt to Fast Quid. How many years had passed? Surely he'd had enough time by now to repay a single payday loan. Surely.

His children's faces, hushed and clustered round to hear what they so little understood, were brighter. It was a happier flat for Ben's death! And if one family, even its children, were reacting this way, how many other thousands of people around the world were also reacting with joy?

Perhaps this was why Graham had feared the Future Ghost. Perhaps, although he could easily best her in a fight, he found what she represented deeply disturbing: a future without him in it, where any inflated significance his ego had once bequeathed him was diminished in the cold light of passing time.

But Ben was not his father, and was not as susceptible to ham-fisted shenanigans like this. He scowled at the Future Ghost. "I see what you're trying, taking me here," he said. "You're nothing but a more melodramatic version of Ralph. Everyone dies. I knew I'd die eventually. Take me to my funeral, take me to my dead body so I can watch it burn in the cremation oven, for all I care. Marley's dead, and nothing else matters."

The ghost had truly thought knowledge of his death would make him a better person? Why did she care what type of person Ben was? Another lecture on his mistakes was the last thing he needed right now, with Marley's death a fresh wound.

He'd felt so triumphant, saving her at the football match. Doing something selfless, for once. In the wake of such an act, it was easy to imagine he cared not only about Marley, but about everyone. Ben was supposed to stay with her, to become a man less afraid to acknowledge his vulnerabilities, to right the wrongs he'd done. He was supposed to nurture the latent kindness within him that decades of cut-throat competition had strangled.

But with Marley gone – and with Ben not long for this world, either – what good was any of that? Who cared if people celebrated his death? Even in death, he'd keep his station. He'd be remembered as the man who'd invented payday loans, a titan of the UK's finance sector. Not bad for a sensitive boy who'd delighted in acting in church plays, who used to rock his baby sister to sleep because comforting children was beneath their dad.

Anyone else whom that boy could have become was now unattainable to Ben. *I am who I made myself, and I should be proud of it. Switching tracks this late in the journey won't take me far.*

But that wasn't what Marley had thought.

"Is this the unchangeable future?" Ben blurted without thinking. He gestured to the family on the sofa, a little happier now that Ben was in the ground.

The spirit inclined her head as if trying to get a read on Ben. "This is currently the highest-probability future," she said.

So it can be changed. Even now.

But no. Why did this future seem so instinctively bad to him? He'd be dead in any future!

Wasn't it enough to enjoy what time he had left as best he could without Marley? He could afford to live like Bortley now. Party his life away. Or he could continue on the familiar road of expanding Fast Quid, building the fortune that insulated him from future pain but did nothing to protect him from the past, no matter how fiercely he tried to force it to. *Whoever has the most money when he dies wins.*

"Why try to become a different man now?" Ben asked as if to Marley, as if arguing with her memory might bring her back. He got up and paced the room. "What good will it do me? I'm an innovator, not a saint. Tell me, spirit. I'm listening. You've clearly brought me here to try and teach me some godforsaken lesson. But I don't want your sermon, ghost. I don't care about your future. I want to go back

363

and grieve, then live my life. I have no need to listen to people who think they know better than I do. I've always known what's best for myself, and it's never changed."

The spirit blinked, passed her staff from one hand to the other. "Knowledge of what's best increases with time," she said. "It would be surprising if our morals never changed as we learned more, as the future unfolds."

"Bah!" Ben said. "It's all blind guesses. There's no way to really know what the future will think is right or wrong. We'll all be wrong someday. Even you, who apparently comes from the future. The *more* distant future will look back and see you as a moral abomination, too. We may as well not even try."

The spirit flickered again, briefly winking away then reappearing, like a guttering candle flame. She barely reacted to it: a glance down at her body, a frown. For her, Ben was beginning to see, this was a striking display of emotion.

"I don't think you realise what's at stake. What futures await you," she said, "if you get it right."

"Get what right?"

The ghost stood as still as a corpse, betraying nothing of her thoughts – until the corner of her mouth rose, and she actually smirked at him. She offered him her free hand, inviting him to take it. To be led... where? When?

The kids started a programme on the TV, while the parents moved to the kitchen to continue their conversation. The man filled plastic bottles with hot mains water, and commented that he hoped it would keep the kids warm in bed while the central heating was out. A delivery drone descended beyond their small balcony. Farther still, lightning flashed from a storm cloud.

Cold despair pressed in around Ben. To spend the rest of his days sinking into it, to make this flat forever his prison, seemed an attractive future, given Marley's death.

Nevertheless, Ben stepped gingerly towards the smirking ghost. He lowered his hand onto hers. She tightened her grip around his.

Her staff pulsed red.

The flat's walls burst outwards. The family shrank into pinpoints, then disappeared. A brilliant, vibrant day swallowed the night.

Vertigo seized Ben. He grabbed the spirit's hand with both of his to keep from falling what was suddenly a vast distance beneath them. A moment later, he realised there was no need for this, and withdrew one hand.

A verdant landscape yawned beneath them. A hilly countryside saturated with trees and fields, devoid of roads and field boundaries. They flew swiftly towards a magnificent city, its skyscrapers four times taller than any Ben had ever seen. Spires and pyramids and ovular towers, all painted white, all connected by innumerable footpaths filled with people and greenery. The solar farms surrounding the city limits were giant petals, the buildings pistils and stamens stretching to the heavens.

"Where are we?" Ben asked. "What city is that?"

The ghost's smile hadn't left her face. "London," she said.

London? With no roads connecting it to other cities? No traffic clogging its streets? No industrial zones? And where were the Shard, the Gherkin, the Eye? A cornucopia of varied tree species flourished everywhere: on the tops of buildings, at the edges of every roadway.

The urban sprawl had been completely replaced with architectural splendour dwarfing even that of London of the twenty-first century. Each building had a distinct style and shape, as if the architects had crafted them over decades with the devotion of true artists.

But there, in the centre of it all, was the familiar shape of the Thames, winding next to the Houses of Parliament and Big Ben.

"London," Ben repeated, trying to process what he was seeing. Wishing Marley was here to see it with him. He let go of the ghost's hand but continued zipping along beside her, as he had with Ralph.

Before his very eyes, an honest-to-God starship blasted off from Heathrow in the distance, climbing rapidly towards space. Nearby, cars flew from building to building, some upwards, some downwards.

"It's incredible," Ben said in defiance of his grief as the spirit led him between skyscrapers.

"There are many people working hard to make this future come to pass," the spirit replied. "We'd love for you to join us."

Ben chuckled at this. He'd got so used to so-called altruists sneering at him, he didn't know how to react when one did the opposite.

"It's not just London," the spirit continued. "Kinshasa and Port-au-Prince look just as amazing. Every city does. People in this future live at least twice as long. There's no illness, war, poverty, hunger. No bias in the legal system. Climate change and factory farming are things of the past. There is disagreement on many ideas, but everyone has a say in how their governments and businesses are run. All viewpoints are taken into consideration when decisions are made."

All of this seemed a preposterous fantasy to Ben. A fiction. This wasn't how the world worked. Humanity's goals weren't supposed to be achievable like this. They were supposed to be unattainable mirages of the mind, meant to paint the real world harsh by comparison. Tenacious people relished this discrepancy – they let it forge them, surfed the harshness like a wave – while the fragile wallowed in the fantasy and were rightly mocked for it.

And yet here was that fantasy, come to life before Ben's eyes. The ghost was right: how differently would Ben have lived his life had he known such a future was possible?

"It's not," Ben said.

"I'm sorry?"

"None of this is possible. People are selfish. There must be a catch. Brainwashing, or some dystopian attempt to change what a human being is."

"Biology may not change quickly, but culture can. All on its own." The spirit smiled as if proud of her species.

"Bah." Disagree with her though Ben might, maybe it was safe to try thinking of something besides Marley, at least for another minute or three. Maybe Ben could sink his teeth into something in this future after all.

"How am I thought of here?" he asked. When the spirit didn't respond, he added, "Am I thought of at all? Do people remember me?"

The spirit's continued silence left Ben to ponder the limits of anyone's legacy, no matter how much one achieves during a lifetime. Far enough in the future, the names of every Roman emperor and US president would be forgotten. Da Vinci, van Gogh, Beethoven, and the Beatles... eventually, no one would remember them, either.

Conquest in search of truly lasting greatness... how many great men have sacrificed all their life's time and energy on the altar of this unreachable goal?

Am I content to be another one of them?

Fine. If the spirit wouldn't play nice with him, he wouldn't play nice with the spirit. He distanced himself from her and fell through the city. Leaving her was irrational – she could easily reach him again. But her lack of sympathy for what had happened to Marley emphasised to Ben that she had ulterior motives: she wasn't showing him this for his benefit, but somehow for hers. The sooner she saw he wanted no part of her machinations, the sooner, hopefully, she'd let him leave and tend his wounds.

But still, this future sparked Ben's curiosity.

Beneath him, children capered in a splash park. Families cheered at an orator's story on a street corner. A field trip of what looked like secondary school students entered a museum with a yin and yang above its door. No two people down there had quite the same colour of skin – a few were even blue, green, purple, rainbow, some with multicoloured hair and eyes and nails. One woman roller-blading down the pavement appeared to have TV screens in place of her skin: a radiant display that was currently treating onlookers to a recording of a fireworks show. A few were giants, two storeys tall, while others were tiny, less than two feet tall. People whose limbs had been replaced by machines. People with wings like those of angels. No dirt, no homeless, no one rushing, no one fighting.

Why does this future provoke such visceral suspicion in me? Is something wrong with what I'm seeing... or is something wrong with me?

Ben touched down in a lush courtyard, next to two young men who were speaking to a computer terminal built into a building's outside wall.

"... it since you're first in our class, Jorwick," the smaller boy was in the middle of saying. "You don't have to do this."

The older boy – Jorwick – elbowed his friend. "Relax, mate. I've got you." He waved a hand in front of the computer terminal. "Uh, hello, AI that runs the school system. Are you there?"

"Hello, Jorwick and Fenton," said a gender-neutral voice from the terminal. "How are you feeling today?"

"Better than last week, thanks. And yourself?"

"I'm well. What can I help you with?"

"Yeah, about that. My mate Fenton here is busting his bum to pass trigonometry, history of the Tudors, and... well, pretty much all his classes. But he's not passing any of 'em. Since he finishes school this year, I'm wondering if you could maybe set him up with some of that ongoing learning. At his level, of course, plus a comfortable flat and a monthly stipend."

Ben practically jumped out of his skin. So much about the barbaric interaction he was seeing disturbed him. For starters: *An AI runs their school system, with no human oversight? And...*

"What kind of society rewards a student for poor performance?" Ben asked when the spirit touched down next to him.

"He's not capable of being a better student. Should he go without housing and food, just for that?"

"I—" Ben sputtered for a moment before finding the right words. "Society needs to reward greatness. Otherwise we'll lose all incentive to achieve."

"Jorwick continues to achieve," the ghost said. "He is not disincentivised, even though no one needs to work here. Could it be possible that people achieve for the thrill of achievement itself, rather than for rewards in status or money?"

Ben snorted. "Spend a few minutes in one of my board meetings, then get back to me."

"Let me rephrase. Could it be possible that in a world where everyone has status, and enough money to meet basic needs, the people who achieve will be those who have an innate desire to do so, rather than those who are driven by the dictates of competitive survival?"

Ben chewed on the question, but couldn't see what was wrong with a little hardship in life. The intelligent boy laughed at a joke the stupid one told, and patted him on the back. The smart one, Jorwick, seemed to have much more going for him than Ben had had at his age. Yet instead of parlaying that advantage into greater advantage, he was helping a lesser boy who might have struggled without his help.

"Show me whatever utopia you want, but you can't deny that our world was built on hierarchies. They have tremendous benefits."

"Might they also have tremendous costs?"

Ben laughed. This was a child he spoke to. What could she know about such things? "Costs, like Fenton's feelings getting hurt?" Ben asked.

"Costs, like this future and those adjacent to it having only a 3.28 per cent probability of coming to pass."

Ben observed the pedestrian traffic around him. Most people walked in groups of two or more. Happy, healthy, rich, free.

"This future is unlikely?" Ben asked. Did he dare ask the obvious follow-up question? He swallowed. He dared. "What is the most likely future?"

"Based on humanity's current trajectory?" the ghost asked. She lifted her staff. Red light beamed from the top, a crimson lighthouse beacon, bright even during daytime. The skyscrapers around them sank into the earth. The urge to flee struck Ben once again.

But what future would I be fleeing into?

"Even in your time," the ghost continued, "you live in a world of abundance. Yet your social traditions and your unchecked evolutionary heritage drive you to see the world as a zero-sum competition for status and survival. Needless scarcity is artificially created so you can climb the hierarchies you crave. In the most likely future, this craving is worshipped. Never questioned. Never kept in check."

Ben and the ghost ascended past flying cars vanishing in showers of sparks. The egalitarian future receded, and below, a vast shanty town erupted beside the Thames. Dirt roads littered with plastic rubbish and broken glass twisted between improvised roofs of corrugated iron, wood planks, tarps. Thick smog rendered all in sepia tones, reducing visibility beyond a mile or so. But this London had no lights, not even any power lines. Did it have any power at all? It was plain to see that the City and its skyscrapers were gone, replaced by slums. As far as Ben could see in all directions, he couldn't spot a single tree or bush.

They drifted above the ramshackle dwellings in ruddy dusk. A group of women heaved a large bucket of water up a rocky incline near the river. Two men pummelled each other in a fist fight right next to a mostly fruitless fruit stall. Passersby ignored their fight entirely. Children roamed atop a landfill, picking through rubbish. At the foot of the landfill, a pack of street dogs was discovering a dead body lying in the road.

This was the most probable future? London had been stable, rich, a global city. Where had all the wealth gone? What calamity had befallen Ben's home? Ben's rage at his father, his heartache at Marley's passing, seemed strangely small concerns all of a sudden.

"What *is* this?" Ben asked the spirit, flying beside him.

"Since my death, I have spent generations of time studying, learning, so I can answer that question," she said. "The answer is that this future is a reversion to the historical mean. What do you know about the distribution of poverty in the static economies between the Neolithic and the Industrial Revolution?"

The question was almost gibberish to Ben. Did the spirit expect him to have taken a graduate course in it? "Uh, lots of people were very poor," he guessed.

"Yes. Only a small elite held wealth."

"I can see where this is going," Ben said. "Spirit, London was *built* by selfish men looking out for their own interests. The very thing that built London couldn't tear it down, much less tear the world down."

The ghost continued as if Ben hadn't objected. "The Industrial Revolution showed states and corporations that having a working class made them competitive with other states and corporations. So they educated their people, kept them healthy, paid them, gave them a say."

"The miracle of capitalism," Ben remarked.

"Indeed. But none of that holds after artificial intelligence automates all labour. In this future, productivity doesn't depend on human beings. The automation fulfils the roles of both producer and consumer, consuming in order to produce, growing wealth for its owners without any need to pay people or keep them satisfied.

They have no economic value as workers or as customers, and thus no political power, either."

Ben surveyed the squalor as they flew farther north. Emirates Stadium loomed like a giant in the mist. Huge chunks of it had crumbled off, and thousands of tents and other makeshift dwellings covered what was left of the rest.

A crisis of a future where most humans were locked out of power? Science fiction, surely.

"I'm confused," Ben said. "In the good future we just visited, no one needed to work, either. Automation controlled everything. There's clearly some gigantic difference between the two futures, but it has nothing to do with AI."

The glowing suggestion of the sun in the smog behind the ghost next to him cast her in eerie darkness. "It takes very wise leaders, very judicious and ethical *CEOs* in particular, to make the transition into the better futures."

Ben gave her a sidelong stare at her emphasis of the word *CEOs*. "Surely some people here are okay?" he asked. "With all the work the machines are doing, it can't be terrible for everyone."

The ghost led him to an estate – no, a fortress – atop a hill. Humanoid robot security guards patrolled a two-storey-tall concrete wall ringing an expansive, Scandinavian-style house. Gardens, stables, a pool as long and wide as the house, a protective drone swarm flying over it in the shape of a giant dome... *If Bortley lived in this future, he'd live here.*

Beside the pool, a middle-aged man in swimming trunks and a bathrobe was trying to shoo away a dozen or so talking drones, which were apparently trying to sell him various "premium-quality" job titles – literally sell him titles, for money. £19 million for "Director of Executive Strategy", £23 million for "Governance Partner", and most cringeworthy of all, to Ben's ears, £28 million for "Thought Leader".

What organisation, if any, were these titles for? What did the man actually do, if anything? Were the prices so high because of inflation, or simply because the man had so much wealth? And perhaps most importantly, why were these drones so aggressively marketing to this one man rather than meeting the great needs, and presumably market demands, just outside the walls? Did they think they could get more money out of him than from the population outside?

If so, were they right?

Ben watched the commotion for ten minutes, and still couldn't answer these questions. The man in the bathrobe seemed to be enjoying the absurd game, teasing the drones as he ran round his expansive pool.

"Why don't people try to bargain with society's leaders?" Ben asked. "Change things?"

"They do, often," the ghost replied.

"Then why don't they try to overthrow them?"

"They do, often." She snagged one of the drones as it passed. It whirred louder in her immaterial grip, trying to muscle its way free. She examined it with the curiosity of an anatomist dissecting a particularly unusual creature. "Again, few people have power here. There's far more wealth here than in your time, but almost all of it is parked in banks and never used. There's no growth. Any would-be innovators or entrepreneurs are too busy trying to get enough food."

She let the drone go. Ben meandered to the thick wall, then through it to the hilltop outside, beneath which the destitute and polluted city spread like a wound on the Earth. Part of Ben wanted to walk door to door and offer people help. Another part of him wanted to raze the whole eyesore to the ground, get rid of the surplus population to make a better living space for himself.

This last thought was ludicrous, though: Ben didn't live here. He bore no ownership of or responsibility for this future. Surely if he did live here, he'd be one of the lucky ones. Surely his descendants were as well-off as he, after the ample inheritance he'd leave Rhys and Frieda one day.

He shook his head to rid it of these bitter worries. "This is all a lie," Ben said to the spirit, who'd followed him. "A fabrication meant to dupe me."

The Ghost of Christmas Futures flickered, her whole body distorting, then vanishing, then abruptly flashing back into being. "The seeds of this world are already found in your present," she said. "Look beyond London if needed. Look to those whom your economic systems exclude, and will, depending on the choices that are made, continue to exclude, forever."

The dismal future around Ben swallowed him. He was an ant and it was a giant, enveloping him without effort. His lips quivered. He refused to believe his eyes. "Surely the seeds of the good future are found in our present, too."

"They are," the ghost said, beckoning for Ben to follow her down the hill. "But they are not taking root. There is a 57.44 per cent probability that the future you see before you, or one close to it, will come to pass."

This statement would normally have shocked Ben, but it barely registered to him as he trundled after her. This was all too much.

What do I care if the world crumbles after I die? What responsibility do I have? None at all. None at all.

He recognised these thoughts as coping mechanisms, but kept repeating them. The apparatus of social and economic security he'd spent his adult life so carefully erecting around himself was gone here. If he were to somehow become stranded in this future, he'd have nothing.

But my descendants must. My descendants must.

They stopped in a dusty courtyard surrounded by a score of shanties. People of all ages slept on thin mats, or on the ground, inside the open dwellings. Flies whizzed around them in the unnatural warmth. In one of the shacks, many people coughed sporadically, shivering in defiance of the heat. They'd covered themselves in threadbare blankets and built an indoor fire. Was an epidemic sweeping through London, just as they'd scourged it in the past? The fire smelt terrible, as if they were burning manure. It clogged the hut with smoke three times as thick as the smog outside, amplifying the sick people's coughing.

Even in the depths of Ben's own supposed poverty, he'd never experienced, or even seen, destitution like this. In many ways, he'd never truly been poor.

One young girl, dressed in a dusty T-shirt that went down to her ankles, carried a metal can under her arm as she tiptoed close to the squat buildings. Sneaking. Her furtive motions took her to a sheet of corrugated metal that looked like part of the wall behind a hut but was actually a door. Ben and the spirit followed her inside and found a hand pump and tap attached to a pipe that jutted into the ground. A well.

The girl held the can beneath the bucket and rapidly pumped. A meagre rivulet of water tinkled into the can.

The ghost pointed to a corner that, at first glance, looked empty. But when a drone there, no bigger than a fingernail, lifted off, Ben caught a glint of dull light reflecting off it. He tried to examine it closer, but it fled through a crack in the wall.

No sooner had it left than a robotic hand ripped the metal sheet off the structure and flung it aside. It crashed into another hut with a bang.

The child dropped her can of water. Two humanoid robots – the same models Ben had seen at the rich man's fortress – entered. One grabbed the girl while the other dismantled the well with inhuman speed.

The girl didn't shout for help. She stood, trembling under the machine's cold grip, as it told her, "You have violated the City of London Water Tax Ordinance of 2190. Fresh water must be paid for at a local water dispensary. Public wells are prohibited."

Ben gaped at the robot and at this ghastly world. As the last of the water spilt from the can into the dirt, a word engraved on the side of the can demanded Ben's attention. A mark of ownership.

"This well was considered a great luxury," the spirit said. "Now she'll have to fetch water from the Thames, like most people here. It's polluted with sewage, and countless chemicals and diseases."

Ben bent down and lifted the girl's can. The robots and the child were apparently too occupied to notice it floating in the air. Even if they had noticed the supernatural event, Ben wouldn't have cared. The name etched on the can transfixed him: *SCROOGE.*

"One day," the ghost continued, her gaze on the girl, "she'll get so thirsty that she'll stab two people in their sleep to steal their water."

Ben spun to face the spirit. "She's-she's you. You're..."

The ghost nodded solemn acknowledgement. "My name is Imogen Scrooge. Or rather, that will be my name, in many futures. I will be your great-great-great-great-great-great grandniece."

Ben grasped her shoulders and studied her face. His family's long eyes, slightly hooked noses, dark hair... all absent in this girl. Either she was lying, or the generations between them had erased all physical similarity.

The robots left the ghost's terrified younger self, and she collapsed on the wet ground, her well uprooted and its pump destroyed.

"Prove it," Ben said to the ghost. "Prove you are my family's progeny."

Prove that I have to reckon with the hazardous, dog-eat-dog world I left you.

"It's your responsibility, spirit," Ben said, his thoughts bleeding into spoken words. "Not mine. Not mine. Prove to me that what you say is true."

Her stoic gaze remained immovable, implacable. He shook her to force a reaction, but her eyes remained hard, and deeply sad.

Red light beamed from the top of her staff. The walls of the pump room fell outwards, and the shanty town disassembled itself around them. Beyond it, the rest of London's indistinguishable remains folded in on themselves.

This is the most likely future. Ben tried to get the thought through his head. A thousand psychological defences tried to shoot it down.

"You're just... You're trying to eradicate *my* feelings, *my* needs, *my* aspirations to squeeze me into your box of a false utopia. It's not emancipation from selfishness; it's a prison of its own."

The spirit said nothing, and the weak excuse died in Ben's mind as soon as it left his lips.

He longed for the community of yes-men who'd assuaged his fears. Perhaps, if he were as well-connected in this future as he was in his present, he could find people like them here. The political pundits Ben had placed his faith in. The Chamber of Commerce. His finance team and legal team. The men from the Garrick Club and the golf course with whom Ben exchanged gossip. The representatives from the universities and museums he donated to.

Where were they now? Where were they in this future? Couldn't they come and share some soothing words with Ben?

London flattened. The Thames, in the distance, dried up. Cacti sprouted from the earth like Hell's fingers. The smog vanished. The sun sank to the horizon in the western sky. Not a human was in sight, but the bones of old buildings could still be seen here and there. One corner of the Tower of London was still standing, as it had stood for a thousand years before Ben's time.

The Ghost of Christmas Futures surveyed the desolation with Ben, the light atop her staff fading. "In this future, which will happen with 57.44 per cent probability, human potential is squandered. We become so consumed with being better than each other that we never become the best we could have been, if we'd worked together. Instead, we stagnate. Our population slowly shrinks for as long into the future as I have looked. Our diminishment is due not to war or technological accident, but to a stubborn piece of our psychology we just couldn't overcome."

The sun was brighter, larger in the sky than during Ben's present. Even at dusk, heat baked the landscape.

"This, too, is one of your descendants," the ghost said, and at first Ben didn't know who she was talking about, but then he saw, in the collapsed husk of a nearby building, a figure lighting a candle. Ben drew closer. It appeared to be a man in his thirties, but his face and body were mostly covered in wrapped cloth, presumably to protect himself from the sun. He set the candle in a pock in the floor, next to a tree fighting upwards through another hole in the bare concrete. Ben didn't recognise the tree's species – it looked more like a misshapen vine, twisting at odd angles and mostly bare of leaves – but the man took a crude copper-coloured metal star and hung it from the top of the plant by a thin string. Despite his grim surroundings, a genuine smile crossed his face. He sat next to the tree and candle, munched on a hard foodstuff of some kind, and hummed a halting, yet dreamy tune. It took Ben a few lines to recognise it as 'Silent Night'.

"This is the last Christmas," the ghost said. "Few people are still alive, and this is the last one who remembers Christmas. In this future. The most likely future."

In the shade of deteriorating walls and huge slabs of an upper floor that had collapsed to the ground, Ben sat next to his descendant, humming and eating happily. Alone. *An encyclopaedia of survival knowledge must live in this man's mind, to allow him to subsist here.* In his face, as in Imogen's, Ben found no familial similarities to himself.

But this was ill comfort. The man had plenty of similarities with Ben: eyes, nose, a mouth. A mind. He'd been born into a time when he was helpless to defend himself against the perils Ben's generation, and others after his, had passed forward. For the first time in Ben's life, he saw another person's disadvantages not as signs of personal failing, but instead as the result of misdeeds inflicted upon him by others.

By Ben.

Yes, the sum total of actions Ben had taken in his life were but a breath in the gale of all human actions. He'd only contributed to this future in a small way. But with his wealth, his power, and his influence, his breath had been the breath of a demigod. Even surrounded by the gale, he'd affected the future far more than most people ever got the chance to affect it.

All at once, Ben's defences disintegrated like the London of the future, leaving him helpless against the colossal weight of shame he'd been keeping at bay. A trickle back when he and Marley had first explored his memories, it had grown into an ocean, and Ben's subconscious had been expending increasingly great effort to ignore its presence dammed above him.

Here, with his descendants in this desolate place, celebrating the last Christmas, he could ignore it no longer, and it all came flooding down.

I have not been a good person. He hadn't built his empire because he had to defend himself against his father, against the disapproving glares of his peers. He hadn't offered a single loan for the purpose of helping another person. He'd done it all – pilfered from the UK's poor, from his dying father, from the more fulfilling career Marley could have had apart from Fast Quid, from Annie's very life, from Imogen Scrooge and the rest of his successors – because he wanted the money. Because he wanted the power, and the prestige, and the safety, and he simply didn't care about anything or anyone else. People like this man, far in the future, least of all.

"I could have done so much more good," Ben said aloud, and was surprised at how strained and frail his voice sounded. "I've treated others so poorly." He wiped a tear from his face, and found his entire cheek damp. "I'm sorry," he whispered. "I'm so sorry."

But even the realisation that Ben had spent his life in wanton pursuit of his most selfish ambitions struck Ben as wantonly selfish. Who cared what Ben felt at having hurt so many people so deeply? Someone needed to care for the people he'd hurt!

"I need to..." His train of thought fizzled. He clutched at disparate strands of ideas, trying to connect them. "I need to erase the mark I made on the world. And of men like me. Men like my dad."

Wind whistled through the building's upper bones. A scavenging lizard emerged from the rubble in front of Ben and climbed down to investigate the candle. From behind Ben, the spirit rested a hand on his shoulder. "You can't go back and live your life over," she said. "But you can do things differently now."

Now? Now that it was beyond his reach to spend the rest of his life with Marley, and Ben would receive no obvious reward for inner growth, his instinct was to abandon any thoughts of it. But seeing the sick people in their shanties... and this man and his dying world...

Marley and Ralph had described Hell as "facing all the people you've ever hurt." Apparently, Ben had built for himself a Hell on Earth.

Could preventing this future not be its own reward?

Ben could protest all he wanted that it wasn't his responsibility. So could anyone.

"Can you find it within yourself to give to the world when it took so much from you?" the spirit asked. "You may have suffered, but your legacy need not be that you paid that suffering forward. Your legacy can be that you stood firm and stopped it before it reached anyone else."

"No," Ben said, turning to the spirit. Just a child, she towered above him, wise beyond her years. Likely wise beyond even his years. "The world is too big, its views too entrenched. I'm just one man."

The ghost leant down. Her hand darted out from her body and snatched the lizard. She examined it like she had the drone she'd caught. Did she perceive each era of time as Ben might see a wing of a museum: a collection of artefacts that gave glimpses of who and what was here?

"In stories about time travel," she said, rotating the frightened lizard before her gaze, "characters fret about changing one tiny thing in the past that will make large changes to the present: the butterfly effect." She set the lizard back on its rock, away from the candle and its flame. It rushed into the safety of a crevice, out of view. "It's strange, then, how so few people in the present believe their small actions will ripple long into the future."

The ghost flickered. Her body warped and faded, but returned in less than a second. "All of my futures, both good and bad, are not certainties yet. In some, I never exist at all. I never become a ghost, and I'm not here talking with you now. This – all of this – is a probabilistic wave function contingent on previous human choices. Everything is."

But some futures are more likely than others.

"What can I do to help? Anything, spir—" Ben stopped, corrected himself. "Imogen. Anything. How can we stop lives like the life I lived from being the most desirable path?"

How can we build a world where young men don't feel like they need to be king in order for anyone to ever love them?

Imogen leant her staff against a rock, stepped in front of Ben, and held out her hands. Ben stared at those hands, at her invitation to climb out of his morass of self-flagellation. *What can she do? What can either of us possibly do?*

His wrinkled old hands tentatively touched those of his future grandchild. She grasped them, lifted him to his feet. Ben's other descendant, oblivious to their presence, finished his song and his food and sat still in the expansive silence of the place.

"I've been watching you," Imogen said. "I see what Ralph saw in you. What Marley saw in you. Fear directed your life down a certain path..." She let go of his hands, turned her palms upwards. A band of light flared between them. As it faded, a long object was left in its place, resting on her hands. A staff.

Ralph's staff. The one Graham had rewound and turned back into a tree, now its normal self again.

"... But even now, there are other paths," Imogen finished.

Ben's gaze flicked back and forth between Ralph's staff in her hands, and Imogen's own staff resting against a rock, the many branching paths at its top flaring outwards. She was offering him Ralph's staff? She was offering him...

"Only a Ghost of Christmas can create another Ghost of Christmas," Imogen said. "And I'd rather do it before your dad gets around to it."

Ben's stomach, or whatever was down there in his ghostly bowels, twisted. He stepped back, his feet passing through the candle and the feeble tree. "I couldn't," he said.

"You already know more than I did when I first became a ghost. And I believe you now recognise the importance of achieving balance between the future, present, and past. I believe you realise what's at stake."

Ben paced pointedly away from her, out into the dry air. Sand shifted beneath his feet between buildings' decayed foundations, where pavement might once have been. Stalwart cacti stood here and there, lonesome guardians. The sun had sunk beneath the horizon, bringing violet to the sky, dotted with the night's first stars.

I can't replace Ralph. The very thought was insane. Ben had proven himself irresponsible, vain, selfish. Time and time again. Why would he be a reliable candidate to serve as a time ghost?

Because I genuinely want to atone.

But no! He could atone as a leader in the finance world, as a living man. If he failed to pay enough penance before the time of his death, he'd continue working towards absolution in his afterlife. Maybe he could become a ghost then, to work off his debt to the world faster. If he became a ghost now instead of then, who would gain?

Ben gazed up at the stars, so much more visible in this depopulated world. He knew who would gain.

"Will I get to see Marley again?"

Holding two staffs, Imogen drifted up beside him and regarded the stars with solemnity. "Sometimes. In fleeting minutes between assignments, you may be able to visit her."

Ben allowed the idea to fully enter his mind. He examined it from different angles. Dissected it.

He would have to die. Abandon his mortal body and whatever time it had left. Such was the price of the power and responsibility of serving as a time ghost. But oddly, this didn't bother Ben. *I'm getting on in years. How much time do I really have left?*

More concerning, becoming a ghost would open Ben to further attacks from his father. Graham hadn't exactly followed the normal rules of ghost-human interaction, but at least there'd been rules. If Ben, too, descended into ghosthood, no rules would protect him, and Graham might assault him as he had Ralph.

And despite the ability to travel through time that would come with the job, Ben would not be able to change the past. As much as he'd have loved to go back and kill Hitler – with apologies to Lord Bortley – he'd be condemned to repeatedly suffer the part of his recent travels he'd hated the most: seeing the horrors of the human world yet having little power to change them. Moreover, if he left his mortal life behind, he'd be remembered as a selfish monster. He certainly didn't want all his money to go to a son who couldn't stand him.

But the desire to leave a legacy was itself selfish. Ben had more important things to consider. His decision came down to: would he be able to do more good as a human, or as a ghost?

"I would serve people?" he asked. "Help mortals in their everyday lives, and assist their transitions after death?" The mere concept of subservience felt caustic to Ben. Wouldn't embracing a helping role brand him as a failure?

No, my old self is the true failure. I had all that influence and I never helped a soul.

"You *will* be the lowest of the spirits," Imogen admitted. "Squeezed under the boots of the Ghosts of the Past, reviled as an enemy collaborator by the Ghosts of the Future. You will be looked down upon. Mocked for your inadequacy."

"But I'll be able to help people. To try and stop this future from happening. And I'll be able to see Marley. Yes?"

Imogen brought her gaze down from the stars, keeping a bit of their light in her eyes, and at the edge of her smile. "Yes," she said.

So Ben stood at the edge of another precipice, all of time stretching out in a valley far below him. If he returned to his everyday life, the temptation to chain himself back to status-seeking would always be there, no matter how hard he tried to dedicate himself to undoing the damage he'd done throughout his life. Alternatively...

What kind of man am I? What kind of man do I want to be?

Ben reached his hand towards Imogen. He would do this. For everyone he'd hurt. But mostly, for Marley.

"You really want a bloke like me as your colleague?" Ben asked.

Imogen's smile widened. "I want a colleague like the man you've been becoming."

Ben whistled. "Brave girl. Must run in your blood."

She almost placed Ralph's staff in his outstretched hand, but Ben shifted his hand at the last moment to point his finger upwards in a gesture saying *wait*. "I will accept the role as a Ghost of the Present on one condition."

Imogen withdrew the staff, eyed him cautiously. "What condition?"

"You're going to visit every single ghost you're on good terms with, and you're going to tell them all to come to a specific place at a specific time. Can you do that for me?"

"What place, at what time?"

He almost told her. But her eyes were a bit too piercing, perceptive. "You already know, don't you?" Ben asked. "You've seen this conversation before, you've heard me say these exact words. You know exactly what I have planned."

She stepped towards him. "You can't use the power you'll receive for your own gain," she said, confirming Ben's suspicions. "They'll take it away from you. Send you to the underworld."

"It's not for my gain," Ben said. "I won't use my wibbly-wobbly, timey-wimey magic for myself. And if I do, then Devil take me."

Suspicion tainted Imogen's face. Ben should have known better than to try and deceive her, given both the shrewdness she must have developed growing up in such a harsh future, and that she could see the future to begin with.

Ben let his expression grow grave. Honest. "I know you're trusting me with a great burden," Ben said. "I will do things my own way. But I will not betray your trust. And I don't think you'd have offered this power to me if you didn't already know what I intend to do with it."

In fact, I'm starting to wonder if it wasn't your plan all along.

Imogen pursed her lips, then relaxed them and exhaled sharply. She shook her head. She slowly, cautiously set the staff in Ben's hand.

He'd expected a longer initiation. Instead, his awareness of the universe around him instantly bloomed to encompass impossibly fine details. Where that grain of sand would be in another eighty-six seconds. The entire history of that building, from its construction in 2063 until the last concrete in its foundation wore away in the elements. The birth and death of his descendant inside with the candle and tree. The radioactive decay of the potassium in that man's muscles, the currents of heat and cold in the atmosphere, a trillion potentialities for every object he chose to fixate on.

Ben laughed, gripped the staff tighter. When the staff had been a tool, he could use it to pick scenes from his past as if out from a photo book. Now, the staff felt like an extension of his own mind, and no time was clearly bounded from any other time. Past, present, and futures all flowed together in an unending stream. If Ben chose, he could dive anywhen into that stream.

The future was confusing, murky, difficult to see or navigate clearly, just as Ralph had said. But the time from the Big Bang up until Imogen's rescue of Ben outside the Houses of Parliament was as transparent as a ghost.

"Thank you," Ben said. "For saving me. For showing me these futures. For giving me this gift, this chance. It means more than you could possibly know."

Imogen stepped back, as if aware Ben would soon depart. "Everything we do sends out ripples," she said. Then she was silent.

Ben glanced one last time at his descendants: the ghostly girl, and the lonely man, who was now curled up beside the candle, trying to fall asleep. Ben was newly aware of their four-dimensional nature, that he was only seeing them at one point in time, in one possible future. What loves and losses had they experienced? Had their lives in any way echoed his? Did they have their own black holes?

Parting ways with Sandra. His father's death. And now Ben's life had a third black hole, a night that would scar him forever. Unless...

Ben's staff pulsed red. Imogen vanished. The world dissolved and reformed around him.

His feet stepped past pulverised asphalt and burning shrubs, down a wide street where a battle had just taken place. Clouds had grown low and thick in the dead of night. Behind him, a sculpture of Boudica atop her chariot raised its spear high, silhouetted against the London Eye – and in his mind's eye, he saw the actual Boudica leading her army from nearly the exact same spot, long ago. With a thought, he could travel to her time.

Ahead of him, Big Ben towered on the left. After a two-minute walk, a graveyard came up on his right. Its headstones caught the city lights and cast long shadows deep into the unlit churchyard. Centuries of wind and rain had worn sculptures of what had presumably been saints and angels down into faceless apparitions posed in sorrow or in protective dominance.

Down the street from the cemetery, beneath the streetlamps, a hulking phantom draped in a cloak lumbered away from the scene of his crime. Ben let his foot interact with the physical world. He kicked a lump of asphalt and it thumped down the pavement. The ghost stiffened. With the menace of a night owl rediscovering its prey, Graham's hood pivoted towards his son just as Ben sank into the graveyard's shadows.

Watch me. Follow me.

Now that Ben was also a ghost, he could have found his father at any other time. But returning at this time, just after the Ghost of Christmases Yet to Come had stolen Ben away into the future, guaranteed Graham's fury would be at its rawest. *If I must confront him at some point, let it be now. Let it be when he can see this.*

But how do you kill a ghost? Even Ralph, battered and beaten far beyond what would've killed a living human, hadn't died; Imogen had sent him to the afterlife. *And if I found a way to kill a ghost, could I even go through with it?*

Ben didn't know all the rules of being a time ghost, but certainly what he was about to attempt was a severe crime that broke many of them. He'd be punished, possibly sent to Hell, as Imogen had suggested. He didn't even know if this would work.

But he had to try, now that he had the powers of a time ghost. After a lifetime of selfishness, he had to attempt this one thing for someone else. For someone he loved.

Ben had been gifted an expansive view of time in the present, of every object's past and future. He strode among simple gravestones and markers centuries old, and newer obelisks and crosses dotting the graveyard. He soon found the grave he was looking for, beneath a large English oak about halfway between the church and the street.

Marley Jacobs.

Her headstone was wider than the others, but cut from limestone that matched the graveyard's other markers, save for the lack of erosion and her name's crisp text. For all her strength and intelligence, this was where she'd ended up. *Where we all end up.*

What was happening to Ben's physical body, back in the flat? Had he breathed his last? Would his cleaning service discover him, stiff and cold, when they returned after Christmas?

"I'm looking forward to spending a lot of time with you," said a deep voice cutting through the gloom. His silhouette loomed a distance away, near a bench and a streetlamp at the graveyard's edge. "The Future Ghost got tired of you?"

Ben knelt next to Marley's grave. Wilted flowers lay next to it. Ben had paid for a hundred bouquets to decorate the grave at her burial, but apparently the groundskeeper had discarded them. These flowers would soon be taken, too, and eventually there would be no more flowers for Marley.

"Let her go, lad. I always said she was a bad influence. Can't be your own man with a lass like her running about with you."

Graham's voice seemed to compress Ben, as if pushing him beneath the ground, as well. *Should I have come back here? Did I walk right into my own demise?* He was in his dad's domain now. Ben Scrooge, a subservient Ghost of the Present. *Is this truly how I can best make amends?*

How did it come to this? Marley, oh, Marley...

Graham entered the graveyard and drifted unhurriedly towards his son. The imminent removal of Ben's freedom lent him clear eyes. He'd come here to do one thing, and one thing only. He didn't need to fight his dad. *How do you kill a ghost?*

Wind picked up around Ben as he tested the air molecules nearby, sending them briefly into other times and bringing them back. *How do you kill a ghost?*

Ben gritted his teeth, pressed his hands to the earth atop Marley's grave. He sensed the worms beneath the surface, the bacteria and fungi, a tunnel built by black ants, the roots of the huge tree. Deeper, a layer of concrete, and then...

Bones. Embalmed skin decaying to leather. Marley's favourite silk dress, just beginning to biodegrade.

"I knew you'd come back, lad. Even when your feet run away from me, your mind's always known I'm right about you."

Ben reached out with his mind and felt what was left of her. He felt the decomposition process. How her remains would deteriorate in the coming days and weeks.

And he felt who those remains had once been. A lovely smartass of a woman, gazing up at him next to an aeroplane window, waiting for a kiss, London's lights reflecting in her eyes.

"Come with me to our past, lad. Let's make it all better. Let's make me the CEO of Fast Quid, and you my number one."

A memory played and replayed in Ben's mind: Ralph, outside Sandra's house, fast-forwarding a *Camellia* flower into decay, and then back into verdure. Ben reached beneath the soil teeming with life, beneath the concrete barrier, touched Marley's remains with his mind, and *pulled.*

How do you kill a ghost?

You leave it where it belongs.

In the past.

Ben stabbed his staff into the grave. The earth split open. What appeared to be smoke erupted from the fissure, rushing into the air, circling down, forming a pool above the grave.

Not smoke. Ben strained to contain the molecules churning before him and revert them to their previous identities: glucose, lipids, haemoglobin, DNA. The chemistry of life.

Ben sucked in air and held his breath. He couldn't hold the near-infinite complexity of the task in his mind at once. He focused on it piece by piece, now stealing an electron from an acacia in Tehran that had once been part of a calcium phosphate molecule in Marley's humerus bone, now plucking a water molecule from halfway to the bottom of the Atlantic that had once lived in Marley's brain, now rewinding these molecules' histories until they made their way back into Marley's body.

Ben lifted his staff to the sky. A geyser of biochemical reactions surged from the grave. It formed a pillar, a cylindrical tornado, rotating faster, faster. Piece of flesh, drop of blood, strand of hair, chunk of bone. All were caught up in it. All reconfigured themselves in midair.

"The blazes are you doing?" Graham yelled above the seething noise. "She made you one of us? You're a ghost now, too?"

Ben could scarcely spare part of his brain to deal with Graham, but he took a cue from Ralph and quickly searched through history. There, fifty million years ago. The land that would eventually become London had been at the bottom of the sea. Ben summoned a tiny speck of that sea.

Graham bellowed at the deluge of seawater crashing down on him, as if the rage in his throat alone could forestall it. Ben invoked a wall of earth from when the land here had been higher before the last Ice Age to keep the water away from his supernatural workspace. The flood washed Graham back out to the street. He flew upwards and spun, flinging a ring of water outwards from his cloak, and darted back into the graveyard.

"No more tricks, boy! You look me in the eyes and fight me like a man."

Every muscle in Ben's body was reaching maximum tension. Stamina drained from him as the tornado thrashed before him. At its centre, hovering above the ground, a human body began to form.

To *re*form.

"I'm done fighting you," Ben said. "I want to heal."

He conjured the Great Smog again to block Graham's view, but kept the area around Marley's grave clear.

A wisp of smoke attached itself to her head and condensed into fluttering hair. Lifeless eyes materialised. Water, oxygen, and a thousand proteins and chemicals formed into a hand at the end of an arm.

The tornado's spin slowed as the body took its form. The nape of her neck. The soft skin of her lips.

The tomb below was empty now. Every piece of her was here, in front of Ben's eyes, and he was bringing them all back together.

Leaves crunched as Graham struck ground in the smog. He rampaged forward, mere yards from Ben, who snatched a horse-drawn cart from 1635 to block Graham's way. Graham was moving with such reckless speed that the cart cracked when he hit it.

Ben's body shuddered. Convulsed with effort. *Just a bit longer. Hold out just a bit longer, Ben.*

His staff beamed with multicoloured light. His teeth ground together. He ignored searing pain tearing into his muscles. Even when the pillar of smoke imploded, rushing inwards into the body, Ben kept going. He couldn't just bring Marley's body and mind back; he had to rewind the plaque in her arteries, had to restore her to health.

It'll be you, Marley. I'm entrusting you to prevent the horror of a future Imogen showed me.

His father leapt over the horse cart. Ben placed a small medieval tenement that had once stood here around Graham, trapping him inside, but the wood planks that formed its wall started to give way the first time Graham pounded against it.

Ben's strength left him. With one final burst of exertion, he lifted his staff and sparked Marley's brain and heart with just the right amount of electricity, in the right places, at the right rhythms – he used the electricity in his own body as a guide.

Her body fell to the fresh dirt beneath it. Utterly drained, Ben collapsed next to her and gasped. His muscles were fire, agony. His vision blurred and darkened. Every cell in his body screamed in distress.

Am I dying?

If death was coming for Ben, he was too weak to fight it. All he could think of was the feeling that every part of him was so fatigued – so impossibly beyond mere mortal fatigue – that the exhaustion registered as pain. Lying there in the dirt with Marley, surrounded by gravestones, in the dark, he couldn't bring himself to care that Graham was about to burst through the wood of the old building's wall. He couldn't care enough to flee. The wall splintered and shattered, and the hooded phantom rushed through to find his quarry gasping for dear life.

He slowed. Loomed over his son. *I've made a horrible mistake*, Ben realised. He'd got caught up in the moment. His radical gambit to resurrect Marley had been a fool's errand. Her body wasn't moving. Not even a breath. And now Graham had absolute control of them both. Ben's staff felt a hundred kilos heavier, but he lifted it against his father, who plucked it away from him and casually snapped it in two over his knee.

The barest suggestion of a rotting face peered down from the darkness beneath Graham's hood. The crescent of a satisfied smile etched itself across that face like cracking glass.

What will my life become, with this man in charge of it again? If Graham succeeded in changing the past, in preventing Ben from leaving home at age seventeen, would Ben's whole present revert to the course on which his life had been set during teenagehood? No way to even know a life outside Graham's shadow was possible? How many of the memories through which Ben and Marley had adventured would be erased? How much of their whole relationship would be erased? Would he have ever even met her?

I'd live a diminished life. A life in which I never knew how much of an impact I could have on the world, for good or ill. Any impact he could have would be surrendered to his dad. How much more likely would Imogen's darkest futures then become?

Graham stooped, reached to Ben's face, brushed it with fingers that would have looked lifeless were they not moving. Thin, rough skin stretched too tight over the bones beneath.

"Greatness is ours," he whispered.

A crimson light beamed at the top of Graham's staff. Illness deeper than any physical malady took hold of Ben as the present began to slip away from them.

The red light flickered out like an electrical short had hit it. Graham scowled at it, struck the staff against the ground.

Behind him, two cloaked phantoms rose from the ground. He didn't see them – just kept shaking his staff, trying to get it to work. They billowed upwards like inflating balloons, their robes drifting in a breeze Ben couldn't feel. He still couldn't muster the strength to move. He could only watch as they lurched forward and grabbed Graham's wrists. He yelped, dropped his staff. It thudded into the dirt.

Up from behind tombstones, down from the tops of trees, around the sides of the church, they came. Spirits. Of all sizes and shapes, young and old. Some hooded phantoms, others flickering in and out as Imogen had. An old woman in a nightgown. A short, ageless spirit with a flame above its head. A bald, demonic-looking man in a formal suit. And even the Ghost of Christmas Present, just as she'd appeared outside Suresh's house. Hundreds of them. Ghostly and transparent.

Every single one carried a staff.

Thank you, Imogen. She'd got so many of them together, and they must have seen it all. Graham tried to yank himself away from his captors, but two additional phantoms joined to hold him at bay.

"What do you want from me?" he yelled at the assembled spirits. "Leave a man to his own business, yeah?"

Others drifted silently closer, surrounding him. Ben finally found the strength to lift himself up and lean back against a tree. He was still catching his breath.

A particularly tall spirit, hooded in a ripped and tattered cloak, stepped forward from the gathering. Leaves crunched under its feet. It glanced at Ben as it passed him, the dull orbs of its eyes deep inside the hood, each a moon shadowed by the Earth at night. It turned its gaze to Graham, stopped, and spoke in a hardy, masculine voice.

"Ghost of Christmas Past."

Graham sneered at Ben. Again he thrashed against the spirits holding him, but they had him well restrained. "Did you do this, lad? You called for your mummy to come save you?"

"And how would you have it?" the big ghost said to Graham as it stepped close to him. "You'd prefer no recourse for those in dire straits, so that the aggressive can freely run roughshod over the peaceful?"

Graham tried to spit in its face, but his dry mouth produced no fluid. "I'm doing my job, mate. You go do yours." When this received no response, he continued: "We're on the same team, Ghosts of the Past. What's your business holding me up like this?"

The tall ghost appraised him. It reached out a hand, just as emaciated as Graham's, and picked up Graham's gnarled staff. Graham tried to pull it away, but the other ghosts held his arm tightly.

"*Our* business," the tall ghost corrected him, gesturing to the multitude of spirits behind it, "is that you are in the present, outside your jurisdiction."

A noise partway between a snort and a laugh escaped Graham. "So are you. There's been an escapee on the loose, in case you hadn't heard."

"But you captured her. And yet you're still here. And we've been told you've been trying to harm a living person, your son here, for some time now."

"He's a ghost, too! He's not alive."

"As of ten minutes ago, yes. But it seems…" It twisted its hands around Graham's staff as if to choke the life out of it. A *snap*, and a long crack climbed from the hand up to the staff's tip. "… now you're trying to take him to the past. To change it."

"Fake news," Graham said. "A lie."

"A lie out of your own mouth, before you knew we were listening? I suppose the bombs that just dropped all across London were also fake." Under its grip, Graham's staff aged, first warping from fungal decay, then crumbling as generations of insects chewed through it. In seconds, the staff was reduced to a pile of humus on the cemetery floor.

Graham jolted like he'd been shot in the chest. A quick gulp of air. Shock on his reddening face. He looked like he wanted to tear the spirit apart with his bare teeth.

"What," Graham said, enunciating each consonant like he was stabbing it as he spoke it, "did you just do?"

"We have rules," the spirit said. "We may have our differences with one another, but it is absolutely central to our code of honour that we help living humans. And yet you have gone past error, past negligence, into active pursuit of harm."

And how serious must Graham's violation of those rules be, to get Ghosts of the Past and of the Futures together like this, collaborating peacefully just so they can collar him? Ben had thought that a battle among the ghostly factions would be a useful distraction for his father while Ben resurrected Marley. But that no longer seemed necessary.

Graham leant forward as much as he was able, bringing his face so close to the spirit that its hood touched Graham's forehead. "Some men are above the codes of normal men." From Ben's angle on the ground, the tall ghost partially obstructed his view of Graham, but he still caught a smirk and a wink, like Graham was telling the spirit that it, too, was part of Graham's elite club.

The spirit raised its face to look down its nose – if it had a nose – at Ben's father, as if emphasising how beneath it Graham was. "It is for men who think such," it said, "that the rules were made."

The ghost's shredded cloak flapped outwards as it spun away from Graham. "It has been decided," it said. "You are hereby stripped of your ghosthood and all your powers so that you may cause no more harm. You will be sent back to the netherworld."

"Are you mad?" Graham bellowed. "I'm the goddamned Christmas Ghost! You're the ghost of what, May the twenty-first? I'm better than you!"

Graham's raving continued as the tall ghost slunk towards Ben. A fearful part of him wanted to watch his father being taken away, to get visual confirmation that Graham was gone and Ben was safe. But the tall spirit's eyes mesmerised him, deep in its hood. It had no irises or pupils, just dull white holes peering out at Ben through the dark.

By the time it stopped above him, Graham's ranting had ceased.

The spirit and Ben regarded each other for a long time. Ghosts dispersed around them, some lighting their staffs and vanishing in a flash, others wandering off into the night. A handful drew closer, seemingly curious about Ben. Perhaps wondering what would be done with him. These were all cloaked Ghosts of the Past. It seemed to be true that the Future and Present Ghosts avoided them.

"You've been through quite an ordeal," the tall ghost eventually said.

Ben swallowed, inhaled. "I have."

"We should have been watching. We should have prevented your struggle." It knelt before Ben. Even kneeling, it was as tall as a normal man. "What can we do to atone for our neglect?"

Ben had to exert effort to keep his brain from spilling out his ears. The spirits – these hostile forces who'd been hunting Marley for weeks – were now asking him how they could help him? Perhaps more of them were like Ralph and Imogen than he'd imagined, and fewer were like his father.

As soon as Ben got his composure back, he didn't hesitate a moment to answer. "Marley. Let her live. I've got her this close. Surely you can resurrect her fully."

A quick glance at Marley's prone form revealed she hadn't moved. But did Ben detect weak breathing? The faint rise and fall of her back?

The tall ghost hung its head, shook it slowly. "You are not the first to use our powers to try to bring back the dead. This is against our rules. Under normal circumstances, you'd be harshly punished. It may be all I can do to belay that punishment."

Ben's heart sank. He stared at Marley, searching for further signs of life. Wishing she'd get up and run away. That all his efforts hadn't been for nothing.

A few additional spirits had left, so now only the tall ghost and two others were gathered around Ben, slumped against his tree among the headstones. One of the other ghosts said, "Seems that this one stumbled into ghosthood. More of a mistake, really. One of Imogen's activist stunts."

The tall ghost drew its whole torso around to face its compatriot, rotating a bit farther than a normal skeleton should've allowed. "What are you suggesting?"

"I'm just saying. Most of us will be busy with his father right now. Those others won't know what we do here. Maybe we should... undo the mistake."

The tall ghost rose to its full height and hovered close to the other's face, the movement just as intimidating as when it had done this to Graham. "We have rules," it said.

"But the rules were broken so many times to put this bloke – this Scrooge – in the position he's in. Wouldn't putting him back be sort of like *unbreaking* the rules?"

For a long moment, the tall spirit didn't react. The three of them were silent and still. Ben tried to gather his strength with minimal success. His effort to resurrect Marley had emptied him of all vitality, and he wanted nothing more than to curl up here and sleep for a day.

So when the tall ghost reappeared in Ben's face, Ben stared into its flat eyes, and waited. "Do not stop thinking about tomorrow," it said. "Yesterday is gone."

Its hand darted forward and pushed Ben's head with such force that it should have collided with the tree. But all Ben felt behind his head was a pillow. Morning called. The last shroud of deep sleep fell away.

STAVE XVIII

Christmas Day

en's sunrise alarm clock's randomly selected song of the morning was 'Don't Stop' by Fleetwood Mac. The light faded on, dawning on him like a caress. He opened his eyes.

His bedroom – Marley's bedroom – was settled around him in plain normality. Morning light leaked in through gaps in the heavy curtains and lit a sheet of dust motes that spanned from the window to the chandelier to the double doors. All was still, but neighbours outside were speaking cheerily with their kids, and an aeroplane's hum was receding in the distance. A normal morning.

Ben peeled his bedsheets off himself like they might swallow him if he moved too fast. Was this real? The bed he sat on felt firm enough, the wood floor solid beneath his feet. He felt perfectly well rested. A peek at his mobile revealed the date to be December twenty-fifth.

Any other morning, he'd have grabbed his laptop, checked his shares, checked his emails, then rushed downstairs to scoff down whatever breakfast his chef had cooked up. But after a savage argument, Ben had agreed to give his chef today off. He'd have to cook his breakfast himself today. His laptop beckoned and his stomach growled, but still he sat there, running his hand over the top of his sheets, staring at the beam of light.

The last Ben remembered, he'd lain on the carpet in the second-floor lounge after watching that old VHS tape, and Ralph had whisked him out of his body into the second leg of the night's adventure. Yet he'd awoken just now in his bed on the upper floor.

It had all been a dream. A vivid, disturbing dream, one he remembered with uncommon clarity. But a dream nonetheless. Marley climbing his staircase from Hell, their repeated flights from his ghostly father, Ben's glimpse of the future's hope and terror... all of it. It had all been a dream.

"Ha," he said aloud. His voice felt small and muted in the large room. In fact, Ben himself felt small, no longer the titan of industry he'd built himself up to be. As Imogen had said, he was a man who'd made choices that had propelled him down a very particular life path. Somehow, as he slept, he'd imagined dissecting those choices. Why had he made them? Did he still value the same things that had led him to make them?

Perhaps Ben needn't let the unchangeable, unyielding past affect his present and future quite so much any more. Maybe Ben's deference to his fears from the past were chains he'd chosen to put himself in, and maybe, after his extended dream last night, he could turn the past into a pint glass instead of an ocean. If it still propelled him in a certain direction, Ben could change that direction. He could become any type of man he wanted. The fear of loss, of not being good enough, didn't need to drive his life if he didn't want them to.

Ben cocked his head. *Astounding, the changes one night of deep sleep can bring.* If it had all been a dream, then what a dream.

If it had all been a dream, though, then Marley was still dead. Maybe she wasn't in Hell, at least, but she was still in the ground. She'd have enjoyed so much of Ben's adventure through the past, had it been real.

Had he truly felt those things for her? Had he ever actually loved her, deep down beyond the business dealings and professional courtesy they'd let calcify around their relationship so they never had to examine it?

Did he love her still?

If she'd felt for him as he'd imagined in his dream, the lost opportunity yawned like an immense void in his life. He'd spent all those decades, all those marriages, ignoring the woman his authentic self truly wanted, all because he'd been terrified to let that authentic self surface. Because he'd been terrified of looking weak. Had Marley known this about him and so resigned herself to her role as his stoic business partner? If she were here now, would she despair with him that they'd wasted their chance, wasted their lives?

No, not Marley. If she were here now, and if she felt and knew the things he now suspected she had, she'd tell him to get off his bum and choose to live differently. Choose goals aligned with the part of Ben that didn't live in the shadow of his father, that wanted not to acquire nor conquer but to explore, to connect, to help. Imogen, figment of Ben's imagination though she might have been, had wanted him to serve as a time ghost so he could apply his newfound generosity to shaping the present and the souls who lived there. But that was dream logic, and Ben was awake now. He could do so much more living as a mortal man, even as an old mortal man. He'd wasted so much time. But not a moment more.

Not a moment more!

Ben leapt off his bed, padded over his Aubusson rug, and flung the curtains open. Morning light assaulted his eyes, but they adjusted. Snow! Thick particles of it drifting lazily downwards. A thin layer of it covered roofs, lawns, trees. Cars were pulling up to the neighbour's flat for a Christmas gathering.

Motion drew his eye towards another flat across the street. Inside, a group of people were assembling round their tree, drinking hot chocolate while some kids tore open presents.

Ben had never enjoyed Christmas, had never really wanted a family, but now he inhaled it all through his eyeballs like a diver starved for air. He ran downstairs, called his bodyguard, and gave him the day off. Forget breakfast, forget his shares. He threw on slippers and coat and marched out into the snow.

"Happy Christmas!" Ben said to his driver, a little too boisterously.

"Uh, happy Christmas, Mr Scrooge," said the man, waiting by Ben's idling car at the kerb.

"Aleksey, right? That's your name? You've been with me for three or four years, now?"

The man had been rubbing his hands together to keep them warm, but now his body froze. Probably unsure whether he was about to be treated to a telling off, a psychotic episode, or both. Ben walked right up to him and plopped a hand on his shoulder – the first time he'd ever touched the man.

"Do you have a family, Aleksey?"

"I... Uh..." He stammered like Ben was an investigator from the Fraud Office interrogating him over professional misconduct. Not that Ben had any personal experience with such a thing.

"How would you like to take your family on an all-expenses-paid, month-long holiday to any destination your hearts desire?"

Aleksey's eyebrows creased and his mouth turned down in a grimace. He actually cowered as if expecting a physical strike. "Mr Scrooge, I'm so sorry if I—"

"I'm not mocking you, Aleksey! You've done nothing wrong. You've only ever done things right. I'm the one who's been a royal arse to you. Which is why *I'll* drive *you* and your family to the airport myself. And you can tell them I'm tripling your salary."

Aleksey dropped to his knees atop the thin layer of fresh snow. "Please let me keep my job, Mr Scrooge. I need this job. What have I done wrong? You can be honest."

Ben gaped. Had the man not heard him? How conditioned must he have been to Ben's unpleasantness that he'd interpret his praise as criticism?

Well, he can't be the only one. I'll have to get used to this, and I have to start somewhere.

"Take the day off, Aleksey. Rest at home. I'll see you tomorrow, and the next day, and when your next pay cheque arrives, you'll know I'm being honest."

"Uh..." He stammered again, starting and stopping a few times. "My name is Pavel."

"Pavel! Give me the keys, Pavel. I'm driving myself today."

Pavel fumbled in his pocket. "Are you—" He found his keys, held them out to Ben with a shaking hand. "Are you quite all right, Mr Scrooge?"

Ben flung open the driver's door, jumped in the car, lowered the window. "Of course I'm all right!" No more than a second passed from when Ben started the car until he jammed his foot on the accelerator. The car squealed out of his driveway. "It's Christmas!" he shouted to his alarmed driver as he sped away. "It's Christmas, I'm alive, and there's still time!"

Outside the memories he'd relived with Marley, Ben hadn't driven a car in years. He tore through London's traffic-free streets like a madman, belting 'Deck the Halls' at the top of his lungs. He screeched to a stop by the kerb across from Frieda and Haddad's flat.

As it happened, a Fast Quid shop squatted on that kerb, and was open for business, as always. He tried to persuade the clerks he was the boss and that they should go home for Christmas, but even after showing them his ID, they thought it was a trick. *Oh well.* He'd send a memo closing all the shops today later. Upon exiting, he found a man in a bandana with tattoos down his arms – probably a drug dealer – loitering out front. Ben gave him a thousand pounds and told him to find better work elsewhere.

Oh, this is brilliant fun! Ben raced across the street in his pyjamas and coat, free from concern for wealth or propriety. *At any time, I could've simply stopped thinking status meant everything, and been free. Any time at all.*

But better late than never.

Bells from a nearby church chimed as Ben bolted into the block of flats' foyer and rang the intercom.

"Hello?"

"Frieda! It's your Uncle Ben. Happy Christmas!"

"Uncle... What?"

"Let me up!"

"Uncle Ben, you shouldn't be wandering round the city, what with everything going on. Is your security with you?"

"No. Now let me up!"

A minute later, he burst through their front door. They'd been eating omelettes for breakfast with their kids, but now both parents stood between Ben and the children as if guarding them from an eccentric intruder.

Ben heaved to catch his breath. "Frieda! I am here to let you know I will take you up on your offer of dinner tonight."

A confused glance passed between Frieda and her husband. "You could've just phoned."

"I could've. But you're my closest family – closer than my own son – and I've neglected you for far too long." He nearly tripped over Haddad's mandole resting against the wall on his rush to the windows looking down on Mayfair. He spread his arms wide to take in the whole view, all of London, the world. "I want to take the kids ice skating, I want to get to know you both and help you build your careers." Not out of guilt about Annie, he found, but because he genuinely cared about Frieda and her family's wellbeing. That was new. And welcome.

"And!" Ben said, stopping at the Christmas tree to face them. "And I will personally redo our financials and send them to you by New Year's. The numbers will be honest. I'm so sorry for asking you to lie for me. I've been a cantankerous old profit-obsessed curmudgeon, but I promise you I'm changing."

The kids liked this. They'd risen from the table and looked ready to run circles round this weird old man who'd shown up, their Christmas-morning energy feeding off his. Frieda stared, blank-faced. Haddad had taken a bite of food right as Ben had entered and still hadn't chewed it.

"Are you broken, Uncle Ben?" Frieda asked.

Ben barked a laugh. "I'm fixed! I want to stop taking and start giving. And I want to start with your family. I love you all – even you, Haddad – and I have so much I want to give."

Sooner or later, he'd have to tell her what really happened to her mother, of course. That Ben had stolen Annie's inheritance and it had driven her into poverty, deepened her depression.

But that was a future conversation. For now, all he had to do was get Frieda on board with the new Ben. If she wanted to keep him at a distance, as a business colleague only, he'd certainly understand.

But thankfully, she simply smiled at him and said, "Okay. I think that's great. Let's, uh, make some plans at dinner tonight."

Haddad finally swallowed his food. "What's happening right now?" he asked.

Frieda smiled that breezy smile that looked so much like Annie's. "I've no idea. But it's great, whatever it is. I told you Uncle Ben would come around."

Ben's attention splintered into a million tangents as he left their flat. *So much to do, so little time.* His stomach was crying out for a morning eye-opener, but that was something he'd need to change, too. How much *did* he drink? Eight, nine spirits per day? *Am I an alcoholic?* He'd never before asked this of himself.

And what of that consistent feeling of tightness in his chest that was so conspicuously absent now? Would he need treatment for anxiety? Would his new outlook on life free him of it all on its own?

Change would take time, yet Ben felt such urgency! Who else did he need to set things right with? Or at least, with whom could he dip his toes in the water of setting things right?

Lauren answered surprisingly quickly when Ben knocked on their mansion's front door. Rhys was in the kitchen far behind her, rooting through the fridge. The fortysomething woman crossed her arms and leant on the doorframe. "What do you want?"

"I want to apologise to you for being a right bastard," said Ben. Her eyebrows creased deeper, but he pressed on. "Whatever we had, it wasn't love, or really even affection... or really even tolerance. We were terrible together from the get-go, and that was my fault. I was a dirty old man who pursued you for your body, then I ignored you for my career, I disrespected you constantly, I put in zero effort to be a good partner. But in spite of all the nasty things I've said about you, you're actually quite a good person, and you deserved better than me." She'd deserved better than a partner who'd fixated tirelessly on a fictitious memory of a youthful romance gone wrong, while neglecting any current relationship that might have gone right, had he only put some effort into it. The list of things Ben could have apologised for was endless, so he stopped his stream of consciousness and put his hands into his coat pockets. Lauren deserved to hear his apology, but he couldn't help but feel she also represented a number of other women who also deserved a similar apology. "I'm not expecting any response from you," Ben went on, "I just wanted you to know I'm sorry, and I'm going to try to change. And if there's anything you feel I owe you, please feel free to ask."

Rhys was approaching the door, wearing only boxer shorts and a T-shirt, sipping from a Robinsons soft drink. Lauren's whole face had scrunched up into a visage of suspicion. Calculations coursed behind her eyes: was Ben playing a joke? Had he gone mad? What was he trying to get from her? Had Ben known he could so immediately flummox people just by being a decent person every now and then, he'd have started doing it sooner.

"Oh my days," Rhys said. A hostile little chuckle shot out from his throat. "Are you about to ask us to do family therapy, Dad? I think that ship sailed."

Ben regarded his son. Lanky. Not a teenager any more. How often had Ben seen him since the divorce? Two, three times? And before that, he'd spent so much time at the office, he scarcely remembered Rhys growing up. He'd missed it. Perhaps part of him had wanted so badly to avoid being as overbearing as his own father that he'd overcompensated in the opposite direction and become a neglectful one – though overbearingness certainly did come out of Ben on the rare occasions when he wanted something from Rhys.

"I've probably sent you some bad messages over the years, haven't I?" Ben said, wringing his hands.

Rhys chuckled again. "What, like that if you're not the alpha, you might as well kill yourself? You gave me that one so many times, I thought you were quoting the Bible."

Even though this was a joke, Ben couldn't meet his son's eyes. He thought of the baby he'd once held in his arms. He'd damaged another young man similarly to how Graham had damaged him. *Shame on me.*

But Ben was not his father. Rhys was still young, and Ben still had precious time on this Earth. Maybe he could repair some of the damage.

"I get it," Ben said. "I get that there are good reasons why you feel safer in your room, playing your Xbox, than being out on your own in the world. You can't lose the games you don't play, I suppose it is."

"If you think—"

"Let me finish, let me finish. Uh, look, it was wrong of me to try and shape you into a cut-throat businessman, clumsy as my attempts at that have always been. Clearly I need coaching on how to be a parent. But it's also wrong of both your mother and me to let you wallow in your room all day wasting your life. What I mean is, you'll regret it once you're my age. You'll be angry we didn't help you grow into someone more fulfilled. If you'll let me, I'd be delighted to help you find what's important to you, and engage with that part of the world."

Now Rhys's face was scrunched up exactly as his mum's had been. He lowered his arms from his hips to his side. "Well, it's interesting that you're saying all this," he said slowly. "But I can't see what you hope to gain."

"Nothing," Ben said, checking his mind to make sure it was true. "Nothing for myself, at least. Well, I suppose a real relationship with you would be nice, if I can earn it."

"Maybe we can..." Lauren began. Her voice drifted off, but she quickly returned to the thought. "Maybe we can make a contract. Set some boundaries. Maybe to earn every hour you spend playing Xbox, you spend an hour doing something outside the house."

"Mom, come on. You're falling for this?"

"Well, he's not wrong."

"He's here to weasel his way back in and assert his authority, that's what he's up to. You can't see that?"

"He just told me all the reasons he's not a good partner for me. I don't think he's trying to get back in. It sounds like he's just trying for the first time in his woebegone life to actually be a dad."

Rhys scowled at them both, blew out a big puff of air. "Whatever." He took a gulp from his soft drink and plodded back towards the stairs. That one would be hard to win over, if Ben ever could.

"Well," Lauren said, "thanks for trying, at least. What's got into you? Is it all that business on the news? What are you getting up to?"

Ben didn't have time to explain the elaborate dream that was making him rethink his life. Nor would his ex-wife find him sane if he did explain it. So instead he grinned at her and said, "For one thing, I'm about to go close my company."

"Happy Christmas!" Ben shouted as he burst through the Fast Quid doors on the fortieth floor, still in his nightwear. Admin assistants and post-room staff stopped in mid-step to gawk at him. "Everyone go home! Fast Quid is no more. I'm liquidating the whole damned global empire, starting immediately." The women at the front desk exchanged confused glances, but Ben didn't have time to convince them he was serious. He strode down the hallway, past feeble decorations: a tiny plastic wreath here, a shrivelling brown sprig of mistletoe recycled from last year there, a single stocking hung on an office door.

Ben *could* unilaterally end Fast Quid. The board would put up a fight, but honestly, who needed boards of directors in this day and age? CEOs were dictators, and no matter what changes Fast Quid's organisational structure had overgone over the years, Ben had always ensured the board's ability to control his behaviour would be frail at best.

"Rob," Ben called upon reaching the man's small office, which was really more of a vestibule between the hallway and Ben's own. "Convene a meeting of the C-suite and upper management. Today if possible. They're all getting redundancy packages for Christmas."

But Rob wasn't there. The ceiling lights were on, though, and a bowl full of steaming porridge sat on Rob's desk. *He must be nearby.* Normally, Ben would've flown into a rage, would've threatened Rob with termination for not being where Ben needed him, when Ben needed him. But Ben would do no such thing today.

It was an odd feeling, to realise he was not, in fact, better than everyone else, after believing this to be so since his thirties. After his wild dream, he could appraise his past honestly now, and so much of his path to prosperity had been determined by luck: recovering from a long-term illness, meeting Marley, accidentally amusing Gilbert enough at a party that he'd thrown the business a financial lifeline. Yet in Ben's memories, he'd rendered those lucky breaks as the masterstrokes of the single-minded force of nature that was his mind, eager to wreak its will upon the world.

Who had he been kidding? He'd invented a legal way to steal from poor people, and he'd harvested his vast wealth from that. To finally admit this to himself felt like knocking the ground out from beneath his feet... *But that's not me any more. I needn't lie to myself to pretend I'm a good person. Better to actually become a good person. Harder. But better.*

How long would it take to remove his payday loan shops? He'd peppered the world with them – he'd needed to, ever since the

Financial Conduct Authority had cracked down on payday lenders in the UK. He had thousands of stores in the States alone, despite payday lending being illegal in many of them. Could he close the stores immediately? The business could keep operating on its contingency fund, but Ben had whittled that fund down to—

In his search for Rob, he'd wandered into Marley's office. Sunlight cast a numinous glow on the beanbag chairs her arthritis wouldn't let her sit in any more. On the old film posters Ben had tried countless times to get her to remove. Above it all, her immense painting looked down on him, flinty, serious, completely unlike her.

This would be her legacy he'd be destroying, too. The ghostly Marley in his dream would surely have wanted that. She'd said herself she regretted what they'd done. But what would the real Marley think of Ben's change of heart? She'd never voiced any scepticism of their purpose – not to Ben, at least. Would she agree with her dream counterpart?

More importantly, had the real-life Marley also held unrequited feelings for Ben?

He'd never know. And yet, her likeness watching him from above was enough that Ben felt her presence. The remnants of her intellect lingering within his own. Thirty-some years of working together had to count for some degree of interpersonal connection, strained though it may have been.

Ben reconsidered his plan. If he closed Fast Quid, wouldn't another payday loan company swoop in to fill the gap his shops had left? Ben had created a market; there was no putting that genie back in the bottle. Fast Quid *was* meeting a genuine need...

"Ah, there you are," Rob said. He entered from the hall, tablet and stylus in hand, the faintest hint of bags under his eyes from a late night at the Arsenal match. Who knew if the man's personal life was anything like what Ben had glimpsed in his sleep, but Ben nevertheless felt sympathy, protectiveness even, upon seeing his assistant again. Did he really have the heart to put Rob, and everyone who worked for Fast Quid, out of a job?

"Happy Christmas, Rob," Ben said warmly.

Rob lifted an eyebrow as he sidled up next to Ben, and spoke cautiously. "Happy Christmas, Mr Scrooge." He followed Ben's gaze, breathed in deep. "She was quite a woman, wasn't she?"

Ben gazed into the painting's eyes, willing them to life. "That she was." He tapped Marley's desk, cleared his throat. "We're going to be making some changes around here, Rob."

"Oh?"

"We're going to lower interest rates to twenty-five per cent, for starters. Everywhere in the world."

Rob snorted a laugh. When he realised Ben was serious, he adjusted his glasses. "Sir? Our average interest rate right now is four hundred. I don't think—"

"Twenty-five, Rob. We'll break even so we can continue serving our customers, and to hell with profit. In fact, let's re-register Fast Quid as a charity. We'll restructure all our loan products to be fair for people on low incomes."

"I—" Rob stammered. "Uh..."

"Write this down, write this down." Ben waved at the tablet. Rob nearly dropped it in his haste to start writing. "In fact," Ben continued, leading Rob out into the hall, "we can do more. I'm going to return several hundred million from my personal investments back to the business. We're going to comb through our records – and I mean do a real, deep audit from every record we still have. And we're going to give refunds to everyone we've defrauded over the decades. I don't care how far back we have to go. If we buggered someone over, even if we did it legally, we'll pay up."

"Mr Scrooge, I don't mean to be rude, but are you having a laugh at me? It's okay if you are. I just—"

Ben spun on his heels to face him. "No, no, no. This is real, Rob. Real! Just like your raise. Triple your current salary. No more using that stupid app I made to borrow from next week's pay cheque. What do you think about that?"

Rob stared, mouth agape, looking deeply concerned for Ben's mental health.

"Raises for everyone!" Ben called down the hallway. "Big raises! Everyone who works for me will have a living wage, and more."

"I— Sir, if we lose all that turnover from our customers, then, uhm—"

"Take it from my salary," Ben said. "It's bloated as a blimp. Hell, take it from my bank accounts in the Caymans. My money won't do anyone any good just sitting there like the world's largest coin collection."

Ben desperately wanted to use it to avert anything even close to the stratified, shanty town London he'd seen in his dream.

"And from now on, Rob, our leadership team will do mandated community work a few times per year, so they can better see the poor's perspective."

They crossed Rob's office into Ben's, where the gloomy countenance of Scrooge the CEO presided from its own portrait. Some interior decorating would be called for. *Throw that thing in a basement.*

Rob scribbled furiously on his tablet as Ben crossed to the window overlooking London. A tight smile was slowly triumphing over Rob's fear.

"And get hold of that man who snuck in yesterday," Ben added. "Forgive his debts and give him ten thousand pounds. And then I'll need to pull us out of the Colombian Drug War somehow."

Rob looked up from his tablet in alarm. "That was real?"

Ben cringed. "That was real." At the window, his eyes ate the city up. Glorious, full, convivial London. In the present day, where it belonged. "We can do better, you and I," Ben murmured to the city. It seemed to reach up to him, embrace him, welcoming him back.

"What was that, sir?"

"Nothing." Ben turned his attention to Rob. Not the assistant, but the man. Ben would have to remind himself daily that his employees were people to work with, not servants to be commanded. The habit would change with time. "And how's your Christmas been, Rob? How's your boy?"

Rob perked up at the mention of his son. The smile that had been fighting to break free bloomed into a full-hearted grin. "Tim's as well as can be. We had a brilliant time last night. Thanks again for letting me leave early."

Ben wasn't sure what at first, but something Rob had said caught in his brain. He spotted the anomaly quickly. "Your son is actually named Tim?"

Rob chuckled as if the answer were obvious. "Yes, of course."

"Huh. You must've mentioned it before." Ben had never paid mind to his employees' personal lives. If Rob had spoken of his son in passing, it would've gone right past him. "And what do you mean, 'As well as can be'? Tim doesn't really have cancer, does he?"

Rob's joy deflated into a puzzled frown. "How did you know?"

Ben paused, reflected. He paced back to the window. Surely Rob had mentioned his son's diagnosis in passing, too.

"I've never said a thing about it at work," Rob continued. "I don't like people to know unless I'm close to them. Got tired of too much pity from near-strangers."

Well, there goes that hypothesis.

"Forget it," Ben said. "We'll get Tim the best treatment available. I'll spare no expense."

He didn't see Rob's reaction, because activity far in the distance caught Ben's eyes. One of the bridges over the Thames was overloaded with parked emergency vehicles. They clogged the whole roadway so no traffic could get through.

"Say, what's that over there?" Ben asked, pointing it out.

"Uh, I'm sorry, what do you mean about treatment for Tim?"

"I said forget it. What's all that activity on the bridge?"

Rob squinted, straining to see. "Oh, all the cop cars on the bridge? You haven't heard?"

"Heard what?"

"There was an attack near Parliament overnight. And other spots all around the City. Bombed somehow. Terrorism is the rumour, except that nothing important was hit. A hotel was the worst, but it's mostly just roads and parks. It's the strangest thing."

Ben pushed through the crowd of gawkers, but they were so dense, he couldn't get halfway to the Heras fencing the police had used to cordon off the area around the Palace of Westminster, from the eastern end of Westminster Bridge all the way to the western end of Parliament Square Garden, where Ben now stood trying to get a glimpse. Over a hundred police and fire personnel crawled over the area like yellow and navy blue ants, some walking springer spaniels sniffing for who knew what. Emergency vehicles abounded, lights flashing. On this side of the barriers, thousands had gathered to raise their phones and capture the historical sight of a massive crater smack dab in the middle of Bridge Street, literally in the shadow of Big Ben.

Ben had confirmed the rest on his own phone: bombs that originated from the World War eras had exploded all over London last night. The tabloids ran interviews with people who claimed to have seen Zeppelins and Luftwaffe planes in the skies. The prime minister had issued a statement. The Underground had been closed for the day. No one knew what to make of it.

Ben let himself get lost in the throng. He wandered for a spell, and so did his mind. Surprisingly, no one had died. Due to Ralph's careful efforts to protect the people of London as they ran?

Ralph had been real. Imogen had been real. None of it had been a dream.

But Ben's waking mind couldn't accept this absurdity. The evidence spoke plainly, yet he couldn't bring himself to believe it. If his dream had been real, and the ghosts along with it, what were the implications for the future of the world, for Ben's own immortal soul?

Was his father still out there somewhere? Rotting in a cell in Hell, maybe, but still out there. What would happen to him? The spirits had implied that even once someone was in the underworld, they could earn their way to a happier afterlife. Could Graham eventually build himself into a man worthy of that?

Could Ben?

"Hey, look who it is," said a woman Ben didn't recognise who carried a clipboard and donation box. She stood on a busy Westminster street corner where Ben had stopped, dazed, to stare at his feet. A charity insignia adorned her coat's left chest. "You look even more lost than yesterday."

Ben blinked. Tried to place her in his memory.

Seeing he didn't remember her, she threw him a playfully dramatic frown. "I asked you to donate to the Future Generations Fund. You said you didn't give a damn about future generations?"

"Ah. Yes." Ben remembered her now. He grimaced in embarrassment. "I've had quite a change of heart since yesterday, if you can believe it."

"Well, that's fantastic to hear. What changed your mind?"

Ben wasn't about to start explaining *that* to her, so he simply took out his wallet and gave her all the money he had. She accepted it gratefully, but grew increasingly concerned as she counted it. "How much is this?"

"I need to get more involved in charity," Ben said, ignoring the question. He needed to phone Suresh, not just to catch up, but to see if he needed funding for his work on malaria. A few of Ben's peers, too, were the uncommon breed of do-gooder billionaire who'd pledged to donate their fortunes to charity. Ben had always scoffed at this and mocked it as virtue signalling – and maybe some of it was. But if striving for status was a human universal, or near to being so, then at least those men were striving for the right kind of status. He couldn't wait to give them a ring, too.

There was so, so much more than the petty, acquisitive world Ben had thought he lived in. With the blinkers of self-interest finally pulled from his eyes, Ben basked in the freedom to find – or create – the sense of community he'd always longed for. Hopefully, he could find people working to make the world a better place. *Incredible that there are groups of people who* actually *think this way.* Ben wouldn't spend one more day of his life avoiding them like the vain social clubs he'd once thought they were.

"What are the best charities?" he asked the woman.

"Uh, this is a lot of money, sir. Do you want some of this back?"

"Is it? I mean, please keep it. I'm new to all this."

"Hmm. Well, if you insist." With physical effort, she stuffed the wad of cash into her donation box. "So, charities that are effective are evidence-based and work in the places they can have the biggest impact. If you have a lot of money to donate, start there. Don't even get me started on what a waste it is to donate a mint just to get your name on some building."

"Like flushing your money down a toilet tied to a lead balloon as it falls off a train wreck into a dumpster fire," said a new voice from beside them.

And there she was.

Dressed casually in white trousers, a cheesy red-and-green Christmas jumper, and a matching bobble hat that mostly covered her crop haircut, her hands rested in the pockets of her huge beige coat. Marley rocked back on her heels, grinning up at Ben, her smile like a warm sun on a cold winter day.

Ben couldn't move. Could scarcely breathe. He wanted to reach out and touch her, but feared she'd evaporate or turn into a ghost if he did. But no, this Marley was flesh and blood, every bit as solid as he was.

"I thought I might find you around these parts," she said, gesturing towards the Palace of Westminster a few streets away.

"You're—" Ben started, but words failed him. Marley let out a girlish giggle at his stupor.

"Everything okay?" the charity collector asked.

"Tippy top," said Marley. "You look for a wire transfer from my legal team tomorrow for half a billion pounds, earmarked for education in low-income countries. This old man's not about to beat me in the altruism game."

The woman blinked in confusion. "Half a..."

But Marley had slung her arm around Ben's back and was leading him away. He put one foot in front of the other, but his brain was still catching up to his eyes, much less his feet.

Marley was alive. Marley was here. Walking with him. Touching him.

After Ben had brought her back, the spirits had let her live.

Thank you, Ben thought to them, though the sentiment seemed wholly inadequate. *Thank you.*

"You might be interested to know, Ben," she said, "that I have spent the last several hours at the police station, where they had some *very* interesting questions about what I was doing naked in a graveyard at two in the morning on Christmas Day. Come on, you could've at least had the decency to bring my silk dress back to life, too – I loved that dress. But what luck, the police had some kind of terrorist incident to deal with this morning, and they decided I'm not a terrorist, so they let me go. I suppose I actually was one of the terrorists they were looking for, but oh well. Their loss."

"I woke up—" Ben stuttered. "I was in bed—" Had the ghosts moved his sleeping body from the lounge up to the bedroom? He'd first discounted his trips through time as a dream only because he'd woken up in bed, and he'd last left his mortal body downstairs. But clearly that had been a hasty assumption.

"I see you're still catching up," Marley said. She stopped, faced him. She ran her hands tenderly up and down his arms, looked into his eyes. "Hey. Ben. I'm here. We made it. We're both alive. And we have the rest of our lives ahead of us."

Ben lifted his gaze to meet hers. He started to believe it. That the dream had not been a dream. That this truly was his best friend, here with him, alive. That after so long fighting for survival, he was suddenly, miraculously safe.

The promise of companionship after so long alone swept over Ben and through him, washing away the last cobwebs of the unwinnable competition that had once ensnared him.

I'm home now.

He tried to speak again, but only jagged breaths came out. He touched Marley's cheek. She reciprocated, wiping away one of Ben's tears.

"I love you, you know," Marley said. "Warts and all."

"I—" Ben expended great effort to speak. Still his voice came out shaky. "It is my sincerest hope that I can give you love like that in return. But Marley…"

A cyclist rang her bell as she sped deftly between them and some pedestrians. A cab honked, seagulls yammered, a siren shrilled in the distance, and construction work thumped and rattled from the building across the street, but in that moment, Ben's entire world was the woman in front of him.

"Marley, I've been so, so horrible to you. For so many years. I don't know how I can even begin to ask for forgiveness. I—"

She shifted her hand from his cheek to his mouth, extinguishing the words he'd been about to say. Her smile lit her face yet again. "You're forgiven," she said. "But for both of our sakes, please do better in future, yeah?"

Ben laughed. "I will," he said. Having only today truly digested the fact that people other than himself were worthy of moral concern, Ben was sharply aware he'd need to fight his own instincts in order to keep that circle of moral concern as wide as it had grown. And in order to grow it farther.

My life is not a script, and I have agency to change myself. I will live in the past, the present, and the future. The spirits of all three will thrive within me. I will not shut out the lessons they teach.

Ben's life moving forward would be a constant battle with the selfish man inside him. Sometimes he might lose that battle. But it was a battle he was now determined to fight. Until his dying breath, and beyond.

"I'll do better, too," Marley said.

Ben took one of her hands in each of his. "I can't believe I was too cowardly to admit I loved you. When the business started taking off, I had all these fool ideas in my head about who I was supposed to be. But you fit me. You fit me so well. You always have."

Marley beamed at his words. "And I was too cowardly to pull your head out of your bum all these years. Sorry. I should've tried harder. It was pretty deep up there, though."

Ben groaned and shook his head. "I'm so impossibly glad to have you back, you ridiculous woman."

He caught her plucking a hair from beneath her bobble hat. She probably hadn't realised she was doing it, but she caught him catching her, and grinned awkwardly. She flicked the hair away.

She took his head in both her hands, gave his cheeks a nice little pat, then resumed strolling down the busy street. Ben walked with her, side by side.

"Well," she said, "we'll need to come up with a story for the government and the company for why I'm still alive."

"Life insurance fraud," Ben suggested. "You faked your own death to give your next of kin a huge payout."

Marley grimaced. "What next of kin? And why do I need to commit fraud? I'm already richer than God."

"Many a judge has wondered the same of the accused in their courtrooms."

"Maybe the doctors flubbed my death certification. I punched through my coffin and dug my way to the surface."

"Believable." Ben smirked at her.

"Ah, we'll think of something," she said, stretching her arms as if just waking up for the day. "Regardless, it's good to be back. Lots of life left to live. Speaking of which, I do want to hear more about that kinky billionaire sex. I haven't forgotten about that."

Ben sighed. "Marley, we are too old for such things."

"Age is just a number. Viagra's just a pill."

"I've just got over using all sorts of toxic sludge as models for my life, and now you're asking me to use billionaire romance books as the new models for my life?"

"No, not at all. I just want to use them as models for the sex part of our lives."

Snorting a laugh, Ben covered his face with a hand. "What have I unleashed upon the world, bringing you back to life?"

"You'll have to find out, I think. It's been ages since we've chatted about anything that isn't business. I bet there's enough we still have to learn about each other to fill Santa's bottomless sack."

Ben held her hand as they walked into St James's Park. "I look forward to it, Marley."

A Note from the Author

Thanks for reading! Truly. It means a lot.

Now comes the part where I shamelessly beg: please leave a review. Seriously—it helps more than anything else. Indie authors like me survive on reviews, and it lets more readers discover the story. Please take just a minute to leave a short review of *A Christmas Carol* on Amazon.

If you like my stuff, I'd also love for you to join my three-emails-per-year newsletter at joshuaingle.com. I'll send you my short story collection for free when you join.

If you're in the mood for another redemption story (and you don't mind heavy profanity and violence), you might enjoy my **Thorn** books: a horror trilogy about a demon who realizes he has a conscience and tries to defect to the angels.

Or, if you fancy a sci-fi mystery, you'll like *Dead Links*, my book set in a cyberpunk future in which a private eye's murder case gets personal. An excerpt from this book starts on the next page.

Here is a preview of Josh's sci-fi thriller

DEAD LINKS

Beyond the wide circle of crime scene tape, a forensic analyst lifts the sheet and I get a peek at the body of this Emilio Cassano—this bigwig from Beverly Hills I've been hearing so much about. Coagulated streams of dried blood paint burgundy lines across his face. Looks about sixty, maybe older. He's still wearing his fancy beige business suit, like he's trying to hide his rotten flesh from his customers, who've all turned into lookie-loos peering through the lobby's tall windows.

For just a second, I see the bullet hole between Mr. Cassano's eyes. I zoom in and try to snap a picture for our records, but my glasses are too slow and I miss my chance. Forensics has laid the sheet back over his head. Oh well. Paul still has some connections inside the department; maybe he can talk the five-O into lending us the crime scene pics.

Cops are crawling all over the lobby, giving me dirty looks. "Who's this loser and how'd he get in here?" I can almost hear them asking. I ignore them, try to fit in, look like I belong.

They've blocked off the whole ground floor. Even though they're erecting tarps over the windows, the lookie-loos persist. I can see indoor walkways four stories above me where curious employees peer down at the body of their boss's boss's boss's boss, dead under a sheet, smack dab in the center of the lobby of his own skyscraper. Which one of you vultures did it, huh? I scan their faces for guilt, but most of them just look entertained, like they're watching the best episode of their favorite TV show. They're all wearing glasses, probably taking pictures, probably selling them to the news. The cops don't even bother to walk up there and shoo 'em away. I guess we're all paparazzi at heart.

Becky and Paul are coming in through the front doors, Becky in shorts and Paul in his Hawaiian shirt, looking for all the world like tourists lost on vacation. They're halfway to me when a cop steps between us—a big guy looking down at me like I'm a roach in his kid's lunchbox. The same guy who's been directing the other officers. He's not in uniform. Maybe he had to hurry over here on his day off.

"Nice coat," he says, gesturing to my ratty trench coat, which, in the middle of all these uniforms, is starting to feel less like my standard work attire and more like a costume in a school play.

I nod at him as if I belong, but of course he wants me off his crime scene. So I reach out my hand to shake, to make a solid first impression. "Hey, I'm Guy Rosen, LPI," I say, adding the "L" for "Licensed" to put a stop to the thousand clichés I'm sure are running through the officer's mind. "But you can call me Guy."

"Lieutenant Marcel Jones," the cop says. "You can call me Lieutenant Marcel Jones."

Becky and Paul step up beside us. Present their IDs. "Paul Abramov, Becky Haslett. The three of us have been hired by Mr. Cassano."

Jones's eyes twitch, betraying his disbelief. He turns to the body at the center of the room, then back to us. Sarcasm is thick on his tongue. "I regret to inform you that Mr. Cassano recently passed away."

"Mr. *Claud* Cassano," I clarify. "The brother. Is he around?"

Paul forwards our digital authorization from Claud Cassano's office to Jones's glasses, and the look on his face as he realizes he'll have to live with us is delicious. "Yeah, he's somewhere," he says, doing a shitty job hiding his disappointment.

"Who do we talk to about getting a look at the body?" Paul asks.

"Not me."

As they bicker, I go online and check out Jones. All I can find are his name and officer number on an obscure section of the LAPD's website. Can't even find a picture of the guy. It says he's served for sixteen years, though. He was probably just good enough to make lieutenant but too thick to move up further. Mid-level fuzz. I open another window and search for Jones's commanding officer and—

"Death comes too soon."

The comment catches me off-guard and I take off my glasses. Reality's dull hues suddenly replace the crisp overlay of the internet. Paul and Becky have walked over to the body and they're nagging some cops to let them cross the tape. Jones looks like he's ready to slug Paul in the nose.

The comment came from much closer. I look to my right and find him: a disheveled Latino man in his early thirties, about my age. Jawline like an anvil, skin like a baby, a mop of model-straight hair, eyes that could melt any woman's heart in a second. I could have mistaken him for a pop star if his tie weren't loose and his coat unbuttoned, with stubble on his cheeks and a half-empty bottle of booze in his hand. He's leaning against a marble pillar, staring at nothing in particular. Death comes too soon?

"That it does," I say to him, putting my glasses back on.

The man nods and downs a sip of liquor—smells like spiced rum. "We see ten people die every day in movies and TV. You'd think we'd be used to death. But when it comes knocking at your own door, you're still so surprised, like you didn't expect it'd ever come for you. We're so good at ignoring the inevitable." He gestures to Emilio Cassano's body, half the room away. Two forensic drones are hovering above it.

"Emilio Cassano lived to be sixtyish," I say, trying to gauge who this guy is. "And he had plenty of life under his belt. We among the living can only hope for a life as fulfilled as his."

"My grandfather lived to be ninety-eight," the man says. "That's almost forty years of life the man under that tarp has now lost."

"It is unfortunate."

He looks at me for the first time. Now that I see his whole face, he looks even more distraught. Then, after a second, he grins drunkenly at me, like he just decided I'm his new best friend. Huh. I offer him my hand to shake.

"Guy Rosen. I'm helping with the investigation."

"Juan Cassano. I'm helping with the investigation too."

Ah, got it. The son. For a trust fund baby, Juan has a firm grip, and the look in his eyes is more determined than any cop's. "Mr. Cassano, I'm very sorry for your loss."

"Thank you. You know my father was a visionary. He built this company to escape the poverty he was born into. He built it from nothing." Juan's words are slightly slurred. He takes a swig, then shuffles around in his pocket and presents his business card. I reciprocate with one of my own. "You find who did this, Guy. Of all the families this could happen to, mine is the least deserving."

"I'll do everything I can to bring the perp to justice, Mr. Cassano."

"Call me Juan. And don't speak official with me. I don't want you to just bring him to justice. I want you to gut the bastard. Can I count on you to do that?"

Before I can respond, Claud Cassano calls my name. He's a well-groomed man in his fifties, walking toward us with a small entourage of other businessmen. Or are they lawyers?

"You're with Paul?" he asks me.

"Uh, Paul's with me."

Claud nods to Juan, behind me. "I see you've met my nephew."

"Yes. Pleased to meet you as well."

He turns to his nephew. "Juan, the captain in charge would like to question you."

Juan stares coldly at Claud, and something deep and hostile passes silently between them. Juan takes another drink and strolls off toward the cops.

"Walk with me," Claud tells me as soon as Juan is out of earshot.

The businessmen-or-maybe-lawyers trail us as Claud leads me away from the crime scene on a scenic tour of the Cassano Building's ground floor. We pass a dozen small fountains in a shallow marble pool, several semicircles of cushy lounge chairs, an elaborate winding staircase, numerous virtual advertisements for razors, shoes, movies, fast food, beverages, more, only visible through glasses. I try to find the app I use for blocking ads, but it's missing from my menus.

Claud's probably using some kind of tech that fucks with my glasses' functionality so I can't record this conversation.

"This is the worst time for something like this to happen," Claud says. "With the Omni launch and all. If I didn't know better, I'd think one of our competitors is trying to sabotage us."

"The Cassano Corporation *has* competitors?" I ask.

Claud doesn't even snicker at the joke. "What do you know about us Cassanos and our company?" he says.

Cassano is a household brand, of course, right up there with Apple and Microsoft, but since I'm not much of a tech enthusiast, I only know what Paul has told me, plus what I researched this morning after Paul got the call about this job. Still, I make a good show of awareness. "I know that you're innovators, that you're highly respected businesspeople who built a small R&D startup into one of the top research firms in the world. I know you branched out into tech and medicine and a half dozen other industries, especially the entertainment industries. I know you're charismatic and LA loves you. I know you're filthy rich. And I know you're my new boss."

"Do you know how the company makes its money?"

"Uh, selling things?" I guess. I'm not one for the formalities of the business world. "Implants, glasses, smartcars, the works. You have a billion and one contracts, even more patents, and every other day I read about one of your breakthroughs in science and tech. And I don't even read."

"Did you know that we also sell doughnuts?"

"Doughnuts? Ha, no."

"You wouldn't think it, but it's true." Claud points to a random bit of empty air as we walk past it, and like magic, an advertisement for "Donas Norte" appears there. What a show-off. As if I care that his implant controls all the tech in the building. Given that he owns the building, does he expect me to be surprised?

"It's a modest chain of doughnut restaurants," Claud says. "They're only in Mexico now, but forty years ago, the first tiny location was right here in LA. My father owned it."

"Juan says he lived to be ninety-eight years old."

"He never ate the doughnuts, is why." I glance sideways and catch a faint smile at the edge of Claud's mouth. So he does have a sense of humor. But on his own terms.

I chuckle politely. I liked Juan better; he seemed honest. Claud comes from a whole different world, a world of moves and countermoves, where life itself is a game you can win. Why the small talk? Let's talk about the murder. That's what I'm here for.

I keep pace with him as he tells the inevitable story of his humble beginnings. "Emilio once had an assignment in elementary school that asked him to research nutrition. He came running into the doughnut shop one night, wide-eyed and grinning, and he asked me what I thought the two most essential nutrients for human life were. This was a fifth grader asking, mind you. Naturally, I answered air and water. But Emilio said that air and water aren't nutrients, and guess again. So I guessed Vitamin C and Vitamin D. My ten-year-old brother said nope, guess again. Do you know what the answer was, Guy? What the two most essential nutrients for human life are?"

"Some kind of protein?"

"Good guess, but the answer is fat and sugar."

"Fat and sugar?"

"Mm-hmm. We evolved to crave them because they're so rare in nature yet so vital to our health. Which is why Donas Norte sells so many doughnuts."

Okay, okay, get to your point. "And your big brother figured all this out on his own?"

"At ten years old, yes. He was fascinated that the most unhealthy food seems to sell the most, because of our evolutionary addiction to its contents, which are, in fact, healthy. In small amounts. Ah, here we are."

We stop next to a massive window looking up at downtown Los Angeles just outside. I see traffic, street vendors, palm fronds swaying in the wind, but I hear none of it; the window is soundproof. Claud waves a hand, and all the ads floating between us and the view dissipate.

"I always suspected that Emilio ran this whole business by the same principle he discovered as a child. What do humans crave? He was always trying to discover what humans crave, so he could give it to them in spades. So he could immerse them in it. And not just to sell products and earn a profit. To truly add value to his customers' lives. He was a good businessman."

"But ain't too much junk food a public health concern?" Paul says from behind us. We turn to greet him. Crooked teeth showing through his wide smile, Paul shakes Claud's hand. Vigorously. "Good to see you again, Claud."

I've been meaning to ask Paul how he knows Claud. He's mentioned him before as an old drinking buddy, but the scruffy PI and the Latino billionaire have nothing obviously in common. Claud seems genuinely glad to see him, though.

"Emilio was no predator, my friend," Claud says to him. "It is the individual's responsibility to educate himself that too many doughnuts is a bad thing."

"Is it? I guess I misedumacated myself, then." Paul pats his own ample belly and laughs.

Claud returns the laughter, and now it's my turn to disregard a joke. When the men see I'm not laughing with them, they get serious again.

Claud says, "I tell you this doughnut story both to endear you to my brother, may he rest in peace, and also because I know someone who craved what Emilio had to offer. Someone who craved it enough to kill him for it."

"Have you told the police?" I ask.

"No. I trust Paul, and you by association, but I have no trust for the police. I don't want them to hear a word of what I'm about to tell you, and I don't want you working with them on this case. Do you understand?"

"Absolutely. But I should point out that the LAPD have resources we don't, and they can—"

"The LAPD can be bought. I've seen it before. Look, I just came down from an emergency board meeting and they've elected me interim CEO, but even with the extra shares I'm nowhere near as wealthy or powerful as Emilio's side of the family. And especially with his newfound inheritance, Juan's pockets run deep. Far deeper than mine. Deep enough to buy the police. Most of Emilio's estate was left to Juan, you know. More even than to Emilio's wife."

And you just happened to have the will readily available immediately after learning Emilio bit the dust? I think it, but I don't say it. The money Claud's paying us is reason enough for me to be interested in this case, but now, all of a sudden, I'm personally intrigued. "What makes you think it's Juan?"

"Because up until a month ago, I hadn't seen him since he was sixteen years old. He's been off the map for most of his life, chasing women and fame. Then out of the blue, the prodigal playboy returns just in time to witness the death of his father—the father he wanted nothing to do with for most of his life. He's lazy, entitled, and he has a violent past. Paul can tell you all about that. I have no evidence that he did it, though, and that's why I need you."

A foregone conclusion? Nice. It just makes my day when clients pull stuff like this on us. They know their spouse is cheating on them and want us to prove it. When they're right, they say they knew it all along, so what good were we? When they're wrong, they tell us we're doing a shitty job, because they know better. Makes me wonder what the point of hiring a PI even is. If I could propose one, it's this: we don't care about anyone's family drama.

This *is* a fascinating job, but I'll have to be delicate with it.

"We'll look into it," I say.

"Don't tell Leah that I suspect Juan," Claud says to Paul.

"Ha, like Leah and me still talk."

"We'll have to at least question her," I say.

"Fair enough," Claud responds.

"I'm curious about something else, though. When I talked to Juan a few minutes ago, he spoke of his father like he was a saint. Seems like he really admired him."

"I'm sure he speaks that way," Claud replies. "He wants to avoid suspicion. So you must follow him. Eavesdrop, plant bugs, I don't care. Don't communicate with law enforcement unless you have to. Don't trust them. I want you to discover the truth for me."

"Mind if we ask you some questions? Just a standard interview we do with every client?"

Claud's eyes dart from side to side, distracted by something in his glasses. He takes a moment to respond. "You certainly may. A few minutes first, though. I have to make a call."

"Sure thing."

Claud paces back toward the fountains, flanked by two of his maybe-businessmen-maybe-lawyers, who by now I've deduced are probably bodyguards. As he begins his call, I turn back to the huge window and gaze out at the city with Paul. My implant starts itching like it has been for the past couple days, so I scratch the back of my scalp. In the mirror this morning, there was a nasty red mark underneath my hair from all the scratching. Damn thing has never given me problems before, and it's good tech, less than a decade old. I paid a small fortune for it. Who wouldn't, to be able to talk to technology telepathically? But I guess everything malfunctions sooner or later. I should probably get it looked at.

"You talk with the forensic lady?" I ask Paul.

"And a few others. Turns out Emilio's been missing for a week, but nobody cared because apparently, he disappears for weeks on end all the time. Last person to see him was his wife when he left home."

"Hmm. Time of death?"

"About a week ago. And the body's pretty well preserved. The fuzz thinks it was dropped off here last night, but so far we've got no witnesses."

"So the killer had access to the building. What'd they find on the security footage?"

"*Nada.* The security footage was erased, the guard bot shut down at midnight."

"What the hell?"

"My thoughts exactly."

"So the killer *really* had access," I say, leaving the obvious question unspoken: Why keep the body for a whole week only to dump it in the lobby of the Cassano Building? Is the killer trying to say something, to put on a show, or does he have some other motive?

"It's all too weird, man. I've been here fifteen minutes and I've heard only good things about Emilio. Claud always spoke highly of him. He seems like a man with few enemies."

"Why didn't his implant notify the police when he died?"

"Killer shot him point blank, right through the chip in his head. Bullet went straight through and they still haven't found it. So the killer either knew what he was doing or was a damn lucky shot. Shot him straight through the glasses, too. The victim's got pieces of 'em in his brain."

"Jesus."

"Yeah."

———◇———

Dead Links can be purchased on **Amazon**.

Acknowledgments

This was a fun one, and I'm immensely grateful to those whose thoughts helped me shape these characters and this story. Sincere thanks to my wife Stacy, my parents Rick and Elyse, and Fedor Steer for their advance reading and criticism. Kevin Kendrick really went the extra mile with ultra-thorough feedback that helped shape one of the book's earliest drafts. Rutvij Padhair offered extraordinarily helpful insight into Indian culture, and Richard Sheehan gave the book a marvellous edit and corrected all the Americanisms that slipped through my previous drafts.

I'm also, of course, deeply indebted to the genius of Charles Dickens, who told a story for the ages. As the centuries tick by, I'm sure many other authors will write their own versions of *A Christmas Carol*. I fully intend to appear to those authors as a ghost and tell them what's what, but if that should prove impossible, I hope I've made at least a small contribution to the evolution of this ever-changing story that they'll find valuable.

I hope you've had a blast with Ben and Marley, my dear reader! Thanks for taking a chance on an indie author. You're the whole reason any of this exists, so my heartfelt gratitude goes to you most of all.